The
Faithful
Spy

THE FAITHFUL SPY

A NOVEL

Alex Berenson

RANDOM HOUSE

NEW YORK

The Faithful Spy is a work of fiction. Any resemblance
between these fictional characters and actual persons,
living or dead, is purely coincidental.

Published in the United States by Random House, an imprint
of The Random House Publishing Group, a division
of Random House, Inc., New York.

RANDOM HOUSE and colophon are registered trademarks
of Random House, Inc.

LIBRARY OF CONGRESS CATALOGING-IN-PUBLICATION DATA
Berenson, Alex.
The faithful spy: a novel / Alex Berenson.
p.   cm.
ISBN 0-345-47899-1
1. Terrorism—Fiction.   2. al Qaeda (Organization)—Fiction.
3. Intelligence service—Fiction.   I. Title.
PS3602.E25F35 2006   813'.6—dc22   2005044689

Printed in the United States of America on acid-free paper

www.atrandom.com

2 4 6 8 9 7 5 3 1

First Edition

For the 1-5 Cav
and the rest of the men and women
of the United States Armed Forces
serving with valor in a complex world
—and in honor of Fakher Haider,
who died for the truth

had
the
that
cou
tect
hor
iba
wat
this
wou

Uni
alre
pos
bon
B
Wel
the
veh
mor
tran
and
Tali
T
outl
unt
His
all
wan
thre
take
for
no
V

God is on the side with the best artillery.

—NAPOLEON

The
Faithful
Spy

PROLOGUE

JOHN WELLS TIPPED his head to the sky, searching for a pair of F-15s circling slowly above in the darkness. Even during the day the American jets were difficult to spot. Now, with the sun hidden behind the mountains, they were all but invisible. Wells could only hope their pilots hadn't seen him either, for the bombs on their wings could obliterate him and his men in an instant.

From the cockpits of those jets, the war looked like a video game, Wells thought. Little gray men ran silently across computer screens an inch at a time until bombs landed with white blasts. The reality on the ground was messier, bones and blood replacing pixels. Wells's mind slid to a Sunday morning many years before, his dad, a surgeon, the best cutter in western Montana, walking into the kitchen after a night in the operating room, washing his hands compulsively in the sink.

"What happened, Dad?" Wells had said that morning. "Was it bad?"

He was ten, old enough to know that he wasn't supposed to ask those questions, but curiosity overcame him. Herbert turned off the sink and dried his hands, poured himself a cup of coffee, and fixed Wells with his weary blue eyes. Wells was about to apologize for overstepping his bounds when his father finally spoke, the answer not what Wells expected.

"Everything depends which side of the shotgun you're on," Herbert said. And sipped his coffee, as if daring his son to press him further. Wells hadn't understood then, but he did now. Truer words had never been said. He wondered what his father, two years gone, would think of the man he'd become. He had just started down his path when Herbert had passed on, and if his dad had had any thoughts on the matter he'd kept them to himself.

"You've got the hands to be a surgeon, John," Herbert said once when Wells was in college, but when Wells didn't respond Herbert dropped the subject. His dad always told him that he'd have to make his own path, that the world was no place for weaklings. Wells supposed he'd learned that lesson too well. A killer, not a doctor, aiming to make wounds no surgeon could undo. Yet somehow he thought that Herbert would understand the need for men like him. Hoped, anyway.

WELLS GAVE UP looking for the jets but kept his eyes raised. In this land without electricity the stars and moon glowed with a brightness he had grown to love. He silently named all the constellations he could remember, until a blast of wind filled his eyes with dust and pulled his attention to earth.

Ahmed, his lieutenant, stepped across the firepit and stood beside him. "Cold," Ahmed said quietly in Arabic.

"*Nam.*" Yes.

The wind had worsened by the day, an icy breeze sweeping down from the north with the promise of the bitter winter to come. Tonight the gusts were especially strong, kicking up ash from the fire Wells and his men had built, mocking their efforts to stay warm. Wells cinched his blanket around his shoulders and stepped closer to the men huddled around the low fire. He would have liked a stronger flame, but he could not risk the attention of the jets.

"It will be a long winter."

"Yes," Wells said.

"Or perhaps a short one." A grim smile crossed Ahmed's face. "Perhaps we will be in paradise before spring."

"Maybe the sheikh will send us all on vacation," Wells said, indulging himself in a rare joke. "Or a hajj," the pilgrimage to Mecca that every devout Muslim was supposed to make at least once.

At the mention of the hajj the sneer disappeared from Ahmed's lips. "*Inshallah, Jalal,*" he said reverently. If God wills.

"*Inshallah,*" Wells said. The Taliban and Qaeda guerrillas called him Jalal. He had taken the name years earlier, after he became the first westerner to graduate from the Qaeda camps near Kandahar. Fewer than a dozen men knew his real name. A few others called him Ameriki, the American, but not many would do so to his face. Many of the younger recruits, in fact, didn't know he was American at all.

And why would they? Wells asked himself. After years fighting jihad in Afghanistan and Chechnya, he spoke perfect Arabic and Pashtun. His beard was long, his hands callused. He rode a horse almost as well as the natives—no outsider could truly ride like an Afghan—and he played *buzkashi,* the rough polo game they loved, as hard as they did. He prayed with them. He had proven that he belonged here, with these men.

Or so Wells hoped. What bin Laden and the other senior Qaeda leaders really thought of him he did not know. He was not sure he ever would. Especially now, with his country at war with theirs. He could not truly prove himself except by dying for them, and that he did not plan to do.

Wells shivered again, from the inside this time. Enough second-guessing. He looked at his six men, their AKs slung over their shoulders, talking quietly in the darkness. Three were Afghan, three Arab; the pressure of war had brought the Taliban and Qaeda closer than ever before. Usually, they were chatty and loud, born storytellers. But Wells was not a talker on missions, and his soldiers respected that. They were friendly enough, and battle-hardened, and they followed his orders quickly and without question. A commander couldn't ask for more. What would happen to them tonight was unfortunate, worse than unfortunate, but it couldn't be helped.

To the south, a bright flash lit up the night. Then another, and another.

"They've started again," Ahmed said. The Americans were

bombing Kabul, the Afghan capital, thirty miles south. So far, they had ignored the Shamali Plain, the flat ground north of Kabul where the Taliban faced the Northern Alliance—the rebel Afghan army that since September 11 had become America's new best friend.

Wells and his men had camped in a nameless village, really just a couple of huts, on a ridge overlooking the plain. They were protected by mountains to the north and west, and they had ridden horses in rather than driving the Toyota pickups favored by the Taliban. No one would bother them up here, and they could easily watch the plain below. And Wells had another reason for choosing this place, one he had not shared with his men. With any luck, there would be an American Special Forces unit in the next village north.

"Harder tonight," Ahmed said, as the flashes continued.

"*Nam.*" Yes. Much harder. After a month of shadowboxing, the United States had opened up on Kabul. A bad sign for the Taliban, already reeling from the collapse of its defenses in the north. Supposedly impenetrable cities had fallen after a few days of American bombing.

But tonight the Taliban had a surprise for the Northern Alliance. Wells looked south, where a rutted road rose out of Kabul and onto the plain. There they were. Headlights, streaming north. A dozen vehicles in close convoy, a break, and a dozen more. Pickups with mounted .50-caliber machine guns in their beds. Five-ton troop transports holding twenty soldiers each. The moon rose in the sky and the headlights kept coming. Another dozen, and another. The Taliban were grouping to attack the Northern Alliance front line.

The trucks cut their lights as they approached the line. Wells pulled out his night-vision binoculars—his only luxury, taken off an unlucky Russian major in Chechnya—and scanned the valley below. Hundreds of trucks had massed. Maybe three thousand soldiers in all, Afghan and Arab. Here to defend Kabul from the infidels who wanted to let women show their faces in public. If the Talibs broke through the Northern Alliance's front line, they might be able to retake much of what they had lost. Wells's unit had been sent to look for signs that the Alliance had learned of the attack. So far, he saw no defensive preparations.

Wells handed Ahmed the binoculars. "It is true, then?"

"*Nam.* We attack tonight."

"Can we win?"

A month ago Ahmed's question would have been unthinkable. The American bombing had hurt the confidence of the Taliban more than Wells had realized.

"Of course," he said. "*Inshallah.*" In truth, Wells admired the plan's boldness. The Taliban would take the fight to the enemy rather than waiting to die in their bunkers. But the massed Talib soldiers would be a ripe target for the jets overhead. To succeed, the Taliban troops would need to punch through the Northern Alliance front lines quickly. Then Talib and Alliance soldiers would be mixed in close combat. The Americans would be unable to bomb without destroying their allies as well as their enemies.

The Taliban troops below broke into company-sized groups, readying themselves to move forward.

They never had the chance.

The bombs began falling almost as soon as the last truck of soldiers reached the front line. Blasts tore through the night, exploding white and red on the plain below Wells like upside-down fireworks. Sharp cracks and long heavy thumps came randomly, three or four in quick succession followed by long pauses. Their force shook the huts where Wells and his men stood, and one blast lit the night with a huge red fireball.

"Must have been an ammunition truck," Wells said, half to himself, half to Ahmed.

THE BARRAGE SEEMED to last for hours, but when it ended and Wells checked his watch he found that only forty minutes had passed. He raised his binoculars to examine the plain below. Fires licked the wrecked bodies of pickups and five-ton trucks. Men lay scattered across the hard ground. The Americans had been waiting all along, and the Talibs had driven into the trap. Which meant that a Special Forces unit was hidden nearby, directing the bombardment. Just as Wells had hoped.

His men were silent now, shocked by what they had seen. Below, the Talibs were trying to regroup, but now the Northern Alliance had opened up with machine guns and mortars. And another round of bombing was surely coming. Without surprise, the Taliban had no chance.

Wells lowered the binoculars. "Let's go," he said.

"Back?" Ahmed said.

Wells shook his head and pointed north, over the folds of the ridge. "Americans are up there aiming the bombs." Ahmed looked surprised but said nothing. Wells had been right before, and in any case as commander he could do what he liked.

They saddled up and rode north in the darkness. Unlike the spectacular mountains of northern Afghanistan, the Shamali ridge was stunted and uneven, low hills of crumbling stone and dirt. They traveled in single file at a steady trot, led by Hamid, their best horseman. Beneath them the bombs fell again. A few headlights were already moving south toward Kabul, the Taliban's attack fading before it even began.

"Slow," Wells said, as his squad neared the crest of a hill north of their encampment. He was sure the American unit had picked a position similar to the one he had chosen. Wells and his men came over the hill and stopped. Ahead, the ground dipped, then rose again. Wells looked through his binoculars. There they were, a half dozen men standing beside a cluster of mud huts, peering down at the Taliban front lines. They could be villagers, roused by the bombing . . . but they weren't. They were American. The proof was in the pickup half-hidden behind a hut.

The truck meant that the SF guys would have a SAW—a light machine gun—or maybe a .50-caliber, a bigger weapon than anything his men carried. But Wells and his squad would have surprise on their side. Wells waved his men forward, warning them to be quiet. They were excited now, excited at the chance to attack Americans. And Wells, though he hated to admit it, was excited too.

U.S.S. Starker, *Atlantic Ocean*

The ride out had been smooth, but Jennifer Exley felt her stomach clench as the helicopter landed and she stepped onto the gray metal deck of the *Starker,* fifty miles east of Norfolk, Virginia. In international waters, of course, so its precious cargo would remain outside the jurisdiction of American courts.

An old navy amphibious assault ship, the *Starker* was now a brig, a floating jail. Today the vessel held just one prisoner, Tim Keifer, a.k.a. Mohammed Faisal, a twenty-two-year-old American who'd been captured fighting for the Taliban near Mazar-e Sharif in northern Afghanistan. Fighting for the Taliban *against the United States*. Exley was still trying to get her mind around that one.

The capture of John Walker Lindh, the other American Taliban, had been broadcast worldwide. But Keifer's detention had stayed quiet. President Bush had signed an order declaring Keifer an "enemy combatant" and suspending his rights, including his access to American courts. Now Keifer was literally floating in a steel limbo, a place where U.S. laws did not apply. Exley wasn't sure she liked that decision, but maybe this wasn't the time to worry about little things like the Bill of Rights. The ship twisted beneath her, and she yelped as she lost her footing on the slick metal deck. Her guide, a friendly young ensign, reached out a hand and steadied her.

"You okay, Ms. Exley?"

"Fine."

He led her off the deck and down a brightly lit hallway. "Mohammed's in the hospital," the sailor said. "We try to be careful, but he keeps having accidents. Banging his head on doors, sh—" He remembered he was talking to a woman and caught himself, she saw. "*Stuff* like that."

How predictable, Exley thought. As long as they didn't kill him.

"I suppose the crew would rather just throw him overboard?"

"We'd draw straws for the chance," he said brightly. "Here we are."

She showed her CIA identification and special navy pass to the two sailors posted outside Keifer's room. They eyed both carefully, then saluted her. The ensign pulled a thick metal key from his pocket and slid it into the heavy lock on the door. He pushed the door open slowly, and she stepped into the windowless room.

"Take as much time as you like, ma'am," the ensign said, closing the door behind her. "Mohammed's not going anywhere."

Keifer lay on a narrow hospital cot, hands and legs shackled to the side of the frame, an intravenous drip flowing into his arm. His beard had been shaved roughly and his hair cropped close. A yellow bruise ringed his left eye. He was skinny and small and looked like a philosophy grad student or something equally useless. He wasn't much of a flight risk, but just to be sure, a camera in the corner was trained on the bed, and two more sailors stood by the door. Either could have tossed Keifer into the Atlantic with one hand. For one tiny moment Exley felt sorry for him. Then she didn't.

UNDER NORMAL CIRCUMSTANCES, Exley wouldn't have spoken to Keifer. She was a handler, not an interrogator, and the CIA and DIA—the Defense Intelligence Agency, Rumsfeld's boys—had grilled Keifer for weeks. But after reading the transcripts of Keifer's interrogations, Exley and Ellis Shafer, her boss, the section head for the Near East, decided she should talk to Keifer herself.

Exley decided to be his mother. She was old enough, and he probably hadn't seen a woman in a while. She walked to the bed and put her hand on his shoulder. His drugged eyes blinked open. He shrank back, his shoulders hunching, then relaxed a little as she smiled at him.

"Tim. I'm Jen Exley."

He blinked and said nothing.

"You feeling okay?"

"What does it look like?"

Unbelievable. This dumb kid still wanted to play tough. All hundred and forty pounds of him. Fortunately, the sodium pentothal and morphine running through his veins had softened him a little. Amnesty International might have objected, but they didn't get a vote. Exley tried to arrange her face in sympathy rather than the contempt she felt. "Can I sit down?"

He shrugged, rustling his cuffs against the bed. She pulled over a chair.

"Are you a lawyer?"

"No, but I can get you one." A little lie.

"I want a lawyer," Keifer said, his voice slurred. He closed his eyes and shook his head, slowly, metronomically, seeming to draw comfort from the motion. "They said no lawyer. I know my rights."

You're gonna have to take that up with somebody a lot more senior than me, Exley thought.

"I can help you," she said. "But you have to help me."

Again he shook his head, sullenly this time. "What do you want?"

"Tell me about the other American over there. Not John Walker Lindh. The third guy. The older one."

"I told you."

She touched his face, moved his head toward her, to give him a look at her blue eyes—her best feature, she'd always been told, even if crow's-feet had settled around them.

"Look at me, Tim. You told someone else. Not me."

She could see the fight leave his eyes as he, or the drugs in him, decided arguing wasn't worth the trouble. "They called him Jalal. One or two guys said his real name was John."

"John?"

"Maybe they had him confused with John Walker Lindh. I'm not even sure he was American. I never talked to him."

"Not once?" She hoped her voice didn't reveal her disappointment.

"No," Keifer said. He closed his eyes. Again she waited. "The place was big. He was in and out."

"He was free to come and go?"

"Seemed that way."

"What did he look like?"

"Big guy. Tall. Had a beard like everybody else."

"Any distinguishing features?"

"If there were, I didn't see any. It wasn't that kind of camp."

She leaned close to him and smiled. His breath smelled rank and acrid at the same time, like a rotten orange. They probably weren't brushing his teeth much. "Can you remember anything else?"

He seemed to be thinking. "Can I get some water?"

Exley looked at the sailor by the door. He shrugged. A stack of plastic cups sat beside a metal sink in the corner of the room. She filled one and brought it to Keifer, tipping it gently to his lips.

"Thank you." Keifer closed his eyes. "The American—Jalal—guys said he was a real soldier. Tough. He'd been in Chechnya. That's what they said." He opened his eyes, looked at her. "What else can I tell you?"

What she really wanted to know were questions she wasn't supposed to ask. How much of the Koran have you read? Do you really hate America, or was it just an adventure? By the way, when are your friends going to hit us next? Where? How?

And as long as she was chewing over unaskable, unanswerable questions, how about this one: Whose side is he on? Jalal, that is. John Wells. The only CIA agent ever to penetrate al Qaeda. A man whose existence was known to fewer than a dozen agency officials. A singular national asset.

Except that the singular national asset hadn't bothered to communicate with his CIA minders—in other words, with Exley—in two years. Which meant that he had been of zero help in stopping September 11. Why, John? You're alive, and not a prisoner. This kid had confirmed that much, if nothing else. Did you not know? Or have you gone native? You always were a little crazy, or you never would have gone into those mountains. Maybe you spent too many years kneeling on prayer rugs with the bad guys. Maybe you're one of them now.

"What else?" Exley said. "I can't think of anything." She put down the empty cup and stood to leave. Keifer's eyes met hers, and now he really did look like a scared kid. He's just beginning to understand how much trouble he's in, she thought. Thank God he's not my problem.

"What about the lawyer? You promised—"

"I'll get right on it," she said, walking out the door. "Good luck, Tim."

WELLS AND HIS men now stood a mile from the Americans. They had left their horses a few minutes before. He led his men into a narrow saddle, a rock ridge that hid them from the American position. Once they left it they would have no cover, only open ground between them and the enemy. Exactly what Wells wanted. He had no illusions that his squad could get closer without being spotted. The ridge was nearly treeless, and the Special Forces had night-vision equipment far superior to his goggles.

He split his men into two groups. Ahmed would lead three men north in a direct attack on the position, while Wells, Hamid, and Abdullah—the unit's toughest fighter—would dogleg to the northwest, moving higher up the ridgeline, then swoop in from above.

"We must move quickly," Wells said. "Before they can call in their planes. Without those they are weak." His men clustered around him, fingering their weapons excitedly.

Now the important part. "As your commander, I declare this a martyrdom mission," he said. The magic words. They were to fight until they died. No retreat, no surrender. "Does everyone understand?" Wells looked for signs of fear in his men. He saw none. Their eyes were steady. "We fight for the glory of Allah and Mohammed. The enemy has put himself within our grasp. Praise Allah, we will destroy him. *Allahu akbar.*"

"*Allahu akbar,*" Wells's men said quietly. God is great. They were afraid, but excited too, Wells saw. There was no greater glory than to kill an American, or die trying.

Ahmed chambered a round into his AK and led his men out of the saddle. Wells followed, angling up the ridge. Minutes later, still a quarter mile from the Americans, he lay down behind a crumbling boulder, signaling Hamid and Abdullah to do the same. "Wait," he said. "Ahmed attacks first." Things would happen very fast now. He peeked around the rock. Through his binoculars, he could see the Special Forces readying for the attack, setting up their .50-cal and spreading out behind huts and boulders, not quite running but moving quickly and precisely, their training evident in every step.

When Ahmed and his men closed to one hundred yards, the Special Forces opened up on them with a fusillade that echoed across the hillside. Ahmed survived the first wave of fire. The other three men went down immediately, their bodies mauled by the .50-caliber, dead before they hit the ground.

"*Allahu akbar,*" Ahmed shouted, brave and doomed. He ran toward the American position, fire flashing from the muzzle of his AK. He was dead in seconds, as Wells had expected. Wells couldn't help but admire the Americans' skill.

Wells double-checked Ahmed and his men. They were silent and unmoving. He stood and crouched, careful to remain in the shadow of the boulder. For a moment he paused. He had known Hamid and Abdullah for years, broken bread with them, cursed the cold of these mountains with them.

He pulled out the Makarov he carried in a holster strapped to his hip. Pop. Pop. One shot into Hamid's head, one into Abdullah's. Quick and clean. They twitched and gurgled and were still. Wells closed his eyes. *I'm sorry,* he murmured through closed lips. But there was no other way. He hid himself behind the boulder and listened. Silence, but he knew the Americans had heard his shots and were looking his way. He would need to move now, or never.

"American," he yelled down the hill in English. "I'm American. Don't shoot. I'm friendly."

A burst of machine gun fire whistled close above his head.

"I'm American," he yelled again. "Don't shoot!"

"If you're American, stand up!" a voice yelled. "Where we can see you. Arms over your head."

Wells did as he was told, hoping they wouldn't cut him down out of fear or anger or just because they could. He could hear men walking up the slope toward him. Two searchlights popped on, blinding him. "Step forward, then lie prone, arms out."

Wells planted his face in the rocky dirt and kissed the earth. His plan had worked. He'd made contact.

BEHIND WELLS THE soldiers scuffled around. "What the hell?" someone said as they found Hamid and Abdullah. A spotlight illuminated the ground around Wells as a rifle muzzle pressed into his skull.

"Stay very still, Mr. American," the voice said, close now. "Who the fuck are you? And what happened to your friends back there?"

"I'm agency," Wells said. "My name's John Wells."

The muzzle jerked back. A sharp whistle. "Major," the voice above him said. A whispered conversation, then a new voice. "What did you say your name was?"

"John Wells."

The muzzle was back on his skull. "What's your EPI, Mr. Wells?" Emergency Proof of Identity. A short phrase unique to each field agent, allowing him to prove his bona fides in situations like this. Normally not to be revealed to anyone outside the CIA. But Wells figured he'd make an exception, because they'd obviously been briefed that American agents might be operating behind the Taliban lines. And because of the rifle poking at his cranium.

"My EPI is Red Sox, Major." More seconds went by. Wells heard the soldier above him paging through papers.

"No shit," the voice said, friendlier now. A light southern accent. "So it is. I'm Glen Holmes. You can stand."

Wells did, and Holmes—a short, muscular man with a crew cut and a reddish-blond goatee—shook his hand. "I'd love to offer you a beer, Agent Wells, but they're back in Tajikistan."

"Call me John," Wells said, knowing Holmes wouldn't. Wells could see that the Special Forces didn't really trust him. They took his rifle and pistol and the knife strapped to his calf for "safekeeping." But they seemed to believe him when he told them how he had maneuvered his men into their ambush so that he could talk to them. In any case, they didn't hog-tie him or put a bag on his head to make him more cooperative.

So he told them what he had come to tell them, what he knew about the Qaeda camps, the training that the jihadis received, Qaeda's experiments with chemical weapons. "It was tenth-grade chemistry. Mix beaker A with beaker B and see what happens. Kill a couple dogs."

"What about bio? Nukes?"

"We didn't even have reliable electricity, Major. We—they—" As Wells switched pronouns, confusion overcame him. He was American, now and forever, and he would never betray his country. But after years in the camps he had grown to like some of the men in them. Like Ahmed, whom he had just helped kill. Wells shook his head. He would sort all this out later.

All the while Holmes watched him, saying nothing.

"They would have loved to get that stuff, biological weapons, nukes, but they didn't know how."

"Does it feel weird to speak so much English?" Holmes said suddenly.

"Not really," Wells said. "Yes. It does."

"You want to take a break?"

"I'm fine. Only . . ." Wells hesitated, not wanting to seem foolish. "Do you have any Gatorade? I really miss it."

"Fitz, we have any Gatorade?"

They mixed him a packet of orange-flavored Gatorade in a water bottle and Wells guzzled it like a conquistador who'd found the fountain of youth. He told them what he knew about bin Laden's inner circle, which was less than he would have liked, about the way Qaeda was financed, where he thought bin Laden had fled. The SF guys taped everything. He poured out information as fast as he could, clocking the hours as the moon moved across the sky. He wanted to get back by morning. The more confusion when he returned, the fewer questions he'd face about what had happened to his squad. Hundreds of Talibs and Arabs had died this night. Who would notice six more?

The sky began to lighten, and Wells knew he had to leave. "That's it," he said. "I wish I had more time. But I have to go back."

"Back?" For a moment Holmes's eyes widened. "Don't you want an exfil?"

An exfiltration. Don't you want to go home? Somehow Wells had forgotten even to consider the possibility. Probably because it seemed about as likely as going to the moon. Don't you want a box seat at Fenway? A look at the ocean? Don't you want to see a woman in a miniskirt? Don't you want to leadfoot across Montana toward home? Don't you want to kneel in front of your father's grave and apologize for missing his funeral? Don't you want to see Heather and Evan and your mom?

The answer to all those questions was yes. Home was life, his real life, and suddenly the pain of losing it hit him so hard that he closed his eyes and dipped his head in his hands.

"Wells?" Holmes said.

Then Wells remembered the glee that spread through the camps on September 11, the singing and boasting, the prayers to Allah. He had known something big was coming, but not the details. He should have tried to find out more, but he'd assumed Qaeda was aiming for an embassy somewhere, a Saudi oil pumping station. He hadn't wanted to raise suspicions by asking too many questions.

Not the World Trade Center. It was so grand, so destructive. His imagination had failed, like everyone else's. And thousands of people had died.

Wells had made a promise to himself that day: This will never happen again, not as long as I'm alive to stop it. Nothing else mattered. Not that he had much else. Heather had remarried, and Evan probably had no idea who he was. Would he even know Evan? He hadn't seen a picture of his son in years. His real life, whatever that was, had vanished. What he'd done tonight proved that. Killing the men he commanded in cold blood.

How would his family recognize him when he couldn't recognize himself?

"No exfil," Wells said. "Can I have a pen and paper, Major?"

Holmes handed him a pad and a pen. Wells scribbled: "Will pursue UBL"—the agency's initials for Osama, which it called Usama. "No prior knowledge of 9/11. Still friendly. John."

He bit his lip and added one more line. "P.S.: Tell Heather and Evan and my mom I miss them."

He tore off the page, folded it, wrote "Exley" across the front. "Will you get this to Jennifer Exley at CIA? My case officer."

"Yes, sir."

"I'd rather you didn't read it." He handed the page to Holmes.

"Roger that." Holmes pulled out an envelope from another pocket and sealed the paper inside.

"Major, can I ask you something? What was it like?"

"What?"

"Two months ago. September eleventh."

"Nine-eleven?" Holmes shook his head, seemingly replaying the day in his head. "Like the whole country got smacked in the gut. People just sat home watching TV. Watching those towers fall, again and again. The jumpers, the second plane hitting. . . . It was unbelievable. I mean, I really couldn't believe it. If Tom Brokaw had come on and said, 'Hey, America, we were just fucking with you, ha ha,' I would have said, 'Well, okay.' That would have made more sense than what actually happened."

"These guys, they'll do anything." Wells knew it was a less than profound insight, but he was suddenly bone tired.

"My mother died two years ago," Holmes said. "Cancer. Awful. That was the worst day of my life. This was second. And it was like that for everybody. Some of the Delta guys started driving up to New York, to dig people out, but I didn't bother. I knew they'd want us at the base."

Holmes looked at Wells. "You okay, John? Maybe Freddy should check you out."

"Beat, that's all," Wells said. "I should go." He stood and looked down at the plain. "That front line isn't gonna hold much longer."

"Your guys won't last a week," Holmes said.

"My guys." Again Wells felt a strange vertigo.

"No offense."

"No," Wells said.

"Look," Holmes said. "When you make it home, call me. I'm under my wife's name—Debbie Turner. Siler City, North Carolina. I'll take you fishing. Beautiful country."

"Almost as nice as Montana."

"When you get home, John."

"Might be a while," Wells said. He stood. Holmes gave him back his weapons. Wells strapped on the knife and pistol and slung the rifle over his shoulder. Holmes put out his hand and Wells clasped it in both of his.

"Major," he said. "One more thing."

"Yessir?"

"I need you to shoot me."

Holmes took a step back, suddenly wary.

"In the arm. It won't look right otherwise. I can't come back in perfect shape and all my guys gone."

"No chance," Holmes said.

"Major. Then I'll have to do it myself."

"Christ."

"A flesh wound. A through and through. No bone."

Holmes hesitated, then nodded. "Okay. Turn around and start walking."

"Start walking?"

"I'm Delta, Agent Wells." Holmes used his best Carolina drawl:

"I can shoot the dick off a possum at one hundred paces. Which arm?"

"Better make it the left," Wells said. He turned and walked away, slowly, holding his arm out. A few seconds later the shot came, burning through the skin and muscle of his left bicep as if a hot knitting needle had been jabbed into him. "*Cosumaq,*" Wells said, a nasty Arabic curse, as the blood sputtered out. Your mother's cunt. He sat down and looked at Holmes, who was still cradling his pistol. Just in case.

"Nice shot, Major." It was true. The wound was clean and neat.

"Want another?"

Wells laughed, at first slowly, then harder, the breath coming out of him in short gasps as his blood pulsed down his arm. Holmes surely thought him crazy. But Wells couldn't help himself. The Taliban didn't make jokes like that.

"One's fine," he said, his laughter slowly subsiding.

"Want a bandage?"

"I better do it myself." Wells ripped off a piece of his robe and tied a loose tourniquet around his arm, cutting the flow of blood to a trickle. The pain returned, burning intensely up his arm and into his shoulder. He'd felt worse. He'd live. He stood, feeling lightheaded. He closed his eyes until the dizziness subsided.

"Siler City," Holmes called out after him. "Don't forget."

Wells turned away and trudged south into the Afghan night.

Langley, Virginia

EXLEY'S OFFICE WAS standard issue for a midgrade analyst. No windows, a wooden bookcase filled with histories of the Middle East and Afghanistan, two computers—one for a classified network, the other linked to the Internet—and a safe barely concealed behind a generic print of the English countryside. She did have a couple of pictures of her kids on her desk, and a cute birthday card from Randy, but the CIA discouraged its officers from showing too much individuality. The implicit lesson: here today, gone tomorrow.

Wells's note took four days to reach her. She supposed the Special

Forces had more important things to do. In the interim, Kabul had fallen to the Northern Alliance. The Shamali battle had proved that the Talibs—like everyone else—could not stand up to American airpower. Now Exley sat at her desk, reading the cryptic note and the even more disturbing after-action report that had arrived with it. "Wells requested that Maj. Holmes shoot him in the arm so that he would appear to have engaged American forces . . ."

Exley squeezed the bridge of her nose and closed her eyes, but when she opened them nothing had changed. David and Jess would be asleep when she got home, and Randy would be watching television and very obviously not sulking, very obviously not asking how long he would have to put up with her late nights and weekends at work. Saving the world was hard on a marriage. Especially when the wife was doing the saving.

"He's not coming back."

She looked up to see Shafer, her boss, standing in her doorway. He enjoyed showing up unannounced in her office. One of his less attractive traits. Along with his uncertain grooming. He held up his own copy of Wells's note.

"He's not coming back," Shafer said again. "He's gone over. Or maybe he's just loco. But I'll bet you a fresh cup of coffee this is the last we hear from him. Too bad." Shafer didn't exactly look broken-hearted, Exley thought.

"I'm not so sure."

"Reasons?"

"The postscript. 'Tell Heather and Evan and my mom I miss them.' "

Shafer shrugged. "Last will and testament."

"Then he'd say he loves them. He says he misses them. He wants to see them again. Maybe he'll die over there, but he's not trying to."

"Hmm," Shafer said. He turned and walked down the hall, yelling, "It's almost ten. Go home, get some rest," as he went.

"Tuck your shirt in," she muttered. She looked at Wells's note one more time before locking it inside her safe. She and Shafer and even Wells—they'd just have to wait, wouldn't they? They'd all just have to wait.

PART ONE

THE
HOMECOMING
KING

1

North-West Frontier, on the border of Afghanistan and Pakistan

SHEIKH GUL SCOWLED at his congregation. "These days every Muslim must fight jihad," he said in Pashtun, his voice rising. "When the Mongols invaded Baghdad, it didn't help the people of Baghdad that they were pious Muslims. They died at the swords of the infidels."

The sheikh threw his hands over his head.

"Now Islam is under siege again. Under siege in the land of the two mosques, and the land of the two rivers"—Saudi Arabia and Iraq. "Under siege here in Pakistan, where our leader works for Americans and Jews. Everywhere we are under siege," said the sheikh, Mohammed Gul. He was a short, bearded man with a chunky body hidden under a smooth brown robe. His voice seemed to belong to someone much larger. Inside the mosque, a simple brick building whose walls were covered in flaking white paint, the worshippers murmured agreement and drew together. Brothers in arms. But their assent enraged the sheikh further.

"You say, 'Yes, yes.' But what do you do when prayers are finished? Do you sacrifice yourselves? You go home and do nothing. Muslims today love this world and hate death. We have abandoned jihad!" the sheikh shouted. He stopped to look out over the crowd and wipe his brow. "And so Allah has subjugated us. Only when we sacrifice ourselves will we restore glory to Islam. On that day Allah will finally smile on us."

Except it sounds like none of us will be around to see it, Wells thought. In the years that Wells had listened to Gul's sermons, the sheikh had gotten angrier and angrier. The source of his fury was easy to understand. September 11 had faded, and Islam's return to glory remained distant as ever. The Jews still ruled Israel. The Americans had installed a Shia government in Iraq, a country that had always been ruled by Sunnis. Yes, Shias were Muslim too. But Shia and Sunni Muslims had been at odds since the earliest days of Islam. To Osama and his fellow fundamentalist Sunnis—sometimes called Wahhabis—the Shia were little better than Jews.

Al Qaeda, "the Base" of the revolution, had never recovered from the loss of its own base in Afghanistan, Wells thought. When the Taliban fell, Qaeda's troops fled east to the North-West Frontier, the mountainous border of Pakistan and Afghanistan. Wells had narrowly escaped an American bomb at Tora Bora, the last big fight of the Afghan war. He liked to imagine that the bomb had been guided by Glen Holmes, who had swung it away from the hut where Wells hid.

But the United States hadn't closed the noose at Tora Bora, for reasons Wells had never understood. Thousands of jihadis escaped. In 2002, they reached the mountains of the North-West Frontier, so named by the British, since the area was the northwest border of colonial India. The North-West Frontier was a wild land ruled by Pashtuns, devout Muslims who supported Qaeda's brand of jihad, and was effectively closed to Pakistani and American soldiers. Even the Special Forces could operate there only for short stretches.

So Qaeda survived. But it did not thrive. Osama and his lieutenants scurried between holes, occasionally releasing tapes to rouse the faithful. Every few months the group launched an attack. It had blasted a train station in Madrid, blown up hotels in Egypt and subways in London, attacked oil workers in Saudi Arabia. In Iraq, it fought the American occupiers. But nothing that had shaken the world like September 11.

Meanwhile Wells and his fellow jihadis eked out a miserable existence. In theory, Qaeda's paymasters had arranged for Pashtun villagers to house them. In reality, they were a burden on desperately poor families. They had to earn their keep like everyone else. Wells and the half dozen Arabs living in this village, just outside Akora Khatak, survived on stale bread and scraps of lamb. Wells did not want to guess how much weight he had lost. He had hardly recognized himself the few times he had seen himself in a mirror. The bullet hole in his left arm had turned into a knot of scar tissue that ached unpredictably.

The winters were especially difficult, even for Wells, who had grown up playing in the Bitterroot Range on the Montana-Idaho border. The cold sank into his bones. He could only imagine what the Saudis thought. Lots of them had been martyred in these mountains, but not from bombs or bullets. They'd died of pneumonia and altitude sickness and something that looked a lot like scurvy. They'd died asking for their mothers, and a few had died cursing Osama and the awful place he'd led them. Wells ate fresh fruit whenever he could, which wasn't often, and marveled at the toughness of the Pashtuns.

To keep sane he practiced his soldiering as much as possible. The local tribal leader had helped him set up a small firing range on flat ground a few miles outside the village. Every few weeks Wells rode out with a half dozen men and shot off as many rounds as he could spare. But he couldn't pretend he was doing anything more than passing time. They all were. If America vs. Qaeda were a Pop Warner football game, the refs would have invoked the mercy rule and ended it a long time ago.

Gul stepped into the crowd of worshippers. He looked at the men around him and spoke again, his voice low and intense. "The time for speeches is done, brothers," he said. "Allah willing, we will see action soon. May Allah bless all faithful Muslims. Amen."

The men clustered close to hug the sheikh. Waiting his turn, Wells wondered if Gul knew something or was just trying to rally the congregation. He poked with his tongue at a loose molar in the back of his mouth, sending a spurt of pain through his jaw. Dental care in the North-West Frontier left something to be desired. In a few weeks he would have to visit the medical clinic in Akora to have the tooth "examined." Or maybe he'd just find a pair of pliers and do the job himself.

Lately Wells had dreamed of leaving this place. He could hitch a ride to Peshawar, catch a bus to Islamabad, and knock on the front gate of the American embassy. Or, more accurately, knock on the roadblocks that kept a truck bomb from getting too close to the embassy's blastproof walls. A few minutes and he'd be inside. A couple days and he'd be home. No one would say he had failed. Not to his face, anyway. They'd say he had done all he could, all anyone could. But somewhere inside he would know better. And he would never forgive himself.

Because this wasn't Pop Warner football. The mercy rule didn't exist. The men standing beside him in this mosque would happily give their lives to be remembered as martyrs. They were stuck in these mountains, but their goal remained unchanged. To punish the crusaders for their hubris. To take back Jerusalem. To kill Americans. Qaeda's desire to destroy was limited only by its resources. For now the group was weak, but that could change instantly. If Qaeda's assassins succeeded in killing Pakistan's president, the country might suddenly have a Wahhabi in charge. Then bin Laden would have a nuclear weapon to play with. An Islamic bomb. And sooner or later there would be a big hole in New York or London or Washington.

Anyway, living here had a few compensations. Wells had learned the Koran better than he ever expected. He had a sense of how monks had lived in the Middle Ages, copying Bibles by hand. He knew now how one book could become moral and spiritual guidance and entertainment all at once.

After so many years in Afghanistan and Pakistan, Wells found that his belief in Islam—once just a cover story—had turned real. The faith touched him in a way that Christianity never had. Wells had always been skeptical of religion. When he read the Koran at night on his bed alone he suffered the same doubts about its promises of paradise as he did when he read the apostles' description of Christ rising from the dead. Yet he loved the Koran's exhortations that men should treat one another as brothers and give all they could to charity. The *umma*, the brotherhood, was real. He could walk into any house in this village and be offered a cup of hot sweet tea and a meal by a family that could barely feed its own children. And no one needed a priest's help to reach the divine in Islam; anyone who studied hard and was humble could seek enlightenment for himself.

But Islam's biggest strength was its greatest weakness, Wells thought. The religion's flexibility had made it a cloak for the anger of men tired of being ruled by America and the West. Islam was the Marxism of the twenty-first century, a cover for national liberation movements of all stripes. Except that the high priests of Marxism had never promised their followers rewards in the next world in exchange for their deaths in this one. Wahhabis like bin Laden had married their fury at the United States with a particularly nasty vision of Islam. They wanted to take the religion back to the seventh-century desert. They couldn't compete in the modern world, so they would pretend that it didn't exist. Or destroy it. Their anger resonated with hundreds of millions of desperately poor Muslims. But in Wells's eyes they had perverted the religion they claimed to represent. Islam wasn't incompatible with progress. In fact, Islamic nations had once been among the world's most advanced. Eight hundred years ago, as Christians burned witches, the Muslim Abbasids had built a university in Baghdad that held eighty thousand books. Then the Mongols had come. Things had gone downhill ever since.

Wells kept his views to himself. Publicly, he spent hours each day studying the Koran with Sheikh Gul and the clerics at the village madrassa. His Qaeda superiors had taken notice. And that was the other reason Wells stayed in the North-West Frontier. He believed that he had at last convinced Qaeda's leadership of his loyalty; the other jihadis in the village had begun to listen to him more carefully. Or so he hoped.

Wells's turn to greet Sheikh Gul had come. Wells patted his heart, a traditional sign of affection. *"Allahu akbar,"* he said.

"Allahu akbar," said the sheikh. "Will you come to the mosque tomorrow morning to study, Jalal?"

"I would be honored," Wells said.

"Salaam alaikum." Peace be with you.

"Alaikum salaam."

. . .

WELLS WALKED OUT of the mosque into the village's dusty main
street. As he blinked in the weak spring sunlight, two bearded men
walked toward him. Wells knew them vaguely, though not their
names. They lived in the mountains, second-tier bodyguards for
Osama.

"*Salaam alaikum,* Jalal," they said.

"*Alaikum salaam.*"

The men tapped their chests in greeting.

"I am Shihab," the shorter one said.

"Bassim." The taller of the two, though Wells towered over him.
His shoes were leather and his white robe clean; maybe life in the
mountains had improved. Or maybe Osama was living in a village
now.

"*Allahu akbar,*" Wells said.

"*Allahu akbar.*"

"The *mujaddid* asks that you come with us," Bassim said. Mujaddid. The renewer, a man sent by Allah to lead Islam's renaissance.
Bin Laden was the mujaddid.

"Of course." A battered Toyota Crown sedan was parked behind
the men. It was the only car in the village that Wells didn't recognize, so it must be theirs. He stepped toward it. Bassim steered him
away.

"He asks that you pack a bag. With everything you own that you
wish to keep."

The request was unexpected, but Wells merely nodded. "Shouldn't
take long," he said. They walked down an alley to the brick hut
where Wells lived with three other jihadis.

Inside, Naji, a young Jordanian who had become Wells's best
friend in the mountains, thumbed through a tattered magazine
whose cover featured Imran Khan, a famous Pakistani cricketeer-
turned-politician. In the corner a coffeepot boiled on a little steel
stove.

"Jalal," Naji said, "have you found us any sponsors yet?" For
months, Naji and Wells had joked to each other about starting a
cricket team for Qaeda, maybe getting corporate sponsorship: "The
Jihadis will blow you away." Wells wouldn't have made those jokes

to anyone else. But Naji was more sophisticated than most jihadis. He had grown up in Amman, Jordan's capital, paradise compared to this village. And Wells had saved Naji's life the previous summer, stitching the Jordanian up after Afghan police shot him at a border checkpoint. Since then the two men had been able to talk openly about the frustrations of living in the North-West Frontier.

"Soon," Wells said.

Hamra, Wells's cat, rubbed against his leg and jumped on the thin gray blanket that covered his narrow cot. She was a stray Wells had found two years before, skinny, red—which explained her name; *hamra* means "red" in Arabic—and a great leaper. She had chosen him. One winter morning she had followed him around the village, mewing pathetically, refusing to go away even when he shouted at her. He couldn't bear watching her starve, so despite warnings from his fellow villagers that one cat would soon turn into ten, he'd taken her in.

"Hello, Hamra," he said, petting her quickly as Bassim walked into the hut. Shihab followed, murmuring something to Bassim that Wells couldn't hear.

"Bassim and Shihab—Naji," Wells said.

"*Marhaba,*" Naji said. Hello. Shihab and Bassim ignored him.

"Please, have coffee," Wells said.

"We must leave soon," Bassim said.

"Naji," Wells said. "Can you leave us for a moment?"

Naji looked at Bassim and Shihab. "Are you sure?"

"*Nam.*"

As Naji walked out, Wells stopped him. "Naji," Wells said. He ran his fingers over Hamra's head. "Take care of her while I'm gone."

"When will you be back, Jalal?"

Wells merely shook his head.

"*Hamdulillah,* then," Naji said. Praise be to God, a traditional Arabic blessing. "*Masalaama.*" Good-bye.

"*Hamdulillah.*" They hugged, briefly, and Naji walked out.

BASSIM AND SHIHAB looked on as Wells grabbed a canvas bag from under his cot. He threw in the few ragged clothes he wanted:

his spare robe, a pair of beaten sneakers, a faded green wool sweater, its threads loose. A world-band radio he'd bought in Akora Khatak a year before, and a couple of spare batteries. The twelve thousand rupees—about two hundred dollars—he had saved. He didn't have much else. No photographs, no television, no books except the Koran and a couple of Islamic philosophy texts. He slipped those gently into the bag. And his guns, of course. He lay on the dirt floor and pulled his AK and his Makarov from under the bed.

"Those you can leave, Jalal," Bassim said.

Wells could not remember the last time he had slept without a rifle. He would rather have left his clothes. "I'd rather not."

"You won't need them where you're going."

Wells decided not to argue. Not that he had much choice. In any case, he always had his knife. He slid the guns back under the bed.

"The dagger as well," Bassim said. "It will be safer for all of us."

Without a word, Wells lifted his robe, unstrapped his knife from his leg and tossed it on the bed. He looked around the room, trying to remember what else he might want. He had no computer or camera or cell phone. His cherished night-vision goggles had broken during the bombing at Tora Bora.

He had held on to a piece of shrapnel from that battle, shrapnel that had gashed a hole in a wall inches above his head. But he had no desire to take it with him. Had his life narrowed to this? Yes. Wells supposed that was why he didn't fear what would happen next. He zipped his bag. "Good-bye, Hamra," he said, stroking her thin fur. She arched her back, jumped off the bed, and strolled out of the hut without a second glance. So much for animal intuition, Wells thought.

"That's all?" Bassim said.

"My good china's in the other hut." Immediately he wished he hadn't made the joke, for Bassim looked blankly at him.

"Good china?"

"Let's go."

AT THE CAR Shihab opened the front passenger door and waved Wells inside. "*Shukran jazeelan,*" Wells said. Thanks very much. Shihab said nothing, just shut the door and climbed in the back.

Bassim slid into the driver's seat, and they rolled off. Wells wondered if he was being taken to bin Laden again—though if he was, they were using very different tactics this time.

He had met Osama twice before, in visits that left him no chance to carry out his vow to kill Qaeda's maximum leader. The first came just before the United States invaded Iraq. Wells had been picked up outside Akora Khatak, blindfolded, and driven for hours over potholed roads. Then he was transferred to a horse-drawn cart and shuffled over rock paths for hours more. When the ride finished, he was stripped to his tattered T-shirt and shorts and searched. His blindfold was removed and he was led up a mountain path that ended at a stone cave.

Inside, a small generator provided light and three prayer rugs decoration. A half-eaten plate of lamb and rice sat on a rough wooden table; bin Laden sat behind it, flanked by bodyguards slinging AKs. The sheikh looked gaunt and weak, his long beard grayish white. Wells knelt, and bin Laden had asked whether he believed the United States would go to war with Iraq.

"Yes, Sheikh," he'd said.

"Even if the rest of the world does not agree?"

"The crusaders are anxious for this war."

"And will they win?"

"You saw what their bombs can do. They will be in Baghdad before summer."

"So it would be foolish for us to send soldiers?"

Wells reminded himself not to be too negative. "We cannot stop them from destroying Saddam. But afterward, when they have taken over, they will be more vulnerable. *Inshallah,* we can hit them every day, small attacks, grinding them down." At this Wells felt a pang of guilt, wondering how many American soldiers would die in the kind of war he had proposed. But bin Laden would surely have reached that conclusion anyway. Guerrilla wars were the only way to fight the U.S. Army.

Bin Laden stroked his beard, looked away, looked back at Wells with cunning narrow eyes. Finally he smiled. "Yes," he said. "Yes. Thank you, Jalal." And with that the sheikh waved him out.

·　·　·

TWO YEARS LATER Wells had been taken to a different cave for another meeting, where bin Laden had asked him about the Hoover Dam. "Is it a great symbol of America?" he had said. Wells had answered honestly. Most Americans had no idea what or where the Hoover Dam was.

"Are you sure, Jalal?" bin Laden said. He sounded disappointed.

Wells looked at the guards flanking bin Laden and wished for a gun or a knife tipped with rat poison. Even a chip in his shoulder so a B-2 could drop a bomb on this stinking hole. "Yes, *Mujaddid*," he said.

Bin Laden nodded. *"Shukran,"* he said, and the guards escorted Wells out. He did not know how much credit he deserved for the fact that the Hoover Dam was still in one piece.

NOW, AS HE sat in the Toyota, Wells wasn't sure what to think. If they had wanted to kill him they could have taken him into the mountains, or even shot him while he slept. The Pakistani cops wouldn't exactly launch an all-out investigation. The police hardly came into the North-West Frontier without Pakistani Army escorts.

But they weren't going into the mountains. They were heading toward Peshawar. Wells figured that increased his chances of survival. As long as they didn't get hit by a bus. The roads in Pakistan were a constant game of chicken, and Bassim drove as though he wanted to catch afternoon tea with Allah. Wells's head snapped back as Bassim swerved into oncoming traffic to pass a truck stuffed with cheap wooden furniture. As an oncoming gasoline tanker blasted its horn, Bassim cut in front of the furniture truck and back into his own lane, nearly sliding off the road and into a ravine.

"Easy, Bassim," Wells said. Bassim turned to stare at him, ignoring the road. The Toyota accelerated again, closing in on a tractor dragging a cartload of propane cylinders.

"You don't like how I drive? You want to drive?"

Jesus Christ, Wells thought—a mental tic he supposed he would never lose. The whole Muslim world suffered from a massive testosterone overdose, and the jihadis were the worst. "Of course not," Wells said, careful to keep a straight face. If he as much as smiled

Bassim really would take them into the ditch, just to prove he could. "You drive great."

A long honk pulled Bassim's attention back to the road. They were about to slam into the back of the propane cart. Bassim stamped on the brakes and the Toyota skidded to a stop by the side of the road. "See," Bassim said. "There is nothing wrong with my driving. My reflexes are superb."

"*Nam,*" Wells said.

"My father was a famous driver. I learned from him."

"Your father," the otherwise silent Shihab said from the back seat, "died in a car accident."

Bassim turned to glare at Shihab as Wells bit his lip to stifle his laughter. Finally Bassim tapped the gas and they lurched back into traffic. No one said anything the rest of the trip.

TWO HOURS LATER the Toyota rolled into Peshawar, the biggest city in the North-West Frontier, a million-person jumble of crumbling concrete buildings and brick huts. Bassim nosed the sedan through a slum clogged with donkey carts hauling propane tanks and garbage. The roads became so crowded that the car could go no farther. In front of a tiny shop whose windows were filled with dusty tins of condensed milk, Bassim killed the engine. Shihab hopped out and opened Wells's door.

"Come," he said, tugging Wells down the street. The rich heavy stench of sewage and mud filled the air. Wells stepped through piles of rotten fruit and donkey shit. Children ran around them, kicking cans and a torn sphere that had once been a soccer ball. So many children. They were everywhere in Pakistan. They sat on the streets, selling toys and overripe bananas, eyes shining with hunger. In neighborhoods like this one they surrounded anyone standing still, their hands out, smiling and asking for "rupees, rupees." The lucky ones found their way to the madrassas, Islamic schools that educated them well in the Koran and badly in everything else. What would they do when they grew up, if not join the jihad?

Bassim pushed open the rusting steel door of an apartment building and pulled Wells inside. "Third floor." He and Shihab seemed desperate to get off the street. Wells wondered whether bin Laden would really risk living here.

The stairwell was dark and smelled of piss and onions. When they reached the third floor, Bassim tugged Wells toward the back of the building. He knocked twice on a steel door, then paused and knocked twice again.

"*Nam?*" a voice said from inside.

Bassim said nothing but knocked twice more. The door swung open. A man in a turban waved them in with his AK.

The room was dark and dreary, lit by a trickle of fading daylight that leaked through the dirty window high on the back wall. Beneath the window, a small poster of bin Laden had been pinned up carefully.

"Sit," the guard said, pointing to a bench covered with tattered red cushions. Wells took a closer look around. Behind a blue beaded curtain, a narrow corridor led to the back of the apartment. In a corner, water boiled on a stove beside scissors, a razor, and a blue plastic mirror. The only other furniture was a wooden chair that had been placed atop a bunch of newspapers.

The minutes ticked by. No one said a word. Wells had never seen Arab men quiet for this long. He wondered if they really planned to shoot him in here. So be it. He had done his best. Nonetheless, he looked around, half-consciously plotting escape routes. That boiling water would come in handy.

Wells heard the shuffle of footsteps in the corridor. "Stand," the guard said quickly, gesturing with his rifle. As they jumped up, the curtain parted and four men walked in, led by a heavy man wearing square steel glasses. Ayman al-Zawahiri. Wells understood why his minders had been so nervous. Zawahiri was bin Laden's deputy, a man almost more important to Qaeda than the sheikh himself. He knew the details of the group's operations, its financing, where its men were hidden. Bin Laden set broad strategy and spoke for the organization, but without Zawahiri Qaeda could not function. Zawahiri hugged Shihab and Bassim and nodded to Wells.

"*Salaam alaikum,* Jalal."

"*Salaam alaikum,* Mujahid."

"*Allahu akbar.*"

"*Allahu akbar.*"

"We have much to talk about. But first you must shave." Zawahiri pointed at the pot of water.

"Shave?" Wells was proud of his thick, bushy beard, which he had not trimmed since coming to the North-West Frontier. Every Qaeda member wanted "a beard the length of a fist," which fatwas—religious edicts—had decreed the minimum acceptable length. Wells's was even longer.

"The Prophet would not approve," Wells said.

"In this case he would." Behind the glasses, Zawahiri's eyes were flat.

Wells decided not to argue. "To the skin?"

"*Nam,*" Zawahiri said. "To the skin."

So while the other men watched, Wells clipped his long brown beard with the scissors, leaving tufts of curly hair on the counter by the stove.

He looked in the mirror. In place of his beard, a pathetic coat of peach fuzz covered his face. Already he hardly recognized himself. He dipped the razor—a plastic single-blade—in the pot and scraped it over his skin. He had to admit he enjoyed the sensation of shaving, the heat of the blade on his face. He took his time, using short smooth strokes, tapping the razor against the pot to shake out the stubble. Finally he was done. Again he looked in the mirror.

"Very handsome, Jalal," Zawahiri said. He seemed amused.

Wells rubbed his newly smooth face. "It feels strange," he said. More than strange. He felt young and soft without the beard. Vulnerable.

"Sit," Zawahiri said, pointing at the chair with the newspapers beneath it. "I will cut your hair." Wells sat silently as Qaeda's No. 2 went to work. He tried to remember the last time someone else had cut his hair; in Afghanistan and the North-West Frontier he had done the job himself. In Washington, maybe, the night before he had left the United States to join the camps.

The night he had stayed at his apartment instead of meeting Exley for a drink after work. Just a drink, say good-bye before I go, he'd said, and they'd both known he was lying and had laughed to cover their nervousness. Yes, he thought. Had to be that night. He had gotten the haircut for her. But then he hadn't shown up. He'd been ashamed, embarrassed, for his wife and for Exley's husband. He'd driven home after the haircut, hadn't called to cancel, and the next morning he had left on a trip that hadn't stopped yet. He had forgotten that night, or shoved it into a corner of his mind where he put all the things that didn't help him survive over here. Now the memories came flooding back. Exley. Was her hair still short? Did she still have that long blue dress?

He'd been gone a long time.

ZAWAHIRI TAPPED HIS shoulder. Wells looked down to see clumps of his curly brown hair scattered over the newspaper. "Now you don't look so Arab. Good," Zawahiri said. He handed the mirror to Wells. A little ragged, but surprisingly decent.

"Stand here," Zawahiri said, pointing to the beaded blue curtain. "Waleed, take Jalal's picture." One of the men who'd come in with Zawahiri held up a portable passport camera. Wells wondered whether they were taking a death shot, to be FedExed to Langley along with a dozen black roses.

"Look at the light," Waleed said. Click. Click. Click. "*Shukran.*" He walked down the corridor.

"Sit," Zawahiri said to Wells, tapping the bench beside him. "Jalal, what would you do if the sheikh said your time for martyrdom had come?"

Wells looked around the room, readying himself. Only one gun out, though the others were surely armed. He might have a chance. Yet he thought trying to escape would be a mistake. Zawahiri's manner seemed professorial, as if he were genuinely interested in Wells's answer. They wouldn't have brought him all this way just to kill him; they could have done that easily in the mountains, and Zawahiri wouldn't have bothered to come.

"If Allah wishes martyrdom for me, then so be it," Wells said.

"Even if you did not know why?"

"We cannot always understand the ways of the Almighty."

"Yes," Zawahiri said. "Very good." He stood. "Jalal—John— you are American."

"Once I was American," Wells said. "I serve Allah now."

"You served in the American army. You jumped from airplanes."

Don't argue, Wells told himself. He's testing you. "My past is no secret, Mujahid. They taught me to fight. But they follow a false prophet. I accepted the true faith."

Zawahiri glanced at the man sitting in the corner, a handsome Pakistani with neatly trimmed black hair and a small mustache.

"You have fought with us for many years. You study the Koran. You do not fear martyrdom. You seem calm even now." Zawahiri took the AK from the guard. Almost idly, he flicked down the safety, setting the rifle on full automatic. He pointed the gun at Wells.

"Every man fears martyrdom. Those who say they don't are lying," Wells said, remembering the men he had seen die. If he was wrong about all of this, he hoped Zawahiri could shoot straight, at least. Make it quick.

"So you are afraid?" Zawahiri said. He pulled back the rifle's slide, chambering a round.

Wells stayed utterly still. Either way he wouldn't have long to wait now. "I trust in Allah and I trust in the Prophet," he said.

"See?" Zawahiri said to the mustached man. He again pulled back the slide on the rifle, popping the round out of the chamber. He clicked up the rifle's safety and handed it back to the guard.

"If you trust in the Prophet, then I trust you," he said. "And I have a mission for you. An important mission." Zawahiri motioned to a fat man who had sat silently in the corner during the meeting. "This is Farouk Khan. Allah willing, he will have a task for you."

"*Salaam alaikum.*"

"*Alaikum salaam.*"

Then Zawahiri pointed to the mustached man. "And this is Omar Khadri," he said. "You will see him again. In America."

Khadri wore Western clothes, a button-down shirt and jeans. "Hello, Jalal," he said. In English. *English* English. He sounded like he'd come straight from Oxford. Khadri put out a hand, and Wells shook it—a very Western greeting. Arab men usually hugged.

"They're ready," Waleed said from the corridor.

"Bring them," Zawahiri said.

Waleed walked back into the room and handed two passports to Zawahiri.

"Very good," Zawahiri said, and handed the passports to Wells: one Italian and one British, both featuring the pictures of Wells taken a few minutes before, and both good enough to fool even an experienced immigration agent.

"Today is Friday," Zawahiri said. "On Tuesday there is a Pakistan Airlines flight to Hong Kong. A friend in the ISI"—the Inter-Service Intelligence, the powerful Pakistani secret police agency—"will put you on it. Use the Italian passport for Hong Kong customs. Wait a week, then fly to Frankfurt. From there you should have no problems getting into the United States with the British passport."

"Your skin is the right color, after all," Khadri said. He laughed, a nasty little laugh that scratched at Wells. He would have been glad to watch me die, Wells thought.

"And then, Mujahid?" he said to Zawahiri.

Zawahiri pulled out a brick of hundred-dollar bills and a torn playing card from his robe. He handed Wells the bills, held together with a fraying rubber band. "Five thousand dollars. To get to New York." He held up the card, half of the king of spades.

"There's a deli in Queens," Khadri said. "Give them this. They'll give you thirty-five thousand dollars."

Hawala, Wells thought. The bane of American efforts to clamp down on Qaeda's finances. The informal banking system of the Middle East, used by traders for centuries to move money. The other half of the card had been mailed from Pakistan to Queens, or maybe brought over by hand. The two halves functioned as a unique code, a thirty-five-thousand-dollar withdrawal waiting to be made. Eventually the accounts would be evened up; Zawahiri would funnel thirty-five grand in gold bars—plus a fee—to the deli owner's brother in Islamabad, or diamonds to a cousin in Abu Dhabi. The owner might be a jihadi, or just a man who knew how to walk money around the world without leaving footprints.

Zawahiri handed the card to Wells. He looked at it—an ordinary red-backed playing card—then tucked it into the brick of bills. "I'll do my best not to lose it," he said. "How will I know the deli?"

"We've set up an e-mail account for you—SmoothJohnny1234@ gmail.com," Omar said. "All one word."

"Smooth Johnny?" Wells said. "I'm not so sure about that, Omar."
He laughed as naturally as he could. Best to get on the guy's good
side. "And then?"

"Then you move to Atlanta," Zawahiri said.

"And wait. It may be a few months. Practice your shooting,"
Khadri said. "Get a job. Keep out of the mosques. Blend in. It
shouldn't be hard."

"Can't you tell me more?"

Khadri shook his head. "In time, Jalal."

"Good luck," Zawahiri said.

Wells hoped his face didn't betray his fury. They had shoved him
to the edge of a thousand-foot drop, made him see his own death.
And he had passed their test. So he was alive, with five grand in his
pocket and a ride to Hong Kong. But they still didn't trust him
enough to tell him what they had planned.

Fine, Wells thought. In time. He tapped his chest. "I won't fail
you, Mujahid," he said. *"Salaam alaikum."*

"Alaikum salaam."

Zawahiri and Khadri stood to leave. At the door, Khadri turned
and looked at Wells. *"Alaikum salaam,* John. How does it feel to be
going home?"

"Home?" Wells said. "I wish I knew."

2

United Airlines flight 919, above the Atlantic Ocean

THE LITTLE GIRL in 35A saw them first. Angela Smart, of Reston, Virginia, flying home with her family from a spring break trip to see her grandparents in London. Angela was glad the trip was almost over. She missed her friends, and Josie and Richard—her grands—were nice, but they smelled funny. She looked out the window again and wondered when they'd be home. When she asked her dad, who was in the seat behind her, he just said, "Not far now, Smurfette," and snorted like he'd said something funny. She didn't even know who Smurfette was. Her dad was goofy sometimes.

At least she had a window seat. The empty blue sky was beautiful; maybe she would be a pilot when she grew up. Being up here all the time would be fun. Then she saw it, a speck in the sky at the edge of the horizon. She pressed her face to her window. Was it? It was. A plane. Two planes, far away but coming closer. They looked like little darts with wings. She nudged her mother, sleeping next to her in 35B.

"Stop it, Angela," Deirdre Smart muttered.

The darts were definitely getting bigger. Angela poked her mother again. "Mommy. Look."

"What?"

"Look."

Deirdre opened her eyes. She was annoyed, Angela could see. "What, Angela?"

"Outside." Angela pointed.

Her mother looked. "Oh good Lord," she said.

She grabbed Angela's hand.

"Is something wrong, Mommy?"

"No, dear. Everything's fine."

The big jet's speakers crackled to life. "From the flight deck, this is Captain Hamilton. You may have noticed that we have some company to the left and right. Those are F-16s, the pride of the United States Air Force. They'll be riding with us into Dulles. No reason to be alarmed." The captain sounded utterly confident, as if fighter jets escorted his flights home all the time. He clicked off for a moment, then clicked back on.

"However, I am going to have to ask you to remain in your seats the rest of the flight. No exceptions. Not for any reason. And please turn off all your laptops, CDs, any electronic equipment. If you're in the bathroom now, please finish your business and return to your seat. If you do notice any of your fellow passengers using electronic devices or doing anything that seems . . . unusual, don't hesitate to signal the flight attendants. I appreciate your cooperation. We've got a little weather coming up, but we should be on the ground in an hour and forty-five minutes."

"Unusual? What the fuck does that mean?" Angela heard someone behind them say.

DEIRDRE SMART SQUIRMED in her seat and craned her neck to see her fellow passengers. Most of them were doing exactly what she was, eyeing one another warily. Had anyone on the plane struck her as "unusual"? Obviously that guy with the beard and the robe across the cabin. But no terrorist would dress that way, right? He'd get so much attention. Unless he figured that the security guys would think that too. A double cross. Whatever you called it. How was she supposed to know? It wasn't her job to look for terrorists, for God's sake.

I don't want to live this way, Deirdre thought. I want to be able to take my kids to see my parents without worrying if we're going to get blown to bits at thirty-five thousand feet. She figured she was like most people. In the years since September 11, her fears of terrorism had faded. Sure, she knew the bad guys were out there. Once in a while, like when she went through security checks at the airport, or watched *24*, she thought about the possibility of another attack. But she didn't really expect one, not in America, and certainly not in the Virginia suburbs.

Now she was flooded by the feeling of powerlessness that had overtaken her on September 11. My family never did anything to any of you, she thought. Why are you trying to hurt me? She supposed that feeling of fear was what they wanted, what they lived for. She'd read somewhere that when planes blew up in the air the force of the wind tore your whole body apart. A second of awful pain. Or maybe they'd be alive the whole way down, until they hit the ocean and got pulverized into shark bait.

Deirdre looked out the window at the fighters shadowing their jet. Dear God, I know we haven't been going to church every Sunday, she thought. But if You get us through this we will. We'll give more to charity. . . . She stopped herself. This was no way to pray. Prayer wasn't about making deals with God. She remembered what her pastor had said two weeks before: We pray to celebrate God's majesty and our faith in Him. Not to negotiate. Fine. She wouldn't negotiate. She began to murmur to herself. The Lord is my shepherd; I shall not want. He leads me down into green pastures . . .

"Mommy," her daughter whimpered. "I'm scared." Angela was crying. "I don't know why, but I'm scared."

"Hold my hand, baby," Deirdre said. "We'll be home soon."

DAVID MADE A nifty move, sliding the ball between his defender's legs and carving himself a slice of open field. As the defense closed in on the void he'd created, he passed the ball off and cut toward the goal for a return pass. Perfect, Jennifer Exley thought. Her son was nine, and the best player in the Arlington junior league. At least she thought so, based on her limited experience as a soccer mom. She admitted she might be biased.

"Great play, David!" she yelled, feeling like a real mother for the first time in a while. He shot her a quick look, embarrassed and proud.

Her pager and cellphone went off simultaneously. A bad sign.

"Jennifer?" It was Ellis Shafer. A very bad sign. "I need you."

"Fuck, Ellis." Another Saturday with David and Jessica spoiled. Another pathetic call to Randy and his fiancée, asking them if they could take the kids on a weekend when she was supposed to have custody.

"It's a priority, Jennifer." That word meant something. Shafer shouldn't even have used it on a nonsecure line.

"Just let me call my husband—"

"Ex-husband?"

"Thank you, Ellis. I'd forgotten about the divorce. David's playing soccer. Lemme see if Randy can pick him up."

"We'll get the goons"—the internal CIA security officers—"to babysit if we have to. Just get in here."

"Such a charmer, Ellis."

"See you soon." He hung up.

"I love you too, honey," she said to the dead line. Cheers erupted around her. David ran down the field, his skinny arms over his head, hooting, as the other team's goalie sheepishly fished the ball from the net. "Did you see it, Mom? Did you see me score?"

Of course not.

"Of course," she said.

THE VIEW OF the Potomac from the George Washington Memorial Parkway usually calmed her, but not today. She tore down the narrow road, flashing her brights at anyone who didn't move aside, swerving left to right like a trucker on a meth binge.

She should have been driving a Ferrari, not a green Dodge minivan with an American Youth Soccer Organization sticker plastered to the back bumper, she thought. No, the minivan was perfect. It made the absurdity of the situation complete. Soccer mom by day, CIA bureaucrat by night. Or was it the other way around?

She came over a rise at ninety miles an hour. The van got air, then thudded back to the pavement, springs grinding, tires squealing. A hard storm had passed through in the morning, and the road was slick with moisture. Exley took a deep breath. She needed to relax. Wrapping the van around a tree wouldn't do her or her kids any good. She eased off the gas.

AT HER OFFICE, she found Shafer standing by her door, cup of coffee in one hand, sheaf of papers in the other. She shook her head at him as she walked in. He set the coffee on the desk and handed her the papers. "One Splenda, the way you like it. Sorry about the soccer."

"Ellis. You feel sorrow? Did they upgrade your software?"

"Funny."

The papers were marked with all the usual secret classifications. Exley had long ago grown cynical about the agency's zest for classifying documents. Secret, Top Secret, Triple Secret with a Cherry on Top—most of it was dreck, and the rest was usually in the *Post* and the *Times* if you looked hard enough. But not always.

"Tick shipped these an hour ago," Shafer said. Tick was the Terrorist Threat Integration Center, created to amalgamate data from the CIA, the FBI, the National Security Agency, Defense, and any other government agency that might have information on potential attacks. "The latest Echelon."

Echelon: a worldwide network of satellite stations maintained by the United States, Britain, and friends. Built during the Cold War to listen in on the Soviets, now used to monitor e-mail and Internet traffic as well as phone calls and faxes. The names of Echelon's stations—Sugar Grove, Menwith Hill, Yakima, a dozen others—were known to spy buffs and conspiracy theorists the world over. They seemed to believe that the network was some sort of electronic god, seeing and hearing every conversation ever held, tracking every e-mail ever sent.

If only, Exley thought. For its original purpose, Echelon had worked well. In the new world, not so much. There was just too much information moving across the Internet. No one could read every e-mail, even if they could all be captured. The National Security Agency, the geeks in Maryland who ran Echelon, had developed the most sophisticated language filters in the world to cull spam and other low-value e-mails from their intercepts. The filters allowed the

NSA to discard the vast majority of the traffic Echelon picked up without showing it to human analysts. Even so, millions of potentially suspicious e-mails in dozens of different languages were sent every day. Reading all of them was impossible. And the problem was getting worse. In the race between the spies and the spammers, the spammers were winning. Penis-enlargement pills had turned out to be Osama's best friend.

The stack Shafer had given her held printouts of intercepted e-mails from Islamabad, Karachi, and London, with cryptic allusions to an important game . . . players in town . . . the team preparing for a glorious victory after Eid—a Muslim festival that had ended a couple of months before.

Shafer poked a finger toward her. "The last one's what counts," he said, his left leg twitching.

"Ellis," she said. "Easy." He had a jumpy, dazzling mind and a habit of intuiting connections on the slimmest evidence. She preferred to work methodically, building cases on the real rather than the invisible. Faith-based intelligence had gotten the country into trouble more than once

Still, she wished that the agency had listened to Shafer during the summer of 2001, when he'd insisted that al Qaeda was planning something big, most likely on American soil. The next year he'd been transferred out of the agency's Near East section and into the Joint Terrorism Task Force, which combined officials from the CIA, FBI, Department of Homeland Security, and every other government agency responsible for stopping terrorism. JTTF was supposed to break down the bureaucratic walls that separated the agencies, so that Langley knew what the Feebs were doing, and vice versa. Sometimes it worked, sometimes it didn't.

Officially, Shafer was an assistant director of the JTTF. In reality, he was the closest thing to a free agent inside the government. He didn't have a lot of analysts, but he had what he really wanted: access to every scrap of data the JTTF possessed. He functioned as a B-reader, a provider of second opinions. His memos went straight to the agency's deputy directors for operations and intelligence. With any luck, they even got read. Shafer and Exley both knew that the agency did not like Shafer. It feared his potential to cause trouble;

the headlines would be awful if he complained publicly that the agency had marginalized him: INTELLIGENCE OFFICER WHO WARNED OF 9/11 SAYS CIA AGAIN IGNORING DANGER SIGNS.

Exley had moved with Shafer to the JTTF, leaving behind her field agents, who had never met her expectations anyway. Shafer had told her that having her with him was his only condition for taking the job. She understood why; their minds meshed. But working with him could be exhausting.

She sipped her coffee, ignored Shafer's twitching leg, and kept reading. "Sixes and sevens," she said. The NSA classified the intercepts on a scale of 1 to 9, based on the likelihood that they represented real al Qaeda traffic. As far as she knew, no e-mail had ever been rated 9—certain. Only a few had ever been classified as 8, extremely likely.

"I wouldn't have bothered you otherwise," Shafer said.

Like any surveillance tool, Echelon was most useful when it could be targeted, sifting through a million e-mails instead of a trillion. So NSA paid very close attention to the handful of al Qaeda–affiliated Web sites that received anonymous postings calling for jihad and hinting at attacks. The CIA and NSA didn't particularly care about what was said on the postings themselves. Everyone assumed al Qaeda would be too smart to give up an ongoing operation on a public Web site.

What the bad guys did not know, or so the agencies hoped, was that the United States had convinced Jordan and several other countries to let the NSA tap into the Web-hosting companies that ran the sites. Thanks to those taps, the NSA could catalogue the Internet addresses of anyone who posted to or even just viewed the pages. Echelon looked for e-mails sent from the hot addresses, then targeted the people who received those e-mails, tracing a steadily widening web of connections. The NSA hoped to find nexuses, e-mail accounts that were hubs of suspect traffic, hidden connections that might reveal the path of al Qaeda's orders.

Exley and Shafer worried that al Qaeda was deliberately using e-mail as a source of misinformation. The same Arab intelligence agencies that had let the NSA install the taps might have tipped the bad guys to what the United States had done. Still, the taps had turned up enough interesting tidbits that the CIA and NSA took them seriously. In the absence of decent human intelligence on al Qaeda, Echelon was the most consistent source of information the United States had.

AS SHAFER PROMISED, the last e-mail was the most important—and the shortest. Five letters and three numbers, nothing more. Echelon would have ignored it as spam, except that it had come from a hot address. U 9 1 9 A L H R. United Airlines flight 919. London Heathrow. The NSA had rated it a 6/7—likely/highly likely.

"What do you think?" Shafer said.

"I think if I was on that plane I wouldn't be paying much attention to the movie," she said. "Why'd the Brits let it leave?"

"The flight number was only sent today. NSA caught it two hours ago." Shafer pointed to the e-mail's time stamp. "They were already in the air." He handed her another piece of paper, the flight's passenger manifest: 307 names. Not quite full.

"How many matches?" Exley said. How many passengers on the flight had names that matched the Terrorist Threat Integration Center's combined watch list?

"Two. Maybe three. You know how it is."

She knew how it was. Most Arab names could be transliterated into English a dozen ways. Mohammed Abdul Lattif. Mohamad Abdullattif. Mohamed Abdullatif. Muhammad Abdul Laitef. The NSA hadn't found a foolproof way to cover all the possible translations without making the list too big to be useful.

Making matters worse, all the agencies had built separate watch lists over the years. Melding them into a master list was a top priority for the threat center. But the project, like so much else in the terror war, had not gone smoothly. The agencies had different secrecy classifications, different thresholds for inclusion. Some used photographs and fingerprints when available, others didn't. So far only about half the names on the lists had been combined.

Again Shafer wagged his finger at her. "Anyone jump out?"

"I'm looking," she said. Jim Bates . . . nope . . . Edward Faro . . . not likely . . .

What went unsaid was the fact that the government's various

divisions, including the CIA, didn't want to share everything they had. Like the fact that the agency was paying close attention to several guys who were confidential informants for the FBI. If the snitches' names wound up on a combined list, the Feebs might accidentally-on-purpose tell them that they'd been targeted. The history of tension between the two agencies ran so deep that even terrorism couldn't make it go away entirely.

In darker moments, Exley wondered if the watch list itself wasn't simply bureaucratic ass covering. After all, what hijacker or suicide bomber would be dumb enough to book a ticket under his own name? Except that the 9/11 boys had done just that. Al Qaeda wasn't always brilliant either.

She focused on the list. Yusuf Hazalia . . . he was probably getting some dirty looks about now . . . David Kim . . . not unless he was North Korean . . . Mohammed al-Nerzi. She stopped.

"Al-Nerzi. That rings a bell," she said.

"The computers picked him too," Shafer said.

"Didn't the Egyptians arrest a guy named al-Nerzi a year or so ago? Said he was planning to take out a Nile tourist cruise. His name wasn't Mohammed, though. Aziz. Aziz al-Nerzi."

"I'll have someone call the Mukhabarat"—the Egyptian secret service—"and find out if they're related." Either way, Mohammed al-Nerzi would have some questions to answer when the plane landed. If the plane landed.

"There was one more matching name who was supposed to be on the plane, but he didn't show up," Shafer said. "Didn't cancel either. No explanation."

"How long's it been in the air?" Exley said.

"Took off from Heathrow at noon London time. About seven hours ago."

"So it's scheduled to land—"

"At Dulles. Forty-five minutes. F-16s are escorting it in."

"Dulles? Why haven't we ordered it down already?"

"An emergency landing? We decided against it. There's no date specified. Just the flight number."

"Oh, just the flight number."

"That's why we scrambled the jets. Why I called you."

Her voice rose a little. "F-16s won't do the people on that plane much good if it's a bomb."

The truth was that the fighters wouldn't do the passengers much good in a hijacking either, she thought. The jets were there to stop the White House from getting turned into firewood, not to save the plane. They would shoot it down if they had to. If you were on United Airlines 919, those fighters were nothing but bad news.

"If they'd wanted to blow it, they'd have blown it already. Over the Atlantic where we couldn't find the pieces. It's a hijacking if it's anything."

"Then there should be at least five hijackers on board, Ellis. And they should be in first class, not all over the plane. It's a bombing if it's anything. Maybe they're planning to blow it on the approach. You know, just for a change of pace—"

"The agency doesn't want to disrupt commercial aviation without a good reason."

"This isn't a good reason?"

Shafer sighed. "Do I have to spell it out for you, Jen? When that plane lands on time at Dulles, it'll get thirty seconds on CNN—fighter jets escorting a plane in. It happens. An emergency landing? Much bigger deal. Especially in New York. The airlines have told the White House that their bookings drop whenever that happens. They're begging us not to overreact. Not saying I agree. That's just how it is."

"How much will their bookings drop if that plane blows up?"

"It's not my decision."

"You could get it down if you wanted to."

"This time."

This time. Shafer's influence was real, but it wasn't infinite. His prescience about September 11 still protected him, but he was no longer invulnerable. In the wake of the 9-11 Commission report, many of the agency's most senior officials had resigned. Their replacements considered Shafer a relic. Plenty of them would be happy to see him screw up. He wasn't a team player. He was too smart. He could make them look bad.

So Shafer needed to be sure that he didn't pull any false alarms. *That Ellis Shafer. He kept crying wolf. Got paranoid. Wanted to be a hero. We had to stop listening to him.* Exley knew all of this, but she couldn't help herself. If that 747 went down, they'd have blood on their hands.

"Fine, Ellis. Then why'd you ruin my Saturday? So I could keep you company while we cross our fingers?"

"That's exactly why."

"Sorry," she said.

"I'm the one who jumps to conclusions. You're supposed to hold me back. All we know is that the flight number came across and a couple names match. It happens all the time."

As usual, Shafer had put his finger on the real problem, Exley thought. This was the third serious alarm since January. Of course the agency was getting lazy. We let this one go to Dulles instead of making it land right away. Eventually we'll just radio the pilot—"Hey, guy, you may have a couple hijackers on board, we're not sure, have a nice day"—and let it go at that.

"This seems different. The way the flight number didn't come through until the plane was up." Exley shook her head. "I hate this."

"What?"

"We have to be right every day. They only have to be right once."

"Life isn't fair," Shafer said. He crossed his fingers. "Let's go to my office, get an update."

UNITED AIRLINES 919 had remained eerily quiet since the captain's announcement an hour before, the hum of the ventilation system the loudest sound on board, aside from an endless stream of Hail Marys being whispered somewhere behind Deirdre Smart in the main cabin. The only movement came from the flight attendants, who paced the aisles without any pretense of friendliness. A few minutes before, a man a couple of rows up had raised his hand and asked about immigration forms.

"We'll hand those out when we're on the ground," a flight attendant had hissed. "Thanks for your cooperation."

Outside, the F-16s continued to shadow the jet. But as the minutes ticked off without incident, the plane relaxed just a bit. Deirdre turned to smile at her husband and their son Aidan in the row behind. "It's going to be okay," she said.

. . .

AND THEN THE plane shuddered and dropped with terrible speed.

Deirdre's daughter Angela screamed, and so did everyone else on board, a sickening chorus of moans and exclamations to God. A flight attendant yelped as she was thrown into the bulkhead. A man two rows ahead of Deirdre retched, a low glottal sound that made her own stomach rise. A moment later the smell of his vomit wafted to her. She choked back the bile in her throat and waited for the plane to dive.

Then the jet steadied. More bumps followed, but nothing like the first. It was just turbulence, Deirdre thought. Just turbulence.

"It'll be okay, baby." She wiped the tears off her daughter's face.

"Something smells, Mommy."

"Try to pretend it's not there."

The intercom ticked on. "From the flight deck, this is Captain Hamilton. I'm sorry about that. It's going to be bouncy the rest of the way—there's some weather between here and Dulles. A spring squall. Normally we would have detoured around the worst of it, but in this case our priority is to get you home as quick as possible. Again, I apologize. We should have warned you. The next ten minutes will be the bumpiest stretch, so please make sure your seat belts are securely fastened. Again, no need to be alarmed. It's just chop. We'll have you on the ground safely in a half hour. Thank you."

He still sounded totally smooth, Deirdre thought. If they landed—*when* they landed, she corrected herself—she'd gladly give him a thank-you hug, and she'd bet she wouldn't be the only one.

The plane shook again, even harder this time, a series of jolts that would have been nerve-racking under the best of circumstances. Deirdre could see the Boeing's wings shake. The three-hundred-ton jet heaved up and down like a swimmer fighting to stay afloat in heavy surf. Deirdre couldn't remember turbulence like this, but as long as that was all it was, she'd deal with it.

Everyone around her seemed to feel the same. The cabin was silent, 307 people willing themselves home. Deirdre noticed a searing pain in her hands and looked down to find that she had clenched her fists so tightly that her nails had cut her palms. She opened her hands slowly, her fingers shaking. She glanced over her seat at her husband.

"Next year we're going to Florida," she said. "And we're driving." He didn't smile.

The minutes passed. Slowly the bumps faded, and the 747 began to descend. A few minutes later a ping in the cabin sounded as the jet dropped below ten thousand feet, and the intercom came to life.

"Captain Hamilton one more time. We're just a few minutes outside Dulles, and as you can see the chop has lightened. Under normal circumstances I'd ask you to turn off all your electronic devices, but those should be off already, so I just need you to stay in your seats with your seat belts securely fastened. We'll be on the ground shortly. Thank you."

Deirdre rubbed her daughter's hand.

"Almost home," she said.

IN SHAFER'S OFFICE, the phone rang. He listened for a moment, then hung up.

"They're on approach," he said to Exley. "Everything seems normal. No word from the Egyptians—it's almost ten P.M. in Cairo. I told you it would be okay."

"It's not okay yet," Exley said.

IN 42H, ZAKARIA Fahd—the bearded man who had for the last ninety minutes been on the collective mind of the main cabin—stepped into the aisle. A flight attendant ran toward him.

"You need to sit down, sir."

"I need to use the restroom," Fahd said.

"Get back in your seat!" Two more attendants moved in to block his path.

"Please—I need the toilet," Fahd said.

"If you don't sit down by the count of three, you'll be arrested. There's a marshal on this plane. One—two—"

In the midst of the fracas, no one noticed that Mohammed al-Nerzi, the quiet man with close-cropped hair in 47A, had turned on his cellphone, a prepaid model that had been bought in New York a month before. The phone found a working cell and blinked its eagerness to serve. Al-Nerzi held down the 4 key, automatically dialing a number that he had programmed into the phone the night before.

The number belonged to another cellphone, a phone that not co-incidentally was also on board UA 919. No one could answer the second phone, but no one needed to. It was hidden in a red canvas bag in the baggage hold below. The bag had been slipped on board by Uday Yassir, a Syrian who had been hired three months before to join United's ground crew at Heathrow after a routine background check found nothing untoward.

Unlike the passengers' luggage, the canvas bag hadn't gone through a security screen. It wouldn't have passed. The phone inside it was hooked to a detonator wired to a pound of C-4, the plastic explosive preferred by armies and terrorists. The squat grayish brick had the power to tear a ten-foot hole in the plane's aluminum skin, destroying the Boeing's structural integrity and breaking the 747 apart in midair.

Across the cabin, the flight attendant said, "Three."

Zakaria Fahd sat down.

And Mohammed al-Nerzi looked at his phone. The call hadn't gone through. He couldn't understand what had happened. He should be dead. The plane should be in a thousand pieces. Something was wrong. He silently cursed his misfortune, then tried to dial the number twice more before turning his phone off and slipping it into his pocket. The man in 47B never noticed.

What al-Nerzi didn't know, what investigators discovered only after the 747 landed and they found the bomb in the plane's hold, was that the turbulence over New Jersey had smashed the second phone, preventing it from receiving the call to detonate the C-4. Only the sudden violence of a late-March squall had saved UA 919 from destruction.

"WE'RE ON OUR final descent into Washington Dulles International Airport. Flight attendants please be seated for landing," Captain Hamilton said. In 35A, Angela Smart craned her neck as the jet passed through three thousand feet, two thousand. They broke through a heavy layer of clouds, and she could see thick woods, roads heavy with traffic, the brown waters of the Potomac. The ride was mostly smooth now. One thousand feet. Five hundred.

Touchdown. The jet bounced once on the runway, then landed

for real. A giant cheer erupted across the cabin, whoops and ap-
plause. The captain threw on the brakes, and the big Boeing came
smoothly to a stop. The cheering continued for a full minute before
finally slowing down.

"We're glad to have you home," the captain said, and the ap-
plause exploded again.

SHAFER'S PHONE RANG. He listened for a moment, then hung up.

"They're down," he said to Exley. "But something happened on
the approach. They want to scrub the hold, talk to some people."

An hour later, with the 747 still on the tarmac at Dulles, an FBI
agent found the red canvas bag, and the truth of what had almost
happened to UA 919 finally became clear.

Finding the would-be bombers wasn't hard. Inexplicably, al-
Nerzi didn't even try to get rid of his phone. And the timing of
Fahd's stunt appeared strangely coincidental, as did the fact that
both men had bought their tickets the same day, through the same
travel agent. Exley had little doubt that both men would end up in
federal prison, or Guantánamo. But somehow she didn't feel any
better. Only an incredible stroke of luck had saved the lives of 307
people today.

IT WAS NEARLY midnight when Exley and Shafer shuffled through
the agency's deserted underground parking garage, their heads low.
Five cups of coffee had not hidden her exhaustion, just covered it
with a layer of jitters.

"It was too close this afternoon," she said.

"We need better intel," Shafer said. "Turbulence isn't a reliable
fail-safe." He laughed mirthlessly. "Where's John Wells when you
need him? The great Jalal."

After his cryptic note in 2001, Wells had gone silent. The agency
had all but forgotten that he existed, but at particularly stressful
moments Shafer liked to invoke Wells's name. He joked of Wells as
a magic bullet, a talisman who would reappear when needed to res-
cue the agency single-handedly. The joke had a bitter edge. Shafer
and Exley both knew that the agency desperately needed someone

like Wells, someone who could provide reliable information from inside al Qaeda.

"I still think he's alive," Exley said as they approached her Caravan.

"Prove it."

"Prove he isn't."

"I'll bet you a hundred bucks we never hear from him again."

"I'll take it," she said. She squeezed her alarm key and the Dodge gave her a friendly blink.

"See you tomorrow," he said.

Tomorrow. Sunday. Another chance to disappoint her kids. "Tomorrow," she said. "Great."

He touched her arm as she slid into the van. "Think more's coming, Jen?"

"This was a one-off. Otherwise at least one more plane would have gotten hit today. But—"

"But?"

"I think they're trying to distract us," she said. "Something is coming. Big. They're waking up."

"Strange, isn't it?" Shafer said. "Nerzi didn't even have to be on the plane. He could have made that call from anywhere. He wanted to be there. He wanted to die."

"I wish we understood them better."

"I don't know how anyone can understand that." He started to close her door, then stopped. "You know what, Jennifer? Take tomorrow off. Hang out with your kids. We're going to have plenty to do."

She didn't argue, just slipped her key into the ignition as he shut the door.

JANET AND LORI were out tonight, Exley saw as she nosed the Caravan down Thirteenth Street to her apartment building. When she and Randy separated, she'd moved into D.C. proper, doubling the length of her commute and subjecting herself to Washington's insanely high taxes. But she'd wanted to put some distance between them, and she didn't regret the choice. She had bought an apartment just off Logan Circle, a once-iffy neighborhood that had gentrified, thanks to Washington's hot housing market. Still, on Saturday nights a couple of prostitutes sometimes cruised Thirteenth, looking for behind-the-times johns who had missed the news about the area's renaissance. She'd gotten to know them—or at least their names—while buying gas at the BP Amoco down the block from her building. She gave them a wave and got a halfhearted nod from Janet in return.

She parked the Caravan in the building's underground garage and trudged to the elevator. Her legs ached from the hours she'd sat at her desk. She wanted nothing more than a glass of red wine, maybe two, before bed. In fact, that wasn't entirely true. She wanted lots of things more than a glass of wine. A backrub, maybe. A boyfriend. A job that didn't leave her constantly exhausted and on edge. But the first two weren't immediately available, and she knew that she would have an awful time leaving the agency no matter how miserable she got. She was fighting for the United States. She couldn't picture herself working for some private risk-management company, even for double the pay and half the hours. Maybe a couple more years of this would burn her out so badly she'd have to leave, but not yet.

No backrub, no boyfriend, no new job. A glass of Shiraz would be it instead.

Inside her apartment, a tidy one-bedroom in the corner of the building's third floor, Exley flicked on the Ella Fitzgerald in her CD player, opened a bottle of wine, and stretched out on her couch. She caught a glimpse of herself in the mirror across the room. God, she looked tired. She could remember being beautiful. She had the pictures to prove it. But age wasn't fair to women, unless they were actresses or trophy wives with fantastic amounts of money for their upkeep. She still had a good figure, and her eyes could light up a room, but only Botox would erase her crow's-feet and the lines on her neck, and she couldn't see herself getting plastic surgery. She wondered if most men would care or even notice. Probably not. But the wondering was the problem. The wondering dammed your confidence. That and the endless pictures of twenty-something models in every magazine.

She finished her wine and poured herself another glass. The irony was that Randy's fiancée was dumpy, to be blunt, even if she was a couple of years younger. And she knew he was still attracted to her. No, he had just gotten tired of her putting the agency first. She couldn't blame him. But the job didn't allow for compromises. And how could it, when the bad guys could hit anytime?

Like this afternoon. If they'd only followed her advice—

"Oh shit," she said aloud to the empty room.

Shafer had known, of course. For once he'd been too tactful to say anything. No wonder he'd given her Sunday off. He knew she would get it eventually. If they'd only followed her advice this afternoon, 307 people would have died. Because if they'd landed UA 919 in Boston or Hartford, before the turbulence over New Jersey, the cellphone in the hold would have worked, and the plane would have gone down.

"God," Exley said. She gulped down the wine and poured herself another glass. She sank down into the couch and closed her eyes. Of course she couldn't have known. No one could have. Even so. She had almost killed 307 people.

What a perfect way to end the evening, Exley thought. She drank the last of the wine and headed for her medicine cabinet to look for an Ambien. She had an old prescription, from the worst of the divorce.

She would need a pill to sleep tonight.

3

LEARNING HOW TO be an American again came harder than Wells had expected.

His first shock came even before his flight landed in Hong Kong, as the Pakistan Airlines A-310 circled over the city's lights. Wells hadn't seen a functioning electrical grid in a long time. The tribal elders in his village had owned two diesel generators, loud stinking beasts that dribbled out enough power for bulbs and a few televisions. But nothing like the sea of yellow-orange lights that glowed below Wells's window, the blinking red beacons that capped the radio towers on Hong Kong Island, the white shine of the skyscrapers. I've forgotten that humans can build as easily as destroy, Wells thought.

The jet landed, and around him passengers stood and grabbed their bags. He could not move, owned by an emotion he could not name, not fear or hope but a sense that time had unfrozen and he had aged a decade in an instant. He knew he should be happy. He was free. Only he wasn't. He had only moved to a new battlefield, one with even higher stakes. Weariness overwhelmed him, and he sat motionless until the cabin emptied and a flight attendant tapped his shoulder.

"Are you all right, sir?"

"Fine." He shouldn't call attention to himself. He took his bag and walked off.

Glossy billboards for Hyatt and Gucci and IBM and Cathay Pacific and a dozen other companies filled the air-conditioned arrival hall. Every woman in the ads was more beautiful than the next, and they all displayed enough skin to merit a whipping or worse in the North-West Frontier. Wells pulled his eyes from the billboards and looked around the hall's polished floors. Women were all around him, Chinese and white and Indian and Filipina. They walked alone, no male escorts, with faces and arms and legs uncovered. Some even wore makeup. A beautiful Japanese teenager, her hair dyed a shocking red, hurried past him, and Wells swiveled his head to watch her. As he did he felt an unexpected irritation. Couldn't these women be a bit more modest? They didn't need to wear burqas, but they didn't have to wear miniskirts either.

On a bench in the arrival hall outside a Starbucks, he puzzled over his reaction. After a decade of celibacy he should be thrilled at the feast of skin before his eyes. Nothing about the Taliban had troubled him more than the way they treated women. He supposed he had internalized the fundamentalist credos more deeply than he had realized. Or maybe he just needed to get laid. Sex had been nearly impossible in Afghanistan and Pakistan; the villagers weren't interested in marrying their daughters to Qaeda's guerrillas, much less an American. And sex outside marriage wasn't worth the risk; the Talibs and Pashtuns were endlessly inventive in their punishments for prostitution and adultery. Wells had seen a man buried alive, and a half dozen others hanged. He had kept his libido locked down. He couldn't even remember what a woman smelled like.

He would have to change that. Muslims were supposed to save sex for marriage, but Wells knew he couldn't be chaste forever. He had decided that he would not pay for sex or look for a one-night stand, but if he found the right woman, someone he cared about, he would not wait for a wedding.

He looked at a tall blonde strutting by and hoped he would find the right woman soon.

. . .

HE SPENT THE next week at an anonymous hotel in Kowloon. To pass the time he walked Hong Kong's teeming streets each morning, then spent afternoons at the city's Central Library, a massive stone and glass building across from Victoria Park. He paged through newspapers and magazines to catch up on his lost years. Monica Lewinsky and Newt Gingrich. The Internet bubble. The euro. Britney Spears. The 2000 presidential election and the Florida recount. The years before September 11 were as calm as a Montana lake on a hot summer day.

Then the attack. In the yellowing newspapers from 2001 the shock was still palpable. Wells learned about the flyers that the families of the missing had plastered across New York, paper memorials more eloquent than any monument. And about Rudy Giuliani's answer, that first day, when a reporter asked how many people had died: "More than we can bear."

What about next time? Wells wondered. What will we have to bear then?

Meanwhile the United States had struck back, stomping into Afghanistan and Iraq, hoping to put its enemies on the defensive. America's soldiers had punished the forces of the Taliban and Saddam Hussein. But Wells worried that the United States had stirred a generation of rage among a billion Muslims. Every time an American soldier stepped into a mosque, a jihadi was born. And now the United States seemed trapped in Iraq. Weighing the possibilities gave him a headache. Finally he returned to the safety of the sports pages, reveling as his Red Sox overcame the Yankees and won the World Series. Theo Epstein was a genius.

At night he drank Cokes in the bar of the Peninsula Hotel, looking across Victoria Harbor at the lights of Hong Kong, eavesdropping on expats chattering on their cellphones. Everyone talked all the time, a hypercharged English Wells could barely follow.

"It better happen this week or it's not going to happen at all—"

"Yeah, Bali this weekend, back here and then San Francisco—"

"These new Intel chips are unbelievable—"

He felt as though he was the only one in the entire city not having sex or making money. Or at least talking about it. For these people globalization was a promise, not a threat. They knew how to surf the world, and they didn't get paid to notice the folks drowning in the undertow.

Nonetheless Hong Kong did him good. The city's energy flowed into him, and he felt his own blood beginning to move. He found a dentist to fix his ruined molar. She frowned as she looked inside his mouth. "They don't have toothbrushes in America?" He showered three times a day to make up for the weeks that had passed between baths in the North-West Frontier, and watched races at the Sha Tin track. He didn't gamble, but he enjoyed the pageantry of the place, the billionaires walking beside women half their age, the sleek thoroughbreds nearly prancing as they approached the gate. And the roar of the crowd as the horses neared the finish.

One morning he found himself outside the American consulate on Garden Road and felt a pang of guilt. He should already have contacted the agency officials inside. But he couldn't bring himself to give up his freedom so soon. As soon as he presented himself to the agency he would have a new set of minders. There would be weeks of debriefings, endless questions: Where have you been all these years? Why didn't you contact us? What exactly have you been doing?

Underlying them all would be a deeper doubt: Why should we trust you anyway?

No. He wasn't ready. He would report in when he got back to America. Nothing would happen before then anyway. He walked on, leaving the consulate behind.

HIS PASSAGE TO Frankfurt and then New York went smoothly. He felt none of the elation he expected when his Lufthansa 747 touched down at Kennedy, only the knowledge that he couldn't escape his duty much longer.

The immigration officer hardly glanced at his passport, and he spent his first morning in Manhattan wandering as he had in Hong Kong. But he couldn't help but see the city through Khadri's eyes, as one big target: the tunnels, the bridges, the New York Stock Exchange, the Broadway theaters, the subways, the United Nations.

And Times Square, of course. When he'd last seen it, the square—really a bowtie-shaped intersection where Broadway meets Seventh

Avenue—had been seedy and rundown. Now it matched its claim to be the world's crossroads. At Forty-fourth Street and Broadway, he watched tourists and locals crawl over one another like ants at a messy picnic. Oversized neon advertisements glowed from the new office towers. News crawled endlessly on digital tickers, the world reduced to dueling strips of orange and green. Drivers leaned on their horns and street vendors tried to outshout them, hawking Statue of Liberty keychains and drawings of Tupac. A huge Toys 'R' Us store occupied the corner where he stood, proof that the place had become an all-ages attraction. Wells remembered what some-body—he didn't know who—had supposedly once said about Times Square: "It must be beautiful if you can't read." Business got done here too. The headquarters of Morgan Stanley, Ernst & Young, and Viacom were within two hundred yards. Plus, you could drive a truck right through it. If the World Trade Center was Ground Zero, Times Square was Ground One.

Wells could feel a timer counting down somewhere. He headed into the subway and looked for a train to Queens. Eight hours later he was on a Greyhound bus headed for Charleston with twenty thousand dollars in his pocket. He'd stashed the other fifteen thousand in a safe-deposit box in Manhattan, just in case.

TWO DAYS LATER, Wells walked through the Minneapolis airport with a brand-new South Carolina driver's license in his pocket, thanks to that state's liberal rules for issuing licenses. He was headed for Boise, and from there through the Idaho backcountry to Missoula. He had two stops to make, three people to see: his mom, son, and ex-wife. His last errand before he reported in.

He hadn't told anyone he was coming. He wanted to surprise his ma, show up in Hamilton and sit in her kitchen while she brewed a pot of coffee and scrambled some eggs. He would kiss her cheek and tell her he was sorry he'd been gone so long. She'd forgive him as soon as she saw him. Mothers were like that. At least his was. As for Evan and Heather . . . he'd have to see.

He had two hours to kill before his flight to Boise, so he found a TGI Friday's and sat at the bar to watch the NCAA men's basketball final, Duke versus Texas. After a few minutes, the man at the next stool turned to look at him. Early forties, a faint tan, close-cropped hair, a thin gold chain around one wrist. "Duke or Texas?"

"Duke," Wells said. He wasn't keen to talk, but the guy looked harmless enough.

"Me too. Where you headed?"

Wells shrugged and looked up at the television. The guy didn't take the hint.

"Me, I'm going to Tampa. I hate Northwest. I flew a hundred and twenty thousand miles last year. They didn't even upgrade me out of Tampa. I couldn't believe it. They *owe* me an upgrade."

"Yeah," Wells grunted. The guy must be a salesman. Not that he planned to ask.

"You married?" the guy said. "I'm married. Five kids."

"Congratulations."

"Hey, you don't mind shooting the shit, do ya?"

Wells found himself unable to tell the guy to get lost. He seemed kind of sad, and Wells hadn't had a casual conversation with another American in a long time. Call it field research.

The guy downed half his beer in a single gulp. "I better switch to shots. Lemme buy you a beer. Name's Rich, by the way."

"I don't drink," Wells said.

Rich looked at the bartender. "Double shot of Cuervo for me and a beer for my friend—"

"I told you I don't drink."

"Sorry, man. Just being friendly. A Coke then." Rich nodded to the bartender. "You know, I never minded flying before 9/11. Since then I get hammered every time. Even still."

Wells wondered again if he should leave. He didn't feel like talking about September 11. He thought about it plenty on his own. But he supposed airports were a natural place for the topic.

"I think to myself, what would I do if somebody pulled out a box cutter?" Rich said. "Tell you what, I'd go down fighting. Be a hero, like those guys on flight 93."

"Hero?" Wells couldn't keep the disbelief out of his voice.

The bartender set a generous helping of Cuervo in front of Rich. "You don't think those guys were heroes?" Rich looked insulted.

Wells didn't know much about what had happened on flight 93, but he knew this: trying to save your own skin didn't make you a hero. Everybody wants to live. You were a hero when you risked your life to save someone else. Usually. Sometimes you were just stupid. He had seen men throw their lives away just to prove they were tough.

Still, some famous battles were remembered for the courage of one side against overwhelming odds. Take Pickett's charge at Gettysburg, the Confederates swarming Cemetery Hill against the Union Army. The attack had been a disaster, but the Rebs would always be known for their bravery. Were they heroes or fools? Did the fact that they were fighting for slavery change the answer?

But Wells didn't feel like debating heroism with Rich the salesman. "Sure. They were heroes."

Rich raised his shot to Wells. "*Salud.* Let's roll. You know what's weird?"

I'll bet I'm about to find out, Wells thought. Rich tipped the Cuervo down his throat and pounded the glass against the bar. "My marriage is so messed up."

Wells tried to look sympathetic.

"My wife, Barbara, she caught me screwing the maid. Consuelo. She's so pissed. Barbara, that is. Consuelo doesn't care much."

Wells racked his brain for an appropriate response. He failed to find it. America seemed to have gotten a lot chattier in his absence. He vaguely remembered television talk shows like *Jerry Springer.* Now the whole country seemed to be auditioning for one of those reality programs. What kind of person told a total stranger that his wife had walked in on him with the maid?

Rich looked at him and pressed on. "I mean, Barb wasn't supposed to be home. She comes in, she starts screaming, 'Fuck you fuck you,' really screaming—"

So much for being polite, Wells thought.

"You have any dignity?" Wells looked Rich in the eye, a stare that had frozen guys in places much tougher than this. "You even know what that word means? Telling some guy you never met about how you cheated on your wife and got caught. I don't know you and I don't want to. Thanks for the Coke." Wells picked up his bag.

"You don't understand," Rich said. "I'm under so much pressure.

You know what it's like trying to pay for two houses and three cars? I can't remember the last time I slept with my wife. I just needed to touch someone. My life sucks—"

"You know what sucks?" Wells said. "Stepping on a land mine and getting your legs blown off. And you're four years old. Riding around in a Humvee waiting to get torched by a bomb you can't even see, like our guys are doing in Baghdad right now."

"I know—"

"You don't know shit. You don't have a clue. You can't imagine how most people in this world live. And most of 'em have never in their lives bitched as much as you did in the last five minutes. Divorce your wife. Quit screwing the maid. I couldn't care less."

"What the fuck do you know about how tough the world is?" Rich said. "You're sitting here watching TV just like me."

"Not anymore," Wells said. He slapped a ten-dollar bill on the bar for his Coke and headed for his gate.

WELLS SAT OUTSIDE gate C-13 furious with himself. What if the guy had swung at him? So much for keeping a low profile then. But Wells didn't understand his countrymen anymore. They owe me an upgrade, Rich had said. No. They don't owe you anything.

Wells knew he needed to relax. Rich the salesman was an alcoholic with a lousy marriage. He would get his act together. Or not. It wasn't Wells's business. Yet as Wells looked around the bright, clean airport he wondered whether he would ever belong in America.

BUT WHEN HE woke the next morning in Boise he felt almost elated. He hadn't imagined he would ever see Montana or his ma again. He could have flown straight to Missoula, but he'd wanted to drive, to be alone in the Rockies. He remembered driving down with his dad over Lost Trail Pass for weekends fishing. They'd go to Boise to watch the Hawks, the Class A minor-league baseball team, and buy his mom a present from the jewelry store downtown. "Don't tell," his dad always said. "It's a surprise."

His dad had been a surgeon at the hospital in Hamilton, south of Missoula. His mom was a teacher. His father had wanted a big family, Wells knew. But his mother had almost died when Wells was born—she'd been hospitalized in Missoula for a month—and her doctors said she could never get pregnant again. So they were three: Herbert, Mona, and John.

Wells had respected his dad, a gruff taciturn man whose skills as a surgeon were renowned across western Montana. Most days, Herbert exhausted his energy in the operating room; when he got home, he would sit in his high-backed leather chair in their living room, sipping a glass of whiskey and reading the Missoula paper. He was never mean, and he wasn't exactly distant either. He always cheered for Wells at football games. But Herbert had rules, in and out of the operating room, and he expected those rules to be followed.

Now his mom, she was something special. Just about every kid Mona taught fell half in love with her. She was tall and beautiful and always smiling. She'd grown up in Missoula, the product of a crazy love match. In 1936, Wells's granddad Andrew had been a sailor in the navy. On shore leave in Beirut, Andrew had fallen for Noor, the daughter of a Lebanese trader. Somehow Andrew had convinced Noor—and her family—that she belonged with him in Montana. Noor was the reason for Wells's dark hair and complexion. And the reason he had known about Islam long before he studied the religion at Dartmouth. He was one-quarter Muslim by birth. Noor had given up her faith when she came to the United States, but she had taught Wells enough for it to intrigue him.

Not that he had much chance to see Islam in action growing up. Hamilton had been a country town when Wells was a kid, a few blocks long. He had loved growing up there, riding his bike everywhere, learning to handle a horse and build a fire. Things had changed about the time he hit puberty. MTV came along to show him and his friends what hicks they were. A lot of kids stopped feeling self-reliant and started feeling bored. Drugs crept from Seattle to Spokane to Missoula and then down U.S. 93 to the Sinclair gas station on the edge of town. He feared that the infestation had only worsened since he left.

ON HIS WAY out of Boise, Wells had seen clouds covering the mountains. Still, he'd decided to take the shortest route home, through the mountains on Idaho 21. Now he headed northeast past Boise's scattered suburbs, the subdivisions packed tight on the open prairie, like cows clustered against an approaching storm. The road turned north and rose toward the clouds beside a fast-running creek. The scrubby ponderosa pines thickened, and snow began to fall. As Wells crested the Mores Creek pass at 6,100 feet, fog swirled over the road. Dead trees clotted the hillsides; Wells remembered vaguely that a huge fire had devastated the area decades earlier. Even now the forest had hardly recovered. The fog grew so thick that he could no longer tell the road from the hills. He did not usually think himself superstitious, but suddenly he felt that he was passing through a netherworld, and nothing on the other side would be the same. Still, he had come too far to turn back. He eased off the gas until his Dodge was hardly moving and crept down the mountain to Lowman. Four hours to drive sixty miles.

After Lowman the weather eased. The road turned east and followed the Payette River along a valley thick with firs. Wells shook his head at his moment of weakness. Since when had the weather dictated his moods? To the south the Sawtooth Mountains cut through the clouds, fierce and broken and looking uncannily like, yes, a hacksaw's teeth. We westerners are literal-minded, Wells thought. With land as beautiful as this there's no need to embellish.

At Stanley he swung onto Idaho 75, alongside the Salmon River. The day brightened as the sun tore apart the clouds. Crumbling red sandstone hills gave way to mountains covered with yellow scrub grass that glowed in the light. Beside the road, men in waders cast lures into the river, hoping for steelhead. Wells felt his heart swell. He hadn't felt so free since he'd joined the agency a decade before. He nearly pulled over and asked to borrow a line for a few minutes, but instead pressed on toward Hamilton.

But by the time he reached Salmon, the last decent-sized town before Hamilton, the sun had set. Wells stopped at the Stagecoach Inn and rented a room for forty-two dollars. He was still nearly three hours from Hamilton, and he didn't want to wake his mother in the dark.

Salmon was a flyspeck western town, its main street a low row of battered brick buildings. Wells found himself at the Supper Club and Lounge, a dank bar with a karaoke machine and cattle skulls nailed to the walls.

"What can I get you?" the bartender said.

Wells felt his mouth water at the rich greasy smell of meat on the grill.

"A burger," he said. The meat surely wasn't halal—slaughtered under Koranic rules, which required the draining of all blood from the animal—but Wells found himself unable to care. He couldn't remember the last hamburger he had eaten, and suddenly that missing memory seemed to symbolize everything else he had left behind during his decade of war.

The burger came fast. He chewed slowly, making each bite last, and listened to a forty-something woman two stools over joke with an old man in a Minnesota Timberwolves cap. "Fishing's almost better than skydiving," she said. "And that's a hell of a lot better than sex, 'specially when you're my age." She laughed, and Wells found himself smiling. She caught him looking and raised her eyebrows. She had streaked blond hair and a wide pretty smile. She slid over and held out her hand. "Evelyn."

"John."

"Do you sing, John?"

"No, ma'am," Wells said, a touch of country slipping into his voice.

"Don't tell me you don't sing, handsome."

"My voice is terrible."

She patted his hand and turned to the bartender. "Come on, punch up 'You Are So Beautiful.' "

He had no intention of singing for this woman. Fortunately, he didn't have to. Instead Evelyn belted out the song, her voice sliding across the notes like a car on an icy road. What she lacked in skill she made up in spectacle, shaking her hips as she leaned toward him, ending with the microphone cradled in both hands. "You—are—so—beautiful—to—me . . ." The half dozen barflies in the place cheered when she was done, and Wells felt a broad grin crease his face, his first real smile in far too long. She bowed to him and walked back to his stool.

"You were great," he said.

"You're up next."

He shook his head.

"Maybe later, then," she said, waving the subject aside. "What brings you to Salmon?"

"Passing through," Wells said. "On my way to Missoula."

"Where you from?"

This was what he'd feared. Maybe she was just being friendly, or maybe she was bored and looking for fun on a Tuesday night. He shouldn't feel so skittish. It would be easy enough to lie, and maybe even go home with this woman. But he didn't want to lie. Not the night before he saw his family.

"I gotta go," he said.

"Hey, I don't bite." She winked and put her hand on his arm. "And I like sex better than skydiving any day." Wells felt himself flush and stir simultaneously. He had forgotten how shameless American women could be.

"I have to get up real early tomorrow."

"Whatever." She turned away. Wells took a last bite of his burger and drove the three blocks to the Stagecoach. In the motel's parking lot he very nearly turned back to the bar. He could not forget the feeling of Evelyn's hand on his arm. His skin seemed to burn where she'd touched him. He turned off the engine and trudged up to his room. He had waited a long time for a woman, and he supposed he could wait longer. But not forever.

THE PHONE RANG precisely at six A.M., knocking him out of a dreamless sleep. He showered, then quickly dressed and prayed, bowing his head to the floor and reciting the first verse of the Koran. *"Bismallah rahmani rahim al hamdulillah rabbi lalamin . . ."* Outside the sun rose and the stars disappeared as the sky turned from black to blue.

Wells had the highway to himself as he headed north toward Lost Trail Pass, the border of Idaho and Montana. Lewis and Clark had followed this route on their way to the Pacific, and the mountains had hardly changed since. At the top of the pass, Wells got out of the Dodge and stood in the quiet air, looking down at the Montana hills ahead. They seemed softer and rounder than those behind.

He reached Hamilton an hour later. The town was bigger than he remembered, and new supermarkets and fast-food restaurants—a Taco Bell, a Pizza Hut—stretched along 93. He turned left on Ravalli Street. There it was. 420 South Fourth. The big gray house on the corner of Ravalli and Fourth.

Except the house wasn't gray anymore. It was blue. And there was a tricycle in the front yard.

He walked to the door. "Ma?" he shouted. No one answered. He rang the bell.

"May I help you?" A man's voice.

"It's John."

"John who?"

Wells wanted to be somewhere else. Anywhere. He wouldn't have minded if the earth itself had opened and swallowed him whole.

"John Wells. I'm looking for my mother."

The door opened a notch to reveal Ken Fredrick, who'd been two years ahead of Wells in high school. Penny Kenny, the nastier kids called him, because his family was always flat broke. He and Wells had been something like friends. Kenny was football manager during Wells's first two years on the team, and he had taken a lot of abuse, especially on the long bus rides to away games. The worst moment came one Friday night near the end of Wells's first season. Three linemen opened the emergency exit and held Kenny out, his face a few inches above the asphalt of Interstate 90 as the bus hurtled along. Wells could still remember Kenny screaming, maybe the first time he'd heard real panic. After that, Wells invited Kenny to sit with him. Even in ninth grade Wells had been starting middle linebacker and running back, so Kenny got picked on less after that.

"John Wells? Bonecrusher?" Wells hadn't heard that name in a long time. He had gotten the name because of the way he hit, jaw-dropping tackles that popped off helmets and left guys flat on the field. Running backs and wide receivers hated coming over the middle on him. Wells wasn't especially big, but he was fast and he knew the secret, the one that coaches couldn't teach: *Don't slow down.* Most defenders pulled up—just a bit—before they made a tackle. They got nervous. It was only natural. Wells never slowed down.

"Man, it's good to see you," Kenny said. "Been a long time." Penny Kenny opened the door and offered up his hand.

"What are you doing here?" Wells unwilling to admit the truth to himself even now.

"I live here, John," Kenny said. "My wife and I bought the place from your mom years ago. I'm a vice president, at the Ravalli County Bank. People call me Ken now." The pride in his voice was unmistakable.

"Where's my ma?"

Kenny swallowed hard. "You didn't know? She passed on, John. Breast cancer."

Wells found himself staring at Kenny's perfect teeth, which had been twisted and uneven when they were kids. You could be in a Crest ad, Wells thought. No Afghan dentists for you. And what are you doing in my house?

Wells wanted to live up to his nickname. His fist clenched as he looked at Kenny and Kenny's white teeth. But none of this was Kenny's fault. Kenny was a nice kid.

"She's at Lone Pine," Kenny said. "With your dad."

"I know where my family's buried, Kenny. Ken."

"I'm sorry, John," Kenny said. "I don't know what else to say. Can I invite you in? Get you some coffee?"

But Wells had already turned away.

TEARS ROLLED SILENTLY down his face as he drove south on 93 to the Lone Pine Cemetery in Darby. Wells couldn't remember the last time he'd cried, or even when he'd wanted to, but he was crying now. He hadn't allowed himself to think that his ma might have . . . passed on. Died. Gone to the Great Prairie in the Sky. Ha. Good one, John.

She couldn't have died. He'd gone to the end of the world and he hadn't died. All she had to do was play bridge with her friends and tend the flowers outside her big old house. She couldn't have died. But she had, and the proof was in the granite gravestone that stared up at Wells near the back of the cemetery. Mona Kesey Wells, 1938–2004. Loving wife, cherished mother, honored teacher. A cross engraved in the stone. His father lay beside her, Herbert Gerald Wells, 1930–1999. Wells knelt before them and closed his eyes, hoping to feel their presence, to feel anything at all. He murmured the eighty-second sura of the Koran, an invocation of Judgment Day:

When the sky is torn
When the stars are scattered
When the seas poured forth
And the tombs burst open
Then a soul will know what it has given and what left behind . . .

But all he heard was the traffic rolling by on 93 and the graveyard's American flag flapping in the morning breeze. Wells knew he ought not to blame God for the loneliness he felt, but he couldn't help himself. God, Allah—whatever His name, He was gone at this moment when Wells needed Him most.

Wells walked to the cemetery's edge. No fence marked its border. The graves simply stopped a few feet before the ground sloped down to a set of railroad tracks. He looked east into the sun until his eyes burned. He could almost see his faith coming loose, pouring out and floating away in the wind. In the distance a locomotive whistle sounded. Wells waited, but no train came. He walked back to his car. He had never felt so empty.

HE DROVE INTO Missoula slowly, trying to escape the feeling that he ought to give up this foolish journey and head for Washington. Missoula had grown even faster than Hamilton. Subdivisions crawled up the hills where Wells and his family had ridden horses. His ma had loved to ride. His ma. Again he felt tears coming, but this time he choked them back. He had sacrificed those years for a reason. No one in Qaeda would have trusted him if he had come back to the United States on his own. His mother had never questioned his decision to become a soldier. Now he needed to control his emotions and do what he needed to do. He didn't know how else to honor her.

He edged his way into town. At least he knew Heather wasn't dead—he had called her from New York. He'd hung up when she answered, feeling slightly dirty.

He parked outside Heather's house, a nice white two-story. As he looked at the place he felt sure he wouldn't be welcome. He walked slowly to the front door and rang the bell. A little boy opened the door. "Is your mom here?" Wells asked.

"Mom!" The boy ran off.

He heard Heather's small feet padding toward the door.

"Yes?" She slipped the chain and opened the door. She was as beautiful as he remembered, a country girl with honey-blond hair and deep brown eyes, tiny and perfect. He towered over her, and he had loved to pick her up and carry her to their bed. They had been wild together. But there had always been part of him that she couldn't reach, and they had drifted apart after he joined the agency. When he said he was going underground and couldn't promise when he'd be back, she gave him an ultimatum: the job or me. The job or Evan, who at the time had just turned two. She told him she wouldn't wait. And she didn't. He couldn't blame her.

When she saw him her eyes opened wide and a low sound—half-sigh, half-grunt—came from her throat. She opened her mouth as if to speak, then closed it.

He reached out for her. She hesitated, then gave him half a hug, holding her hips back so they wouldn't touch him.

"John," she said.

"Can I come in?"

She motioned him in. The living room was nicely furnished, Wells saw. A handful of children's books lay on the coffee table. Nineteenth-century drawings of men in robes and wigs hung on the walls. A life that had no intersection with his own. He bit his cheek and tried to think of something to say.

"What's with them?" He pointed to the drawings. Then, feeling as though he'd already stumbled, he tried to make the question less hostile. "They're neat, is all I mean."

"Howard's a lawyer."

"Howard?"

"My husband." She pointed to a picture: Heather, a handsome paunchy man who must be Howard, Evan, and two young children, a boy and a girl. "That's George, and Victoria. Howard has a thing for English royalty."

"Do you?"

She shook her head. It wasn't an answer to his question. "I figured you must be dead when you didn't come to Mona's funeral."

"No such luck."

"She missed you, John. She thought you'd come back."

"I didn't know."

"They didn't tell you on super-spy radio or something? Give you the bat signal so you could come home?"

Wells tried not to think of his mother in her hospital bed, waiting and dying. Then just dying.

"I'm sorry, John. I didn't mean that. You always were a mama's boy, that's all. I figured if you were anywhere on the planet you'd be back."

"I never thought of myself as a mama's boy." But he couldn't deny that some of his fondest memories growing up were of Mona baking in their kitchen, while Herbert worked at the hospital or read in his study. Wells smiled. "Maybe I was. So this is your life?"

A look he couldn't read crossed her face. "This is my life. Married. Three kids. Boring."

"Heather—"

"Whatever you're gonna say, just don't."

"Can I see Evan?"

"He's at Little League practice at the YMCA."

"He plays baseball?"

"Third base. He doesn't even know who you are, John."

Wells felt as though she'd slapped him. "Tell you what. Stay here a year, be his dad, you can see him. Heck, you can teach him all that spy stuff."

"Heather—"

"Six months?" Pause. "A month? Is your son worth a month to you, John?"

Wells was silent. She was right. He couldn't begin to tell his son what he'd done, where he'd been. And what if the boy accepted him and then he disappeared again? What then?

Heather's face softened as she saw him nod.

"What do you tell him?"

"That you're a soldier. That you're fighting a war that we have to win. The truth."

She smiled as she said the last two words, and he wondered if she still loved him. Not that it mattered. "Do you remember—" she started to say. She broke off as the phone rang, an electric trill that went six rings and then stopped.

"No answering machine?" he said.

"Voice mail."

Huh. Voice mail had been much less popular when he'd left. A meaningless glimmer of a thought, but for a moment it pulled his mind from this miserable day. "What were you going to ask me?" he said.

But her smile had disappeared, and he knew she wouldn't say. The phone had pulled her back to her life now, and she had no place for him in it.

"You should go, John."

He looked around the room, trying to imprint it in his mind so he would have something of her to remember. Suddenly she cocked her head, a tic he knew well. "Why'd you come home?"

"What?"

"You're still working for the agency." It wasn't a question. He wondered if she'd been asked, or told, to call in if she saw him. "So why are you here? Why now?"

"You know I can't say."

"Do they know that you're here? In America?"

"Of course."

But he had never been able to lie to her, and he could see she knew he was lying now. Her face showed her uncertainty. He wished he could explain, tell her how he had ended up here without a person in the world he could trust. Instead he walked to the door. As he stepped through, he felt his hand on her arm. He turned, and she hugged him, for real this time. He closed his eyes and hugged her even harder.

Then she let him go.

WELLS SAT IN his rented Dodge and tried to burn his son's picture into his mind. Finally he slipped the car into gear and rolled off, driving slowly toward the YMCA. But when he reached the fields he didn't recognize Evan.

HEATHER WATCHED HIM leave. When the Dodge had disappeared, she pulled a business card from her wallet and picked up her phone to make a call that would push the United States closer to the deadliest terrorist attack in history. She punched in the numbers. The phone rang twice.

"Is this Jennifer Exley?" Heather said. She paused. "Jennifer? It's Heather Murray. . . . Yes. John Wells's ex-wife."

4

AT TWO A.M., weary travelers filled the arrivals hall at Miami International Airport. Omar Khadri was pleased to see that he fit in easily; everyone was his shade or darker. He joined a long line for non-U.S. citizens, carrying a black leather briefcase that held a copy of *Don Quixote* in Spanish to match his passport.

An hour later, he was still waiting. Meanwhile, the lines for Americans moved smoothly. Khadri seethed. You show us your contempt even before we arrive, he thought. Maybe if he shouted his delight at reaching the United States, Allah's gift to the universe, he would be jumped to the front of the line. Finally he reached an agent. She looked briefly at his passport, then at him.

"Are you here for business or pleasure, Mr. Navarro?"

"Business," Khadri said. Definitely business.

"Where will you be staying?"

"Miami." With a side trip to Los Angeles.

"How long?"

"Two weeks."

She handed him his passport. "I just need a fingerprint and photo and you'll be on your way."

"Excuse me?" Khadri said.

"Your fingerprint and photo. It's standard procedure."

Khadri did not want his prints and picture on file with the United States government. As far as he knew, no intelligence service had ever taken his photograph. He was as close to anonymous as anyone could be: medium height, medium weight, straight black hair, relatively light skin for a Pakistani, and an uncanny ability to mimic accents, a great gift in his line of work. He could pass for Egyptian, Iranian, Filipino, maybe even Italian. Even so, giving up a fingerprint would lock him into using this passport every time he came to America. He much preferred being able to change names.

"Sir? That a problem for you?"

"It's a rule?" Khadri wished he weren't so tired. Fatigue muddied his thinking, and he felt an unexpected fear, not for himself, but for this week's operation.

"Same for everyone, sir." A hint of a smirk crossed the agent's face. If you don't like it, tough, she didn't quite say. You can always go home.

Khadri fought down his irritation as he looked at her black face. He did not like black people, especially black Americans. This woman was a trained monkey, a combination of American arrogance and African savagery. But Khadri decided to be polite; he didn't want the trained monkey looking too hard at his passport. "I'll be glad to," he said.

The procedure took only a few seconds. He put his index finger on a digital reader and looked into a small digital camera. A few seconds later the agent's computer beeped and she waved him on.

"Welcome to the United States."

"Good to be here," Khadri said.

ON HIS FLIGHT to LAX the next morning, Khadri silently raged at himself. He should have been familiar with the new fingerprinting rules, which had been publicly announced. He couldn't make mistakes like that. In their paranoia, Americans seemed to think that al Qaeda was an all-powerful killing machine. But Khadri knew the group's weaknesses all too well.

True, al Qaeda was in no danger of going broke. Sheikh bin Laden had squirreled away tens of millions of dollars around the world during the 1990s, and new cash still flowed in quietly. But money alone was not enough. Al Qaeda's biggest problem was finding good operatives. Plenty of men wanted to die for the cause. But only a handful had gotten inside the United States before America clamped down on immigration from Muslim countries. Even fewer could be trusted for difficult missions. One bad decision, a moment of panic, could destroy a plan years in the making.

A flight attendant rolled her cart up. "Coffee? Tea?"

"Coffee. Two sugars and milk." Naturally, Khadri did not drink or use drugs, but—like many devout Muslims—he had a sweet tooth and a serious coffee habit.

He sipped his coffee and wondered how history would judge him. He fully expected that one day the world would know his name, his real name. Biographers and historians would examine his life. But if they were looking for a traumatic event, something they could "blame" for clues to his "crimes," they would be disappointed, he thought.

He had grown up in Birmingham, England, the oldest child and the only boy among six children. His father, Jalil, was an engineer who had emigrated from Pakistan, a sour man with a quick temper. His mother, Zaineb, had trained briefly to become a nurse's aide but never worked. Jalil and Zaineb were deeply religious, and strict. Khadri had felt the lash of his father's belt more than once as a child, and he had learned quickly not to disagree. He was a mostly solitary child; his father didn't allow him to spend time outside school with unbelievers, and Jalil's definition of "unbeliever" included most Muslims. So Khadri had escaped into his math and science textbooks, and the Koran. At the school library, where his father couldn't see, he turned to philosophy, trying to understand power, looking for clues in Nietzsche and Machiavelli and Hobbes. Infidels all, but they showed him how strong men forced their will on the weak. One day he would prove his strength to the world, and his father.

As the years passed, his hatred of Britain and the West grew fiercer. Unlike some al Qaeda soldiers, he could not point to a specific incident that had turned him against the *kafirs* and onto the path of righteousness. Sure, like everyone in England with tea-colored skin, he'd been called a raghead by yobs on the street. But he'd never been seriously threatened, or even spat on. No, he had simply grown sick of the moral corruption around him, drug taking and homosexuality and pleasure seeking at all costs. And the *kafirs* did not merely insist on polluting themselves. They wanted to force their ways on the rest of the world, while piously pretending to spread freedom.

Yet Khadri's religious fervor had limits. Yes, he believed in Allah, believed that Mohammed was the last and truest prophet. He prayed five times a day. He never polluted his body with alcohol or drugs. He hoped to see paradise when he died. But when his companions sang tales of black-eyed virgins who would pleasure them for eternity, Khadri turned away to hide his embarrassment. Paradise wasn't an amusement park, and only fools were eager for their own deaths. Khadri did not try to build his faith by promising himself rapture. Jihad was an obligation, not a game. Paradise might await in the next world, but Islam needed to triumph here and now. As always, Mohammed had set a fine example, Khadri thought. He had been a commander, not just a prophet. His armies had swept Arabia, and though he was a wise and just ruler, in battle his ferocity knew no bounds. He had aimed for conquest, and had viewed martyrdom as a tool to that end, not an end in itself.

Khadri made good use of the fanatics. Any man willing to die could be a dangerous warrior. But he did not fully trust them. They were irrational, and rational men like him were needed to win this war. America, Britain, and the rest of the West might be rotten, but they were still fierce enemies, none fiercer than the United States. Thousands of American agents dreamed of sending him and his men to Guantánamo or the execution chamber. They had tools and weapons that he could hardly imagine. So he needed to be perfect. Because he and al Qaeda spoke for a billion Muslims. For every Iraqi killed by an American soldier, every Palestinian torn apart by an Israeli missile. We speak for Islam, he thought. And on September 11 we spoke loud and clear. The attack that day had been genius. Using the enemy's own weapons to destroy its biggest buildings. He did not mind that the targets were civilian office towers, the missiles passenger planes. Only by bringing the war to American soil could al Qaeda succeed. One day armies of Muslim soldiers would fight the crusuaders everywhere, as they already did in Iraq. Meanwhile, al Qaeda would fight with the weapons at hand, and if they happened to be jets like this one, so much the better.

Khadri had only one regret about September 11. He had wanted to target the Capitol and the White House, not the Pentagon, but the sheikh had insisted on attacking the American military directly. Unfortunately, the Pentagon was too big to be seriously damaged, even by an airplane. Destroying the Capitol would have killed hundreds of congressmen and senators. The American government would have fallen into chaos.

Nonetheless, the attacks had been a strategic triumph. In their wake America had sent its Christian crusaders into two Muslim countries. The whole world could see the battle between the Dar al-Islam and the Dar al-Harb, the place of peace and the place of war. But September 11 was slipping from the world's memory. Al Qaeda needed to remind the *kafirs* of its power. Khadri wanted to hit this fat rich country in the face a dozen times, until blood flowed out of her eyes and nose and mouth. Then he would hit her a hundred times more, until she pulled back her armies and begged for peace. He would show the Americans just as much mercy as they had offered the Japanese they vaporized in Hiroshima, the Vietnamese they burned up in the jungles. No more. No less.

We must win, Khadri thought. And we will. For Allah is with us. He drank the last of his coffee. He felt refreshed, invigorated. The thought of attacking America always excited him.

EXLEY SAT AT her desk, sifting through Wells's file, looking for something new and knowing it wasn't there. She rolled her head, trying to relax the tension that had been building in her since Heather Murray called the day before. The call had sent a jolt through the CIA or, more accurately, through the handful of officials to whom the name John Wells meant something. Vinny Duto, the chief of the Directorate of Operations, had immediately dispatched a couple of internal security officers to interview Heather and Kenny, but they hadn't gotten much from either one.

Exley looked again at the polygraph test and psychiatric interview Wells had taken when he'd joined a decade before. He had smoked pot but nothing harder, he'd said. He drank occasionally. He had never had a sexually transmitted disease. He had never had sex with a man, though he had been involved in a ménage à trois in college. Despite prodding from the examiner, Wells had declined to be more specific. Good choice, Exley thought. Stuff like that got all over Langley in a hurry, confidentiality agreement or no.

More from the poly: Aside from the marijuana and two speeding tickets, Wells had never broken the law. He felt that dissent was an essential American right. He would quit before carrying out an order he believed immoral. He had never seen a psychiatrist. He rarely had nightmares. He believed in God but would not call himself Christian. While playing football at Dartmouth he had broken the leg of the Yale quarterback. He had not felt remorse. The hit was clean and violence was part of the game. About the only time Wells had responded unusually was when he'd been asked whether he loved his wife. Yes, of course, he'd said, but the poly hadn't agreed.

The agency shrink had hit the obvious points in his evaluation. Wells had a high tolerance for risk. He was self-reflective but not overly emotional. He was very self-confident. He had no pedophilic or psychopathic tendencies, but he appeared capable of extreme violence. In sum, he was an excellent candidate for the Special Operations Group, the agency's paramilitary arm, its most covert operatives.

None of this was news to Exley. She looked at Wells's picture and remembered when she'd first seen him. She had come back to Langley after a frustrating posting in Islamabad. She hadn't recruited anyone important; despite her best efforts, the Pakistani intelligence officers had refused to take her seriously. If she'd whored herself to the generals who'd groped her at embassy parties she might have gotten somewhere, but she'd refused.

After three long years, Exley had decided to come home, get married, have kids. She'd requested and received a transfer to Staff Ops. She always judged herself too harshly. She'd been disappointed with her time in Islamabad, but her bosses said she was a rising star; she'd recruited more agents in Pakistan than anyone since.

Which showed how badly the CIA had ossified since the end of the Cold War, Exley thought. Despite its swashbuckling mystique, the agency had become merely another Washington bureaucracy. Like all bureaucrats, its senior officers found the real action at headquarters, not in the boring grunt work of actual spying. They happily brought Exley home, where she read cables from field officers who somehow missed the fact that Pakistan was developing nuclear weapons under their noses.

THEN SHAFER CONVINCED the Directorate of Operations that the agency needed someone to recruit inside the Taliban. He picked Wells, and Exley understood why the moment she saw him on a trip to the Farm, the agency's training grounds at Camp Peary in tidewater Virginia. Wells looked swarthy and vaguely Arab. He was tall and strong, maybe six foot two and two hundred and ten pounds, but he didn't hold himself like a soldier. Instead he had a sleepy-eyed confidence that seemed unshakable. In fact—and even now, a decade later, the memory brought a flush to her cheeks—her first impression when she met him was that he carried himself like a man who was a very good fuck. And knew it. Highly inappropriate, she knew. Totally inappropriate, especially for a professional and a happily married woman. But there it was.

More to the point, Wells spoke Arabic, was learning Pashtun, and had studied the Koran. He eagerly agreed to a recon trip to Kabul and Kandahar. Exley would be his handler, although in truth she had little to do but hope Wells's performance matched his pedigree.

Wells disappeared to Afghanistan for six months, a month longer than he was supposed to, and returned to Langley without a single agent. Recruiting was impossible, he said. The Taliban wouldn't accept outsiders. Exley was disappointed, but not surprised. Then Wells talked about bin Laden. The agency was monitoring him as a terrorism financier; Wells insisted he was more. Bin Laden was building training camps in Afghanistan and planned a jihad against the United States and Saudi Arabia, Wells said. But he was short on specifics. He hadn't seen the camps. His information was hearsay. Exley remembered the moment vividly.

"Everybody hates us," she'd said. "What makes this guy different?"

"I saw him once in Kabul," Wells said. "There's something in his eyes. We need to take him seriously."

"Something in his eyes?" Shafer didn't hide his sarcasm. "You didn't even get inside the camps, son. For all you know they're roasting marshmallows and singing 'Kumbaya' in there."

Wells grunted as if he'd been hit. He's never failed like this before, Exley thought. Her sympathy was limited. No one was right all the time, and the sooner Wells learned that lesson the better. Welcome to the real world. Wells stood and leaned over the conference table where she sat beside Shafer.

"I'll go back. I'll get in."

"You can't."

"Authorize it, sign the waivers. I'll get in."

"Okay," Shafer said. He had wanted Wells to say that all along, Exley realized later.

WELLS DID GET in. He never said how and Exley never asked, since the answer no doubt included violations of agency regs and U.S. law. Langley didn't know what to do with Wells; most field agents looked for informants at dinner parties. Wells was simply trying to prove himself to al Qaeda, while sending back what he could about the group's structure and plans.

In 1998, after months of silence, Wells reported that al Qaeda planned to attack U.S. interests—most likely an embassy—in East Africa. But he didn't have specifics, and the agency could not correlate his warning. Without much interest, the CIA dutifully told the State Department about the report, and State dutifully filed it away. Two weeks later, suicide bombers blew up the American embassies in Kenya and Tanzania. More than two hundred people died. The agency started taking bin Laden, and Wells, more seriously.

Just before the millennium Wells helped disrupt a planned bombing of two hotels in Cairo on New Year's Eve. The plot was in its final stages; the agency believed it would have succeeded if not for Wells. In his final contact with Exley, Wells said he was going to Chechnya. He had volunteered for the mission to reestablish his bona fides; after the Egyptian plot failed, a Qaeda lieutenant had wondered openly whether he was responsible. I have to prove myself to them every day, he had said; they don't fully trust me, and I'm not sure they ever will. Exley could not even imagine the pressures he faced.

Then silence. Wells's connection to the agency was strictly one-way; Exley had no way to reach him. Still, after the millennial plot, Langley viewed him as an ace in the hole, the last fail-safe if everything else went wrong. Except on September 11 the ace turned into a joker. Or so Wells's former fans believed, especially when he vanished after his cryptic note in the fall of 2001. Exley had the distinct impression that Vinny Duto wished that Wells were dead. Dead, he was a hero, an agent who'd made the ultimate sacrifice. Alive, he was a failure at best, a traitor at worst. Of course Duto was too smart to set Wells up as a scapegoat for his failure to prevent 9/11. But Duto would be out for blood if Wells ever turned up.

Now, looking again at Wells's file, Exley wondered if Duto might be right. She could not understand why Wells had come back to the United States without telling the agency. Without telling her. She thumbed through the poly.

Q: Were you sorry you had broken his leg?
A: It was a clean hit. Violence is part of the game.
Q: So you weren't sorry?
A: Not at all.

What if Wells had been doubled? What if he had decided that violence against the United States was part of the game? Exley shook her head. If Wells had wanted to stay hidden, he wouldn't have contacted his ex-wife. Still, Exley wished he would report in. Soon. Before something blew up.

JOSH GOLDSMITH DIDN'T want to be nervous, but he couldn't help himself. This morning was Thursday. His bar mitzvah was in two days, and even before that he'd have to speak on Friday night. For what felt like the thousandth time he looked at the photocopied section of the Torah he was supposed to read, making sure he had it memorized.

A knock on his door startled him. "Ready for school, sweetie?"

He shook his head, annoyed. "I'm studying, Mom."

"You'll miss breakfast."

"I just need a couple minutes." His voice broke. God, he was pathetic. Would he ever get through puberty like a normal kid?

"At least put your socks on—"

"Okay, okay." Like most Reform Jews, the Goldsmiths were not particularly religious. But Josh was a studious child, and he had worked hard for the ritual ceremony of his bar mitzvah. Still, he was nervous, both for the ceremony on Saturday morning and the party afterward. Most of the kids at school had turned down their invitations. Josh tried not to feel too bad about it. His real friends would be there anyway. He looked at the poster of Shawn Green—a Jewish first baseman, once of his beloved Dodgers, now traded to Arizona—taped above his bed.

"Think Blue," Josh whispered to himself, the Dodgers' motto, the giant letters visible in the hillside beyond the parking lot at Dodger Stadium. "Think Blue, Blue, Blue." Think Blue. He reached up a fist and tapped Shawn Green. He knew his reading perfectly. He'd be fine.

THE STEEL DRUMS shone dully under the van's overhead light. Holding a handkerchief over his mouth so he wouldn't swallow too much dust, Khadri stepped into the van's cargo compartment. He lifted the rusted top of the drum by the van's back doors and ran his fingers through the small off-white pellets that filled about three-quarters of the drum. The van held a dozen similar drums, about twenty-seven hundred pounds of ammonium nitrate in all. Khadri had already checked out the first bomb, which was even larger and hidden in a panel truck in a shed in Tulare, fifty miles north.

Khadri smiled to himself. No one would ever mistake Aziz or Fakhr for brilliant, but building a good ANFO bomb didn't require brilliance, just patience and steady hands. His men had both. As they had been taught in the camps, Aziz and Fakhr had wired the barrels with dynamite charges that would set off the initial explosion and arranged the nitrate barrels in a shaped charge to maximize the force of the blast. Khadri checked the wires again. Everything was in order. They just needed to pour in fuel oil, stir, and blow.

ANFO was a bomber's dream, Khadri thought. Governments could crack down on antiaircraft missiles and machine guns. But as long as farmers needed fertilizer and truckers had to drive, the ingredients for an ammonium nitrate–fuel oil bomb would be available everywhere. Even better, ANFO wasn't volatile. After it was mixed, it could be driven hundreds of miles without much risk of accidental detonation. Which was convenient when your targets were inside a major city—say, Los Angeles. And ANFO was shockingly effective. A truckful of the stuff would take out an office building, as Tim McVeigh and Terry Nichols had proved in Oklahoma City. During the 1970s, the U.S. military had even used it to simulate nuclear explosions.

Still, Khadri was not sorry that he had taken the time to examine the bombs for himself, just as he had done his own target reconnaissance the night before. After the problems on the United flight, he intended to see to the success of this operation himself. These bombings would be a crucial diversion from the mega-attack coming next, and he could not allow another mistake.

He had planned the attack carefully. The truck and van were untraceable, bought for cash under fake names. Similarly, Fakhr and Aziz had built their cache of ammonium nitrate a hundred pounds at a time, while keeping a low profile. Until two weeks before, they had worked as cabbies and lived in a basement apartment in the Rampart district, a gritty neighborhood north of downtown Los Angeles. They rented month to month, always paid cash, always paid on time. It was their fifth apartment; Khadri insisted they move every year, so the neighbors never got friendly. Not that Rampart was known for its warmth.

Now Fakhr and Aziz were staying in a flophouse motel on Sunset Boulevard that wasn't picky about identification. They lived in separate rooms and pretended not to know each other. Still, to maximize security, Khadri had spent only a few minutes with them. He would visit them just once before the mission tonight, to make sure they were ready. After the bombs went off there wouldn't be much of them left to see.

" . . . TWELVE . . . THIRTEEN . . . FOURTEEN!"

Daunte Bennett hoisted the metal bar over his chest, arms shaking with effort. "One more. No help," he grunted to Jarvis, his spotter. He lowered the bar, then pushed it up again, groaning as he fought the weight. Fifteen reps at 255 pounds was no joke.

"Almost there," Jarvis said. Finally Bennett extended his arms to their limit and grunted in triumph. He steered the bar into its metal cradle with a loud clank.

"Two-five-five."

"Coaches be begging you to sign."

Bennett was twenty, a former linebacker for the Crenshaw High Cougars who was a step slow and a couple inches short for big-time college ball. He had tried to bulk up since he'd graduated the year before, hoping to add thirty-five pounds and become a D-lineman. But he knew Jarvis was blowing smoke. Despite protein shakes and daily workouts, he was still only 240, twenty pounds short. Without steroids, he had no chance, and he refused to put needles in his body so he could play third-string tackle for UCLA.

To pay the bills while he figured out his next move, Bennett had found a job as a bouncer at the Paradise Club in Hollywood. He might be too small for Div. I football, but in the real world, he looked plenty intimidating. And he had an even temper, a useful trait for a bouncer. He liked the job. The pay was good—$150 a night, cash, plus a twenty now and then from drunk white boys hoping to jump the line—and he liked watching people when they were trying to get in, or realizing they might not. Some stayed cool, some got huffy. All this for the chance to pay a $25 cover to listen to music so loud you couldn't even hear it. Folks were silly sometimes.

But he didn't want to be a bouncer all his life. He'd been thinking about the army, getting the chance for college without a football scholarship. Plus, part of him missed the structure he'd had playing ball. Having somebody to yell at him, work him hard. War was no joke, he knew that—a kid from the Cougars had gotten a leg blown off in Iraq—but he'd seen enough drive-bys to know that everybody died sooner or later. Might as well go down fighting.

KHADRI COULD HEAR the battered television in room 202 playing CNN even before he opened the door. Inside, Aziz and Fakhr sat side by side on the edge of the bed, three feet from the TV, its glow reflected in their eyes. They looked like zombies, Khadri thought. The living dead. When he closed the door Fakhr jumped up. His eyes flickered to Khadri and back to the television before coming to rest at last on a Koran that sat open on a table in the corner. Thin sweat stains soiled the armpits of his blue button-down shirt. The fear did not surprise Khadri. Looking at death was not entirely pleasant, even when the cause was just and heaven awaited. Now that they had picked up their vehicles and thrown out their clothes, Fakhr and Aziz had little to do but contemplate their mortality.

Khadri turned to Fakhr and hugged him, quickly and tightly.

"Fakhr."

"Abu Mustafa." They did not know his real name and never would.

Aziz rose, and Khadri hugged him as well.

"Brothers," Khadri said in English. He motioned for Fakhr and Aziz to sit. "Brothers," he said again. "The sheikh himself awaits this night." He gestured at the television. "Tonight the infidels will have news. Tonight they will see our power for themselves."

Fakhr's left hand twitched uncontrollably.

"Fakhr—"

"What if we fail, Abu Mustafa?"

"We won't fail," Khadri said. For twenty minutes they walked through the plan and its contingencies: What if one of the trucks ran late, or got pulled over, or a bomb didn't explode? Khadri focused on the details so that the attack itself seemed inevitable. When they had discussed every possibility, he picked up the Koran and turned to the eighty-seventh sura, "The Most High."

"Let's read together," he said.

"*Bismallah rahmani rahim . . .*" they chanted. "In the name of Allah, the Compassionate, the Merciful . . ."

All three knew the sura by heart. Like many Muslim boys, as children they had memorized important verses of the Koran even before they could read. They slowed as they reached the climax of the prayer, the lines Khadri wanted them to remember.

He succeeds who grows
Who remembers the name of his Lord and performs his prayer

But you prefer the life of the world
Though the hereafter is better and more lasting
Yes, this is set down in the scrolls of the ancients
The scrolls of Abraham and Moses.

Khadri squeezed the hands of his men. The fear had left Fakhr's eyes, he saw. "The hereafter is better and more lasting," Khadri said. "I envy you, brothers. Soon you will be in heaven. As is said in the twenty-second sura: Praised be Allah, for He is the truth."

"He quickens the dead, and He is able to do all things," Aziz said, finishing the verse.

"*Nam,*" Khadri said. "Now send the *kafirs*"—the unbelievers—"to hell."

THE SERVICE WAS taking forever, Josh Goldsmith thought. He sat on the bimah, the raised stage at the front of the Temple Beth El synagogue, trying not to look at his parents. He was nervous, although he had no reason to be. Everyone in the sanctuary tonight was a relative, a friend, or a regular at temple. Josh wore a new gray suit, a white shirt, and a red tie with tiny blue rabbits that he had picked out himself. He was trying not to be too nervous. He peeked at his watch: 9:35. He'd be on soon.

THE TRIP HAD taken exactly as long as Fakhr expected—no surprise, since he had driven the route a dozen times in the last month. He guided the white Dodge van down Walton Avenue, heading south toward Wilshire. He wanted to come through the intersection with speed. The light ahead dropped from red to green, and Fakhr tapped on his brakes to put more space between the van and the car ahead. A few seconds later, he pumped the gas. The van leapt ahead.

"I CALL JOSHUA Goldsmith, our bar mitzvah, to the microphone to lead us," Rabbi Nachman said. Josh felt his legs wobble as he stood. In the front row, his sister Becky looked at him and pretended to pick her nose before his mom elbowed her sharply. He smiled at her and felt his stomach loosen up. Those people out there were just family and friends. Think Blue.

FAKHR PILOTED THE van up the steps at the northeast corner of the temple, the corner nearest the intersection. A middle-aged security guard barely had time to stand before the van plowed him down and smashed through the temple's entrance into the hall outside the sanctuary. Fakhr steered toward its doors. He wouldn't be able to get into the sanctuary itself, but that didn't matter.

Don't be scared, Fakhr told himself. Do it quickly. "*Allahu akbar,*" he said aloud.

He had taped the detonator, a small plastic box connected to a thick black wire, to the passenger seat so it wouldn't bounce as he came up the steps. He tore it off the seat, looked at it for a moment, and pressed the button in the middle of the box.

JOSH HAD ALMOST reached the microphone when he heard a loud crash outside. The congregation turned around, and three men stood up to investigate.

THE BUTTON CLICKED. A jolt of electricity ran through the wire to the blasting caps attached to the dynamite in the back of the van. The dynamite exploded, and a moment later the ANFO detonated.

INSIDE THE SYNAGOGUE, the world ended.

The explosion looked nothing like the Hollywood version of a car bomb—a smoky fireball that blows out windows but leaves the body of the car intact. Those explosions are produced by low-velocity explosives like black powder, which burn in small showy blasts. High explosives like dynamite don't burn; they detonate, turning from solid to gas instantaneously and in the process generating tremendous heat.

In a fraction of a second, Fakhr and the van ceased to exist, as the gas produced by the explosion moved outward and created a huge pressure wave that pushed the air forward at two miles a second. Effectively, the bomb created a super-tornado in the synagogue, a tornado with winds fifty times more powerful than those seen in nature.

The pressure wave and the shrapnel it created blew apart the back wall of the synagogue and tore to pieces everyone at the back of the sanctuary. Others burned to death in the flash fireball from the explosion, which reached a temperature of several thousand degrees. No one could run, hide, or duck. Survival was a matter of luck and distance; Josh's parents in the first row had better odds than his cousin Jake six rows back. His uncle Ronnie against the wall had no chance at all.

Then the pressure wave reversed direction to fill the vacuum left where the van had stood. The explosion had blown the ceiling off its walls. As the roof was pulled back down, the walls—now weakened and out of alignment—could no longer support it. The ceiling fell in progressively, from the back to the front of the synagogue, dropping tons of concrete and wood and steel on the survivors of the initial blast.

For Josh Goldsmith, the collapse of the ceiling came as a relief.

Josh had the misfortune to be standing when the explosion occurred, so he took more than his share of shrapnel. Metal fragments from the van turned his face into a bloody pulp. A larger piece sliced into his stomach and cut his liver nearly in half. Lacerations covered his body. Fortunately, his agony lasted only a few seconds, until a slab of concrete from the ceiling crushed his skull.

ON HOLLYWOOD BOULEVARD it was just another Friday night. Convertibles and tricked-out pickups cruised slowly, bass thumping. The evening was unseasonably warm for April, and girls in thigh-high skirts flirted with boys in muscle shirts. A red Lamborghini Diablo competed for attention with a black Cadillac Escalade on gleaming twenty-six-inch rims. Tourists snapped pictures of Grauman's Chinese Theatre. Near the corner of Hollywood and Ivar, dozens of kids had lined up to get into the Ivar, a restaurant and club that attracted the masses from the Valley. Across the boulevard, police barricades held back a hundred fans who'd shown up for the premiere of *Number,* a campy horror movie about a crazed accountant, at Cinespace, a movie theater in the same building as the Ivar.

From a Nissan Altima parked two blocks east, Khadri watched Aziz's van snake slowly west on Hollywood. Aziz was running a few minutes late, though Khadri didn't expect him to have a problem. The police and firefighters would just be reaching the synagogue. They would need a minute to realize they were looking at a crime scene, and their immediate response would be to lock down the city's other synagogues, not to look for a bomb in Hollywood. Still, Khadri wished Aziz would hurry.

Khadri had parked outside the blast zone but close enough to feel the bomb for himself. He knew he should have left Los Angeles already, but he couldn't help himself. He wanted to see his handiwork firsthand. He had his escape route mapped, of course: east to Phoenix, Arizona. He would stay for a few days—no need to rush—then leave the Altima at Sky Harbor International and fly to Mexico City. No one would notice the car for weeks, and it couldn't be connected to him anyway.

Khadri looked at the men and women walking past his car. Those heading east would live; those walking west might die. Their fates were no concern of his, he thought, any more than American generals worried about what happened to the inhabitants of the cities they attacked. This was war, and sometimes war killed people who didn't think of themselves as combatants. These people weren't innocents, though they preferred to imagine themselves that way; no one in America was an innocent.

He drummed his fingers against the wheel, anxious to feel the blast.

ARMS FOLDED, BENNETT stood outside the Paradise Club, a half block west of the corner of Hollywood and Ivar. Paradise was harder to get into than the Ivar, so the lines were smaller but just as unruly. Tonight a crowd had formed early.

"*Puta!*"

"Asshole!"

Near the front of the line, two guys in their early twenties, one white, the other Hispanic, got in each other's faces. Bennett stepped forward. "Easy," he said. They appealed to him simultaneously.

"This *maricón* pushed me," the Hispanic guy said.

"He was checking out my girlfriend."

"That fat bitch?"

Just like that the white guy stepped up and swung wildly. Bennett grabbed his arm before he could connect. This crap didn't usually start until later. In the distance Bennett heard sirens screaming west. A lot of sirens.

The white kid tried to pull his arm from Bennett's hand. "What's your name?" Bennett said.

"Mitch."

"Mitch, you're walking this way," Bennett said, and pointed west. He turned to the Hispanic guy. "What's your name?"

"Ricky."

"Ricky, that way." He pointed east.

"Man—"

Bennett shook his head. "Start walking."

They looked at Bennett's huge arms and walked. He watched them go until the blare of horns down the block grabbed his attention. Hollywood was always loud on Friday nights, but this was ridiculous.

COLD AIR POURED out of the vents of the Mitsubishi panel truck, but Aziz couldn't stop sweating. The cab stank with the acrid smell of his fear, overwhelming the faint scent of the rosewater he had dabbed on himself as he prepared to make his journey to paradise. Nine forty-five, five minutes late, and he still wasn't there. Far worse, he could feel his resolve weakening. He had felt confident in the motel room, but as the moment approached he could no longer control his terror. Would it hurt when he pushed the button? What if he didn't get to heaven? He knew he would, of course. The Koran said so. Abu Mustafa said so. He would be a *shahid*, a martyr, surrounded by the most beautiful virgins, drinking the purest water, eating the sweetest dates.

"Allah hath bought from the believers their lives and their wealth because the Garden shall be theirs," the ninth sura said. "They shall fight in the way of Allah and shall slay and be slain."

So he knew he would get to heaven.

But what if he didn't?

The light ahead turned green but no one moved. Aziz leaned on his horn, and finally the cars ahead crawled forward. He looked at the street around him. These people walked around in a haze while their soldiers raped prisoners in Iraq. They sucked up the world's oil and lived like kings while Muslim children starved. They treated their bodies with disrespect. They believed in a false god. They were pigs in slop. Everything they did was *haram,* forbidden. Anger surged in Aziz. He had no reason to fear. They deserved to die. It was Allah's will.

The light dropped green again, and Aziz inched through the intersection of Hollywood and Ivar. Crowds filled the sidewalks. This was the spot. Aziz stopped the truck. He picked up the detonator and turned it back and forth in his hand.

I can't, he thought. Allah forgive me, I can't.

INSIDE THE TRUCK, time moved very slowly. Aziz knew he had to decide. People were looking at him, and a police officer would tell him to move along soon. But he felt paralyzed. He wormed his thumb over the detonator, pressing down on its button ever so slightly, feeling the tension under his finger. He looked out the windshield and silently murmured the first sura to himself.

"In the name of Allah, the Compassionate, the Merciful . . ."

Now, he told himself. Now or never.

He pushed the button.

THE SECOND BOMB proved even more devastating than the first. The explosion blew a crater fifteen feet deep and thirty feet around, and shot a cloud of smoke, debris, and fire hundreds of feet into the sky. With no walls to slow it, the overpressure wave killed everyone in an eighty-foot radius. The people nearest the truck were blown apart and barbecued; farther away the bodies were left recognizably human, although many lacked arms and legs. A few of the dead appeared basically unhurt; the blast wave had left their bodies intact but shaken their brains to jelly.

The blast partially knocked down four buildings, including the

Ivar-Cinescape building directly across the street. Inside the Ivar, a fire began, and with only one emergency exit left, panic set in. Eighty-five more people were crushed or burned to death.

FOR JUST A moment after the explosion a shocked silence descended on the street, a false peace splitting before from after. Then chaos: car alarms ringing, fires roaring, screaming. So much screaming, most of it hardly recognizable as human: a high-pitched keening that started and stopped at random.

Bennett found himself on the ground. He pushed himself to his feet and ran toward the wreckage, not even noticing the blood dripping from his face. He didn't know where to turn or what to do; he wished that he had taken that first-aid class at Crenshaw.

He slowed down, crunching broken glass under his feet, then nearly tripped over what he thought at first was a blue denim bag. He looked again and discovered that the bag was a leg, a leg that wasn't attached to a body, not anymore. Hell. This was hell on earth.

A few feet away, a man lay trapped under a black Jetta, groaning softly. Ricky, the guy from the line. Oh God, Bennett thought. I told him to walk this way.

Ricky motioned feebly. "Shit, help me."

Bennett threw his shoulder into the Jetta. It didn't budge. He tried again.

"How 'bout some help!" he yelled.

Ricky was starting to shake, Bennett saw.

"Just be cool," he said. A big white guy joined Bennett. They lifted together, inching the Jetta higher. Another man grabbed Ricky under his arms and began to pull him out.

Ricky screamed in agony, the worst sound Bennett had heard yet. The Jetta had masked his pain by crushing the nerves in his hips. Now they could fire again, and Ricky was learning the truth of his injuries.

"Ricky, Ricky—" Bennett said. The scream became a whimper. He grabbed Ricky's hand and squeezed. "Ambulance'll be here soon. Just—" Ricky's hand went limp as he slipped into unconsciousness. Bennett looked at the other two men and wordlessly they decided to leave Ricky and see if they could help anyone else. Help? Bennett had never felt so helpless.

At that moment Bennett decided he would sign up for the army the next morning. He would kill whoever had done this. It was all he could do.

IN HIS REARVIEW mirror, Khadri saw the truck disappear. A moment later the blast wave rattled his car.

He drove off, careful not to speed. He and his men had dealt America a mighty blow tonight. KNX was already reporting a massive explosion at a Westwood synagogue. But even before he reached the highway, his jubilation faded. He had so much more work ahead.

And his next mission would put this night to shame.

RICKY GUTIERREZ MIGHT have lived if he had reached a hospital in time, but the twin blasts overwhelmed the Los Angeles police and fire departments. They had drilled for one bomb, not two explosions miles apart. By the time ambulances arrived in force at the Hollywood explosion, Ricky and dozens of others who survived the initial fireball had died.

Two weeks later, when the last victim died at Cedars-Sinai and reports of the missing stopped coming, the death toll from the Los Angeles bombings reached 336: 132 at the synagogue, 204 in Hollywood. It was the worst attack since September 11, and no one was surprised when al Qaeda took responsibility.

EXLEY WOKE ON the first ring. She hadn't been fully asleep anyway. The boundary between sleep and consciousness, once easy for her to cross, these days seemed bounded by barbed wire and broken glass. She grabbed for the phone and heard Shafer's voice. "Jennifer. Get in here." Her clock radio glowed 1:15 A.M. in the dark. "There's been a bombing. In L.A."

Her mind spun.

"It's bad. Two bombs." Click.

On her way to Langley she flicked on the radio to hear the mayor of Los Angeles declaring that an emergency curfew would begin in an hour. "Only police, fire, and hospital vehicles are permitted in the emergency zone. All others are subject to arrest. The emergency zone is bounded by the Santa Monica Freeway to the south . . ."

She turned off her radio and looked at the dark silent highway around her and tried to comprehend why someone would blow up kids out for fun on a Friday night. But she couldn't. She understood intellectually, of course: she knew all about asymmetric warfare, the relationship between terrorists and failed states, the financial and religious motivations of suicide bombers. But in the end those words were as meaningless as wrapping paper for an empty box. Nothing justified these bombs. She couldn't help but feel that these killers were barbarians, something less than human.

Which, she was sure, was exactly how they felt about Americans.

AT LANGLEY, NO one needed to say the obvious: U.S. intelligence and law enforcement had failed terribly. Again. Hundreds of Americans had died, and so far clues were scarce. The bombers wouldn't be talking; they had been so completely obliterated that the FBI would never find enough tissue for DNA samples. For the moment, anyway, they had no leads.

But they did have a suspect, as Exley realized when she arrived at her office and found one of Duto's assistants waiting to demand that she give him Wells's file from her safe. "For Vinny," the assistant said. She said nothing, just unlocked her safe and handed over the file.

She was looking at the first flash reports when Shafer appeared. "What's your gut?"

She didn't need to ask what he meant. "It wasn't him."

"Explain."

"One, he was just in Montana. This thing didn't get put together in a day."

"Two?"

"Two, if it was his, why would he risk blowing it by visiting his ex?"

"Three?"

"Three, even if he's flipped, he would never attack soft targets."

"He's violent."

"Not against civilians. He wouldn't consider that fair."

"Four?"

"I don't have a four."

Shafer held his thumb and index finger an inch apart. "Duto's this close to having Tick flash a bulletin for him." A bulletin to police and the FBI about Wells.

"On what evidence?" Exley said.

"On the evidence that he's scared shitless his own guy just killed three hundred people and he wants to get in front of it. If Wells did this, getting fired is the least of it. You and I could go to jail. On general principles."

"He didn't do it." The conviction in her voice surprised her.

"Come on, let's talk to Vinny."

As she stood, her phone rang.

"Yes?"

"Jennifer Exley?" a man asked. She knew his voice immediately.

"Where are you?"

"Here, Washington."

She couldn't help herself. "Thank God, John."

"I think I need to come in."

"Yes," she said. "You do."

5

"IT WAS A mistake," Wells said again. "I made a mistake."

Exley, Shafer, and Duto sat across from him at a conference table in a small windowless room that wasn't quite standard-issue office space. No clocks, for one. Then there were the cameras in each corner that had deliberately been left visible, and the acoustic padding covering the walls. In theory, the padding was meant to defeat any efforts to listen in on conversations in the room. In reality, it and the cameras were signals, Wells knew: This is a serious room and you're in serious trouble. A man in a suit sat against the far wall. He hadn't introduced himself, but Wells figured him for a lawyer. He didn't have to guess about the no-neck plainclothes security officer who stood by the door, his hand resting on the Glock on his hip.

No one had even pretended to be friendly. The gate guards had searched him head to toe before they'd let him in. He'd been searched again before he'd been allowed to see Exley and Shafer, who had met him with handshakes, not hugs, like he was back from a three-day sales trip to Detroit. Wells couldn't say he was surprised.

"John," Shafer had said. "We're gonna have some questions for you." Wells had picked up a flicker of something more in Exley's eyes when she'd first seen him, but the look had disappeared fast. If she was glad to see him, she was hiding it.

After leaving the YMCA, he had bought a Greyhound ticket from Missoula to Washington, one last chance to be alone before the world started to turn again. He planned to call the agency when he reached D.C. He had met Zawahiri in Peshawar two weeks before. Two weeks of freedom seemed fair after all his years at the edge of the world.

On the bus Wells felt heavy and tranquil, as if his blood had been replaced with something cooler, his veins filled with embalming fluid. He thumbed through his Koran and cataloged what he had lost during his time away. His mother. His ex-wife. His son, though not forever, he hoped. But he still had the chance to protect his country from men who believed that Allah had given them a license to destroy it.

NOW HE WAS furious with himself. The world had been turning all along, and he hadn't noticed. Three hours after the Greyhound pulled into Washington's rundown bus station he heard the bulletins about Los Angeles. He knew immediately he should have checked in as soon as he'd reached Hong Kong. The attack would make the agency's doubts about him boil over.

He promised himself he would stay calm, whatever they said to him. He had to convince them to trust him, or they would never give him another chance. So he sketched out his years in the North-West Frontier, walked them through the weeks since he'd left Islamabad: where he'd stayed, how he'd traveled, the name he'd used to clear immigration at Kennedy. He told them about his meeting in Peshawar with Zawahiri and Khadri and Farouk, how they had sent him to America without a specific mission.

"It wasn't Los Angeles," Duto said.

"No."

"You didn't know anything about Los Angeles."

"Of course not."

In the most even tone he could muster, he apologized. For entering the country without telling them. For not reaching out when he was in Pakistan. For not killing bin Laden. He explained as best he could. But he knew he didn't have what they really wanted: information about the last attack, or the next.

ACROSS THE TABLE, Exley felt her stomach clench. Duto had never met Wells before, so he couldn't tell how much Wells had left over there. But she could. It wasn't just the lines on his face or the scar on his arm. The confidence in his eyes hadn't disappeared, but it was mixed with something else, a humility she hadn't seen before.

And Wells's story made sense. He had wanted to visit his family, to be alone for a few days. Maybe Duto couldn't understand that, but she could. Those weren't crimes. She wanted to grab Duto's arm and say, Can't you see he's on our side? But she didn't. She couldn't conceive of a quicker way to lose what little influence she had. Duto had clearly decided that Wells was worthless even if he was still loyal. He hadn't stopped 9/11 or Los Angeles, so screw him.

Telling Duto that she could see the truth in Wells's eyes would earn her a transfer straight to Ottawa, for the glamorous job of watching the Canadian Parliament. So she kept her mouth shut and listened as Duto fired away. Then the door opened, and Duto's assistant walked in and murmured something in his ear. "Be right back," Duto said, and walked out.

WITH DUTO GONE, Wells looked at Exley and Shafer. He would have liked to know whether they hated him as much as Duto did. But he wasn't going to ask in here, with the tapes rolling and the lawyer scribbling. He didn't want to compromise them. Besides, he might not like the answer.

Exley leaned toward him. "John," she said.

It was all she said. And it was enough. Wells felt a spring relax inside him.

DUTO WALKED BACK in holding a plastic bag, a clear plastic evidence bag sealed with a chain-of-custody tag. He slapped it on the table. "What the fuck is this?"

Wells's Koran.

So they had searched his room. He had given them the name of the hotel where he had checked in that night, of course. "You get a warrant or just break the door down?" Wells said evenly.

Duto pointed to the book.

"I'm Muslim," Wells said. "That's my Koran."

Shafer put his head in his hands.

"You're Muslim?" Duto said. "When did that happen?"

"John," Exley said. "Your file indicated you were studying the religion—"

"Shut up, Jennifer," Duto said, without taking his eyes off Wells. Duto leaned across the table, nearly spitting his words: "You converted? When?"

Wells gave Exley a second to defend herself, but she passed on the chance.

"It didn't happen all at once."

"You admit you're a Muslim."

"Yes," Wells said quietly. He wasn't about to lose his temper to this asshole. "I'm guilty of being Muslim."

"You dumbfuck."

"Curse at me all you like." Again his voice was quiet.

"I'll do whatever the fuck I like."

"Cool it, Vinny," Shafer said.

Duto looked at Shafer but said nothing. Wells wondered if the two men were putting on some kind of show for him, a good cop/bad cop routine.

"Tell us what happened," Shafer said.

"You know about my grandmother," Wells said. "I pretended to believe to get in the camps. But the more I learned, the more kinship I felt."

"So you converted?"

Fatigue and emptiness, the emptiness that had swept him as he knelt before his mother's grave, overwhelmed Wells. But he wouldn't show weakness at this table. His faith might be wavering, but he wasn't telling Duto that. "Converted. Accepted. I don't know what to call it. Islam is more holistic than Christianity—it's not just a religion, it's a way of life."

"Yeah, if your way of life doesn't include freedom and democracy," Duto said.

"Turkey's a democracy," Wells said.

"Not if your boys have their way."

"I hate them as much as you do," Wells said. "They've perverted the Koran. Look, Christianity isn't perfect either. Kill them all and let God sort them out. You know where that comes from?"

"Enlighten me, wise one."

"Eight hundred years ago a Catholic army was attacking this splinter Christian sect called the Cathars in a French town. Béziers, it was called. But the army had a problem. There were Catholics in Béziers along with the Cathars. So the soldiers asked this abbot who was commanding them, 'What do we do when we get in? How do we tell our own Catholics from the Cathars?' Know what the abbot said?"

"Please, continue." A flush crept across Duto's face.

"He said, 'Kill them all. The Lord will recognize those which are His.' "

Duto stood and leaned across the table, his face inches from Wells's.

"Shut the fuck up," he said quietly. "You come in here with stories, fucking parables, whatever they are, on a night when your buddies blew up Los Angeles? If I want history lessons from you I'll ask. What, you looking for converts? You may be even stupider than I thought. Which would be tough."

This time Duto wasn't faking his anger, Wells thought. He wondered if he'd gone too far.

"Vinny—" Shafer said.

"If I were you, Ellis, I'd keep my mouth shut," Duto said, not taking his eyes off Wells.

"Most Muslims don't want bin Laden to win," Wells said. "They only support him because they feel so alienated from us."

"Like you."

Wells wondered if Duto really believed he was a traitor. "That's not what I meant."

"Any more speeches, John?"

Wells said nothing.

"Good," Duto said. "One last time. You know anything about last night?"

"No. But something's coming," Wells said. "Maybe not right away, but something."

"Great tip," Duto said.

"We could all use some sleep," Shafer said. "We've got a room for you, John."

Wells nodded. Sleep sounded like a very good idea.

"We want you on the box this afternoon," Duto said.

WELLS NEEDED A second to remember what that meant. A polygraph. He looked across the table at his inquisitors. Duto had made his feelings clear. Shafer: a crumpled shirt, hair in all directions. Everything about him messy except his quiet eyes, looking at Wells like he was an experiment gone wrong. And Exley. Jenny. Worry creasing her forehead. Those beautiful blue eyes. He thought he saw compassion in them. But maybe he was wrong.

Now she spoke, quietly. "You don't have a choice, John. And neither do we." And fell silent, waiting for Duto to slap her down again.

She was right, he knew. The agency's need to polygraph came from both bureaucratic ass covering and a genuine belief in the power of the box. The CIA liked to believe that the poly's squiggly black lines offered truth, the rarest jewel of all. If he didn't agree to take the test, they would never believe him again. They might arrest him. Though for what, Wells wasn't sure. Possession of false documents, maybe. They might just put him in a corner somewhere. But they would never believe him again.

Of course, they probably wouldn't believe him even after he passed the test. They knew he could beat a poly. They had trained him to do just that.

"Kind of Kafkaesque, isn't it?" Wells said.

"Actually I think it's more of a Catch-22," Shafer said.

Wells couldn't help but laugh.

"This isn't funny," Duto said.

"Jenny's right," Wells said. "Box me."

Duto stood to leave, then picked up Wells's Koran. "You want it back, John?"

"Is this some kind of test?" Wells said. "Yes."

Duto flicked it contemptuously across the table. "I understand," he said. "It's your special book."

EXLEY SAT ALONE at the conference table, her head in her hands, replaying the moment when Duto had shown her just where she stood. He wasn't simply snapping at her, or cursing at Wells. He had wanted Wells to know that he was the alpha. It was the wrong strategy—Wells couldn't be intimidated—but Duto had decided to try. He'd proved his point by picking on the weakest link. On her. Men were intuitive assholes. And no one had bothered to defend her, not even Wells, whom she was trying to help. Because in the shark tank you saved yourself first. Probably the others had hardly even noticed what had happened, not after the way Duto had reamed out Wells, but she couldn't stop thinking about it.

Where had her confidence gone? But she knew. The divorce, the endless work . . . and the feeling that none of it made any difference. She couldn't help but envy al Qaeda's certainty. Always wrong but never in doubt.

WELLS'S ROOM HAD a double bed, a separate bathroom with a steel shower and toilet, even a narrow window that overlooked the agency's lush green campus. Aside from the cameras in the corners, he could hardly tell it was a cell. "High class," he said to Dex, the guard from the conference room.

"I just do what they tell me."

"You and everyone else."

"Get some sleep. I'll be back at noon." Dex left. The door closed with an electromagnetic thunk that let Wells know he was locked in.

Between the Greyhound and the interrogation, Wells had hardly slept since Missoula. But before he lay down he opened his Koran and recited the ninety-fourth sura, a beautiful verse:

> In the name of Allah, the Compassionate and Merciful
> Have we not caused your chest to relax
> And eased you of the burden
> Which weighed down your back
> And exalted your fame

But—truly—with hardship goes ease
Truly with hardship goes ease
So when you are relieved, still toil
And strive to please your God

He lay down and fell immediately asleep.

WELLS HID BEHIND a boulder as a black-robed man walked toward him, whip in hand. Crack! The whip swung toward him. The air was foul and thick. Bats screeched overhead. He was lost in a cave; a distant glimmer marked the world outside. But the man in the black robe blocked his escape route. Who was he? Khadri? Duto? Bin Laden? Wells would be safe if he could answer that question. He shrank lower behind the rock.

Crack! The cave itself was crumbling, its walls shattering. A heavy stone fell from the ceiling and crashed beside him. Smoke seared his eyes. The man vanished and Wells tried to run for the mouth of the cave. But as he did the light receded, and the ground beneath him turned to muck. He stumbled and fell into the mire, which covered him, filling his nose and mouth so he could not breathe—

He woke to find Shafer shaking him.

"Sorry," Shafer said. "I let myself in. You seemed to be having a nightmare."

"I don't have nightmares," Wells said. At least this one was easy to read. He felt trapped. What a shock.

"Most people would after what you've been through. Then again, most people wouldn't have survived what you went through."

"I'm not most people."

"Don't get touchy."

Immediately Wells felt his temper rise.

"Are you saying they let me live because I turned?"

"I meant it as a compliment, John. Believe it or not."

"Sure. Everybody has a job to do, Ellis," Wells said. "Like Duto's the bad guy, you're my real friend."

"Duto doesn't even know I'm here. I'm not sure he'd be happy about it. We have some differences of opinion."

"Yeah?" Wells said. "Like what?"

"Well, I think he's a Class A prick. He thinks he's Class B."

Wells laughed. "As long as you spare me the speech about how it'll go easier if I just tell you everything right now."

"If we really thought you'd flipped we'd be treating you a lot worse than this." Shafer stepped back and pointed to a shirt and a pair of jeans stacked on a chair. "Yours, from the hotel."

"Ellis—" Wells stopped himself. He wanted to ask Shafer about Exley, where she stood, but he would have that conversation with her directly.

"Yeah?"

"Thanks," Wells said.

Shafer looked at his watch. "The poly's in an hour."

"Am I a prisoner, Ellis?"

"That's for the lawyers to decide. Let's say you're a guest."

"Like the Hotel California?"

"You're showing your age, John." Shafer opened the door.

"It's not locked?"

"Not for me," Shafer said. And walked out, closing the door behind him.

WELLS HADN'T TAKEN a polygraph since his agency training, and he was surprised when he realized that a flat-panel computer monitor on the examiner's desk had replaced the paper-and-needles box. Otherwise the room hadn't changed: beige walls, a thickly padded chair, and an obvious one-way mirror on the far wall.

"Sit," said the examiner, a tough-looking guy, early fifties, with the thick forearms and unfriendly squint of a marine gunnery sergeant. He strapped a blood-pressure cuff around Wells's arm, tightened rubber tubes around his chest, and attached electrodes to his fingers. "Pull up your pant leg."

Wells hesitated, then rolled up his jeans. The examiner knelt next to Wells's left leg. He pushed down Wells's sock and pulled a straight razor from his pocket. "Hold still." He shaved a patch of Wells's calf and pasted another electrode to the spot. He stepped back to consult his monitor.

"What's your name?" His tone was harsh, as if Wells were a prisoner.

Wells controlled his temper, visualizing the top of Lost Trail Pass, the Montana mountains.

"Easy, killer," he said. "What's yours?"

"You can call me Walter. What's your name?"

"Walter what?"

"What's your name?"

Wells knew he couldn't win this fight. He could either pull off the electrodes and walk out—and be back where he started—or answer Walter's questions. "John Wells."

"Where were you born?"

"Hamilton, Montana."

"When?"

"July 6, 1969."

"Any siblings?"

"No."

Walter slowly worked his way through Wells's life: the name of his first-grade teacher, the make and model of his first car. Sometimes he moved quickly, sometimes slowly, sipping from a water bottle as he mulled or pretended to mull his next question. The air in the room grew heavy and stale and Wells wondered if the air-conditioning had been turned off to make him uncomfortable. But he stayed patient, knowing Walter wanted to irritate him, distract him, so that the real questions would come almost as a relief. Finally they began.

"When did you first go to Afghanistan?"

"In 1996."

"Are you sure?"

"I don't think I'd forget."

"Are you sure?"

"Yes."

"I don't mean for the agency."

"You mean when Osama called me after I graduated college, said he had a job for me. That time? Come on, Walter."

Walter said nothing.

"I never went to Afghanistan before 1996," Wells said slowly. "I never went to Afghanistan except on the orders of the Central Intelligence Agency."

"How'd you get in?"

"Flew into Islamabad, found a ride over the border. The usual route."

"What was your cover?"

"NOC." Nonofficial cover, the CIA's term for an agent who had no open connection to the U.S. government, as opposed to one supposedly working for the State Department or another federal agency. "Very nonofficial. I was a backpacker, a small-time dopehead."

"Were you nervous?"

Wells laughed. "I was too dumb to be nervous."

"Someone in Kabul knew you were coming."

"Didn't we just go through this?"

"You were in contact with al Qaeda even before your first mission."

"I never even heard of Osama bin Laden until that first trip."

The answer seemed to satisfy Walter. He walked Wells through the details of his first trip to Kabul and Kandahar. Wells answered mechanically, in his mind seeing Afghanistan. The thick sweet smell of a goat roasting over a spit, the moaning of an exhausted horse being whipped to death because it could no longer pull a cart. The Afghans, so hospitable and so cruel.

The snap of Walter's fingers pulled Wells out of his reverie. "Pay attention."

"Can I have some water?" Wells didn't want to ask, but he was badly thirsty. Walter pulled a bottle out of his bag, and Wells gulped from it. For the first time he felt their kinship. They were both pros, just doing their jobs. Of course, Walter wanted him to feel that way.

"WHAT WERE YOU doing in Kabul that first time?"

"Trying to recruit. Unsuccessfully."

"What went wrong?"

"Where should I start? I hardly spoke Pashto. Under U.S. law I wasn't supposed to recruit anybody dirty. Remember that stroke of genius, Walter? I was frigging twenty-seven years old and I was gonna turn these guys who'd been lying to each other for a thousand years?"

"You failed to recruit a single agent."

"I didn't even try. I would have blown my cover, gotten myself killed."

Walter walked toward Wells.

"When did they tell you about 9/11?"

Switching abruptly from a comfortable line of questioning was an old trick, but effective. Wells's pulse quickened. "I found out afterward like everyone else."

"Why didn't you warn the agency beforehand?"

Pretending you hadn't heard the subject's denial was another old trick.

"I told you I didn't know beforehand."

"So you failed."

"I failed."

"What was your role in the Los Angeles attack?"

"I wasn't involved."

Walter stepped back and looked at the monitor. "You're lying."

"No."

"The box says you're lying."

"Then it's wrong."

"When did you enter the United States?"

"A week ago."

"You're lying again."

Wells shook his head. "No."

"How many people have you killed?"

"About fifteen."

"About?" Walter sneered.

"I don't keep an exact count."

"Americans?"

"No."

"How many Americans, John?"

"None. Never."

The questions were coming fast now.

"But you want to kill Americans."

"No."

"Why not?"

"What?"

"That's what al Qaeda does, right? And you're an al Qaeda agent."

"I infiltrated Qaeda on the orders of this agency."

"Did this agency order you to convert to Islam?"

"No."

Walter leaned in close to Wells. "Does al Qaeda have WMD?"

"I don't think so."

"You don't *think* so?" Walter spoke as if Wells were a rebellious but not very bright five-year-old. Wells wished he could jump out of the chair and break Walter in half, but he kept his voice even.

"Getting those weapons was a priority, but I never saw any evidence that they were successful."

"You infiltrated al Qaeda all these years and you don't know if it has weapons of mass destruction? You're not much of an agent, are you?"

"I guess not."

"Or maybe you've been doubled."

Wells stood and pulled off the electrodes and the blood-pressure cuff. The door opened and Dex came in, his hand on his 9mm. "Relax," Dex said.

Wells sat. "Tell Vinny this little show is over," he said. "Ask me whatever you like, call me a fool, but stop telling me I'm a traitor." Walter walked out as Dex sat on the corner of the desk, hand on his gun.

"Let me guess," Wells said. "Just following orders."

IN THE ADJOINING room, Exley and Shafer watched the examination through the one-way mirror along with Regina Burke, another examiner, who was seeing a real-time data feed from the exam.

As the interrogation progressed, Regina, a small woman with short gray hair, leaned closer to her screen. Occasionally she clicked her mouse to mark one of the lines scrolling across the monitor. Exley wished she knew how to read the response charts. But she didn't need to be a professional polygrapher to see that Walter had gotten under Wells's skin.

When Wells blew up, Regina picked up her phone. "Could you inform Mr. Duto that the subject has discontinued the examination?" She paused. "Thank you." She hung up. "Duto's secretary says he'll be here in a few minutes."

Walter walked in.

"So?" Shafer said.

"He's telling the truth," Regina said.

"Yes," Walter said.

"How sure are you?" Exley said.

"You can never know one hundred percent," Regina said. "But his responses are physiologically consistent. He didn't shut down under the stress, which is what he'd do if he were trying to lie."

"If he's faking he's really good," Walter said. "I think he's loyal."

Exley looked at Wells, who was staring into the one-way mirror, his face set and unsmiling. Occasionally he would walk around the room, sliding from corner to corner with slow long strides as Dex watched. A few weeks before, Exley had taken her kids to the Washington Zoo. Now, watching Wells, she recognized the controlled fury of a tiger pacing his cage. If they weren't careful, he might not bother to control that fury much longer, she thought.

DUTO SCOWLED WHEN he heard Walter's assessment. "You let him stop? You let the guys in the chair tell you what to do?"

"It's not there," Walter said. "He's not lying."

"Maybe he's too tough for you. Maybe he needs a more coercive environment."

Coercive. The magic word. Coercive meant weeks without sleep inside a tiny cell with no heat or running water, sensory deprivation in a dark, windowless room until the hallucinations began. Coercive wasn't quite torture, but it was close.

Exley decided that if she didn't say something now she might as well resign. "Vinny, you can't do that." She kept her voice steady.

"Did I ask permission?"

"Forget that he's an American citizen and it's illegal. He can help us."

"Let me spell it out for you," Duto said. "He hasn't produced anything for us in a very long time. And this Islam crap is the last straw."

"He's the only agent we've ever placed inside al Qaeda," Exley said.

"He's not inside anymore. For all you know he's lying about meeting Zawahiri. And even if it's true, what did he get? A few bucks and a ride home? They don't trust him any more than I do."

Duto had just revealed the real reason he was being so hard on Wells, Exley thought. He didn't care whether Wells was loyal. In his eyes Wells had failed, and Duto would do anything to distance himself from failure.

"Vinny. Coercion is unacceptable," Shafer said.

"Unacceptable to who?"

"Drop it."

"Who you gonna tell, Ellis?" Duto said disgustedly. "Your friends in the Senate? At the *Post*?" He looked around the room, as if seeing Regina and Walter and Exley for the first time, imagining what they might say if they were called to testify. "Fine," Duto said. "He goes back on the box."

"He already passed," Shafer said. "Why don't we have a friendly conversation with him tomorrow. Get more on these guys Khadri and Farouk. Maybe Wells can put together a name and a face. Maybe he knows more than he thinks."

"I doubt it. Is that your official recommendation, Ellis?"

"Call it that."

"Put it in writing and I'll consider it. In fact, perhaps we shouldn't detain Mr. Wells at all. What would you think of letting him come and go as he pleases?"

Shafer was taken aback, Exley saw.

"As long as he's under surveillance," Shafer said. "Maybe a monitoring device."

"A monitoring device. He'll love that. Put that in your note as well." Duto turned to Walter. "I want a full report on the poly this afternoon. Thank you." Duto walked out.

Exley was half impressed, half disgusted. These guys played bureaucratic games so hard that it was easy to forget the real enemy.

Shafer had gotten control of Wells, but Duto had forced Shafer to put himself on the line to do it. And none of the infighting made any difference to the kids who'd died in L.A.

"Let's go get our boy," Shafer said.

IN THE CORRIDOR that connected the rooms, Shafer stopped and leaned toward her. "When we go in there, don't tell John he passed the poly. Don't be too friendly."

"Why?"

"Just trust me on this. I don't want him too comfortable."

Then why'd you bother to take him from Duto? she wondered. But Shafer wasn't going to tell her, so she didn't ask. Something important had just happened. She wished she knew what it was.

THAT NIGHT SHAFER moved Wells to an agency safe house in the Capitol Hill neighborhood in Washington. From the outside the place looked like just another run-down town house. Inside, it had cameras and alarms in every room. Still, the surveillance was unobtrusive. Two minders sat outside the house overnight, and Wells wore an electronic ankle bracelet that broadcast his location.

Every day Dex drove Wells to talk with Shafer and Exley. They were decent, but hardly friendly. No one mentioned the polygraph, and he didn't ask. He spent most of his time explaining al Qaeda's structure and trying to identify members from surveillance photos. He was certain he wasn't being shown anything too new or valuable. After he mentioned Khadri's Oxbridge accent, Shafer gave him pictures of every Arab student who had attended a top British university in the last twenty years. None matched. The name Omar Khadri didn't pop up in the NSA database either, they told him. Whoever Khadri was, he had stayed out of sight. Which made him very dangerous.

Privately, Wells seethed at being stuck in limbo. He never mentioned or checked the e-mail account Khadri had created for him, fearing that if Khadri sent a message the agency would immediately try to set him up. That would never work. Khadri didn't trust Wells, or he wouldn't have been so coy about his plans. Wells would have to earn Khadri's confidence, though he didn't want to guess what that might take. And Khadri had surely designed the next attack—whatever it was—to work even without him. They would need to roll up Khadri's network all at once, and only someone on the inside could do that. To beat Khadri, Wells needed some freedom to maneuver, precisely what he didn't have.

Exley and Shafer didn't tell Wells much about the investigation into the Los Angeles bombings either, but he didn't need to ask. From the *Times* and the *Post* he could see that the investigation wasn't going well. The papers were filled with comments from anonymous FBI agents about the difficulties of cracking a case where the perpetrators couldn't be identified, much less questioned. On CNN and Fox, the usual talking heads blamed the FBI and the agency for failing to prevent the attacks, and debated whether they signified a new wave of terrorism or were a one-off. Wells figured he knew the answer to that question. And yet after a week of shock and impromptu memorials, most people—especially outside Southern California—already seemed to be putting the attacks behind them.

"I'm just happy it wasn't worse," one man said in an article in the *Times*. "It's kind of the price we pay for being Americans." The guy wouldn't be so cavalier if he knew what was really happening inside the CIA and the other agencies that were supposed to protect him, Wells thought. The waste, the bureaucracy, the inefficiency. . . . These attacks didn't have to happen. They could be stopped. And instead of helping stop them, he was stuck doing nothing in a safe house because he hadn't kissed Vinny Duto's ass.

After two fruitless weeks, he decided to break out. Maybe he was making a mistake, but what choice did he have? What if Khadri had already contacted him and another attack was imminent?

IT WAS MID-APRIL, and cherry blossoms were blooming across Washington. Already thunderstorms had racked the city, hinting at the torrid summer closing in. But this Friday night was unseasonably cool. Wells pulled on a jacket and left the safe house, walking west toward the Capitol. In his hand he cradled a paper bag that held a hammer and screwdriver he had bought the day before. A black Ford sedan parked three houses down followed him, as it always did when he left the house. A block later another Ford began to roll.

Wells had walked the neighborhood every night since Shafer had put him here, and he was certain the surveillance ended there—no walkers, no truly undercover cars, no snipers or peepers. He was almost offended. They didn't seem to know or care how easily he could lose them. At a little convenience store on A Street, he bought himself a Coke, then walked home, the Fords trailing.

Almost ten o'clock. Wells settled on his stoop and waited for the right cab. Capitol Hill hadn't completely gentrified this far east; he saw the occasional dog walker, but the street was mostly quiet. Televisions glowed their eerie blue in the windows across the street. Wells sipped his Coke and smiled at the surveillance team in the Ford, fighting the urge to wave. He felt like a kid about to go off the high dive for the first time all summer.

A CAB WITH tinted windows rolled up. Perfect. Wells flagged it. "Okay if I sit in front?"

The driver, a black man in his fifties, sized him up. On the radio an Orioles–Red Sox game had just gone into the eleventh inning. "Sure. Watch my hat." A brown fedora lay on the seat.

Wells slid in.

"Where to?"

"East Cap. Benning Road."

"Get out." East Cap, two miles east on the other side of the Anacostia River, was one of D.C.'s poorest neighborhoods, nearly all public housing. Cabbies didn't like going there even during the day.

Wells handed the guy a twenty. "There'll be more."

The guy eyed him suspiciously. "Looking for rock?"

"No."

"'Cause I won't help you."

"No drugs, I swear."

"Pussy?"

"No pussy."

They rolled off.

"What's your name?" Wells said.

"Walter."

Wells laughed involuntarily, a short sharp bark.

"My name funny?"

"I just met another Walter. He didn't trust me either."

"You strange, you know that?"

On the radio an Oriole batter doubled. "You like the Orioles over the Nationals?" Wells said.

"Been rooting for that team too long to change now. Yourself?"

"Gotta tell you I'm a Red Sox fan. But I love extra innings, any game."

"Better than the Yankees."

They swung past RFK Stadium onto the viaduct that crossed the Anacostia and 295, a busy commuter highway that paralleled the river. The Fords followed. The Friday-night traffic on East Cap was heavy in both directions, Wells saw happily.

"You know somebody's following us?"

Wells handed Walter another twenty. "Two of 'em. They're friends. We're playing a game."

"Game." Walter looked at Wells.

"It's called lose the man."

"I want no part of this shit."

"How 'bout for another hundred?"

Walter flopped open his jacket to show Wells a battered revolver. "You starting to piss me off."

Wells shook his head. "What about two hundred? That's all I got."

They came off the viaduct and up a hill. Walter looked hard at Wells. "Man . . . you get in my cab . . ." Walter shook his head. "You not a cop."

"I'll get out now if you want."

Walter pursed his lips. He seemed to be flipping a coin in his mind. Then he nodded. "A hundred's fine. What next?"

"How well you know East Cap?"

"Better 'n you, I suspect. I grew up here."

They cruised down toward the light where Benning and East Capitol intersected. Beyond that another hill led up to the city's worst projects. To their right an overgrown park, really an urban

forest, loomed over the road like a bad dream. Here there be drag-
ons.

"Okay. Stay on East Cap. Come out of the light fast. When we get
up the hill, find a break in traffic they can't make. *Be sure about
that.* Swing left, through the traffic. When we're out of sight I'll roll
out. Should only take about three seconds. When I'm gone close the
door and keep moving. If they find you, let 'em pull you over, but
don't make it easy."

"You gonna roll out."

"I'll be fine."

They waited at the light, the Fords a couple of cars behind. Wells
reached down for the screwdriver. He slid it under his ankle bracelet
and twisted. The plastic strained and gave. No turning back now.

"What's this about?" Walter said.

"There's this song. From sometime in the nineties, I don't know,"
Wells said, more to himself than Walter. " 'Time is all the luck you
need.' "

Walter shook his head in disgust. "Just gimme the hundred, man."

Wells did. The light changed, Walter went.

WELLS ROLLED OUT of the taxi, paper bag in hand. He landed
smoothly on his shoulder and popped to his knees, then scuttled behind a beat-up black Jeep Cherokee. The taxi disappeared. Walter
had already closed the door, Wells saw. The two Fords came by,
flashing their emergency lights, no sirens. Then they too were gone.

The Cherokee would do. No alarm. Wells swung the hammer at
the front passenger window, breaking it with a satisfying crunch. He
swung again to widen the hole, reached through, and unlocked the
driver's door. He jogged around the Jeep and slid inside. He popped
open the steering column with the screwdriver and twisted together
a pair of wires. The engine started on the second try. Wells looked
down the road. The Fords were nowhere in sight. He rolled away.

HE CALLED EXLEY'S apartment from a pay phone on Massachu-
setts Avenue. "Hello," she said on the second ring. Her voice was
quiet and slightly smoky; she had smoked when Wells knew her last,
but she must have quit. A pleasant shiver passed through Wells.

"It's me," he said.

"John?"

"Be on your front steps in five minutes." He hung up. Calling her was a mistake. He should be on the road to New York already. There he would ditch the Jeep, pick up the money he had hidden, and find a Greyhound that would get him to Atlanta without coming through D.C. She could stop him with a ten-second phone call. But he needed to say good-bye to her. He needed to believe there was at least one person he could trust.

SHE TROTTED OVER to the Jeep. He popped open the door and reached out a hand.

"Watch the glass." He'd tried to sweep it onto the floor but hadn't completely succeeded. He was surprised to see she was wearing a knee-high skirt. She ought to wear skirts more often, he thought. Even the Talibs would approve. Well, maybe not.

She swept off the window fragments and arranged herself gingerly on the seat. He drove off, north on Thirteenth Street.

"You stole this?"

"Borrowed." He held up the Jeep's registration. "I guess I owe Elizabeth Jones a few bucks."

"Where are we going?"

"We're not going anywhere. I just wanted to see you. For a minute."

"Where are you going?"

"Away."

"John—"

AND SUDDENLY EXLEY understood. Shafer had set this up, like he'd set up Wells's trip to the camps so many years before. Shafer had known that Duto, out of stupidity or spite, would shut down anything Wells tried to do. So Shafer had taken Wells for himself. Then he'd let Wells twist until Wells believed he had no choice but to run. That was why they hadn't told Wells he'd passed the poly, why they'd kept him at arm's length. Why Shafer had put Wells at that safe house instead of someplace more secure. It was the only way to get Wells out.

"It's so risky," Exley said aloud. What if Duto called out the dogs? But he wouldn't. He didn't think Wells was dangerous, and he'd be happy to let Shafer twist over the loss of his prize pet.

"I know what I'm doing," Wells said.

Do you, John? Exley wondered. She put her hand on his arm.

AT HER TOUCH Wells wanted to pull the Jeep over and have her there, on the side of the street. Let the neighbors watch. Let them call the cops. And then Langley can bail you both out, he thought. She took her hand from his arm.

"John? There's something I've been wondering."

"Yes?"

"Why'd you go see Heather?"

"It wasn't Heather I wanted to see. It was Evan."

They sat in silence for a moment, and Wells wondered if he'd understood the question properly: Do you still love her? Then Exley put her hand on his arm again, and he knew he was right.

"Tell me a story," he said. To distract himself. To hear her voice for a little while more before he disappeared.

"What kind of story?"

"Anything. I don't care. Something personal."

SHE WONDERED WHAT to tell him. All she did was work. Should she explain how her son had yelled at her the last time she'd seen him, told her he liked Randy better than her? About how she kept the radio in her bedroom tuned to sports talk, not because she cared about the Nationals but because if she woke up at three A.M. she could turn it on and be sure of hearing a man's voice?

"You want a story," she said. "Okay." And before she could stop herself she said, "So, the night I lost my virginity. I was fifteen—"

"Fifteen?" Wells sounded surprised, she thought. He didn't know what he'd gotten himself into. She wasn't sure she did either. She'd never told this to any man before, not even her husband.

"You want me to keep going?" She wanted to keep going.

"Please." His voice was steady again.

"Anyway, I was fifteen. My family was going through a rough patch. My dad, he was always a drinker, but about then he started to head off the cliff. Took him five more years to hit bottom, but we could see where he was going. And my brother, Danny, he'd just gotten kicked out of freshman year at UCLA. He was hearing voices and he hit his roommate in the head with a Tabasco bottle."

"A Tabasco bottle?"

She laughed, with an edge. "I know it sounds ridiculous, but it wasn't one of those little ones you see in restaurants. It was big enough to do some damage. He got brought up on aggravated-assault charges. He would have gone to jail if we hadn't convinced the judge he was schizo. Which he was."

"I didn't even know you had a brother, Jenny."

"He killed himself a few years after that. I don't talk about it."

Wells slowed down, put his hand on her shoulder. "Exley."

"Lots of them do, you know. Schizophrenics. He just couldn't bear it." She shook his arm off her. They were still heading north on Thirteenth. The apartment buildings had turned into two-story houses, indistinguishable in the night.

"You're gonna have to drop me off soon," she said. "They're going to call my cell to tell me you're gone, and they're going to wonder if I don't answer. So you want to hear the rest of my story or not?"

"You still want to tell it?"

"Yes. Strange but true." She didn't know why, or maybe she did. Because it would be his when she told him, a gift she wouldn't give anyone else, in its way more intimate than any other. "So I'm fifteen, cutting school, smoking pot, acting out. Wearing black. The whole deal. You know, my brother's crazy, my dad's an alkie, and I'm just ignoring my mom, who's doing her best. And I decide a couple weeks before my birthday that there's no way—no way—I'm still gonna be a virgin when I'm sixteen. Great plan, right, John?"

"Lucky boyfriend."

"Only—no. I didn't have a boyfriend back then. And I didn't want a high school boy. I wanted a man. Somebody who would fuck me. I didn't even know what that meant, but my new girlfriends, the ones I cut class with, they were always talking about guys who fucked them, really fucked them. And some of it was crap, maybe most of it, I knew that. But some of it wasn't. So, about a week before my birthday, Jodie, who was a couple years older, the nicest of them, told me about this party she was going to, in Oakland, across the bay, with some college guys. She said I should go. And then the next day she told me she couldn't go, but I made her give me the address. And so I told my mother I was going to some concert—I remember I was so happy I put one over on her, my poor mother—and I got all dolled up and I went."

He slowed down. "Is it wrong for me to imagine how you must have looked back then?"

"I looked *good*. I mean, I can say it now that I'm old and decrepit: I was hot. And I was wearing this thigh-high skirt and these boots. . . . My mother had a lot on her mind or she never would have let me out of the house."

"You're not old, Jenny."

"Too kind. So, anyway, I catch the BART to Oakland, 'cause I'm not even legal to drive, remember. And I start walking around this kind of crummy neighborhood, because this is before every square foot in the Bay Area is worth a million dollars, and I'm starting to get nervous, and then I find it. And it's loud, amped up, a big party in a big run-down house. There were some Berkeley students, but there were grad students too, and some guys from the neighborhood who'd come by and even some bikers, because that's what Oakland was then. If you were having a party you'd better invite the locals. The girls were a little younger, but they were all in college at least. And I grab myself a beer and take a couple bong hits from this bong that must have been about four feet long. And I start looking for Mr. Right."

"Jenny—"

"Too late. Let me finish." She knew she had to tell him everything. To provoke him, to arouse him, she wasn't even sure. "And I see a blond guy, surfer type, tall, cute. Not rough. Maybe twenty-one, twenty-two. I start heading toward him, but before I can get to him, this guy in a black T-shirt grabs my arm. He's got a couple tattoos on his arms. And he's holding me pretty close. He asks me if I want a beer or maybe something harder, and he's practically sticking his tongue down my throat while he says it. But I shake him off and head for the surfer.

"And Blondie's interested, and it only takes about half an hour before I get him to a bedroom upstairs, and we're making out, and he's good and hard, and I say something dumb, like 'Put it in me, stud.' He looks at me and says, 'What did you say?' Then he looks again, and says, 'How old are you, anyway?' and he's out the door like that, moving even faster when I say, 'But I *want* you to fuck me. I don't wanna be a virgin anymore.' "

"So you didn't lose it that night after all."

"Let a girl finish, John. So I go back downstairs, and I find Mr. Tattoo. And I say, 'How about that drink?' And ten minutes later he's fucking me on this pool table in the basement, with a towel under me because that was his main concern about my virginity, that I not bleed all over the felt, 'cause he knew the guys who rented the house. He probably only went about five minutes, but it seemed like a *long* time. I was lucky I was still a little wet from the surfer, or it really would have hurt."

"Jenny—"

"And the kicker is, when he's done, and I've bled all over that towel, he tosses his condom next to me, pulls up his pants, turns around, and leaves without a word."

WELLS PULLED THE Jeep to the side of the road. A light rain had just begun, misting the windshield, putting halos on the streetlights. Cars cruised by slowly, driven by men and women who worked in malls or hospitals or offices downtown and lived decent quiet lives. People he would never know.

Why, Jenny, he almost said aloud. Why would you? But he held back. She'd done it because she wanted to, and told him because she wanted to, and who was he to judge? His career choice didn't exactly give him a lot of moral authority. "So were you glad you did it?" he finally said.

She moved closer to him in her seat, and he knew he'd asked the right question. "Yeah. Even though I never did anything like that again. It's like dropping acid. A little goes a long way. But the truth is, I was giving something to the guy, even if he thought he was taking it from me. I did it how I wanted to. Maybe it sounds crazy, but it's how I felt. And I never talked to him again. Never even knew his name. Though I'm pretty sure I spotted him years later in Berkeley, when I was back from college. Luckily I was in my car, and I just kept driving. So there's your story, John, and I hope it keeps you warm wherever you're going." She laughed her low smoky laugh.

HE LOOKED AT her, looked away, then back again. "Can I ask you something?" he finally said, his voice so low she could hardly hear him.

"No more stories."

"You didn't show up that night, the night before I went away, did you?"

"No, and I knew you wouldn't either. We keep blowing our chances. Now unless you want to spend some more time with Vinny Duto, you better go."

"Jenny. Jennifer—" And she knew what he would ask before the words left his mouth. Maybe before the thought had formed in his mind.

"Yes. I do."

"Do what?"

"I trust you, John. Of course. Why do you think I just told you what I just told you?" He seemed to want to say something more, but he didn't. He leaned toward her and for a moment she thought he would kiss her. She stayed still, not moving toward him or away, mesmerized, wanting and angry and afraid at once. But wanting more than anything. And then he kissed her, across the miles and the years. A chaste kiss, lip to lip, that turned warm and open-mouthed and sweet until finally she summoned the will to break it off.

"Go," she said.

"Look. You know that park in Kenilworth, the Aquatic Gardens?" he said. The Gardens was a small national park on the east bank of the Anacostia River, near the projects where Wells had stolen the Jeep.

"In East Cap?"

"If I need you, I'll leave you a message with the word 'swimmingly.' That's where I'll be."

"What if I need you?"

He didn't say anything. She ran her hand down his cheek. He raised his chin as if receiving a benediction.

"Take care, John."

He was silent. Finally, he laughed, a rueful sound. "Be seeing you."

She got out. He hesitated, then drove off. She watched the Cherokee go, watched until she couldn't see it anymore, and then kept watching. As if she could bring him back simply by staying still. She wanted more than anything to be in that Jeep.

Be seeing you, John.

Please.

PART TWO

THE
BELIEVERS

6

ON THE BATTALION radio, A Company used the call sign "Mad Dog." As in "Mad Dog 6 to Bushmaster 6, moving out, over." The other companies in the 2-7 Cav battalion, the armored unit that covered northwest Baghdad, had found call signs to match their letters. B Company went by "Bushmaster." C had settled on "Commando" after briefly trying "Crusader."

But no one in A Company could think of a kick-ass word that started with A, except for "Anarchist," which—like "Crusader"— sent the wrong message. For a while A Company had called itself the Angry Dogs, but that sounded stupid. Then Angry Mad Dogs, which was worse. Eventually Jimmy Jackson, the captain of A Company, gave up on alliteration and said Mad Dog would be the company's handle. Good thing too, Specialist J. C. Ramirez thought. Hearing "Angry Mad Dog 6 to Angry Mad Dog 2" over the radio was driving him nuts.

Up in the gunner's sling of Captain Jackson's Humvee, J.C. mopped the sweat off his face. He used to think Texas was hot, but these Iraqi summers were something else. The sun had almost set, but it was still one hundred degrees. His body armor didn't help. He drank a gallon of water a day and never had to piss, because he sweated every drop out. And though he stuffed himself with chow, he'd lost twenty pounds in nine months. The Baghdad diet. His uniform hung loose on his five-ten frame.

"They don't feed you?" his mama had asked him when he came home to El Paso in July for his two-week leave. "They starving you to save money, is that it?" He told her the chow was fine, but she didn't believe him. She was ready to write the president before he calmed her down. He understood. The food gave her something to focus on, something small that kept her mind off the real stuff. Or maybe she was just being a Mexican mama, looking for any excuse to stuff him with enchiladas.

Either way he'd be back with her and his girl again soon. A couple more months, and then he would never have to see this place again . . . until his next rotation. This was his first time over here, but lots of the guys in the 2-7 were already on their second trip. Like most soldiers, J.C. figured this war would go on awhile, no matter what the politicians said.

Almost seven-thirty. They'd been waiting to roll for an hour. J.C. was getting bored. Typical false alarm. They planned four raids for every one that happened. "How much you wanna bet it's off?" he yelled down to Corporal Mike Voss, the Humvee's driver. Voss just shook his head.

Then J.C. saw Captain Jackson walking toward the Humvee, Jackson's quick clipped stride telling J.C. that they would be going out tonight after all.

THE HUMVEE ROLLED to the two-inch-thick steel gates that served as Camp Graphite's front door. J.C. tugged his armor down tight over his shoulders and pulled his pistol from his leg holster. He had cleaned it a day before, but he double-checked the slide, as he always did before leaving the base. The metal slipped back smoothly. Good. He chambered a round and slipped the pistol back onto his leg. Not that he expected to need the 9mm. It was a popgun compared to the .50-cal on the Humvee's roof, much less the machine cannons on the Bradleys or the 120mm main guns on the tanks. If somebody got through all that he was in deep shit, pistol or no. But extra firepower never hurt.

They crossed through the gates, and at his feet J.C. heard the barking chorus of "Who Let the Dogs Out" for the hundredth time:

Who let the dogs out
Woof woof woof woof

Naturally the Mad Dogs used the song as their slogan; they played it every time they left base. J.C. tried to remember when the song had come out. Was he in eighth grade? Ninth? Probably ninth. A smile creased the corners of his mouth. That dumb song was good luck. None of the Mad Dogs had died here. The other companies in the 2-7 hadn't been so fortunate. A car bomb had blown up one of Bushmaster's Humvees, and a sniper had shot Lieutenant Poley of Commando and gotten away clean. Freaking sniper. Maybe the Mad Dogs would have a chance at him tonight.

The Humvee swung through the chicane of concrete barriers that protected the front gate, then accelerated down a wide avenue west of Baghdad's tattered zoo. J.C. concentrated his attention on the zoo's deserted grounds, a natural hiding place for a guy with a rocket-propelled grenade. He had learned the hard way that ambushes could come anytime, anywhere.

J.C. was a gunner. His buddies said he had the worst job in the army: sitting in a harness in a hole in the roof of the Humvee, handling a machine gun that swung 360 degrees. On hot days—which meant every day—he baked in the sun. When they rode the highways he ate dust and diesel fuel and came back to base spitting black clods of phlegm. And gunners had the highest pucker factor around. As in the pucker your asshole makes when you're squeezing back your fear. The tanks and Bradleys had thick steel armor. Even the Humvees had steel plates and heavy bulletproof glass. J.C. just had his helmet and flak jacket, which wouldn't do much good against an RPG.

But he liked the job. He didn't want to be stuck inside a tank. Up here he could spot ambushes and bombs. He had so much to watch for, and yet he couldn't get trigger-happy. A C Company gunner had shot a kid carrying a toy gun, a mistake J.C. had promised himself he'd never make. He knew how to make a crowd back off without firing a shot, and how to tell the heavy thump of a mortar from the deadly hiss of a RPG. Even the officers had figured out he was the best gunner in the company, maybe the whole battalion. So he always rode with Captain Jackson.

The Humvee turned left on Santa Fe, a main east-west avenue in central Baghdad. The Iraqis didn't call the road Santa Fe, of course. They had their own haji name for it, Mohammed Avenue or something. J.C. wasn't entirely sure. None of the soldiers spoke Arabic, so for the sake of convenience the battalion had renamed the roads after American cities.

Now, squinting into the setting sun as the convoy headed west, J.C. wished he had learned more about Iraq. He had picked up a few Arabic words from Salim, Captain Jackson's interpreter, a teenager the Mad Dogs called Harry because he wore little round glasses like Harry Potter. Salim had taught him that *abu* meant father and *umm* mother. He could count to ten: *wahid, ithnien, thalatha* . . . Salim had even told him that *haji*—the word J.C. and every other soldier used to describe anything local—wasn't just some random word. It meant someone who had taken a hajj, the pilgrimage to Mecca, a big deal for these guys.

Even so, J.C. felt like he was on the moon most of the time. He didn't understand this place. Why did the men wear those long robes that looked like dresses? Why did they hold hands? And what was up with the women? He'd been inside Iraqi houses with Captain Jackson, and it was like the women didn't even exist. Once they had served tea, but usually they hid in the back of the house. Not that J.C. had tried to find them. Command Sergeant Major Holder, the senior enlisted man in the battalion, had made that clear. Don't look at the women, don't talk to the women, and never—ever—touch the women.

The Iraqis were hospitable enough, anyhow. Even the ones who barely had furniture made sure to offer up tea and Cokes to Captain Jackson when he visited. But you couldn't trust them much. J.C. had seen the captain lose his temper after one long meeting with a local sheikh. "Just be honest with me. Tell me the truth," Jackson had said. The sheikh had flat-out laughed when he heard Salim translate. "The truth?" he said. "I save the truth for Allah."

. . .

THE HUMVEE HALTED as the cars ahead jammed around a traffic circle. Everyone wanted to be home by dark, when kidnappers and guerrillas ruled the streets, sharks cruising in black BMW sedans with smoked-glass windows. J.C. cursed as he looked up the road at an old Mercedes truck belching diesel smoke. He hated getting stopped in traffic. Anybody could take a pop at them. And he hated dusk, when the shadows offered cover but there was still too much light for his night-vision goggles.

Around him the call to evening prayer echoed through the streets, an eerie amplified chant that J.C. knew he would always be able to hear, no matter how far behind he left this place. The sound of Baghdad.

He angled the .50-cal down a notch and watched the men on the sidewalks, looking for the glint of metal hidden in a robe. The Humvee jerked forward, then stopped again. "Come on, move," he yelled down to Voss.

"You want to drive?" Voss yelled back.

"Fuck no."

"Then shut up."

As they inched ahead J.C. wondered what had happened to this country. Anybody could see it had been rich once. Their base had been one of Saddam's palaces, a huge building with an entrance hall three stories high, marble floors, and gold walls. The Baghdad airport looked newer than the one in El Paso. The highway to Falluja, that shithole, was six lanes wide, good as any interstate. Baghdad had twenty-story hotels and big mosques with beautiful blue domes. J.C. had even seen dusty cracked advertisements for Air France and Japan Airlines. People had once wanted to come here; the Iraqis had once had enough money to leave.

No more. Now the place was a disaster, dying a little more every day. On the streets the men walked slow, with slumped shoulders and angry faces. Not just unhappy. Hopeless, like life had been getting worse for so long that they couldn't even dream it would ever get better. And the resentment in their eyes was impossible to mistake.

In some of the neighborhoods the 2-7 patrolled, the stink of sewage and burning garbage filled the streets. Little boys without shoes begged for candy every time they stopped. After a car bomb a couple months before, the Mad Dogs had wound up at Kindi Hospital in western Baghdad. The place was covered with blood and J.C. had seen flies in an operating room, hovering over a girl whose face was cut to pieces. Even the guys who joked about everything didn't have much to say that day. Baghdad was poorer than Juárez, poorer than any place in Mexico he'd ever seen. J.C. couldn't understand. These people had all that oil, and they lived like this.

J.C. knew he was thinking too much. His buddies kept it simple: Bank your checks, stay down, and hope your girl is keeping her legs shut back home. And they were right. His job was keeping himself and his fellow Mad Dogs alive. Let the hajis take care of themselves. But sometimes, playing dominoes after dinner in the palace, J.C. felt the doubt sneak up: How did this place get so messed up? Is it our fault?

IN THE HUMVEE below, Captain James Jackson Jr. was hoping for a little luck. The tip had come in three days before from the battalion's best informant, a college student named Saleh who wanted an American visa to join his cousins in Detroit. He hadn't led Jackson wrong yet. In fact Jackson worried that Saleh was giving the battalion too much; his life expectancy would be measured in hours if his friends realized that he was ratting them out. But Jackson figured that Saleh knew the risks better than anyone.

Anyway, if this raid panned out, Saleh would be one step closer to 8 Mile Road. He had claimed that several "488s"—military slang for high-value targets—planned to meet tonight at a barbershop in Ghazalia, a suburban Baghdad neighborhood that had become a center of the resistance. Saleh didn't have any names, but he promised they weren't the usual criminals and street fighters. One was a foreigner nicknamed "the Doctor" who had just arrived in Iraq, he said.

If military intel had confirmed the story, the raid would have been handed off to Task Force 121, the Special Forces/CIA operating group responsible for top-level targets in Iraq and Afghanistan. But "the Doctor" didn't show up in anyone's database. So the Special Forces, who couldn't be bothered going after anybody less important than they were, turned the job down. Which was fine with Jackson. The Mad Dogs had five tanks, six Bradleys, and four armored Humvees, enough firepower to take out a small town. He didn't expect any problem grabbing a couple of guerrillas. He just hoped it was worth the trouble. Saleh had been right so far, but there was a first time for everything.

JACKSON NEED NOT have worried. The Doctor's real name was Farouk Khan, the fat man who had met John Wells in the apartment in Peshawar five months before. Although he had earned his title, Farouk was no M.D. He was a physicist, the third cousin of A. Q. Khan, who had overseen the development of Pakistan's nuclear weapons. Farouk had worked for the program too, until he was fired for attending an Islamabad mosque whose imam preached for the overthrow of Pakistan's government.

A year later, Farouk found his way to Osama bin Laden's lair in the North-West Frontier. There the sheikh offered him the exalted title of "director of atomic projects," and Farouk set about trying to pry a bomb out of Pakistan's arsenal. Even with his old connections, Farouk found his mission difficult. Pakistan's generals knew that if al Qaeda blew a Pakistani nuke in New York the United States might respond with its own bomb on their villas in Islamabad. An attack on Delhi would be even more dangerous, inevitably provoking a full-scale nuclear war that would turn India and Pakistan to dust. Farouk had to move cautiously.

Nonetheless, he eventually found three lower-level technicians whose sympathy for al Qaeda had escaped the government's security checks. They could not deliver him a working bomb, but they provided equipment that Farouk found very helpful. Then he discovered Dmitri Georgoff, an out-of-work Russian nuclear scientist looking for hard currency. Farouk and Dmitri attended their first meeting with great caution, Farouk because he feared a CIA sting operation, Dmitri because he preferred that his head remain attached to his body. But both men found the meeting satisfactory, and after some negotiations, Dmitri agreed to provide Farouk with two lead-lined steel boxes filled with useful material. Their cost: $675,000. That sum represented a serious investment for Farouk. Sheikh bin Laden himself had to approve the deal.

Al Qaeda still had nothing close to a working nuclear weapon that could vaporize a city. But one didn't need a nuke to panic the enemy. A conventional bomb laced with radioactive material—a dirty bomb—could devastate the infidels. Radiation frightened people. They couldn't see it, smell it, or feel it, yet it could kill them years after it hit them. Some radioactive isotopes could contaminate an area for decades, making it worthless even if the buildings remained standing. In the proper place—midtown Manhattan, say— a dirty bomb would cause hundreds of billions of dollars in damage and kill thousands of *kafirs*. And unlike a nuclear weapon, a dirty bomb was easy to build. The hard part was finding the dirt, but Farouk had solved that problem. Already he had shipped enough radioactive material to the United States for at least one bomb.

Now he hoped for more. Three weeks before, the man who called himself Omar Khadri had given Farouk a new mission. Iraqi villagers in the desert south of Falluja had found a secret underground building in an abandoned military base. They believed that the building contained radioactive material. They hoped to give their find to Sheikh bin Laden.

So Farouk had made a most dangerous trip, two thousand miles west, from Pakistan to Afghanistan to Iran and then over the mountainous border of Iran into Iraq. Along the way he dodged both the infidel troops in Afghanistan and the Iranian secret police, who did not look kindly on al Qaeda. Farouk could have flown to Jordan and driven to Baghdad, but on a mission as sensitive as this he preferred to avoid leaving tracks on any airline manifests. Besides, he would have had difficulty explaining the equipment he carried to customs agents.

Farouk had warned himself not to get too excited. The men he was meeting tonight were fighters, not physicists. All he had seen so far were blurry pictures of rods and steel drums that looked promising but proved nothing. Still, he couldn't help but hope. If they had truly found new material . . . and under the nose of the United States!

The Americans were fools, Farouk thought. Decades before, the Jews had blasted Saddam's nuclear reactors and destroyed Iraq's effort to build an atomic bomb. The material he would see tonight,

Allah willing, represented the remains of that program, exhumed from a grave in the desert. At best it would be nuclear trash, iodine and cesium that could never have made a real atomic weapon. No government would bother with the stuff. But it would do just fine for al Qaeda's purposes. And al Qaeda would never have had a chance at it if the United States hadn't invaded Iraq. For Saddam had never shared his secrets with Sheikh bin Laden. He was a godless devil, the most useless of the infidel Arab leaders. But America had taken care of Saddam. Iraq's doors had opened to al Qaeda's holy warriors.

Yes, the Americans were fools. You invaded Iraq because you said it was full of "terrorists," Farouk thought. Well, now it is. Allah works in mysterious ways.

THE SUN HAD set when the Mad Dogs rolled up to the concrete blast walls that blocked the entrance to the Khudra police station, a pitted two-story building marked by a tattered Iraqi flag. Suicide car bombs had hit the station three times. Now most cops wouldn't leave the station even to patrol, much less arrest anyone. But a few officers still worked with the 2-7 Cav; Jackson wasn't sure if they were brave or crazy. In any case, they knew the streets of Ghazalia better than he ever would. He hoped to take a couple of them out tonight.

Jackson strode to the station's front gates, where Lieutenant Colonel Ghaith Fahd stood, cigarette in hand. The men tapped their hands to their chests, then shook hands. Fahd was the only officer at Khudra whom Jackson really trusted. *"Salaam alaikum,"* Jackson said.

"Alaikum salaam."

"You heard us coming?"

"Nam."

Jackson was not surprised. His tanks ran on huge engines, modified jet turbines, that announced their presence long before they arrived. Noise was their biggest tactical weakness. But tonight he hoped to turn that flaw to his advantage.

"Cigarette?" Fahd said, offering Jackson his pack.

"Dunhills? Fancy, Colonel." Jackson shook a cigarette onto his palm.

"My raise came through," Fahd said, and laughed.

Jackson lit up and gratefully sucked on the cigarette. Though he didn't smoke. At least he hadn't before he came over here. "You know those things will kill you," he told Fahd.

"No quicker than anything else, Captain."

Jackson marveled at Fahd's cool. For an Iraqi officer in this neighborhood, even to be seen with an American was an act of supreme courage. Yet Fahd never seemed tired or tense, much less afraid. They walked into the street, out of earshot of the station.

"You have plans tonight?" Fahd asked.

"Yes. A raid."

"How many men do you need?"

"Only those you really trust."

Fahd nodded. "Five . . . no, four. Ehab is home today."

"Just four men?" Fifty officers were on duty.

"Yes."

"That bad, huh?"

"Even worse, Captain." Fahd handed Jackson the cigarettes. "Have another Dunhill. I'll round them up."

TEN MINUTES LATER Fahd was back, four men in tow.

"As you like, Captain." An Iraqi expression that meant: Whenever you're ready.

Jackson looked at his watch. Eight-forty. Saleh had said the meeting was supposed to start at nine and last an hour. But he'd also warned Jackson that the guerrillas often ran late. And Jackson knew he couldn't risk watching the barbershop—any American presence would be obvious. He had decided to hit at nine forty-five and hope for the best.

"We have a little while. Where's your flak jacket, Colonel?"

"I don't have one."

"We gave you enough armor for every officer in Khudra." Jackson didn't hide the frustration in his voice.

A brittle laugh escaped Fahd's lips. "Let me tell you a story." He lit a fresh cigarette. "It will be over before this Dunhill."

"Sure."

"My father owned a store in Sadr City. You know Sadr City, of course."

"Of course." Sadr City was a giant slum in northeast Baghdad, on the other side of the Tigris River, a desperately poor place.

"We were not wealthy. No one in Sadr City is wealthy. But we were comfortable," Fahd said. He took a deep drag on his cigarette. "Unfortunately my father—Mohammed—liked to joke. Sometimes he joked about Saddam. In 1987, the Mukhabarat"—Saddam's secret police—"raided his store. They took him and my brother Sadiq to Abu Ghraib. You can guess the rest."

"Did you ever see them again?"

"Sadiq survived, for a while. He died two years later."

"Did he tell you what had happened?"

"He never spoke after they let him go."

"He never said what they'd done?"

"He never spoke at all." Fahd pointed at his mouth. "No tongue."

Jackson felt his own tongue curl inside his mouth as he tried to think of something to say.

"I'm sorry."

"They must have found a very bad Mukhabarat agent," Fahd said. "My father's jokes weren't so much."

"And you escaped?"

"I wasn't there. They never came back for me. I don't know why. Maybe they felt—what is the word?—lazy."

"*Inshallah.*"

"*Inshallah,*" Fahd said. "Instead they sent me to fight against Iran. I survived—the war was almost over—and then I got into the police academy somehow. Now I am a lieutenant colonel in the Iraqi police, respected and loved by my men." Fahd laughed. "A charmed life, wouldn't you say, Captain?" He held up his cigarette, still burning. "And now the story is over, as I promised." Fahd took a final drag on his cigarette, then stubbed it out into his palm and flicked it onto the asphalt.

"So you don't wear body armor," Jackson said.

"If Allah wishes me to stay alive, I will. And if he wishes me to see my father again, I will. Either way I will be grateful for his blessings."

LED BY J.C.'S armored Humvee, the Mad Dog convoy rolled north on Dodge, a broad avenue that stretched through the center of Ghazalia. Bomb holes pitted the road. Patrols here got hit almost every night, though no soldiers had been killed. Yet.

With the streets empty, they had the road almost to themselves. The patrol stretched a half mile nose to tail, with Fahd's Land Rover nestled in the middle, a toy among the Bradleys and tanks.

Through J.C.'s night-vision goggles the world glowed yellow and black. Looming over a field to the east was the Mother of All Battles mosque, a concrete monstrosity with minarets designed to resemble machine gun turrets. Saddam had built the mosque to celebrate his decade-long war with Iran, which had left two million people dead. When the electricity was running, the minarets glowed infernally in the night. But tonight the power was out. The mosque and the neighborhood had gone dark, though generators provided power to a few fortunate houses. The blackout was a good break, and so was the new moon. The darker the night, the better the goggles worked.

A tracer round cut through the night, a single shot as the patrol passed by. They're out there, J.C. thought. Watching us. Waiting for us to make a mistake. Good. Let 'em. His finger crawled around the trigger of his .50-cal.

The Humvee halted as the convoy reached the northern end of the Ghazalia road, where a narrow bridge ran into Shula, a crowded slum. The patrol has to look routine, Jackson had told the Mad Dogs. They can't know we're coming. The convoy made a slow U-turn and headed south.

IN THE NARROW back room of the barbershop in Ghazalia, officially known as Al-Jakra for Hair Cutting and Shampooing, Farouk Khan perched uncomfortably on a cheap blue couch. Boxes of old shampoo bottles lay on the floor, and three AK-47s had been left carelessly under a staircase by the back wall. A noisy generator in the corner powered an overhead bulb and a hot plate boiling water for tea. He looked again at his watch. Nine-twenty. Why hadn't they arrived? Farouk was not a coward; cowards did not last long as nuclear spies. Still, he hated pointless risks.

The door opened, but it was just Zayd, the skinny Iraqi who had guided Farouk from Islamabad to Baghdad. Farouk was thoroughly sick of Zayd. The Iraqi's manners were atrocious. He spat and picked his nose with abandon, and he never washed. Plus, Farouk didn't trust anyone so thin. Eating was a great pleasure; who would forsake it? But Farouk had to admit that Zayd had come in handy. He spoke Arabic, Farsi, Urdu, Pashto, and English. In fact, Farouk hadn't yet heard a language that Zayd didn't understand. And he knew half the tribal leaders between here and Pakistan. So Farouk had accepted the man's medieval personal habits.

"Funny, isn't it, Zayd," Farouk said. "It's easy to tell the wealth of a country from a hospital or a supermarket. But barbershops look the same wherever I've been. Here, Pakistan, Europe. Black swivel chairs, counters crowded with mysterious glass jars, posters of young men with close-cropped hair."

"Umm." Zayd put a knuckle into his nose. Farouk wondered whether the gesture was meant as an answer. For a man of so many tongues, Zayd said surprisingly little. Perhaps great conversations went on inside his head.

Farouk settled back in the couch, feeling it creak under his bulk. Outside he could hear the heavy low rumbling of American tanks in the distance. He jiggled the Geiger counter in his lap and tried to control his nervousness. "Will they be here soon, Zayd?" His companion merely shrugged and poured two glasses of tea, dropping in sugar with his dirty fingers. Farouk grimaced and drank. Then he heard the cars pull up.

CAPTAIN JACKSON'S PLAN was simple. The barbershop sat on the western edge of Ghazalia. When his convoy reached the street that ran to the shop, the Humvees and Land Rover would peel off and race west. The tanks and Bradleys would follow. With any luck the guerrillas wouldn't realize what was happening until the Humvees had already reached the shop. The heavier armor would establish a perimeter when it arrived.

The strategy had risks. Jackson had fifteen soldiers in the

Humvees, along with the five Iraqi officers in the Rover. They should be able to take out four guerrillas. But if the shop had been fortified, they could be in for a fight. Especially before the Bradleys arrived with reinforcements. Normally, Jackson would put his heaviest firepower at the front and keep the lighter vehicles in the rear, but this time he could not risk alerting his targets.

Even after his men got inside the store, their problems would not be over. Jackson didn't know the layout of the shop, or even whether it had a second exit. His patrols had cruised by the store twice in the last three days, but he had feared more recon might spook the target. Still, he had no doubt his men could pull off the mission. They'd been through worse.

Jackson looked through his armored window at the deserted storefronts. Time to give the bosses one last chance to chicken out. He picked up his battalion radio and called the Tactical Operations Center at Camp Graphite. "Mad Dog Six to Knight Six, over." Knight Six was the battalion commander, Lieutenant Colonel Steve Takahashi.

"This is Knight Six."

Jackson looked at his watch. Nine thirty-three. The Humvees should hit the shop in minutes. "Our ETA is Niner Four Tree." "Tree" was army lingo for "three."

"Niner Four Tree," Takahashi said. "Roger that. You're cleared for takeoff."

"Roger," Jackson said. A cold excitement filled him as he put the handset down.

FAROUK WAVED THE wand of his Geiger counter over a narrow steel capsule six inches long. The headphones around his ears clicked rapidly, each click a signal that the capsule was emitting radiation. He put the wand over a second steel capsule and again heard the clicking.

Mazen, the mujahid commander, was a giant, the tallest Arab Farouk had ever met. He spoke a rough, peasant Arabic and carried both an AK-47 and a sword strapped to his waist. Since giving Farouk the capsules he had stood quietly by the stairs at the back of the room, nervously watching Farouk flutter the Geiger counter. He fears that he has brought me junk, Farouk thought.

"How many are there?" Farouk asked.

"Thousands," Mazen said. "Too many to count."

And with that answer Farouk knew his trip had been worth the risk. Thousands of capsules of cobalt. Allah had bestowed a great gift upon his warriors this night. Khadri would be pleased.

The ring of a cell phone startled him.

"*Nam,*" Mazen said, and hung up. "One of our brothers is watching the main road, in case the Americans come this way," he said to Farouk and Zayd. "But they never do. They fear Ghazalia at night."

"So?" Zayd said to Farouk. "What do you think?"

But Farouk wasn't quite ready to share his exhilaration. "Show me the yellow metal."

Mazen handed him a canvas bag, surprisingly heavy and filled with yellow pellets. Farouk waved the wand over them, and again the Geiger counter woke up, clicking loud and fast. The pellets were uranium oxide, he thought. Yellowcake. Slightly enriched, 2 or 3 percent, though nowhere near weapons-grade. Farouk held up the bag.

"You found these in a barrel."

"*Nam,*" Mazen said. "It was very heavy. We could hardly move it."

"It was the only barrel?"

"There were four, Doctor."

Four barrels of yellowcake? Farouk tried to contain his excitement. This was only the start, he reminded himself. They needed to gather the material and then get it to the United States. But there were ways. They would truck the uranium and the cobalt capsules into Jordan. Then to Dubai, or Turkey. East to Pakistan and then Singapore. West to Nigeria and then across the Atlantic to Brazil. He didn't know the details; Khadri would handle that. But he knew there were ways.

"My brothers," Farouk said. "You have answered our prayers."

"*Allahu akbar!*" Mazen screamed. Then his cell phone trilled again.

A FEW SECONDS earlier the Mad Dogs' Humvees had swung west off Dodge, flicked off their lights, and accelerated toward the barbershop. The Humvees didn't have jet turbine engines like the tanks, but then again they didn't weigh seventy tons. They swept down the dark silent avenue at seventy-five miles an hour, the wind pushing back J.C.'s face. He stared down the road through his goggles, looking for movement, but he didn't notice the small man frantically dialing his cell phone from an Opel sedan.

As they closed in, J.C. wondered what they might find. Probably nothing. He hoped that anyone inside would be smart enough not to fight. The first seconds of a raid were the most dangerous. The Mad Dogs had to hold their fire as they sorted out friends and foes.

BUT TONIGHT THAT wouldn't be a problem. Qusay's alert backfired. By the time his call went through, the Mad Dogs had nearly reached the store. The guerrillas—eight in all, including Farouk and Zayd—could only grab their guns and run for their cars.

THE HUMVEE THUMPED over a curb and into the narrow parking lot. J.C. saw three guys with AKs running from the shop. He covered them with his machine gun. "Stop!" he yelled.

They turned and fired wildly. Rounds thumped into the Humvee, and another seared by J.C.'s head. Hostile fire, he thought automatically. Rules of engagement permit lethal force. Even before the words were complete in his mind he had put the .50-caliber on target and squeezed its trigger.

Fire flashed out of the weapon's muzzle. At close range a large-caliber machine gun has unfortunate effects on the human body. One man's head exploded like an overripe pumpkin; the other two were cut nearly in half. Before their bodies had hit the ground J.C. had already turned his gun on the shop's front door, where two more men stood, firing hopelessly. This time one survived his initial burst. But not the second.

Five kills. J.C. felt no emotion at all. The mission wasn't over yet.

MAZEN RAN INTO the storage room, his shirt drenched with blood. "You told them," he yelled at Farouk. "Spy. Jew spy." Mazen swung his rifle at Farouk, who hunched down, catching the blow in his right shoulder. A dull pain spread down his arm.

"I swear to Allah—" Farouk croaked out the words, feeling his bowels loosen.

"Idiot," Zayd said to Mazen. "Look at him. He's more frightened than you."

Zayd pulled a grenade from his belt, ran to the door, and tossed the grenade into the barbershop without looking out. "*Inshallah,* that will give us time," he said. The building shuddered as the grenade exploded in the front room.

"Stay here," Zayd said to Mazen. "Kill as many as you can. Farouk, come."

Farouk reached for his Geiger counter.

"Leave it."

Farouk shook his head. He seemed to have forgotten how to speak.

"Fat fool," Zayd said. "It won't help you anymore." But Farouk held on to the counter like a charm. He would not die in here tonight. Allah would not permit it. Not after what he had found.

Zayd turned away and trotted up the staircase. Farouk followed, huffing with each step up. But at the top of the stairs Zayd cursed wildly. A cheap steel lock held the door closed.

ANYPLACE ELSE, CAPTAIN Jackson would have taken his time, brought up his tanks and reduced the barbershop to rubble, then let the Iraqi cops sort through the pieces. But not Ghazalia, not tonight. Already men were on the street, pointing at the store and his Humvees.

After the initial firefight, the barbershop had briefly gone quiet. Jackson had crept toward the shop, hoping they had killed everyone inside. Then a grenade had blasted out the front window, sending a glass shard into his cheek and a trickle of blood down his face. He was more annoyed than hurt; he shouldn't have left himself so vulnerable.

Now he stood behind the open armored door of his Humvee, his ear cradled to the company radio as he ordered his Mad Dogs into place. Lieutenant Colonel Fahd waited a few feet away, Dunhill in hand. He hadn't said anything, but Jackson could see the eagerness in his eyes.

The company's tanks positioned themselves at the corners of the block, cordoning off the stores so no one could enter or leave. Three cars were parked in front of the barbershop, and J.C. had already taken out five guys by himself. Only a few jihadis could be left, Jackson figured. He clicked on the company radio.

"Blue Six to Blue Tree," he said. "Tree, it's your perimeter. We're going in."

"Roger that, Captain."

Jackson clicked off and looked at Fahd. "Ready, Colonel?"

Fahd flicked away his cigarette. "As you like, Captain."

CRADLING HIS M16, J.C. crept along the building toward the door of the barbershop. Corporal Voss, Captain Jackson's driver, hid a few feet away on the other side of the store's busted-out front window. The Iraqi cops were a half step behind him, which J.C. didn't like. They had no way to communicate if something went wrong. But Captain Jackson had ordered it.

The shop had been quiet since the grenade. But unless it had gone off on its own, guys were still alive in there. J.C. poked his head around the corner of the door to check inside. The store looked like a tornado had blown through it: mirrors cracked to shreds, barber chairs flipped over, and two bodies lying on the floor. Then he saw the door at the back of the shop, open an inch, a shadow fluttering behind. He looked at Voss to be sure Voss had seen too. Voss pointed at J.C., then back at himself. J.C. nodded, and just like that they had a plan.

Voss held out three fingers. Two. One.

J.C. ran across the front of the store toward Voss, a motion guaranteed to draw fire. Sure enough, the door opened and a guy stepped out, AK in hand. Voss shot, popping the guy—a huge man with some kind of *sword* attached to his belt, J.C. saw as he ran—in the shoulder before he could get a round off. The guy spun around and went down as J.C. dived for cover behind Voss.

"Go!" Jackson yelled at the Iraqis. The cops poured into the store, firing wildly, skidding on the pools of blood and bone fragments scattered across the floor. The first cop, the lieutenant colonel, stepped into the back room. A second cop followed, then—BOOM!

The store shook as a grenade exploded somewhere in the back, sending metal shards over J.C.'s head. The cop who'd been in the doorway was blown backward by the blast. He landed on his back and didn't get up.

J.C. crept into the store, Voss a step behind him. He heard only a faint moaning from the back room, and he didn't think anyone could have survived that second grenade in shape to fight. But he wasn't taking any chances. Anything that moved was going down. Then Captain Jackson stepped past him and strode toward the door.

"Sir," J.C. said. Too late. Jackson was inside.

FAHD WAS DEAD. Jackson knew as soon as he stepped into the back room. The shrapnel from the grenade had shredded Fahd's chest; his uniform, once a powder blue, was stained wine-dark with his blood. Even body armor might not have saved him. His legs were torn apart, the left one blown in half at the knee. Only his face was undamaged, its expression strangely peaceful. He seemed to have died instantly. But in the corner under the stairs another man had not quite stopped moving, a huge jihadi who had avoided the worst of the grenade.

Jackson knew he should call a medic for the guy, insurgent or no. Then he looked again at Fahd and decided to wait. Someone touched his arm. He turned, startled, to see J.C.

"Sir. It's not secure." J.C. pointed to the stairs.

J.C. was right, Jackson thought. He shouldn't have been the first man in this room. He wouldn't be much use to his Mad Dogs dead. He pointed to the stairs. "You and Voss," he said. "Go."

FAROUK AND ZAYD crept along the roof, trying to find a way down while staying hidden from the American soldiers who surrounded that block beneath them. From the street, the storefronts looked like part of a single big building, but up here it was clear that each store had been built separately. Walls separated the roof of the barbershop from its neighbors. In one corner, someone had shoved an empty cigarette pack and a no-name condom wrapper into a hole in the roof's concrete. Both were yellowed from months in the sun.

Zayd clambered over the wall to the north. Farouk struggled to follow. He came over the wall to see Zayd pulling on a locked door. Beyond it the roof was flat, no staircases down.

The low thump of a grenade sounded from the barbershop. Mazen must have made his last stand, Farouk thought. Zayd seemed unfazed. He turned around and climbed back over the wall they had just scaled. But Farouk felt his spirits sag. They wouldn't get off this roof unless Allah himself sent a chariot.

J.C. HUSTLED to the top of the stairs, where a door to the roof hung crookedly, its lock shot open. Voss was just behind him. J.C. kicked the door open and spun right. Voss followed and moved left. J.C. saw two men climbing a wall thirty feet away. But before he could follow, Voss kicked over a grenade that Zayd had tied to the door as an improvised booby trap. The grenade's handle locked in place.

"Down!" Voss screamed. He desperately kicked at the grenade. J.C. dropped to the roof and covered his face. The world turned upside down as he felt an explosion so loud that it seemed to come from inside his head.

J.C. crawled behind the door toward Voss, but Voss didn't seem to be there anymore. At least not in one piece. Something else was wrong too. The world had gone silent. "WHO LET THE DOGS OUT?" J.C. yelled. Or imagined he did. "WHO? WHO LET THE DOGS OUT?"

J.C. stood and tried to fire at the guys who'd gone over the wall, but his rifle wasn't working. Fuck this, J.C. thought. He pulled his pistol and charged the wall just as two more Mad Dogs came up the stairs. They yelled for him to stop, but he couldn't hear them. Even if he had, he would have kept running.

THEY WERE TRAPPED, Farouk could see that now. A crazy American soldier ran toward them carrying only a pistol, as Zayd made a last stand, his AK on full automatic, shells pouring out, the gun jumping crazily in his hands, scattering rounds through the night.

Farouk stepped backward. He wanted to surrender, but Zayd would kill him if he tried. He would wait for Zayd to be shot and then, if he was still alive, put his hands up like he had seen in the movies. He supposed he was a coward after all. But he preferred a Guantánamo prison cell to dying on this roof.

The American staggered but then kept coming, firing away. A shot hit Zayd in the shoulder. And just like that the American was over the wall. Zayd turned toward him and kept shooting. Farouk couldn't believe that he had missed. But the soldier seemed invulnerable. He raised his pistol and fired, hitting Zayd in the chest, then squeezed the trigger again and again.

Farouk dropped the Geiger counter and raised his hands. The soldier was already turning toward him. "Surrender," Farouk said. "Give up. Give up."

THE FAT MAN was saying something, but J.C. couldn't hear him. He aimed his pistol squarely at the guy's chest and pulled the trigger.

THE GUN CLICKED, and Farouk waited for his chest to explode, for the blackness—or whatever happened next—to take him. He ought to feel close to Allah right now. Instead he felt very far away.

Another click. Nothing happened. Farouk sank to his knees and realized he was still alive.

J.C. STARED stupidly at the guy, then at his pistol, which didn't seem to be working anymore. Out of ammo. Must be. All the adrenaline in his body evaporated at once. Instead of reloading he dropped his pistol and leaned forward until his face was only inches from the other man's, the fat man quivering, mouthing words that J.C. couldn't hear or understand, flecks of his spit flying onto J.C.'s uniform. J.C. wanted to tell the guy something, but he couldn't remember what.

They stayed that way until Captain Jackson pulled J.C. back.

BODY ARMOR MIGHT not have saved Lt. Col. Fahd, but it had sure saved J. C. Ramirez. His Kevlar had stopped two rounds. For his busted-out eardrums, J.C. got an early ticket home, though he desperately wanted to stay with his buddies. For killing six insurgents and attacking in the face of close-range enemy fire, he wound up with the Distinguished Service Cross, a military award second only to the Congressional Medal of Honor.

As far as Jackson was concerned, J.C. deserved the big one. The kid was the best soldier he'd ever seen. But Takahashi, the battalion commander, said that some senior officers wanted to keep the raid quiet. A Medal of Honor would attract attention. Jackson wasn't surprised, considering how quickly the guys from Task Force 121 had shown up after he radioed in that his company had captured a man carrying a Geiger counter and a Pakistani passport. They had stuffed the guy into one of their Humvees and told Jackson to take the guerrillas' bodies and cars back to Camp Graphite for inspection. Like he was their damn errand boy.

"We'll make sure you get credit for this," said one of them, a Special Forces officer who called himself a colonel though his uniform had no badges at all. Like credit was all Jackson should care about, and Fahd and Voss didn't matter at all. Jackson hated losing one of his own. Two, depending on how you thought about it.

But when he crashed out on his cot the morning after the raid, the sun already up and the heat rising, Jackson had to admit that he was proud of his company. All these TF 121 guys running around and it was the Mad Dogs who scored. He would make sure his men understood what they had done, even if they weren't allowed to talk about it. Missions like this were the reason they had shipped off to this hellhole. They had disrupted al Qaeda, taken the fight to the terrorists instead of the other way around.

Jackson folded his hands behind his head and stared at the ceiling. Amped up as he was, he knew he needed to sleep. He was supposed to brief a couple of one-stars on the raid tomorrow. Not bad for a twenty-nine-year-old captain. I just hope intel knows what to do with this guy we caught, Jackson thought, as he finally drifted to sleep. And I hope it's not too late.

7

BROWN-SKINNED MEN with cheap mesh caps and hungry eyes stood in clusters in the giant parking lot. Though the sun had risen only an hour before, already the air was hot and sticky, and the men moved slowly, conserving their energy for the long day ahead. But their apparent lethargy was deceiving. When a pickup truck turned into the lot, the men swarmed it in seconds.

A red-faced man in a short-sleeved shirt leaned out of the truck, pushing back the crowd. "Chill, wetbacks." The men grumbled but gave ground. The man in the truck held up four fingers. "Four guys. All day," he said. "Eighty bucks each. Anybody speak English?"

John Wells shouldered through the crowd. "I do."

"You," the man said. "Up front." He pointed to three other laborers. "You. You. You. In back."

As the other men trudged away, Wells hustled into the pickup, a red Chevy crew cab with commercial plates and a white-painted slogan: LEE'S LANDSCAPING: BEAUTIFYING ATLANTA SINCE 1965. "What's your name?" the guy said.

"Jesse."

"I'm Dale. You speak Spanish?"

"Little bit," Wells said. "*Poquito.*"

"Keep these guys in line, you get an extra twenty."

"*Sí, señor.*"

Dale laughed. "*Sí, señor?* That's funny."

The truck nosed out of the lot and onto the Buford Highway, Route 13, a crowded six-lane road that ran from Atlanta to the northeastern suburbs of Chamblee and Doraville. Wells hadn't known what to expect from Atlanta when he'd arrived in April. Outside of his brief stint in the army, he had never spent time in the South. He had vague visions of Scarlett O'Hara and Martin Luther King. Atlanta had surprised him. The city was bigger than he expected, blending into suburbs that sprawled over the low Georgia hills for miles in every direction. And it was not just black and white, as he had pictured, but filled with Hispanics and Asians and even a few Arabs.

Especially here, the Buford Highway, a mélange of strip malls with signs in Vietnamese and Japanese and languages Wells had never seen. Taquerias and Korean saunas and the First Intercontinental Bank—"Tu Banco Local"—sat beside a Comfort Inn and Waffle House, relics of a more familiar America. A mile north was the Buford Farmers Market, which despite its bucolic name catered to Central American immigrants, selling oxtails and bulls' testicles wrapped in plastic for $2.99 a pound.

The locals called Chamblee "Chambodia," but that term hardly captured its variety. The Buford Highway was post-American America, the United States at its ugly, tacky best, accepting—if not quite welcoming—immigrants of every color, Wells thought. More practically, it was a good place to hide. Anybody who wanted to work could make a living here, and the landlords didn't fuss over renting to people whose papers weren't quite in order. They welcomed anyone who paid on time and kept quiet, like Wells.

So for four months he had lived in a furnished one-bedroom apartment just off the highway. Every morning he took his place among the Guatemalans and Nicaraguans waiting for work at the parking lot. At first they had suspected him of being an immigration agent or a cop and refused to talk to him, but lately they had loosened up a bit. They still didn't really like him; he got picked for more than his share of jobs because he was white and spoke English.

But Wells figured he knew how to be an outsider. Another fake name, another new identity, another endless wait for orders. He sometimes wondered what guys like Dale the landscaper would do if he told them who he really was. Laugh, probably—"That's funny"—and tell him to get back to work.

THEY HEADED WEST on I-285, the ring road that surrounds Atlanta, leaving the grit of Doraville behind as they passed the giant Perimeter Mall, a shopping center the size of a small city. Even now Wells couldn't get used to the casual wealth of America, the gleaming opulence of cars and office buildings. At exit 24, Sandy Springs, they turned off 285, and a few minutes later Dale swung onto a cul-de-sac with four newly built homes that grandly proclaimed itself HIDDEN HILLTOP LANE: A PRIVATE DRIVE. A truck full of saplings awaited them, along with a teenager wearing a Jeff Gordon cap.

"Kyle," Dale said to the kid.

"Wassup, Dale." They exchanged a complex, fluid handshake.

"Got you some Mexicans," Dale said. "This here's John. He speaks Spanish—he'll tell 'em what to do."

Wells's heart thumped. How could Dale possibly know his real name?

"Jesse," Wells said.

"Whatever," Dale said. "Long as you can dig a hole."

Wells could only shake his head. This cracker had just given him his biggest scare in months.

Dale pointed at the trees in the truck. "Kyle'll show you where to put them," he said. "Make sure you get the roots in deep."

THEY STOPPED FOR lunch around noon, hiding from the sun by the side of the house. The Guatemalans unwrapped homemade tamales and bottles of warm beer; Wells pulled out a bucket of Kentucky Fried Chicken, his secret vice. He munched on a greasy, salty drumstick and rolled his tired shoulders, trying to stay loose. He had sweated through his shirt, but he didn't mind the work. Months of digging and hammering had given him back the muscles that had disappeared in the North-West Frontier.

Wells tilted the bucket of chicken toward the Guatemalans. "You want?"

One of the men reached toward the bucket, then stopped.

"It's okay," Wells said. "Really."

The guy took a drumstick. *"Gracias."*

"Quien es tu nombre?"

"Eduardo. Tú?"

"Jesse."

"You work every day."

"Sí," Wells said.

"But you white."

"Looks that way," Wells said. The beginnings of a smile formed on Eduardo's face, then disappeared.

"And you no *inmigración.*"

"No."

Eduardo looked puzzled as he tried to understand why a *norteamericano* would be stuck working with them. Wells had had this conversation, or something similar, a dozen times. It always stopped here. These men respected privacy and, anyway, most of them didn't know enough English to push further. Sure enough, Eduardo finished off the last of his chicken in silence.

"Gracias," he said again, and turned back to the other Guatemalans.

Wells leaned against the wall and looked at the houses around him, broad and tall, with three- and four-car garages attached. Each one probably had fifteen rooms. For one family. Amazing, he thought. Someone would be glad to live here, or ought to be.

THEY FINISHED UP around five o'clock, with the clouds thickening, promising a heavy summer downpour. "Anybody want a cigarette?" Kyle asked. He walked over to his truck—and suddenly hopped in and pulled away. "Later, bitches," he said. Just like that he was gone. The Guatemalans chased the truck but gave up as it disappeared down Mount Vernon.

"Maricón," Eduardo yelled uselessly down the road. "Fucking *puta.*"

This had happened to Wells once before. Most contractors kept their word, because they were honest or because they knew that word would get out if they didn't. But some were real pricks. Wells wanted to put a rock through a window of one of these fancy houses. But Dale might show up at the Kermex lot with the cops, and nobody could risk that. Least of all Wells. He tossed the box of fried chicken on the lawn—maybe the smell would attract raccoons.

They walked for miles down Mount Vernon in rain that turned into a full-on thunderstorm. Wells forced himself to stick with Eduardo and the others, though he worried that a cop might pick them up. Sandy Springs was the richest suburb in Atlanta, and its police didn't look kindly on brown men wandering the streets. For long stretches, the road had no shoulder or sidewalks, and twice they were forced to jump into brush to avoid speeding SUVs.

Finally they reached 285 and waited interminably for a bus. From now on Wells was bringing twenty bucks and his cell phone on these jobs, so he could call a cab if he got ditched. He had been colder and hungrier plenty of times, but he couldn't remember being quite so furious. He expected more from his country. Beside him the Guatemalans chattered away until finally Wells tapped Eduardo's shoulder. "You speak English?" Wells said.

Eduardo smiled. "Good as you speak Spanish."

"Then can I ask you something? You like it here?"

"Every month I send my family seven hundred dollars. They building a house in Escuintla, where I'm from," Eduardo said. "When it's done, I go home."

"You don't want to stay?"

"You really want to know?"

"I asked."

Eduardo looked at Wells, considering.

"Then I tell you, man. I know all about America before I come. So big, so rich. And also you have demo-cra-cy and free-dom—" English might not be Eduardo's first language, but he understood irony just fine, Wells thought.

Eduardo coughed and spat at the traffic. "You act like this is the only place in the world. And everybody should be sad they don't live here. So I'm glad I came, man. Now I seen America for myself. I won't miss it. This place, for me, it's a job. That's all."

· · ·

DARKNESS HAD FALLEN when Wells finally reached his apartment. Tired as he was, he remembered to check the sliver of tape he'd fastened to the top of the doorsill and the thin black thread at the base; both were intact. He'd escaped his pursuers for another day. If anyone was bothering to pursue him.

His living room looked even duller than usual. A dingy futon and a wooden coffee table marred with cigarette burns. A particleboard bookcase and a television-DVD combo with a few discs, mainly westerns like *Shane*. A motivational poster of an eagle flying above a generic mountain landscape. Except for the DVDs and a few books, the apartment looked as tired as it had when Wells first rented it. No pictures, no trinkets. No clothes on the floor, no dishes in the sink. Nothing that marked the place as being inhabited by a human being instead of a robot. Well, one thing: a few weeks earlier Wells had bought a fish tank and a couple of angelfish.

"Hello, Lucy," he said to the tank. "Hello, Ricky." He had never particularly liked fish, but he was glad to have something alive in his apartment. Half alive, anyway—the fish had been swimming slower and slower the last few days.

He knelt on his prayer rug and unenthusiastically flipped his Koran to the first sura. "In the name of Allah, the Compassionate, the Merciful," he murmured in Arabic. "Praise be to Allah, Lord of the worlds, the Compassionate, the Merciful—"

Wells broke off and set the Koran down. He tried to pray every morning and night, but he couldn't hide from himself the truth that his faith had deflated like a leaky tire since the morning when he'd knelt hopelessly before his parents' graves. He still believed—or desperately wanted to believe, anyway—in God and charity and brotherhood. But he had told Duto the truth when he'd said Islam had been a way of life as much as a religion for him. Being Muslim meant praying five times a day, standing shoulder-to-shoulder in the mosque every Friday, not necessarily believing that Mohammed had risen to heaven on a white horse. Now he prayed alone, and without the comforts of the *umma,* the brotherhood, the Koran seemed increasingly foreign.

In a way the distance made him glad. He knew that when the moment came to stop Khadri, he wouldn't have any doubts. Still, he wished he could believe in *something*. No country, no religion, no family. He had tried to write his son, but what could he say to the boy? "Dear Evan, you don't know me, but I'm your real father, not that nice lawyer who's taken care of you all these years . . ." "Dear Evan, I know I disappeared from your life when you were two . . ." "Dearest Evan, it's Dad. I can't tell you where I am or what I'm doing or even the alias I'm living under, but here's $50. Buy yourself a video game and think of me when you play it." After a half dozen pathetic efforts, he'd given up.

He wouldn't have guessed he'd be lonelier in the United States than in the North-West Frontier. He supposed he believed in Exley. Jenny. He dreamed of her every couple of weeks. Sometimes he was back in the Jeep with her. Sometimes he was with her on the night she lost her virginity. Always he woke with an erection swollen against his boxers. He didn't have a picture of her, but he could almost see her blue eyes and translucent white skin. The hitch in her walk. He was sure he could pick her out of a crowd from a hundred yards away. And he was sure she felt the same about him.

Though what did he really know about her? She might even have made up that story, faked feelings for him on orders from somebody higher up. The agency had used sex as a weapon before. Wells shook his head. If that story was fake, she belonged in Hollywood, not Langley. He had to trust his instincts, or he would wind up seeing FBI agents around every corner. No, Exley wanted him as much as he wanted her. They would see each other again. For now he had to do his job, and that job was to be ready for the moment when Qaeda finally came to him.

With that thought he put Exley aside and for the hundredth time tried to guess why Khadri had sent him to Atlanta. The Centers for Disease Control was a few miles south of his apartment, with freezers full of smallpox and Ebola. But the CDC campus was a fortress, with motion sensors, armed guards, and biometric locks. Khadri was fooling himself if he imagined they could get inside. And Khadri didn't strike Wells as dumb. A sadistic fuck, for sure. The L.A. bombings proved that. But not dumb.

Then what did Khadri want here? Centennial Park, home of the 1996 Olympics? Nobody cared about the 1996 Olympics. The regional Federal Reserve Bank? Ditto. The Coca-Cola building? Sure, the Coca-Cola building. Coke stood for American imperialism. Or maybe Khadri had big plans for Fort Benning, a hundred miles south of here. In truth, Wells had no idea what Khadri was planning, or if Khadri would ever contact him again. Every couple of days he went to the Doraville library to check his gmail account, and every couple of days he found it empty.

Wells rolled his neck, an old habit. Sulking in here with his dying fish wasn't doing him any good. He headed for the door. "Sorry, Lucy," he said, looking at the tank. "Sorry, Ricky. But at least you've still got each other."

The fish said nothing.

WELLS'S FORD RANGER had seen better days; its air conditioning hardly worked, and someone had torn out the glove compartment. But the truck was utterly anonymous, a little white pickup like one hundred thousand others in Georgia. Even if he got pulled over he should be okay; the name on his insurance and registration, Jesse Hamilton, matched the name on his driver's license. He also had an old Honda CB500 motorcycle, bought three months earlier in Tennessee. He had paid cash and never reregistered the bike, so it couldn't possibly be connected to him. Just in case.

Wells steered the pickup off the Buford Highway and into the narrow parking lot of the Rusty Nail, a restaurant with a front door guarded by a six-foot-long black revolver that was actually a barbecue roaster. The Nail was famous for its barbecue, and day and night the revolver's barrel vented a thin stream of blue smoke. Inside the place looked oddly like a ski lodge, an octagonal wooden building with a bar at the center and booths around the outside. The Braves game played on televisions mounted in the corners, and the smell of cigarettes and barbecue hung heavy in the air. On another evening the stale smoke might have chased Wells away, but tonight it felt just right.

Wells posted himself at the bar beside a trivia-game console whose screen blinked brightly. The place was mostly empty, just a few regulars at the bar watching the ninth inning with an alcoholic gleam in their eyes, and some kids from Emory looking for a cheap place to drink. Wells had been to the Nail once before, on a night like this, when the silence of his apartment became too much. He would have liked to eat here more, have dinner and watch a game once a week, but regulars got noticed.

"Whenever you can, be the gray man," Knoxville Bill Daley, the agency's top countersurveillance instructor, had told him during training at the Farm. "Right now people see you when you walk into a room. Be the man no one remembers."

Ever since, Wells had done his best to slow down and keep his mouth shut. Of course he hadn't been the gray man in Afghanistan, where by his very existence he stood out. But even there staying quiet helped. Sometimes Wells wondered if he had taken Bill's advice too far, submerged his personality so far inside himself that he no longer knew who he was. Not that the answer necessarily mattered.

Living in the North-West Frontier, he had wanted to come home. But now that he was back he had no idea what he would do, what he would be, once this mission ended. If it ended. The war on terror showed no signs of losing steam. He would never need another job. He could play the gray man forever.

Knoxville Bill's comment had been the most important piece of training Wells got. Outside the Farm, he had never touched a dead drop or shucked a team of enemy agents. He regretted not having been a spy during the Cold War. Back then the game had possessed a certain formal elegance. The agency and KGB had existed almost outside their governments, playing three-dimensional chess on a board only they could see. Neither side really expected the other to blow up the world, and proxy soldiers in Africa and Central America fought the nastiest battles. A few unlucky Soviet moles got executed, but not the spooks themselves. The biggest penalty for failure was expulsion, maybe a nasty Select Intelligence Committee hearing.

No more. Get caught by the wrong guys today and you wound up dead, a video of your beheading on the Internet for the world to see. And the bad guys really would blow up the world if they could. Invisible ink and pinhole cameras were cute tricks for an easier time.

· · ·

THE BARTENDER SLID over to him, a lanky woman with a stud in her nose, friendly blue eyes, and a long-sleeved Braves T-shirt. "What can I get you?"

She leaned in toward him, and Wells almost fell off his stool. After almost a decade of celibacy, just being this close to a woman set him off. Especially this woman. She looked . . . well, she looked like a younger version of Exley. Taller. A little trashier. No wonder he had come back to the Rusty Nail.

She smiled. He did his best to smile back. "Burger and fries, medium-rare."

Her smile turned into a smirk. "Medium-rare may be a little tough for our 'chef' "—she made quotation marks with her fingers so he couldn't miss the fact she was teasing him—"I'd pick one or the other. I'm not sure what language he speaks, but it isn't English."

"Medium, then," Wells said.

"Good choice."

"And a Coke."

"Coke?"

"No, a beer," Wells said, surprising himself. A guilty pleasure ran through his veins. He hadn't tasted a beer in a very long time. He figured this was how addicts felt when they were about to take the day's first hit.

She gave him a tiny shrug, indicating that his sobriety was no concern of hers. "What kind?"

"Budweiser. Draft," Wells said. "Bring it with the burger."

"Sure. What's your name?"

"Jesse."

"I'm Nicole," she said.

Before he could stop himself Wells had stuck out his hand. She looked at it for a moment, then took it. "Pleased to meet you," he said.

"Hi." She walked back to the kitchen, and Wells watched every step, feeling his cheeks redden. Pleased to meet you? A handshake? She was a bartender, not an insurance agent. But he hadn't known what to say. He just wanted her to come back, so he could look at her some more.

. . .

WELLS SLID A dollar into the game machine and played Entertainment Trivia, amusing himself with his lack of knowledge. "The highest-grossing movie of all time is A) *Star Wars* B) *Titanic* C) *Shrek* D) *Spider-Man*." Wells picked *Star Wars*; he had hardly heard of the other three. The answer turned out to be *Titanic*.

Nicole slid his beer and burger across the bar and rested an easy hand on his shoulder. "You really didn't know it was *Titanic*?"

"Uh-uh." Wells sipped his beer and tried not to say anything stupid. The Budweiser was cold, acrid, slightly bitter on his tongue. Perfect. It tasted like home.

"That movie was so great."

"Never saw it."

"Really? What were you, living in a hole?"

"Something like that."

"Let me see your arms." She took his hands in hers and rolled his arms back and forth. "No tats. You weren't in prison."

"Nope," Wells said. "Do I seem like I was in prison?"

"Sort of," she said. "And like you haven't had a beer in a very long time."

"You're right about that part."

She tapped the trivia game. "Play. It's gonna eat your dollar."

Wells punched up the next question: "This one-hit wonder was the first winner of the television show *American Idol:* A) Jessica Simpson B) Kelly Clarkson C) Ruben Studdard D) Justin Timberlake."

"Who are these people?" Wells said.

"Jessica Simpson. Blond, big tits—ring any bells?" She tapped the screen B and was rewarded with 900 points. "Maybe Ruben's more your liking? Country boy from Birmingham."

"Like Garth Brooks?"

"Sure, only Ruben's fat and black and sings ballads. Come on, you never heard of any of them? You're messing with me."

"I stopped caring about music about the time that Kurt Cobain died."

He hadn't exactly stopped caring, he thought. But rock didn't get a lot of play in the places where he'd been. Wells couldn't claim sophisticated musical tastes; in high school he had adored Springsteen and Zeppelin as well as slightly cooler stuff like Prince. Then in college he'd gotten into grunge and alternative, like everybody else. In Afghanistan and the North-West Frontier he had missed music more than he'd expected he would, though he had burned a few dozen songs into his head before he left and could still conjure them on occasion.

"Where have you been?" Nicole said. "The moon?"

"Worse. Canada."

"Maybe I been stuck in Georgia my whole life, but I know they have TVs in Canada." She gave him a long look, then shook her head. "Canada it is then."

"Hey, Nicole," a guy called from the other side of the bar. "Can a man get a drink, or you gonna spend the whole night flirting?"

"What man? Oh, you mean you," she said.

"You're not as cute as you think," the guy said.

"Yes she is," Wells called out. He was on his second beer and already feeling lightheaded.

"Coming, Freddie." She leaned into Wells and said, "I'd let him pour it himself but he'd suck down the whole bottle."

"I heard that—"

"Then you know it's true," she said over her shoulder to Freddie. And winked at Wells and walked away. Wells sipped his beer and tried not to stare at her ass. He failed.

FOUR HOURS LATER, Wells turned his Ford into the parking lot of a storefront pool hall down the highway from the Rusty Nail where the illegals watched Mexican soccer and drank two-dollar Buds. He checked his mirror. Sure enough, her Toyota pickup was making the same turn.

He knew that he was making a mistake, that getting involved with this woman—even for one night—would cause complications that he didn't need. He knew too that Nicole, whatever her charms, was a poor substitute for Exley. But at the moment he didn't much care. He needed a woman, and the hard truth was that he might never see Exley again. He flicked at his shoulder, envisioning an angel on it disappearing in a puff of smoke.

The guy behind the counter gave them a half-friendly nod when they walked in. Aside from the occasional movie, playing pool was Wells's only entertainment; he had been here twice before.

"We close in a hour, man."

"That doesn't give me much time to kick your butt," Nicole said. "Let's go."

TO HIS SURPRISE, she wasn't joking. She started cold and lost the first game but won the next two and would have taken a third straight if she hadn't scratched on the eight ball. "Should have known a bartender could play," he said, watching her smoothly stroke a ball into a side pocket.

"Hate to get beat by a girl?"

"You haven't beat me yet. It's two–two."

She narrowly missed a double bank shot and walked around the table to him. Even after a few drinks she moved easily. "You're funny," she said. "You pretend you don't care but you hate to lose."

Wells shrugged. "That's true," he said.

"And you're always watching. You never stop watching. What are you looking at, Jesse?"

Even after all these years alone Wells knew the right answer to that one. "You."

She laughed. "That took way too long. You're like a robot that's almost human but not quite. The Terminator."

Wells suddenly felt as though he'd gone to a five-dollar storefront psychic and been told not just that he would die, but exactly when, where, and how. She didn't know how right she was. To cover his discomfort he laughed awkwardly. "That's not nice," he said. He leaned over the table to line up his shot. She slid behind him and put her arms on his. Wells could smell her, whiskey and cigarettes. He turned to kiss her but she pulled her mouth away. For a moment he forgot her entirely and thought of Exley, lying on the table in a dirty basement in Oakland. Then he was back.

"No, I'm helping you. Get closer to the table," she said. "Concentrate. Watch the angle." She laughed again. "I hate it when guys pull that shit, grab me at the table. That's why I always lose the first game, to see if they will."

"Kiss me," Wells said.

"Make this shot and I will."

He missed, badly. "I never should have had that fifth beer."

"That's no way to be a Terminator," she said.

"I'm not the Terminator," Wells said. "I'm the good guy. Trying to stop him. What was his name?"

She picked up her cue and sighted her shot. "Too bad. I always had a thing for Arnold Schwarzenegger."

"Really?"

"Yeah . . . well, I was talking to Britney—my best girlfriend—a couple years back, about men, you know? Their equipment."

"Their penises," Wells said. "Just say it."

"Yes, Professor."

"And?"

She flushed. "I can't believe I'm telling you this."

"As long as it's not about how you lost your virginity," Wells said.

"What?"

"Inside joke. Between me and myself."

"Right. Whatever. Anyway, Britney and I decided there's really no way to know how . . . large a man is. Except for one thing." She shot and missed. "This is distracting."

"You brought it up," Wells said. He was surprised to find that his disquiet had faded and he was enjoying himself. Maybe she'd done this a hundred times, flirted in a bar with the promise of more to come. He hadn't. "Let me guess—height?"

"You wish. No."

"Really? How about big feet, big hands—" Wells held up his palm and she did the same. They touched palms. Her fingers reached barely to his first knuckle.

She giggled. "I'd like to think that's a good sign, but nope."

"Then what?"

"Okay. Well, look, it's not like I've got a ton of experience—"

"Coulda fooled me."

She folded her arms.

"Kidding," Wells said. "What was the tell?"

"German blood."

"What?"

"German ancestry. German men are very . . . well-equipped."

"Really?"

"Would I make that up?"

"How much German blood? Do you have to be all German?"

"It's not like I did a survey, Jesse." She laughed.

Wells wished he could tell her his real name. "So that's why you like Arnold Schwarzenegger?"

"Well, no. I always thought he was hilarious. I mean, you could tell he was in on the joke in those movies. But the German thing added to the intrigue."

"You know he's Austrian."

"Like there's a difference. Your shot."

Wells picked up his cue and leaned over the table.

"Why don't you miss so I can run the table and we can get out of here?"

He did.

THEY WALKED UP the stairs to her apartment, stopping every other step to kiss, Wells running his hands over her hips, pushing up her T-shirt, touching her soft stomach. Outside her door she stepped away from him.

"You can't stay over. You really can't."

He kissed her neck.

"Five, ten minutes. That's all. And promise me you won't be upset. It's kind of a pigsty, at least by girl standards." She unlocked the door and Wells followed her inside. Clothes were strewn across the couch, glasses piled in the sink.

Wells leafed through a textbook sitting on a coffee table—*Introduction to Nursing I.* "You didn't say you're studying nursing."

"Sit. You're making me nervous poking around."

Wells sat. "You want a drink?" she said.

"No thanks." She clicked on the radio. A syrupy ballad filled the apartment. "Hey, Terminator. This is Ruben Studdard."

"Where do you go to school?"

She put two glasses of water on the table and sat beside him. "You got ten minutes. You want to quiz me or kiss me?" He kissed her, put his hands on her face while hers traced his body. He tasted the smoke in her mouth and felt a faint guilt that she wasn't Exley. But mainly a desire so fierce that it seemed the room had shrunk around them until she was all he could see or feel. He pushed her back on the couch and slid his hands under her shirt—

Rap-Rap-RAP! Three sharp knocks at the door. She pulled away from him.

"Who's that?"

"Shit," she said.

RAP! RAP! The knocks came louder.

"I know you're in there. Slut," a slurred voice said from outside. "Open the door."

"My ex-boyfriend," she said.

"What's his name, Heinrich?"

"Not funny. We broke up in July. He didn't take it well." RAP! RAP! "He's come by a couple of times. It's just—nobody's ever been over before."

Wells could feel his erection fade, his desire curdling into anger. "Fuck him," he said. "I'll get rid of him."

"I can handle it."

"Open the door!"

She walked to the door. Wells followed, positioning himself behind the door where the guy couldn't see him. She shook her head and pointed toward the bedroom, but he put his finger to his lips and didn't move. She opened the door a notch. "Craig."

"Nicole—"

"Go home. Please."

"You can't cheat on me." He sounded pathetic to Wells, a whiny little man.

"Craig, we broke up two months ago."

"I know you got a guy in there." The door was shoved open a notch.

"I don't."

"I saw you from the parking lot."

Nicole stumbled backward as Craig pushed her.

Wells didn't try to control the fury rising in his chest. He had seen enough. Enough of men treating women like chattel. Enough foolish machismo for a lifetime. He pulled open the door and turned toward Craig. The guy wasn't so little after all, maybe 210, his face flushed, waves of whiskey rolling off him.

"I knew it." Somehow Craig managed to look triumphant as he said this, as if Wells's presence justified his own.

"Go home," Wells said softly, knowing Craig wouldn't. "I don't fight drunks."

"Fuck off." Craig swung, a looping roundhouse that Wells easily dodged.

"Please don't make me hit you," Wells said. "Go home." The guy swung again. Again Wells slipped the punch. A red fog clouded his eyes. He could almost smell Craig's blood. Too much loneliness. Too much desire, unrequited.

"I asked you nicely," Wells said, pleading for himself as much as Craig.

"Nicely." Craig's lips curled into a sneer. "You go out with faggots now, Nicole?" Craig swung again, another drunk wild punch.

Wells caught Craig's arm and counterpunched, hitting him in the stomach, a vicious right that bent Craig in half. Then a quick left jab to the face. Then another right to the stomach, Craig's hands dropping as he wheezed for breath.

"Jesse—" Nicole said. "Let me call the cops."

Wells hit Craig again, an uppercut this time, stepping forward and getting all his weight behind the punch. Craig's mouth snapped shut and he fell backward onto the second-floor walkway. Wells followed him outside and waited. Sure enough, Craig grabbed the railing of the walkway and tried to stand. Wells kicked him in the ribs. Craig rolled onto his side and moaned, clutching his ribs, spitting blood and teeth, as Wells considered where to hit him next.

Nicole jumped Wells from behind, screaming. "Stop it stop it you crazy psycho stop it!"

"Nicole—"

"You're gonna kill him!" She let go of Wells and knelt over Craig. Wells stepped back. Nicole looked up at him. "You psycho. Leave us alone." She pointed down the stairs. "Go. Don't ever come back to the Nail. I'll call the cops."

He raised his hands and backed slowly down the stairs.

. . .

WELLS DIDN'T SEE another car as he drove home down the Buford Highway. He felt as empty as the road unspooling under his tires. He couldn't understand what he'd just done. First off, he would be in serious trouble if Nicole or Craig called the cops. He should never have taken her to the pool place. Some of the guys at that place knew him from the parking lot. Fuck. So much for being the gray man.

They weren't going to call the cops. Craig wouldn't want to admit how badly he'd gotten his butt kicked. Nicole would want them both to disappear. The cops weren't the real problem. *He* was the real problem. It wasn't the violence that had freaked Nicole out. Not just the violence, anyway. She had surely seen fights at the Nail. But his coldness, his efficiency, had terrified her. These people, these civilians, they didn't understand. And he would be wasting his time if he tried to explain. He had to remember this wasn't a war. This was America.

HE PULLED OVER and reached for his cellphone, a prepaid model he had bought in Tennessee. He would ditch it and buy a new one tomorrow.

"Hello?" Exley's sleepy voice said.

"Jennifer?"

"Who is this?" Recognition filled her voice. "John?"

"Yes."

"Oh my God. Where are you?"

"I need to see you."

"We can do that."

"We? Who's we?"

"I meant—just you and me. That's all."

"Forget it."

"Are you in trouble?"

"I'm not in trouble. But tell me something. How will I know if I've gone too far?"

"You'll know, John." Her voice had a confidence he hadn't expected. "I trust you."

"Because I don't know how much longer I can do this."

"Do what?"

He was silent.

"Why don't you come in so we can talk about it?"

"You'll never let me out again."

"John—"

He hung up.

THE NEXT MORNING he went to the Doraville library to check his gmail account. And, for the first time, he found a message in his in-box, from BigBoyK2@hotmail.com. "Hartsfield. 11:45 a.m. 9/19. DL561. Confirm at this address." Wells hit the reply key as quickly as he could. He felt a strange gratitude to Khadri. At least now he had something to wait for. And somewhere to channel his rage.

8

Montreal, Quebec

THE HOUSE LOOKED like any other, a little two-story wood-frame, its gray paint peeling at the corners after too many years without a touch-up. It sat on a quiet street off Saint-Laurent Boule-vard, the center of Montreal's Muslim community, separated from its neighbors by a few feet of close-cut grass.

A close observer might have noticed that the gray house was less crowded than those around it. No kids. Just one man and one woman, both light-skinned Arabs. But being childless was no crime. The observer might have wondered why the house's blinds were al-ways down, even on summer nights perfect for leaving the windows open to catch the breeze off the Saint Lawrence River. But then the blinds stayed closed in lots of houses in the neighborhood. Muslim women prized privacy.

A *very* close observer might have wondered if the people in the house were running an unlicensed business. Every so often the man dragged cardboard boxes from his minivan to his front door. He usually made these deliveries just after sunrise, when the street was deserted. But, like being childless, starting the day early was per-fectly legal.

Anyway, what an observer might have noticed was irrelevant,

conjecture only. For no one was watching the house. Tarik Dourant could work unmolested.

LIKE MANY OF the Arabs in Montreal, Tarik had come from France. He'd grown up just north of Paris, in Saint-Denis, one of a dozen run-down suburbs where the French government warehouses the Muslim immigrants it does not want and cannot send home.

Even by the bleak standards of Saint-Denis, Tarik had a wretched childhood. His mother, Khalida, was a nurse from Algeria, his father, Charles, a French plumber whose lust for Khalida ended the day he impregnated her. When Khalida refused to have an abortion, Charles tried to beat her into a miscarriage. He failed, but the thrashing left Khalida nearly blind. She quit her job, and for the rest of her life she and Tarik subsisted on disability payments. Over the years, she grew dependent on painkillers, first to sleep, then just to get by. She died when Tarik was seventeen of a morphine overdose, officially ruled accidental. Meanwhile, the French legal system treated Charles with unsurprising leniency. He was out of prison in two years.

The neighborhood kids cut Tarik no slack for his mother's miserable fate. Quite the contrary. Though he had never met his father, they scorned him as French. He was not helped by the fact that he was small and preferred reading to playing soccer. The nurse and the plumber had produced a brilliant child, his aptitude for science obvious from kindergarten. The French educational bureaucracy took note. As a teenager Tarik attended the Lycée Louis-le-Grand, among the top high schools in France, where he excelled in physics and biology. But the better Tarik's grades, the deeper his misery. The rich white students at Louis-le-Grand didn't bother to hide their disdain for the poor Arab in their midst. Meanwhile, the kids in Saint-Denis scorned him as a sellout, calling him "the brain" and "the little prince" and ripping up his homework. His lowest moment came on his fourteenth birthday. No one, not even his mother, bothered to remember.

A week later, Tarik found himself signing up for an Arabic class at a Muslim community center a few blocks from his apartment. To his surprise, everyone at the center encouraged him. Within a few months he was attending a local mosque every morning. Then another mosque, this one more radical. And he found that everywhere he went the believers accepted his prayers. For the first time in his life he belonged.

By the time Khalida died, Tarik had devoted his body and soul to Islam. He hated his father and France and the West for what they had done to his mother, and his mother for what she had done to him. He wanted more than anything to travel to Afghanistan and join the jihad. But the imams wouldn't let him go. He should keep studying, they said.

They had enough fighters. They needed scientists.

TARIK DID AS they asked. He took an undergraduate degree in molecular biology from the University of Paris, then left France for Canada. Now he was working toward a Ph.D. in microbiology from McGill, in downtown Montreal. His advisers considered him diligent, though privately they acknowledged that his second year had been less promising than his first. It happened. Not everyone could make the jump to a graduate-level program. And . . . perhaps Tarik's professors in France had inflated his potential, since Arabs were badly underrepresented in the sciences.

But the McGill professors were wrong. Tarik was every bit as smart as his scores had indicated. Unfortunately, he couldn't devote his full attention to their labs. In the basement of the anonymous gray house, he had his own project.

PLAGUE.

To nonscientists, the word conjures up visions of the end of days, illness and death beyond measure. But for biologists, the word has a more specific meaning: *Yersinia pestis,* the scientific name for the germ that causes the disease called plague, or sometimes the Black Death. During the Middle Ages plague was the most feared of diseases, more terrifying even than smallpox. In the mid-1300s, tens of millions of Europeans, a third of the continent's population, died after being bitten by plague-infested fleas.

"The condition of the people was pitiable to behold," one Italian wrote, recalling the devastation. "Many died in the open street, others in their houses, their deaths known only by the stench of their rotting bodies." Another epidemic began in China in the 1890s and ran for a generation, killing twelve million people.

Since then plague has largely disappeared in Europe and the United States, thanks to better sanitation and aggressive efforts to exterminate rats and fleas. But the *Y. pestis* germ remains widespread in the wild, infecting thousands of people every year. Exotic viruses like Ebola get most of the media's attention, but plague has killed far more people.

In humans, *Y. pestis* causes several types of infections. The best known is bubonic plague. It begins with chills and shaking, followed by a fever spike that can top 105 degrees. The swollen lymph nodes—also called buboes—explode to the size of baseballs as the immune system tries desperately to clear *Y. pestis* from the body. A profound fatigue takes over, so severe that many victims find themselves beyond caring whether they live or die. In the final stages of disease, the explosion of *Y. pestis* in the bloodstream causes septic shock. The blood hemorrhages under the skin, and the arms and legs take on a deep blue-black tint, the signature symptom of the Black Death.

YET THE BLACK Death isn't the most dangerous form of plague. Bubonic plague can't be transmitted from person to person, and some victims recover without treatment. No, the real terror is the Red Death, pneumonic plague, the disease that results when *Y. pestis* infects the lungs. In that warm, moist environment, the germ replicates with furious speed.

An infected person first notices a fever, headache, a slight cough the nuisances of daily life. But in a few hours *Y. pestis* takes over. The headache turns from annoyance to agony. The cough becomes a spiraling pneumonia. A vise of pain constricts the chest as bacteria fill the lungs and the heart struggles to pump blood. The victim spits up phlegm, watery and loose at first, then thick with clotted blood.

Within forty-eight hours, people infected with the Red Death have less than a 50 percent chance of survival even if they are put on a respirator and given intravenous antibiotics. Left untreated, they will die within days of shock or respiratory failure, choking to death as their lungs fill with blood. Living through pneumonic plague without treatment is about as likely as winning the lottery.

Worse, infected people spit up clouds of *Y. pestis* bacteria each time they cough, so the disease jumps easily from person to person. And while modern antibiotics can stop plague if it is detected quickly, no vaccine for the germ exists. In fact, *Y. pestis* is in some ways its own worst enemy. Like Ebola, pneumonic plague kills its victims so fast that it can't spread far under normal circumstances, limiting the danger of outbreaks in the wild.

But that condition doesn't apply if plague is released deliberately as a terror weapon. Scattering *Y. pestis* in the air over a major city could produce hundreds of thousands of infections at once, overwhelming hospitals and causing a worldwide panic. The World Health Organization has estimated that a release of *Y. pestis* in a metropolitan area of five million, the size of Washington, could cause 150,000 cases of pneumonic plague and kill 36,000 people. The WHO didn't venture to guess what the plague might do in a larger city, like New York.

TARIK DOURANT HAD a half dozen vials of *Yersinia pestis* stored in his basement.

He hadn't needed to attack the Centers for Disease Control headquarters to get them, or to sneak into Vector, the giant germ factory in Siberia where the Soviet Union hid its biological-weapons research during the Cold War. Tarik hadn't even needed to leave the house. He had just needed to be home when a FedEx delivery truck rolled up, so he could sign for a package from the Muhimbili Medical Center in Dar es Salaam.

Tanzania had scores of plague cases every year, and its government worked hard to prevent outbreaks. Doctors who discovered a potential case were required to take blood samples to be tested at Muhimbili's infectious disease lab, the most sophisticated in East Africa. There the samples came under the care of a quiet Pakistani technician who had moved to Tanzania to get a job at Muhimbili—on the orders of the man who called himself Omar Khadri. Khadri figured that a Pakistani Muslim would have an easier time getting hired in Tanzania than at the Centers for Disease Control. He was right.

Thus the plague had found its way to Tarik, who at the tender age of twenty-three was the most sophisticated scientist ever to work for al Qaeda. *Inshallah*. God's will. And so Tarik could not give his full attention to his studies at McGill.

THE GRAY HOUSE was silent as Tarik unlocked the front door and stepped inside. "Fatima?" he called out. "Fatima?"

No answer. She should have been home by now, cooking dinner. Acid rose in his stomach. His wife had been late twice in the last week. Her respect for him seemed to be vanishing by the day.

Tarik had met Fatima in Paris during the spring of his final year at the university. She was the oldest daughter of an imam in Brussels, a petite eighteen-year-old whose *hijab*—the head scarf worn by pious Muslim girls—framed her big brown eyes. Tarik was smitten instantly. He was ecstatic when he found she felt the same about him, despite his pockmarked skin and thick glasses. They married four months later, just before he moved to Canada. She followed the next year. For a few months she seemed like the perfect wife, loving and supportive. She didn't question the long hours he worked at McGill or spent in the basement. But then she began complaining that Tarik wouldn't let her work. She was bored staying home all day, she said. In the spring, she had found a job as a secretary for a law firm downtown. He had tried to forbid her from taking it, but she'd just laughed.

"Then divorce me," she'd said. She knew he would never do that. She was the only woman he had ever been with. He was sometimes frightened by how much he wanted her. But her job had increased the distance between them. She hardly listened to him anymore. He couldn't understand this other side to her. She seemed to have forgotten her place since she'd come to Canada. But maybe she had never cared for him at all. Maybe she had seen him as just a chance to escape her father.

A month before, he had hit her for the first time, on a night when he tried to make love to her and she turned away. He had raised his fist, not intending to touch her. Then she smiled. She was mocking him, he thought. Mocking him for his weakness, for his skinny arms and caved-in chest, just like the kids in Saint-Denis had done. He might be weak, but he was still a man. She needed to remember that. He swung his fist into her belly. She cried out, just once, and he wanted to comfort her and tell her he was sorry. But he held his tongue.

When he reached for her later that night, she gave herself to him without complaint. In fact she never mentioned what he had done. For a few days Tarik thought she had learned her lesson. But in the last couple of weeks she'd turned secretive. He'd overheard her whispering on the phone in the kitchen. When she saw him listening she hung up and pretended she hadn't been talking at all. He raised his fist at her again, but she just shook her head, and he dropped his hand and turned away in humiliation.

TARIK TRIED TO put Fatima out of his mind. He would talk to her when she came home. In the meantime he had to work. He unlocked the door to the basement, revealing a narrow enclosed staircase that led to another locked door. Tarik knew the twin locks might look suspicious, but he couldn't take the chance of allowing anyone down here. Besides the plague, he had anthrax and tularemia in his refrigerators downstairs, all classified by the CDC as grade A pathogens, all delivered from Muhimbili.

To preserve his privacy, Tarik kept his distance from the other McGill graduate students, accepting their invitations to socialize only when his absence would be conspicuous. He told classmates that his wife was a devout Muslim who didn't go out, and he told Fatima that the other students were prejudiced and never invited him. He couldn't stop her from meeting the neighbors, but he discouraged her from bringing anyone to the house, one reason she insisted on working. Maybe that had been a mistake; maybe he should have let her have more friends.

Tarik put his key in the padlock at the base of the stairs. He needed to stop thinking about Fatima. Now. If he allowed himself to be distracted down here he might make a mistake, and if he made a mistake he could easily die. He breathed deeply, closed his eyes, and cleared Fatima from his mind.

When he was sure he was ready, he opened the second door and stepped inside.

HE HAD SPENT most of the last two years just setting up the lab. The equipment was expensive, and installing it without attracting attention was difficult, especially since he had to work alone. But this summer, just in time for the arrival of Y. *pestis,* he had finally gotten the space into order.

He had divided the basement into two working areas. Most of the room was open, its floor and walls covered with double layers of clear, heavy plastic sheeting to keep out dirt and grime. Lab benches lined the walls, stacked with his precious equipment: a 1,000-power microscope, a gas spectrometer, fermenters to grow bacteria in solution. A freezer and refrigerator. Mouse cages and autoclaves and Bunsen burners and trays of slides and pipettes. In one corner he had installed a sealed safety cabinet connected through a filter into the house's air vents. He kept goggles, gloves, gowns, and a portable respirator in a cabinet by the door, next to a small shower. Fluorescent lights overhead gave the room a bright institutional shine.

The space was essentially a crude equivalent of a Biosafety Level 2 lab, like the one at McGill and every university in the world. BSL-2 labs handle germs and viruses that are moderately dangerous and infectious, pathogens that might give their victims a bad fever but are unlikely to kill anyone. Ironically, plague can sometimes be handled in BSL-2 labs, because Y. *pestis* is not a hardy germ. It grows slowly and is easily destroyed by sunlight, rain, even wind. Only in the human body does plague turn monstrous.

But Tarik needed more than a BSL-2 lab for his experiments. He wasn't just growing plague and anthrax; he wanted to aerosolize them, turn them into airborne particles that could be easily inhaled. For that he should have been working in a Biosafety Level 3 lab or, even better, a secure BSL-4 lab like the one at the Centers for Disease Control.

The standards for BSL-4 labs run hundreds of pages. They must have their own air supply, double air locks that cannot be opened simultaneously, and filters to scrub the air they exhaust. Scientists must never wear their lab clothes outside the lab. They must always shower before leaving, and the shower water itself must be chemically treated. Germs can be moved only after being put inside a double set of unbreakable containers. And for really tricky projects, scientists must work in a "suit area," a special room where they wear a full body suit with its own oxygen supply, so they will never accidentally breathe the air around them.

Tarik understood the standards. He had seen photographs of victims of smallpox and plague, faces twisted in agony, bodies bloated in death. He respected the power of the vials in his refrigerator. And he would have preferred to run his experiments at the CDC.

But that institution might have frowned on his work. So Tarik built his own suit area. He sealed a five-foot corner of the basement in floor-to-ceiling Plexiglas, then covered the Plexiglas with thick plastic sheeting, creating a plastic bubble whose air could not circulate into the rest of the room except through an intake and exhaust system protected by HEPA filters.

Inside the bubble Tarik needed his own sealed air supply. Because Canada, like other industrialized countries, restricts the sale of full-body positive pressure suits, Tarik couldn't order one. Instead he used a respirator and oxygen tanks like those worn by scuba divers. To avoid contaminating the open part of the basement, he installed a Plexiglas passage off the door to the bubble, creating a crude airlock. He always changed into and out of his respirator in the airlock. Inside the bubble he had installed a stand-alone safety cabinet that held a mouse cage and a nebulizer, a machine that blew air through liquids to produce aerosol sprays. On the bubble's plastic floor he had placed a half-size refrigerator and a cage big enough for a cat or a small dog. He hadn't used the cage yet, but he expected to change that soon.

The space wasn't ideal. Tarik could work inside it for only short stretches, until his tanks ran out of oxygen. And his respirator wasn't as reliable as a genuine BSL-4 pressure suit. Still, the bubble had worked so far. He hadn't gotten sick, and neither had the mice in the open half of the basement, a crude but effective way to measure exposure. Too bad he couldn't show his professors—they'd be impressed.

.   .   .

TARIK FLICKED ON the overhead lights and checked to be sure the benches and beakers and agar dishes were exactly as he had left them. Down here the street and the world seemed far away. Only the faint rustling of his mice intruded on the silence. He counted them, making sure none had gone missing.

He stripped naked and folded his clothes on a chair. Normally he worked first with less dangerous germs before entering the bubble. But tonight he wanted to be close to his "specials," *Y. pestis* and *Bacillus anthracis*—anthrax. He opened the first door of the bubble—the door to the airlock—and stepped inside. He pulled on the shirt, underwear, and sweatpants that he used in the bubble, then slipped a white smock over his clothes. He pulled the door shut and smoothed over the plastic sheeting on the door, sealing off the bubble from the rest of the basement. He picked up his respirator, hooked up his oxygen tank, and pulled the mask over his face. He breathed deeply, making sure the oxygen was flowing smoothly, then cut back on the flow to preserve the tank. Then a cap, booties, and gloves.

Finally he opened the inside door of the airlock and stepped into his bubble.

In here he could have been underwater, or on the moon. Only his breathing broke the perfect silence. He slid noiselessly to the safety cabinet. A week earlier he had grown *Y. pestis* for the first time, placing the bacteria in petri dishes of blood agar at 28 degrees Celsius, about 82 degrees Fahrenheit. Two days later, white colonies of bacteria speckled the red agar, their edges pebbly and uneven. They looked like tiny fried eggs, the telltale shape of *Y. pestis*. They were ugly, Tarik admitted to himself, small and ugly. But anyone who didn't respect them would be surprised. And he controlled their power. The thought gave him great pleasure.

AFTER GROWING THE plague, Tarik injected it into six mice. Only one survived more than two days. Now it, too, lay on its side in the safety cabinet. Tarik put the mouse's carcass in a glass container, then filled the container with hydrochloric acid to destroy the remains. At McGill he would have autopsied the animal to see how exactly it had died, but in here that wasn't important. He simply wanted to prove to himself that he could grow a good, virulent strain of Y. *pestis*. And he had done just that.

But Tarik knew he had taken only a small step toward his ultimate goal. Infecting people with pneumonic plague was much harder than sticking a needle in a mouse. He needed to figure out a way to spray the germ in a fine mist that could be inhaled and caught in the lungs. He would have to test different solutions, different plague concentrations, chemicals that might allow the mist to disperse more easily without killing the bacteria inside it.

That challenge had perplexed scientists in labs much more sophisticated than this basement. Aum Shinrikyo, an apocalyptic Japanese cult, had spent millions of dollars in the 1990s trying to develop biological weapons, and had even sprayed Tokyo with botulism and anthrax. But Aum had never managed to infect anyone. Its only successful attack had come with nerve gas, which was far easier to make than biological weapons.

Furthermore, military scientists weren't exactly publishing reports about their experiments with plague. Tarik would have to make his own mistakes. He wished he could talk to someone about the technical difficulties. But his only confidant was Omar Khadri. Khadri was a typical nonscientist. He seemed to think that unleashing an epidemic should be as easy as growing germs in a beaker and then tossing them on subway tracks. He had been bitterly disappointed when Tarik had explained otherwise.

"You received my present?" Khadri had asked in their last conversation, a few days after the plague arrived. Tarik was at a pay phone at a gas station in Longueuil, on the other side of the Saint Lawrence River, miles from his house.

"Yes. Thank you, Uncle." They always spoke French and never used names or specifics.

"So how long will it be?"

"I can't say, Uncle."

"Your best guess then. A month? A few months?"

"For the purpose you require, a few months at the earliest."

"You know I'm anxious to see your work."

Tarik shifted anxiously from foot to foot. He hated to disappoint Khadri. "I beg your forgiveness. But this job cannot be rushed."

"Will you need more money?"

"Yes."

"How much?"

"The same as January." That was $200,000. Tarik had spent carefully, but the equipment he needed was unavoidably expensive.

"The same?" Khadri laughed, but the sound had an edge. "You think your uncle is so rich?"

Tarik said nothing.

"I'll make the arrangements," Khadri finally said. "And how is your wife?"

"Uncle, I don't know what to do."

"Don't let her become a distraction, my nephew."

How easy for you to say, Tarik thought. "Will you visit soon? I'd like to see you."

"I wish I could," Khadri said. "But I'm very busy these days. You're sure you don't have any competitors?"

"I've been very careful."

"Well. Nephew. In this I am in your hands." Khadri sighed, as if he found that admission particularly painful. "Keep up your work. You know the whole family has great hopes for you. We'll speak again soon."

"I won't disappoint you, Uncle."

Click.

TARIK WISHED KHADRI could see the basement now. He was certain his "uncle" would be impressed. Two days before, Tarik had moved colonies of *Y. pestis* from the agar dishes into beakers of brain-heart infusion broth. Now Tarik saw that the transfer had been successful. The broth inside the vials remained clear, but white rings of bacteria lined their glass walls—the sure sign of a plague colony. Unlike most germs, *Y. pestis* did not disperse readily in solution, preferring to remain clumped.

Tarik poured the broth into a glass mixing dish, carefully scraping the colonies of *Y. pestis* off the walls of the beakers. Using a wire, he gently mixed the colonies until the bacteria were scattered through the broth. Now he would test aerosolizing the bacteria. He connected a simple rubber hose to a small electric pump. He dropped the free end of the hose into the dish and turned on the pump. A moment later bubbles began gurgling out of the broth, as if it were a primordial stew about to boil over.

This was the most basic way to aerosolize bacteria, Tarik knew. But he wanted to see whether Y. *pestis* could survive being moved between the beakers and the dish, and whether this basic aerosol could cause infection. In the scientific vernacular, this was a proof-of-concept experiment. And so Tarik had put six more mice in a cage beside the mixing dish. They crawled calmly around their metal pen, oblivious to their fate.

Tarik worked for another half hour inside the bubble, transferring plague colonies between agar dishes and beakers of broth. He had more experiments planned, and he would need much more Y. *pestis*. He took careful notes, recording the temperature and humidity in the cage, the number of bubbles rising from the dish every second. Simple stuff, to be sure. But most laypeople didn't understand that a thousand hours of tedium in the lab paved the way for every breakthrough. One step at a time, and he would get where he needed to be.

9

THE DOORMAN TIPPED his cap as Exley walked into the Jefferson Hotel, her low heels clacking on the lobby's marble floor, the hotel's air conditioning a relief from the muggy summer night.

"Good evening, Ms. Exley."

"How are you, Rafael?"

"Never better, ma'am."

She turned right, into the lounge, a quiet red-walled room whose dark wood tables seemed as if they should be crowded with politicians and lobbyists. Instead the space was mostly empty. The Jefferson had never matched the glamour of the Hay-Adams, and with the arrival of the Ritz-Carlton and other five-star hotels it had fallen permanently into second-tier status, a dowager whose rooms filled after the rest sold out.

But Exley liked the hotel's faded elegance, the bouquet of flowers in the lobby, the way the doormen knew her. Plus, the Jefferson was on Fifteenth Street, a short walk from her apartment. After a couple of drinks she could wobble home. Tonight she'd stopped in for a special treat, a meeting of the S.L. Club, five professional women who saw each other for drinks every few weeks. One was a reporter for the *Post*, another a lawyer at Williams & Connolly. They were all divorced or never married, all middle-aged or older. Exley hated to define herself as middle-aged. Ugh. But she was, by any reasonable standard. Soon enough she'd be closing in on menopause. Okay, maybe not that soon, but still.

The S.L. Club had no bylaws, no fees, and no real purpose, aside from giving its five members a chance to vent about work and family and sneak a couple of cigarettes that their kids didn't need to see. Exley had met Lynette, its informal leader, at an interminable Fourth of July party three years before.

The five of them were friends, but not a part of one another's lives. So they could be honest with each other about their sputtering parents and complicated children. About ex-husbands who had remarried and decided that they wouldn't pay for private school for their kids anymore. About minor triumphs at work and home, bureaucratic victories or honors their kids had won. In fact, that was probably the best thing about the club. Women weren't supposed to brag, and Exley liked having the chance to celebrate a little when things went right. She looked forward to these gatherings, even— especially—when work became overwhelming, as it had been for months. But tonight she was distracted.

THEY WERE IN the corner, as usual, and she was late, as usual. She took the last seat, a glass of wine already poured for her. "To the Sophisticated Ladies," they all said, glasses raised.

"The Sophisticated Ladies." Clink.

A somewhat bitter joke. The initials stood for Self-Loathing as well. Did they really hate themselves? Probably not. But Exley could always hear a little voice deep in her head, and she guessed the other four women could too: *Your kids don't even think of you as their real mom anymore. You're going to be alone the rest of your life. Worst of all*, words she knew the others didn't hear: *There's a pattern in the intercepts. Something is coming, and you're too dumb to see it.*

She needed to stop this second guessing before she shook herself apart. There wasn't any pattern. She couldn't analyze information that didn't exist. That damn voice. Men didn't hear that voice. Men expected success even when they failed; women awaited failure even after they had succeeded.

Lynette, a slim black woman who was a producer at NBC, caught her eye. "You okay, baby? You look stressed."

"Just fine." Exley tried to smile.

"We find Osama yet?" They all knew Exley worked at the agency, though not what she did.

"You're asking the wrong woman," Exley said. "I'm just a secretary."

"I know you run that place."

"If I ran it, things would be different." The joke was almost automatic, but Lynette smiled anyway, and after a moment Exley did too.

"That is the truth." Lynette raised her glass.

THE AGENCY AND the Joint Terrorism Task Force had worked nonstop in the months since the Los Angeles bombings. But the investigators still hadn't identified the bombers, much less figured out how they had accumulated three tons of ammonium nitrate without anyone noticing. Either they had gotten the stuff through customs or they had built a stash bit by bit while living in America for years. Exley couldn't decide which prospect was worse. And she worried that the attacks had been designed as a diversion. Even the United States government didn't have infinite resources. The FBI had put some of its best agents on the bombing case, pulling them from other open investigations. Exley understood the instinct; the families of the dead wanted answers and arrests at any cost. She just hoped that the cost wouldn't include another attack.

She and Shafer were looking ahead. They had spent the spring and summer poring over the databases the JTTF used to track the movements and communications of every known al Qaeda member, searching for patterns the first-line analysts had missed. So far they hadn't found much. Over the years the intelligence community had accumulated evidence that al Qaeda had at least one sleeper network somewhere inside the United States. Network X, some people at the agency called it. Two or three cells, between six and twenty agents in all. Put in place before September 11. Al Qaeda's secret weapon. Waiting for orders to launch a big attack, presumably chemical or biological or radiological. Or nuclear, God forbid. And last month the NSA had picked up an e-mail that indicated that al Qaeda had somehow gotten nuclear material into the United States. But the message was unconfirmed, and no one knew how—or even if—it tied into Network X.

Not that Exley would mention any of this to the Sophisticated Ladies. Much less the early-morning phone call she had gotten two weeks before. She poured herself another glass of wine and decided to try to relax. "Girls," she said. "It's good to see you."

Gretchen, a petite gray-haired woman, leaned in. "So . . ."

"So?"

"Don't play dumb with us, Jennifer. How was your date?"

Exley didn't feel like having this conversation again. "Isn't it amazing?"

"What?" Gretchen said.

"The five of us, we're all attractive. All financially stable, all reasonably sane."

"Speak for yourself," Lynette said, getting a laugh.

"No, really. And we're lucky to get, what—two dates a month? Not two each. Two for all five of us."

"Hey," said Ann, the lawyer. "I got propositioned just last week at this conference in Atlanta. I mean, he was married, but he did take off his ring before he asked. I thought that was sweet."

This time the laughter had an edge. The Sophisticated Ladies got plenty of propositions from married men at bars—or, worse, at work. They got invitations to cocktail parties from guys who had never married and were probably closet cases. What they didn't get were real dates from divorced men their own age. Unless they didn't want more kids, those guys inevitably wound up with women at least a decade younger.

"Stop stalling," Gretchen said to Exley. "How was it?"

Normally Exley submitted to these interrogations without much resistance, though privately she wished they would spend less time talking about men. Nothing ever changed, so what was the point? But tonight she had no appetite for Gretchen's questions. She wanted to sit and drink her wine.

"Must have been good," Ann said. "You look tired."

"Leave her alone," Lynette said. "Least let the lady finish her wine."

EXLEY HAD MENTALLY replayed the call from Wells a hundred times. She had traced the number—an exchange in Nashville, a cellphone, which meant it could have been made from anywhere. She could easily call a friend at the FBI to find out where. But she wasn't sure she wanted to take that step.

Nor had she told anyone at the agency, even Shafer, about the call. She feared she would lose control if she did. They would tap her phone, monitor her apartment. After all, Wells was a fugitive. Duto had a couple of his goons searching for Wells in the United States without telling the FBI—even though the agency's charter specifically prohibited it from operating on American soil. Duto had somehow convinced his general counsel that the CIA could search for Wells under an exception to its charter that allowed limited investigations of internal security breaches.

Exley assumed that the search for Wells was small and basically for show, so that Duto would have his ass covered in case something happened to Wells. She didn't think Duto seriously considered Wells a threat. In fact, he might be glad to have Wells on the loose. This way Duto would still get credit on the off chance that Wells stopped an attack, while being able to blame Shafer if Wells screwed up or turned up dead. But she couldn't be sure, since Duto refused to give her or Shafer any details about the search—though he had told her that she needed to tell him if Wells contacted her.

"I want to know *personally*," he had said. "You understand, Jennifer?"

Disobeying direct orders from Vinny Duto was a bad idea. But Exley didn't care. She was certain Wells hadn't flipped. She wanted to protect him as best she could, save him from being warehoused in a cell somewhere. If he found anything important, he would reach out.

Meanwhile, she wished she knew where he was now, what he was doing, what he thought of the agency's games. What did he think of the United States, after his years away? And what about her? Did he think of her the way she thought of him? He was a constant presence in her mind, and his call had made her believe that he felt the same, but she couldn't be sure. Perhaps he had reached out to her only because he had no one else. Yet when she'd hung up the phone she'd realized that the call hadn't surprised her at all; subconsciously, she had expected it.

Her overwhelming desire for Wells confused her. She was basically logical, and yet somehow she had fallen for a man she had seen for all of two weeks in the last ten years, a man who had probably lost his mind somewhere in the hills of Afghanistan. But he hadn't seemed crazy in the Jeep; his brown eyes had seemed entirely calm. In any case, he wasn't like anyone else she had ever known.

In her more cynical moments she wondered if she wasn't lost in an escape fantasy. A strong silent man to take her away. If he happens to be a renegade agent even better. She wished she could tell the Sophisticated Ladies about the situation. They would appreciate the irony. She had always prided herself on keeping her feelings out of the office. Women so easily got tagged as weepers who couldn't be trusted under pressure. Even during her divorce only Shafer had known how badly she was hurting. Now she had thrown away her rules for a man she would probably never see again. If the stakes weren't so high, she would have laughed at herself.

For the moment she had decided to think of the call as a dream. That way she didn't have to report it.

A tap from Gretchen shook her out of her reverie. "Come on, Jennifer. Share."

Fine. She would tell them about her date. "There's nothing to share. His name's Charles Li, a cardiologist at Georgetown. Divorced. We went out last week."

"Where?"

"Olives."

"Very nice."

And so very predictable, Exley thought. Olives was an overpriced restaurant on Sixteenth and K with a big-name chef and a fancy wine list. She had to guess that Wells would never take her to Olives.

"So . . . how it'd go?"

"It went fine. I learned a lot about stents. And Lipitor. You all should have your cholesterol checked. Did you know that heart disease kills more women than any other illness, including breast cancer?"

Lynette shook her head. "That bad, huh?"

"Let's just say I didn't get to talk much."

"You know you have to let them talk about themselves on the first date," Gretchen said. "Has he called?"

"Oh yeah." Called, sent flowers, called some more. Dr. Li was persistent. Persistent enough that she had considered giving him another chance, despite his potbelly and comb-over. At least the good doctor was making an effort.

"Well that counts for something—" Gretchen said as Exley's cellphone rang. She flipped it open.

"Pack a bag for warm weather and get in here." It was Shafer. Click.

SHE WAS GLAD for the excuse to go. She quickly said her goodbyes and arrived at Langley an hour later to find Shafer sitting on her desk, a suitcase at his feet.

"What took you so long?"

"Ellis. I set a land speed record getting here."

"I have a special treat. Come on." He grabbed his suitcase and strutted out of her office, leaving her to follow. Evidently she wasn't the only one losing her mind.

At the best of times Shafer was an uncertain driver. Tonight he veered from lane to lane, speeding and tailgating, as they headed south, then east on the Beltway, toward Andrews Air Force Base.

"Where are we going, Ellis?"

"You're an analyst. Analyze the situation."

She felt herself flush with irritation. Shafer must be nervous. He wasn't usually so juvenile.

"Ellis. This isn't a fucking class trip."

"Temper temper."

"Fine," she said. "Looks like we're headed to Andrews. And you told me to pack for warm weather. I'll say Gitmo."

"Guantánamo?" Shafer laughed. "Come on, reporters tour that base. You think we keep anybody important there?"

"Then where?"

"A long way away."

"Kuwait? Oman?"

"A place that doesn't exist."

"Diego Garcia," she said.

"Well done."

Diego Garcia was a U.S. naval base on a British island in the Indian Ocean, one thousand miles from the southern tip of India, even farther from Africa. The base wasn't a secret, but it wasn't exactly well publicized either. The Pentagon always denied holding al Qaeda members there, mainly to soothe British sensibilities. The Pentagon lied, Exley knew; Diego was home to several al Qaeda operatives.

"May I ask why?" she said. "Or do I have to play Twenty Questions again?"

"A month ago we caught somebody in Baghdad. A Pakistani nuclear scientist."

"Why didn't you tell me?"

"I'm telling you now."

"And?"

"And he's got some interesting information. I thought we should see him for ourselves."

THEY SAT IN the upper deck of a C-5 Galaxy at Andrews Air Force Base, a row ahead of two scowling men whose passes identified them only as Mr. Smith and Mr. Jones. Below them, a company of Rangers sat in the aircraft's giant cargo bay, along with pallets loaded high with MREs, ammunition, and even a couple of armored Humvees.

"Can this thing really fly?" Shafer said.

"Scared?"

"I just can't believe how big it is. Did you know it can carry two M-1 tanks? It's the biggest bird the air force has."

"When did you start calling planes 'birds'?"

"We're lucky to get to ride in it. They don't usually take civilians. I had to pull some serious strings."

"I didn't think you had too many strings left."

Shafer leaned toward Exley as the C-5's engines whined to life. "I don't," he said quietly, under the noise of the jets. "Remember that, Jennifer."

Exley didn't know what to say. Was Shafer exaggerating, or did he really have problems? The whine became a roar, and a throb of power ran through the plane's frame. Exley felt the C-5 accelerating slowly, though without windows she couldn't see the jet move.

Shafer handed her earphones and a little white pill. "How about some vitamin A?"

"Vitamin A?"

"Ambien. See you tomorrow."

He popped a pill into his mouth. A moment later she followed him down the rabbit hole.

EXLEY'S PHONE RANG and rang; she knew Wells was calling, but she couldn't answer. An earthquake gripped her bed, lasting longer than any earthquake should, and every time she tried to pick up the phone it jumped away.

Then the phone stopped ringing, and fear gripped her. She'd lost Wells—

She woke up. For a panicked moment she couldn't figure out where she was. Someone touched her shoulder and she yelped.

"You okay?"

The world came back into focus when she heard Shafer's voice. "How long was I out?"

Shafer looked at his watch. "Ten hours. Still a ways to go. You missed the movie."

She needed a few seconds to realize he was joking. She supposed the Ambien hadn't fully worn off yet. The plane was shaking; that accounted for her dream.

Shafer cocked his head toward her. An expression she couldn't read crossed his face.

"What?"

"You and Wells look the same when you're having a nightmare, you know that?"

Exley blinked in her seat. How did Shafer know what Wells looked like when he was dreaming? Was he telling her that he knew about the Jeep? The call? Was he just guessing?

"You're sleeping with him too?" she said.

Shafer laughed. "I saw him asleep once at Langley, that's all."

"Do we have any food on this bird?"

"I saved you dinner." He handed her an MRE, a sealed brown plastic bag whose label informed her that it contained spaghetti and meatballs. She looked at it doubtfully.

"Not bad. Just make sure you use the heater. And you ought to stretch your legs."

"Believe it or not I've flown before."

He handed her a sheaf of papers. "Before we land you need to sign this."

She flicked through them. "A secrecy agreement? Ellis, I have every classification there is."

"Not for this. No one is graded for this."

Exley felt her stomach drop again. This time it wasn't turbulence. She had left the Jefferson a long way behind. "Just what are we doing to this guy?"

FAROUK KHAN WAS having a very bad day. Not that day or night meant much to Farouk anymore; his concept of time had vanished in the weeks since the Special Forces put a hood over his head and took him to an underground cell at Camp Victory. Though Farouk's passport was fake, his Geiger counter was real enough, and Task Force 121 immediately understood his importance.

Within hours word of his capture reached senior officers at both the CIA and Centcom—United States Central Command, which runs American military operations across the Middle East. By the time the sun rose the next day in Washington, the White House had been informed. Before noon the president had signed an executive order designating Farouk as a C-1 enemy combatant.

The United States had used the C-1 label only six times since 2001, when it began exempting al Qaeda detainees from the protections that the Geneva Convention offered to traditional prisoners of war. In legal terms, the designation meant that the United States government had determined that Farouk might have knowledge of imminent (Category C), large-scale (Category 1) terrorist attacks. As a result, Farouk would be excepted from both the Geneva rules and the rights that the Supreme Court had required for prisoners held in Guantánamo.

In less legal terms, the designation put Farouk neck deep in shit.

Of course, the United States government did not condone torture, even for prisoners like Farouk. Civilized nations do not torture captives. But torture had been defined rather narrowly in the manual that specified the permissible interrogation techniques for C-1 detainees like Farouk. The manual, called the White Book because of the color of its cover, noted that interrogators should weigh the harm inflicted on detainees against the potential danger from terrorist acts. Thus the White Book said interrogators could do anything that did not cause "severe *and* permanent" injury. The conjunction was italicized so that the manual's point would be clear. Severe injuries were allowed, as long as they were not permanent. Similarly, psychotropic drugs were banned only if they produced "severe *and* permanent" brain injury or mental illness. The same rule applied to sensory deprivation, restrictive confinement, and denial of food and water.

The White Book also noted that pain was a subjective concept, differing from one person to another. Thus any amount of pain was allowed, as long as it did not produce "severe *and* permanent" injury. The White Book also noted, dryly, that "pain should not necessarily substitute for more traditional methods of interrogation. The threat of pain is often more effective than pain itself."

FAROUK'S JOURNEY HAD begun in Baghdad.

They locked his hands behind his back even as he was still on his knees, on the roof, with Zayd's body a few feet away. A man in an American military uniform pulled a hood over his head and tightened it around his neck. The world went black. The hood was too tight. They surely hadn't meant to make it so tight. He couldn't breathe. He took one shallow breath, then another, fighting for air through the bag. Soon he was panting like a dog. His throat tightened as he began to panic. He was going to pass out. He was going to die up here. His breaths came faster and faster, until he was hyperventilating and the roof seemed to fall away under him.

Stay calm, Farouk told himself. They wouldn't kill you this way.

Relax. Breathe. He slowed down his breathing. And after a few minutes he realized he was still alive. He focused on his other senses, the shouting of the men around him, the rough fabric of the hood touching his face, the wetness where his saliva had trickled onto the inside of the hood.

Two men grabbed him and pulled him up. He stumbled. A moment later he felt a punch into his thick stomach. He grunted and fell. He rolled onto his side. The pain and surprise were enormous, and now he really couldn't breathe. He mashed his face against the rough roof, hoping he could drag the bag off his head.

"Allah," he said. "Allah." He felt the stick of a needle in his leg. A silver peace spread to his brain and his fear vanished. Then the blackness overtook him. The nightmare ended.

BUT WHEN HE woke he found that it hadn't ended after all. He opened his eyes and saw nothing, nothing but the most profound blackness possible. He seemed to be swimming inside it, swimming in a sea of blackness. The hood. He must still be wearing the hood. He tried to pull it off . . . and realized his hands were locked behind his back. With that thought his shoulders began to ache. His legs too, for his ankles were manacled to the floor. And yet his flabby buttocks were exposed to the cool air. The chair he was on had no seat, and his pants had been cut off. Also, oddly, it felt as if a tiny alligator clip was attached to his right index finger, and a Velcro strap to his left ankle. He tried to rub them off but found he couldn't.

And he was thirsty. He licked his dry lips with his dry tongue.

"*Salaam alaikum,*" he said, his voice a rasp.

No answer. He tried again, more loudly this time. "*Alaikum salaam.* Hello." And now a real shout: "*Allahu akbar.*"

But no one answered, and Farouk suddenly realized he could hear nothing at all. Not a sound. Not the rush of the wind or the bark of a dog or the hum of a car's engine. No inside sounds either, like pipes or air conditioning. His ears seemed to have been stuffed with cotton, only they weren't.

Could the Americans have forgotten him here, wherever here was? Would he die of thirst?

Farouk pulled himself back. He needed to stay focused. I'm a scientist, he thought. I must use my mind. My name is Farouk Khan. The *kafirs* have taken me prisoner. How long ago? I don't know. Where am I? I don't know. They drugged me, put me to sleep, moved me somewhere. Fine. He breathed in and out, and realized that someone had cut a hole in the mask so he could breathe more easily. Good.

Why are they doing this to me? They want to know about the Geiger counter. Of course. That beast Zayd had been right. He should have left it in the storeroom, though the Americans would have found it anyway.

He tried to relax. He wasn't an illiterate peasant. He knew the Americans had rules. They could make him wear this hood, but they couldn't hurt him too much. They would ask him their questions, and then would put him on a plane to Guantánamo. If they asked him about the Geiger counter, he would say . . . he would say that he didn't even know what it was. He should make up a name. A Shia name would be best. Hussein, then. He would call himself Hussein. As long as he didn't tell them who he was or what he was doing in Iraq, he would be fine.

The Americans had rules. He just needed to stay calm.

BUT STAYING CALM got harder as the seconds stretched into hours. He thought of his wife, Zeena, of his sons and daughters, of the dirty concrete floors of the lab where he had worked, of the black stone of the Kaaba, which he had never seen except in photographs. Of the glorious moment when he had met Sheikh bin Laden, of Zayd picking his nose as they waited for the peasants to arrive with their yellowcake. Of the lead box that he had bought from Dmitri, and the havoc it would wreak. He smiled at that memory. But always his thirst distracted him, pulled him back to this empty black room. And his bladder had grown uncomfortably full. And what if he needed to empty his bowels? Was that why they had cut open his pants?

"Swine," he said aloud. "*Kafirs*. My name is Hussein. Hussein Ali." His voice rose. "Let me go!" He repeated himself a dozen times, a hundred times, until his voice cracked and crumbled and his face flushed under his hood.

Someone had to respond. But no one did.

. . .

PERHAPS THE AMERICANS really had forgotten him. No, that was impossible. This was a game. They wanted to scare him. But Allah would protect him.

And so he waited, fighting his fear, licking his dry lips and counting slowly to one thousand and back down again. But his dread deepened in the silence, along with his thirst.

"Please," he said quietly. "Please."

LATER. HE DIDN'T know how much later, couldn't imagine, and suddenly a torrent of water drenched him. Freezing water, painfully cold, stinging him through his hood and his clothes. So cold. Yet Farouk turned up his head to drink, thankful even for this, for any sign that they knew he was here.

"*Allahu akbar,*" he mumbled. He had asked and Allah had provided. He drank and drank even after he was full, afraid that the water might not come again.

But the cold flow kept coming, and deliverance quickly turned to a new kind of misery. He squirmed left and right, but he couldn't escape the stream. The water saturated his clothes until they couldn't hold another drop, then soaked his skin. Water trickled along his stomach, down his legs, off his feet. He could feel it pool on the floor and rise to his ankles.

He began to shiver. He hadn't realized how blessed he had been just a few minutes before. To be dry. How he hated these Americans and their tricks. They were laughing at him somewhere, he knew. He should be angry. But he was only afraid and cold. How long would they let him sit here, and what would they do next? "Allah," he said, "I beg your forgiveness." And again: "Please."

LATER. A NEEDLE jabbed into his back. Almost before he could register its sting the blackness had taken him again.

HE WOKE UP on a sagging cot in a small room, a thin blanket over his body. He sat up. He was naked. He could see. His hood had been taken off, and the room was lit by a ceiling bulb. His hands were cuffed in front of him, but his legs were free.

A pile of clothes lay on the floor, a loose shirt and sweatpants with an elastic waistband. He awkwardly pulled on the pants and shirt, and his spirits brightened. They had realized there was no use hurting him. He had survived their test. So he hoped.

He shivered as a cough shook his body. He sat on the cot and tried to think. He felt tired and hungry, slightly feverish. But otherwise okay. They wanted to scare him, these Americans. But he wouldn't give in. He waited a few more minutes. Then, feeling as though he had no choice, he stood up and tugged at the door. To his shock, it opened.

FAROUK HAD KEPT them waiting. Which fit his profile, Saul thought. They could see him on the monitors as he sat on the cot scratching his head. He was rattled and getting sick, and the oximeter and pulse monitors showed that he had reacted badly to his time in the hole, although he had slowly brought himself under control. Saul was not surprised. Farouk was a scientist, not a killer like Khalid Sheikh Mohammed. The hole was deeply disconcerting to anyone who wasn't flat-out psychotic.

But Saul had learned not to underestimate those guys. They were highly motivated. Their faith gave them extra strength. They never broke all at once, not the important ones. They gave up a little, and then they started lying again. Getting everything took time.

Saul was the lead interrogator in Task Force 121, a Delta Force major with a doctorate in psychiatry from Duke. He pushed the limits of the White Book, he knew. Even some other interrogators worried that his methods crossed into . . . the T-word . . . a word that he didn't even like to think to himself. Sometimes, after a particularly draining session, Saul worried too. He didn't want to look in the mirror one day and see Josef Mengele. He wondered what his parents or his wife would think if they saw what he was doing on CNN.

But Saul had never killed any of his prisoners, or hurt one in a way that wouldn't heal. He pushed the limits, but if he wasn't clear on whether a procedure was permitted, he asked Colonel Yates, a military lawyer permanently attached to 121. The questions were never written down; the colonel didn't want to end up on CNN either. Still, Yates's mere presence checked the worst impulses of the interrogators. And they closely monitored the prisoners' health, if only to make sure their techniques were working. The interrogators in 121 had interrogated close to one hundred prisoners, and only one had died, of a huge heart attack that probably would have hit him in any case.

The TF 121 interrogators had other restrictions. They never worked alone, and they took two-month breaks twice a year. Once a year they were interviewed by army psychiatrists and took a long personality test. The rules were supposed to prevent them from developing God complexes—a real risk, Saul knew. Having this much power over another human being, not just the power to kill but the power to hurt, could be intoxicating. Look at the other side, cutting throats on camera. Nothing could be more repulsive. Yet Saul understood the impulse, the sick thrill of making another human being cringe and beg for his life . . . or beg for death because the pain was too much.

Yes, he was on a slippery slope, and he knew it. But he slipped only far enough to get the information he needed. Saul rarely had moral qualms about his job. In his office he kept a paperweight engraved with a quotation from George Orwell: "People sleep peaceably in their beds at night only because rough men stand ready to do violence on their behalf." He had broken Khalid Sheikh Mohammed. He had disrupted at least three attacks, saved hundreds of civilians. He didn't know their names, and they would never know his, but they were still real.

And the men he questioned, the Farouks of the world? They weren't innocent. They weren't Iraqi farmers caught in dragnets and taken to Abu Ghraib. They were terrorists, real ones, who knew the risks they had chosen to take. Saul had nothing but contempt for the Amnesty International types who whined that any coercive tactic was unfair. If those weaklings believed that men like Farouk would give up their secrets over tea and crumpets, they were even more naive than he thought.

The real problem was that the tactics that TF 121 had pioneered had spread much too widely, Saul thought. Coercion should be used only when necessary—under close supervision, and on prisoners who could reasonably be expected to have good information. He didn't understand why twenty-two-year-old corporals from West Virginia who'd never learned basic interrogation techniques were beating up detainees at Abu Ghraib and Guantánamo and Bagram in Afghanistan. Not that anyone at the Pentagon had asked his opinion.

As for the argument that his methods shouldn't be used because they didn't work, Saul could only laugh. Of course they worked. They worked too well, in fact, which was why they couldn't be used in police investigations. After a few weeks with him, most people would admit to anything, even crimes they hadn't committed, simply to get out. Those forced confessions were almost worthless, because even the questioner couldn't tell if they were true.

But Saul wasn't trying to solve crimes. He was trying to stop them. He wanted information about attacks that hadn't happened yet. The location of hidden bombs. The structure of terrorist cells. The real names and addresses of operatives. Concrete, verifiable information. He didn't care how often he was lied to, as long as he got the truth at the end. Lies only drew out the pain. Eventually every detainee understood that, and when they did, they gave him what he wanted.

FAROUK WALKED OUT of his cell and into a larger room that had a table at its center.

Two big men walked into the room. "Sit," one said in English. Farouk saw no reason to pretend that he didn't understand. He sat. One man stood behind him, while the other manacled his legs to the chair. Then they brought out a plate of bread, a bowl of hummus, and a glass of orange juice.

Saliva filled Farouk's mouth. He could never remember being so hungry, not even as a boy when his mother had to make three kilograms of flour last a week. He wondered if the food was safe. One of the men dipped a piece of bread into the hummus and ate. At that Farouk dipped his head toward the table and shoveled food into his mouth with his cuffed hands. The glorious food filled his belly, and he felt a momentary rush of gratitude toward his captors. He stifled the reaction immediately. Don't thank the *kafirs*, he told himself. That's what they want.

After he finished, the men cleared away the plates and walked out, leaving Farouk to sit alone. He suddenly felt strangely fatigued. He wanted nothing more than to put his head on the table and sleep, and a few minutes later he did just that.

SNAP! THE LIGHTS shone brightly as Farouk tried to shake the mustiness from his head. A new man stood over him. Someone else shook him from behind. Why had he fallen asleep? And for how long? The hummus must have been laced with something. He was a fool. He wiped at a line of drool trickling from his mouth.

"Wake up," the man said. He was tall, with dark hair and a neatly trimmed goatee. He set a thick folder on the table. Farouk shook himself desperately. He needed to be clearheaded.

The man sat across from Farouk and took a pack of Marlboros from his jacket. "Cigarette?"

"No," Farouk said, though he badly wanted one.

The man shrugged. "Suit yourself. What's your name?"

"Hussein. What's yours?"

"My name doesn't matter. And I think you're lying to me. What's your name?"

"Hussein. Hussein Ali," Farouk said. "I'm a farmer from Basra. This is all a mistake."

"You're not even Iraqi. Don't insult me." The nameless man smiled a small cold smile. "For the last time. What's your name?"

"I told you," Farouk said as sincerely as he could. "Hussein."

"Do you want to go back in the hole?"

Not that, Farouk thought. Please not that. He swallowed hard and tried to keep his composure as his interrogator tapped a Marlboro from the pack on the table.

"Do you want to go back in the hole? Yes or no?"

"Of course not," Farouk said. "But my name is Hussein." As long as he stayed calm he could outsmart this American.

NOW, SAUL TOLD himself. Show this bastard who's in charge. He opened the folder. "Your name is Farouk Khan," he said. "You were born in Peshawar, Pakistan, in 1954. You attended the University of Delft in the Netherlands as an exchange student. You received a bachelor's degree in physics, and then an advanced degree. Upon your return to Pakistan, you were hired by the government."

Farouk had been foolish to carry a Pakistani passport, even one with a fake name, Saul thought. Pakistani intelligence had identified him and revealed his past to Task Force 121, though only in the vaguest terms. The Pakistanis didn't talk much about their nuclear weapons program, not even to America. But the Pakistani silence didn't matter. Once the CIA knew Farouk's real name, the agency dug up enough information for a psychological profile of him. The goal was to make Farouk believe they knew everything about him and that lying would be a waste of time. To their subjects, the best interrogators appeared all-seeing as well as all-powerful.

FAROUK'S HEAD SNAPPED back as the man read. He had to fight to keep from retching. How could the American know all this?

"My name is Hussein," he said desperately.

The man with the goatee stopped reading, stood, and slapped Farouk across the face. Farouk yelped, from the shock as much as the pain. To be slapped like a woman was intolerable. Yet Farouk somehow knew he deserved the punishment for lying so foolishly.

"Don't be stupid. Your name is Farouk Khan. You lost your government job in 2000. Would you like to tell me why?"

Farouk said nothing.

"It doesn't matter," the man said. "I already know." He stepped back and lit his cigarette. "You are 174 centimeters tall and you weigh 105 kilos." Five foot eight and 231 pounds. "You have a resting heart rate of approximately ninety beats per minute. Your blood pressure is 170 over 110. You are in poor health, and you have reacted badly to the stress you have faced so far. The minimal stress."

"*Allahu akbar,*" Farouk murmured to himself. His blood seemed to have left his body. He could not control his shivering.

The nameless interrogator took a deep drag on his Marlboro. "Yes, God is great," he said. "But God has nothing to do with this." He leaned over Farouk, holding his cigarette close to the prisoner's face. "Farouk, you're a smart man. An educated man," he said. "You know the United States has a prison camp at Guantánamo Bay." He waited.

"Yes," Farouk rasped.

"And it is no secret that detainees in Guantánamo are treated well. They receive three meals a day. They pray freely. You may even have heard that they have lawyers, yes?"

"Yes."

"But you are not going to Guantánamo."

The nameless man slid the burning end of his cigarette toward Farouk's eye.

"No." Farouk shrank back in his chair, blinking furiously, trying to look at anything but the burning ember two inches away.

"I'm glad you agree. No. You are not going to Guantánamo." The man took a last drag on the cigarette, then stubbed it out against the table and flicked it away. "I don't want to hurt you, Farouk," he said. "But you need to tell me the truth. And you will. You're going to tell me everything I want to know."

Farouk found his voice. "There are rules," he said. "You can't."

But even as he said it he knew he was wrong.

"I'll tell you something I probably shouldn't," the American said. "There is one rule. I'm not supposed to kill you. Not on purpose, anyway."

Then he smiled. The expression on his lips scared Farouk more than anything that had happened yet. This man was a devil, a devil in human form. Please, Farouk almost said. I'll give you everything. I'll tell you about Khadri. I'll tell you about the box I got from Dmitri. I'll even tell you the biggest secret of all, where that box is now. Just leave me alone. Then Farouk reminded himself that he must not fear. But maybe he could give this man a little. Anything to make that smile disappear.

"Farouk, are you listening?"

Farouk nodded. He hated himself for answering the man but his will seemed to have melted away.

"I'm not supposed to kill you. But I am allowed to make you wish you were dead."

The American walked out. Even before he closed the door, Farouk felt the hood coming down over his head.

"No," Farouk said. "Please. Ask me something. I'll tell you." His voice became a shout. "I'll tell you! Please!"

But the room went dark, and Farouk knew that the hole awaited.

. . .

THE NEXT FEW weeks were much the same. As the interrogations continued, Farouk's experiences in confinement became even more terrifying; he was shot up with adrenaline until his heart raced so fast that he believed it would explode. He was slipped LSD and left to chase his mind around the silent room. When he tried to sleep he was hit and kicked by men he could not see.

Meanwhile, Saul lengthened the stretches that Farouk spent outside of solitary confinement, in order to make the contrast between the hole and the world even sharper. Saul wanted Farouk to learn that Saul could save or destroy him, could turn day to night, white to black.

The lessons were effective, and Farouk divulged new secrets at each session. He told them how he had met bin Laden. How he had recruited three employees in Pakistan's nuclear program. How he had met an American agent for al Qaeda who was being sent back to the United States to help carry out a major attack. Saul hadn't expected Farouk to give up so much so soon; he simply wasn't as tough as Khalid Mohammed or other senior al Qaeda lieutenants, who had taken months to break. Still, Saul believed that Farouk was holding something back.

AS THE C-5 made its way over the Indian Ocean, Exley worked her way through the transcriptions of Farouk's interrogations and his reactions in solitary. The report's descriptions were cool and clinical: "The subject screamed 'Allah!' for several minutes before losing consciousness. When he was revived . . ." Exley felt herself growing cold, and part of her wished that the jet could turn around and take her home.

"What do you think?" Shafer said.

"I see why I had to sign that security clearance," she said. "Are we keeping a video?"

"Nope."

She wasn't surprised. The Pentagon had learned something from Abu Ghraib, though maybe not the lesson that rights groups had hoped. "I'm not exactly naive, Ellis," she said. "I knew this stuff was happening." She shivered. "But I guess it's different when you read it firsthand. That's all."

Shafer merely grunted, and they sat the rest of the flight in silence. They touched down at Diego Garcia so smoothly that Exley hardly realized they had landed. As the plane's huge rear doors opened and sunlight filled the C-5, the Rangers ran out with a cheer. Exley had never missed being twenty-five so much, though she was consoled by the fact that Shafer looked even worse than she felt, with a scrim of stubble on his cheeks and his eyes bloodshot.

"What day is it?"

Shafer looked at his watch. "Saturday. Saturday morning."

"We left Thursday night."

Shafer yawned gigantically. "Nineteen-hour flight, and we're eleven hours ahead of D.C."

They walked gingerly onto the tarmac. The equatorial sun shone hard on the Humvees parked around them, glaring off mirrors and windows. Exley was glad she'd brought her sunglasses. Coconut palms and ironwood trees were scattered around the runway, a strange juxtaposition with the military hardware. The warm moist air reminded her of Washington, though a light ocean breeze made the humidity here easier to take. Around them the Rangers were unloading their bags and bitching good-naturedly about the flight. For them Diego was just another base. Yet Exley had an overwhelming urge to be somewhere else.

A soldier walked toward them. "Sir? Ma'am? You must be Mr. Shafer and Ms. Exley. Please come with me."

FAROUK SAT IN the evil dark, the evil all-seeing dark. The blackest darkness there ever was. So dark that he could almost convince himself the darkness was light. Only it wasn't.

He knew now that Allah had forsaken him, left him to rot in the claws of the *kafirs*. He had only darkness. This room and the other. They were the same room really, but this room was dark and the other wasn't, and that was everything.

"I can't," he said. "I can't do this. Please." Allah you have forsaken me. You have forsaken me.

Tears rolled down his cheeks. In the diminishing rational corner of his mind he knew that the Americans had somehow built this room to hold him. It was just a cell, a specially designed cell that was silent and dark. Sometimes he tried to envision how they had put it together. But he couldn't keep his thoughts straight for long. Soon enough the darkness took over. The darkness, and the . . . tricks. He didn't know what else to call them. The tricks. They *hurt*.

Farouk had told Saul a lot, more than he'd ever meant to say. But Saul wanted more. "I know that's not everything, Farouk," he would say quietly. And the hood would go back on. Farouk couldn't convince him otherwise, no matter how hard he tried. Because of course he hadn't told Saul the biggest secret of all, about the package from Dmitri. And he needed to keep that secret with him. In the dark.

SAUL WANTED TO break Farouk today, give the folks from Langley a show. He didn't feel any need to hide his methods from them. They weren't from the Red Cross or snot-nosed reporters. They were on the team. They were cleared to see. So let them see.

THE LIEUTENANT ESCORTED Exley and Shafer to a thick concrete building at the northern edge of the compound. BUILDING 12. RESTRICTED ACCESS: LEVEL 1 TF 121 CLEARANCE REQUIRED said a small sign in red letters. A tall, unfriendly man in a floppy hat stood guard by the building's steel doors, trying to find shadow from the afternoon sun.

"Mr. Shafer, Ms. Exley, this is as far as I go," the lieutenant said. "But I'll wait for you there when you leave." He pointed to a building they had passed.

"Thanks, Lieutenant."

"You're welcome, ma'am." He turned and strode away. He couldn't wait to get away from this building, Exley saw.

THE MAN ON the infrared monitors hardly moved. They couldn't see his face, which was covered by a hood. But they could hear his sobbing. "Does he always cry like this?" Exley said.

"He started to cry late in his third session," Saul said. "Now he cries almost constantly after a couple hours."

"And how many sessions has he had?"

"Eight. He's progressing nicely," Saul said.

"When did he mention Wells?"

"About a week ago. I can go back over it with him if you like. He's very cooperative about things we've already discussed."

Saul had shown them the building before bringing them in here. The hole was in its own wing on the first floor, specially proofed against sound and light, he said. Normally such rooms were built underground, but the coral on Diego didn't permit deep construction.

"Please," the man on the screen said. "Please." His sobs thickened. If any of the interrogators noticed, they didn't comment.

"How long has he been in there?" Exley asked as neutrally as she could.

Saul glanced at his watch. "Only nineteen hours. But his tolerance for the room seems to be breaking down."

"That doesn't always happen?" Shafer said.

"Some of these guys get stronger for a while, which makes things tough. But Farouk—I think he's about ready to break completely."

"So now what?" Exley said.

"We typically introduce an additional stress element at some point in his sessions. Sometimes early, sometimes late—we don't want him to be able to anticipate it. Now seems like a good time."

THE DARK DARK dark. Farouk tried to count to one thousand, but he couldn't keep the numbers straight anymore. He had tried to recite bits of the Koran, but each time he said Allah's name he felt more forsaken. So he quit that too, and just sat in the dark.

The American was right, Farouk thought. This was worse than being dead. In fact, maybe he was dead already. Maybe he had died on the roof in Baghdad and he was in hell. But it couldn't be. He had served Allah as best he could. He belonged in heaven.

"Heaven," he said aloud. "Heaven."

As he said the words an intense electrical shock flooded his legs. He threw his head back and screamed in pain. His muscles spasmed uncontrollably, tightening and loosening over and over. He had never felt so much pain, up one leg and down the other.

"STOP STOP STOP!" he screamed.

Finally it did. "Allah," he said. It had lasted only a few seconds, he realized. Thank God. He couldn't have taken much more. His legs were still quivering from the shock, and the muscles felt . . . warm, as if he had been running. He tentatively shook them. They still worked.

Then the pain came again, up his left calf and thigh and across his waist and down the other leg. "STOP! STOP!" He felt his heart thumping, but he couldn't move. Time no longer existed. He couldn't tell, couldn't even guess, how long the shock flowed through him.

The electricity stopped. He had time for three quick breaths before it started again. Somehow it hurt even more this time. He tried to tell himself that they couldn't keep shocking him like this unless they really wanted to kill him . . . but that knowledge didn't help. He wanted to beg them to stop, but the words melted on his tongue and he merely moaned until the electricity stopped flowing.

He could take no more. He would tell them anything, everything, not to have to sit in here and wait for this agony. He wrenched his head from side to side.

"Please . . . please . . . please . . ."

"LET HIM CALM down a little and then get him out of there," Saul said, watching Farouk twist. "I think it's done."

They had just used a Taser on Farouk, an electrical gun that produced 50,000-volt shocks that caused involuntary muscle spasms, Saul said. The gun's barbs were attached to Farouk's ankles and didn't need to break the skin to deliver the electricity, so Farouk probably had no idea where the pain had come from. "I've had it done to me and it hurts," Saul said. "But it works."

EXLEY KEPT HER face straight. She should have been elated. A senior al Qaeda operative cracked. If he *was* a senior al Qaeda operative. If he *had* really cracked and didn't need another month in the hole. But she couldn't take her eyes off the quivering mass on the screen. I don't know if I can face this anymore, she thought. It hurts but it works. And what if it didn't work? What came next?

I just want to live in the suburbs somewhere with my kids and work forty hours a week and have a nice, small life. Someone has to do this but it doesn't have to be me. Or maybe no one had to do it. Maybe they just all needed to relax and treat the guys on the other side like human beings.

Then that little voice of hers: Even you aren't that dumb, Jenny. You want this guy to nuke New York City?

Had Shafer brought her here as an object lesson? Did he believe this torture was necessary? Was it even torture? Farouk would be okay, at least physically. She didn't have any answers anymore, only questions, and she couldn't face any more questions.

Suddenly she knew that Wells was going to die. He would be another human sacrifice on the altar of this war. He would die, and she would never see him again. The thought roiled her gut, and she wanted nothing more than to be back in her little bedroom, lying on her back, looking up at the ceiling, with Wells beside her, holding her. Anywhere but here.

Shafer tapped her. "You okay, Jennifer?"

She wasn't, not at all.

"Fine," she said. "Just thinking about what he's gonna have for us. Great job, Saul."

10

TAP. TAP. A finger poked at Khadri's shoulder. He turned to find a shapeless vagrant standing too close, her stringy brown hair pulled into a ponytail, an oversized cross hanging dully around her neck, her foul warm breath on his cheek.

"Excuse me, sir? Spare some change for something to eat?"

"I'm afraid I can't." Khadri could hear his English accent creeping out. He didn't like surprises, even small ones.

"Please, mister? You look like a nice man."

Khadri fished in his pocket for a dollar so she would go away. The woman's eyes lit up when she saw the bill. She tugged it out of his hand.

"Thank you, sir." Khadri shook his head and turned away, hearing her last words, almost a whisper: "I'm gonna pray for you."

The prayers of an infidel. He mused over the woman's promise as he opened the glass doors to Albany's dingy downtown bus station, walking in for the third time that morning. Would she help the cause, or hurt? He stepped slowly through the station's main hallway, his trainers—what the Americans called sneakers—squeaking on the dirty floor. Besides the trainers, he was wearing jeans and a blue T-shirt, camouflage for this ridiculous country where everyone took pride in dressing as poorly as possible.

A half hour later, after what felt like his hundredth loop through the station, he bought a cup of coffee and plunked down on a wire chair, which rocked under him on uneven legs. Running a hand through his close-cropped dark hair, Khadri cataloged his annoyances. The coffee was acrid and cold. The air was stale and hot.

And he was surrounded by Americans. Sweaty fat poor Americans. Women in cheap white uniforms and hairnets trudged past, their mouths slack, their smiles missing teeth. By day's end they would earn a few dollars, enough to feed their families if they were lucky. This station had lights and running water, but in its rank desperation it reminded Khadri of the most pitiful precincts of Islamabad.

Khadri almost sympathized with these fools. Their infidel religion blinded them to the truth: they were nothing but chattel for the Jews who ran the United States. If only they would realize that Allah was the only God and Mohammed his prophet. If only they would rise against this corrupt country and their devil leaders. But they were caught up in their worship of Jesus. And anyway most Americans weren't so poor, Khadri reminded himself. They enjoyed their lives, supported America's wars. No, the United States would never redeem itself, not until the day when al Qaeda proved beyond doubt that only fools stood against Islam.

Khadri believed that such a day would arrive, believed it as he believed in the beating of his heart. So he tried not to overreact to disappointments, like the bad news he had just received from Tarik Dourant in Montreal. Tarik should worry less about his wife and more about his work, Khadri thought. Tarik was a brilliant biochemist and committed to the cause, but Khadri worried about him. He had come to al Qaeda out of loneliness, a man almost broken by the cruelties of the West.

Khadri didn't trust that type of recruit any more than he trusted the fanatics who begged to blow themselves up. They were mirror images. The fanatics were irrational, though strong. Men like Tarik were weak and prone to panic. A strong man would not have let his wife insist on taking a job surrounded by *kafirs*. Tarik needed to regain control over Fatima, or divorce her, not complain uselessly about the situation as if she were the man and he the wife. In fact Khadri didn't really care what Tarik did about Fatima, as long as he kept working.

Khadri dumped two packets of sugar into the coffee to hide its bitterness. A month earlier Farouk Khan had disappeared in Baghdad after an American raid, and since then he hadn't responded to Khadri's messages. Khadri feared the worst. If the Americans had captured Farouk alive, they might have learned of the packages that al Qaeda had brought to the United States. Khadri needed to know if Farouk had betrayed that secret.

So Khadri had come to Albany to conduct an experiment of sorts. Now he needed a helper. An unwitting helper. Someone who wanted money. Someone who would follow orders without asking questions. Someone expendable. The bus station, in the shadow of the highway that stretched down the eastern edge of this ugly city, had seemed a natural place to look. But Khadri hadn't found anyone suitable. He would never trust a woman for this job, and the men loitering here were old and ragged. He needed someone younger. Maybe a black. They would do anything for money, and Albany was filled with them.

HE LEFT THE station and walked through Albany's decaying downtown. There. A black man sat on the stoop of a vacant office building, a blue baseball cap pulled down over his forehead, a bottle half-hidden in a bag between his legs. A hostile look settled into the man's eyes as Khadri walked toward him. "Hello," Khadri said.

A glare was the only response. Evidently this black had some irritations of his own.

"I'm sorry to bother you. Sir."

"Can I help you with something?" The man's words were polite, but his tone wasn't.

"This may seem strange, but I have a favor to ask."

The man sneered. "A favor." The black drew out the word to show his disbelief. The insolence of these people. Khadri reminded himself to stay calm.

"I will pay." A flicker of interest crossed the black's face. Khadri wasn't surprised. "I need a package picked up."

The interest disappeared, replaced with anger. "You got nothing better to do than hassle me?" The black stood up, towering over Khadri. "You know I just got out and now you wanna send me back—"

The black thought he was with the authorities, Khadri realized. "I'm not a constable—a police officer," he said. "Please, listen for a moment."

"Don't care who you are," the man said. "Just get out of my face."

Khadri decided to comply. As he walked away, he heard the words muttered at his back: "Fuckin' raghead."

How he hated this country.

KHADRI FELT DEFEATED as he sat in his motel room in Kingston that night. He had not expected so much trouble finding help. But he had been scorned three times. These people weren't fools. They could see he didn't belong.

He would have to solve this problem by tomorrow. He didn't want to become known in Albany as the Arab stranger who needed a favor, which was why he had chosen to stay fifty miles from the city in this rundown motel. Of course he could bring his own man to get the package, but doing that would mean risking an operative and compromising the security of an entire cell. He had so few reliable men in the United States. And now he viewed this as a personal challenge. He should be able to dupe an American into doing his bidding.

Khadri sighed and flicked on the room's battered television. His mood improved when a rerun of *The Apprentice* filled the screen. Khadri enjoyed these so-called reality shows, Americans prostrating themselves before their false gods of money and fame.

The show ended, and Khadri looked at his watch. Time for his evening prayer. He checked his compass, spread his rug toward Mecca, and prayed silently, touching his head to the ground, genuflecting before Allah. When he finished the ritual he felt calm and clearheaded, ready for a night's sleep and the next day's work. Then an idea filled his mind, surely placed there by the Almighty. Or perhaps—Khadri couldn't help but smile—by Mr. Donald Trump.

These Americans, they knew he didn't fit in. So he wouldn't try.

. . .

EARLY THE NEXT afternoon, after some research and a stop at a Kinko's, Khadri returned to the streets of Albany, slowly driving through the battered neighborhood north of downtown. In a run-down parking lot, a chunky man sat on a battered gray Ford Focus, the obligatory paper bag in his hand. His T-shirt was rolled up to expose his heavy white biceps. Good. Khadri was tired of blacks anyway. He didn't like them, and the feeling seemed to be mutual.

Khadri, dressed today in a dress shirt and khakis, parked next to the Focus and stepped out of his car. "Hello, my friend." This time he didn't hide his English accent.

The man looked at him suspiciously.

"May I ask your name?"

"Tony."

"And your last name?"

"DiFerri."

"Tony DiFerri, very pleased to meet you."

Khadri stuck out his hand, and after a moment the man shook it.

"I'm Bokar," Khadri said. "How would you like to be on television?"

"Say what?"

"I'm a talent spotter. I work for a new reality television show that's searching for contestants."

Tony looked at Khadri as if he had announced he was an alien. "Why me?"

"It's a British show. We want a mix of contestants. Not the usual Hollywood types. *Diversity.*" Americans loved that word.

"You serious?"

"Utterly, sir. Utterly." Khadri rolled the word out with the plummiest Hyde Park accent he could muster. He was beginning to enjoy himself. Now the tricky part. "But we need to prequalify you."

The man's face went blank. "Prequalify?"

"Make sure you're capable, that you have a realistic chance of winning."

"Sure."

"There are five tasks you must complete. The good news is you'll be paid for each, as well as fifty dollars merely to participate. The bad news is that if you fail even once, we'll be forced to reject you. Are you interested?"

Tony was more than interested, Khadri could see. He nearly snatched the pen from Khadri's hands to sign the ten-page contract filled with legal boilerplate that Khadri had printed out that morning.

The instructions took only a few minutes. DiFerri listened carefully, even borrowing Khadri's pen to scratch a quick note to himself. Then he took the key to locker D-2471 from Khadri, coaxed his Focus to life, and drove off. His destination was a converted warehouse on Central Avenue that was home to Capitol Area Self Storage.

OPERATION EARNEST BADGER had begun a week before, after Farouk Khan sobbed out the last of his secrets to his questioners in Diego Garcia. Looking over the transcripts of the interrogation, Exley almost couldn't believe how much information Farouk had given up: details of bank accounts and e-mail addresses; the location of an al Qaeda safehouse in Islamabad; the names of three al Qaeda sympathizers in the Pakistani nuke program. Farouk had turned out to be the biggest catch for the United States in years.

Most stunning of all, Farouk revealed that he had bought one kilo—about two pounds—of plutonium-239 and another kilo of highly enriched uranium from a Russian physicist, Dmitri Georgoff. The agency and Joint Terrorism Task Force had moved immediately to find Georgoff, only to learn that he had been murdered three months earlier in Moscow. The crime officially remained unsolved. But Russia's Federal Security Service, the successor to the KGB, reported in response to a discreet inquiry that at the time of his demise Dmitri had been deep in hock to the Izmailovsky mafiya, Moscow's meanest gang.

Dmitri was a compulsive gambler with a nose for $2,000-a-night whores, according to the Russians. A real charmer, Exley thought. Still, his death was bad luck for al Qaeda, which had surely hoped to do business with him again. And worse luck for the agency, which had hoped that Dmitri could verify Farouk's confession. Though, having seen Farouk being interviewed firsthand, Exley was inclined to believe him.

In any case, Farouk's information had panned out so far. The oversized canvas bag in locker D-2471 in Capitol Area Self Storage was real enough. So were the traces of radiation seeping from the lead-lined aluminum trunk inside the bag. Farouk had told his interrogators that he had bought the plutonium and uranium the previous summer and turned the material over to the mysterious man who called himself Omar Khadri. Farouk had heard nothing further for almost a year.

Then, just before his trip to Iraq, Farouk had been told by Khadri that al Qaeda had smuggled the stuff through Mexico and into the United States. That route made sense to Exley. The Arizona desert had no radiation detectors, no customs agents, no shipping companies to create a paper trail. The best coyotes had almost a 100 percent chance of crossing the border undetected, and al Qaeda had surely hired the best for this trip.

Exley shook her head as she pictured al Qaeda's careful movements. For the thousandth time she marveled at the patience of these jihadis. They were slow and steady and they never gave up. She'd been thinking lately about selling her apartment, heading back to Virginia to be closer to her kids. Now, reading over the report, she wondered again about listing her place, and soon. Logan Circle was barely a mile from the White House, and radioactive fallout couldn't be good for real estate prices.

IT WAS TWO P.M. in Diego Garcia when Farouk Khan told Saul where the plutonium and uranium were hidden. Two P.M. in Diego Garcia meant three A.M. on the East Coast. On a Sunday. No matter. Secure phones began ringing at homes all over suburban Virginia less than ninety seconds after the Critic-coded transmission reached Langley and the White House. The president heard the news when he woke four hours later, per a standing order that his sleep not be interrupted for anything less than a full-scale attack on American soil.

By the time the sun was rising the Joint Terrorism Task Force had begun an investigation, which it named Operation Earnest Badger. Intelligence agencies seemed to have an unwritten rule that the most serious jobs got the most ludicrous names, Exley thought. The name wasn't the only absurd aspect of that first Sunday morning meeting. The FBI and the agency had argued for an hour over which side should run Earnest Badger. Finally they'd agreed to name coheads: Exley's old friend Vinny Duto and Sanford Kijiuri, the deputy director of the Feebs. With their fight for bureaucratic glory out of the way, Duto and Kijiuri got down to business, deploying fifty members of the Nuclear Emergency Search Team—a.k.a. NEST—to Albany.

The Department of Energy had created NEST in 1975 after a hoax nuclear warning in Boston showed the need for a specialized task force that could quickly investigate atomic threats. The emergency team now had about a thousand members, though only a few dozen were full-time paid employees. The rest were volunteers, mostly scientists from the government nuclear laboratories in Los Alamos and Oak Ridge. NEST even had a few retirees old enough to have seen the power of nukes firsthand during the open-air tests of the 1950s.

Exley admired the courage of the scientists, whatever their ages. They had taken upon themselves the unenviable mission of searching for nuclear and dirty bombs, and the even unhappier job of defusing any weapons they found. They worked alongside FBI counterterrorism agents, as well as Special Forces commandos authorized by a secret presidential directive to kill on sight anyone believed to possess a nuclear device.

During the Cold War, only top-level intelligence and military officials had known of NEST. Now the veil had lifted slightly. Still, the government took extraordinary precautions to prevent the public from learning about nuclear threats, hoping to discourage hoaxes and blackmail. NEST and the FBI never disclosed threats, even—or especially—those considered credible.

The NEST scientists wore civilian clothes on their missions and carried their laptop-sized radiation detectors in briefcases and oversized purses. The detectors could pick up unusual levels of alpha and gamma rays at distances up to forty feet. They sent wireless signals to miniature receivers that the scientists wore like hearing aids. NEST also owned a fleet of trucks that looked like ordinary delivery vans but actually held larger detectors able to pick up radiation from hundreds of feet away. To defuse a bomb, NEST had warehouses full of exotic tools at its headquarters at Nellis Air Force Base, just outside Las Vegas: robots that could be controlled from miles away, the most powerful portable X-ray machines ever created, saws that cut with a high-pressure stream of water instead of metal. In fact, all of NEST's equipment was fabricated from plastic and nonmagnetic metals like aluminum, since strong magnetic fields could scramble the computer chips inside nuclear weapons.

UNTIL NOW, THE most serious threat ever investigated by NEST had come in October 2001. SISMI, the Italian military intelligence service, had warned the agency that al Qaeda had smuggled a ten-kiloton nuclear weapon—a so-called suitcase bomb—into New York.

A ten-kiloton bomb is about as small as a nuclear weapon gets, barely half as powerful as the Fat Man bomb the United States dropped on Nagasaki at the end of World War II. Still, the bomb had enough power to obliterate midtown Manhattan and kill 200,000 people. Most civilians simply couldn't comprehend what nuclear weapons could do, Exley thought. She envied them. Thinking too much about al Qaeda's desire for a nuke was like envisioning the end of the world, or your own death—an exercise in humility that could become a morbid obsession.

Exley vividly remembered the search that had followed the SISMI warning. NEST had frantically deployed hundreds of scientists to check every street in Manhattan, every airport terminal, every floor of the Empire State Building. But NEST never found a bomb. And neither the CIA nor any other intelligence agency could ever confirm the initial Italian report. By Christmas 2001 the investigation had wound down. Four months later NEST and the Joint Terrorism Task Force officially declared the report a hoax. Duto, at the time the No. 2 in the agency's Operations Directorate, flew to Rome to tell SISMI it needed some new sources. Exley wished she could have seen that conversation.

She also wished that the suitcase-bomb episode had given her confidence in NEST's ability to find a nuke if all else failed. But she knew better. During the search the NEST scientists hadn't tried to hide their limitations. Despite their equipment, they had little chance of locating a bomb in a blind search. They faced an almost impossible problem: plutonium and uranium are only moderately radioactive until they detonate. And cities are filled with radioactive hot spots: X-ray machines in dentists' offices; CAT scanners in hospitals; pacemakers, which are powered by minuscule amounts of plutonium. Even freshly cut granite emits enough radiation to cause false alarms.

Three days into the suitcase-bomb search, Stan Kapur, a chubby physicist from Los Alamos who threatened to take Exley to dinner whenever he came to Washington, had said something that Exley still remembered. During a meeting, someone, she couldn't remember who, had asked about the odds that NEST would find the bomb if it existed.

"Looking for one of these in New York, it's like trying to find a needle in a haystack. A haystack made of needles," Kapur had said. No one had wanted to hear that. But Kapur, who was now leading the NEST team in Albany, had told the truth, Exley thought. Without accurate intelligence, all the physicists on earth couldn't find a bomb. Getting inside the enemy's head was the only way to win.

EXLEY FELT A strange frisson as she looked at photographs of the duffel bag on the floor of D-2471, which was called a locker though it was really about the size of a one-car garage. On the Sunday after Farouk's confession came in, the president had considered ordering Albany evacuated. That step had turned out to be unnecessary after the NEST scientists reported that the trunk inside the bag was too small to hold a nuclear weapon.

After inspecting D-2471 with a pulsed fast neutron scanner and a modified CT scanner, NEST's best guess was that the trunk held about eight pounds of C-4 explosive, packed around two small lead-lined steel cases that contained plutonium or uranium. In other words, the trunk was a miniature dirty bomb, capable of killing hundreds of people around Albany if the wind blew the wrong way. But NEST could not estimate exactly how much radioactive material the bomb held, because its lead linings blocked almost all the alpha and gamma rays the material emitted. Meanwhile, the army's explosive-disposal teams reported that the trunk appeared booby-trapped, wired to detonate if it was moved or opened without the proper key.

After two days of debate, the president decided to leave the bomb where it lay and signed an executive order nationalizing the storage center on the vague grounds of a "national security emergency." Not even the White House Counsel's Office believed the order was legal, and Joey O'Donnell, the owner of Capitol Area Self Storage, had balked at giving up his property. But Kijiuri, the FBI deputy director, had not-so-politely explained to Joey that he had an easy choice. He could be a good American and accept the $1 million the government was offering, twice what the place was worth. Tax-free, too. Or he could protect his constitutional rights by filing a lawsuit and pissing off everyone from the FBI to the president himself. "You just won the lottery, Joey," Kijiuri said. "Take the check and take a vacation. You want us looking at your taxes?"

Joey took the check and a vacation. Even before he signed over the building, a combat engineering team had arrived to reinforce the walls and ceiling around D-2471 with six-inch-thick lead-and-steel plates. By the end of September the entire building would have a new roof and walls thick enough to trap the fallout from an explosion.

ALONG WITH A new ceiling, Capitol Area Self Storage got a new workforce. None of the previous staff complained about being fired; they had all received severance checks bigger than they'd expected. The Delta Force commandos who replaced them were unfailingly polite to customers, though their mid-South accents didn't quite fit in upstate New York. Meanwhile, FBI and CIA technicians engaged in a not-very-subtle competition to see who could install fancier surveillance equipment in the center. Because of the rules preventing the CIA from operating on American soil, the agency should have left the job to the Feebs. But that restriction had been lifted by the presidential order that created Earnest Badger, or so Duto insisted.

The dueling teams of techies had locked up Capitol Area Self Storage tigher than—tighter than any cliché imaginable, Exley thought. Four hundred cameras, heat sensors, and motion detectors had been installed in and around the building. A roach couldn't get within twenty feet of the bomb without setting off silent alarms. And God help the person who opened, asked about, or even looked too long at locker D-2471.

Too bad the Joint Terrorism Task Force had no idea who that person might be. The room had been rented two months earlier by a man who had called himself Laurent Kabila, the name of the late and unlamented former president of the Congo. "Laurent" had paid in advance and in cash for a three-year rental. He hadn't come back since his initial visit. Not surprisingly, neither the locker nor the bag had revealed any fingerprints or traces of DNA. Anyone capable of smuggling nuclear material into the United States was presumably also capable of wearing gloves.

So Duto and Kijiuri had decided that whoever came for the bag would be arrested only if he removed it from the center. Otherwise he would be allowed to leave and would be tracked. Of course, by allowing the courier into D-2471 instead of arresting him immediately, the task force ran the risk that he would blow up the bomb inside the storage center. But if they arrested the courier right away, the trail to the rest of the cell would end. And they desperately needed more information about al Qaeda's operations in the United States. On the other hand, they couldn't risk allowing the bomb outside the center.

Exley understood the decision. As an analyst, she wanted as much information as possible. But if her family lived in Albany, she'd have wanted to try the president for treason if he allowed al Qaeda even an outside shot at taking control of a dirty bomb.

EXLEY HAD RESOLVED to leave the office before dark at least once this week, give herself a chance to get some exercise outside, maybe walk down the Mall. Not today, though. She wanted to read Farouk's transcripts again, cover to cover.

At that moment she realized that something really bad was happening to her. No point in lying to herself. Since coming back from Diego Garcia she had turned a mental corner. She had always been obsessed with her job, but as the stakes rose she was *enjoying* it more, enjoying the chance to see what no one else saw and hear what no one else heard. Even the interrogation—the torture; she'd say the word—of Farouk. Her revulsion had faded all too quickly as she watched Saul at work. He was just so good at breaking Farouk, and part of her enjoyed seeing genius in all its forms.

You're just a cog, the little voice in her head told her. You gave up your life to be a cog. Now you're giving up your morals too. But for once she ignored the voice. Fine, I'm a cog, she thought. But I'm a cog in the most powerful machine in history, a machine that reaches everywhere in the world, that can snap you off a roof in Iraq and make you disappear before anyone knows you're gone, that can see through clouds and hear through walls.

Ugh. What nonsense. What shit. And yet her pride was real. At least now I know how it happens, she thought. I know how power corrupts.

A KNOCK ON her door startled her. She looked up to see Shafer twisting his little body inside her office.

"Ellis. I was just thinking about you."

"Only happy thoughts, I hope."

"Always."

"*Qué pasa?*"

Exley stifled a sigh. Shafer's oldest son had been studying Spanish all summer. Now Shafer had gotten into the act, dropping Spanish phrases at random into his conversations. Every mangled word grated on Exley, reminding her of her distance from her own kids. Plus, as someone who had worked hard to learn three languages, she found Taco Bell–style linguistic ineptitude deeply annoying.

She held up the report. "Wondering if I should sell my apartment. Whether a dirty bomb will hurt property values."

"Probably not," Shafer said. "September eleventh was the best thing that ever happened to Washington real estate."

"You're not supposed to say things like that."

"True though."

And it was. The agency and the Defense Department had added tens of thousands of jobs after the attacks, propelling house prices in the D.C. area into the stratosphere. Another unintended consequence of September 11. Bin Laden surely hadn't expected that he would make government bureaucrats rich when he hit the Pentagon.

"Catch anything on the hundredth reading you didn't see on the first ninety-nine?" Shafer asked. "Anything brilliant?"

"I leave the brilliance to you, Ellis. However . . ." She fell silent, unsure if she wanted to talk about Wells right now.

Patience was not one of Shafer's virtues. "What? What?"

"Tell me something. We fix up customs and immigration. We've got gamma-ray detectors at the ports. We spent, what, ten billion dollars on this stuff last year? So why can you still walk in from Mexico?"

"Is this a rhetorical question? Because you know the answer as well as I do," he said. "We want an open border so Mexicans can come in and do the jobs we're too lazy to do ourselves." He cocked his head. "Now, what were you really going to say? That wasn't it."

"You never let me get away with anything, do you?" Shafer knew her well. She had to give him that.

"Out with it."

"You'll think I'm obsessed."

"You are obsessed. That's why I like you."

"I think this stuff from Farouk proves that Wells told us the truth."

At the mention of Wells's name Shafer wrinkled his nose like he'd stepped in a broken sewer. "John Wells?" Shafer said. "Mr. Invisible? The biggest mistake of my career?"

"He's the first one who told us about Khadri. Farouk confimed it. And Farouk confirmed meeting Wells in Peshawar last spring."

Shafer shook his head. "Great. So where's he been since he ran away five months ago?"

"He didn't run away. He escaped." Because you let him, she didn't say.

"Escaped, ran away, whatever. He's gone. I fear the great Vincent Duto may be right about Mr. Invisible. I don't think al Qaeda trusts John Wells any more than we do."

"Do you ever think about him?" She couldn't help herself now. "What it must be like for him. They don't trust him. We sure don't trust him."

"He knew what he was getting into when he signed up."

"He couldn't have expected to be undercover this long. Nobody could. I mean, he's got to be the loneliest guy in the world." She remembered what Wells had said when he'd called that night: *"I don't know how much longer I can do this."*

The disgusted expression on Shafer's face brought her back to reality. "I couldn't care less how lonely John Wells is, Jennifer. I want some actionable intelligence from him. As in, intelligence upon which we can act."

"What if he's just waiting? Biding his time?"

Shafer sucked in his lip. He leaned into her desk and lowered his voice. "Jennifer, are you trying to tell me something?"

She shook her head. He looked around the office. "Do you want to have this conversation somewhere else?"

"No." She was sorry she had brought Wells up.

"Then let's move on to a happier topic," Shafer said. "Why did Khadri tell Farouk where the bomb was hidden?"

"Why wouldn't he? Farouk knows more about nukes than the rest of al Qaeda put together. He'll probably get brought over to put it together."

"But it's already together, right?" Shafer said. "It's sitting in that locker waiting to get picked up."

Exley felt very dumb. "So al Qaeda—"

"Has at least one other person who knows how to play with plutonium."

"Then why'd Khadri tell Farouk where it is? That's a terrible operational breach."

"Maybe Farouk isn't the only one who knows," he said, thinking out loud. "Maybe Khadri wants to be sure the bomb won't rot in the locker if we catch him."

"He can encrypt that info a hundred ways. Telling other people is the least secure system of all. It's not logical."

"Whoever built that bomb is logical as hell."

"Interesting choice of words."

"You want to joke around, fine. I have things to do." Shafer began to walk out.

"Ellis, relax. I'm sorry."

He stopped. "I just hate things that don't make sense," he said. "And this doesn't. This guy Khadri is playing with us."

"There's something else," Exley said. "The bomb's too small."

"It's all they have."

"All the plutonium, maybe. C-4's easy to find. Why not build something bigger? This thing will kill fewer people than a truck bomb."

"Maybe it's for an assassination," Shafer said. "Put it in the Waldorf during a fund-raiser for POTUS." For reasons Exley had never understood, everyone in Washington insisted on using the term POTUS—which stood for "President of the United States"—instead of just calling him the president.

"If it's a target like that, why bother with a dirty bomb? Use a stand-alone package of C-4 and be done with it. Dead is dead, right?"

Shafer frowned and tugged at his hair. Exley wished he wouldn't. One day he was going to pull off a chunk of scalp.

Finally he nodded. "Dead is dead. Right. No need for plutonium in a bomb this small. So what's he doing?"

"Maybe he made a mistake."

Shafer shook his head violently. "He's too smart to make mistakes," Shafer said. "I think he doesn't like anyone to know what he's doing. Not even his own guys."

"He's a control freak."

"Keeps his secrets as tight as he can. He knows his guys are vulnerable, that we can catch anybody the way we caught Farouk."

"Then why'd he tell Farouk?"

"I asked you first, Jennifer."

And Shafer walked out, leaving her with another unanswerable question.

CIGARETTE IN HAND, Tony DiFerri walked into the front office of Capitol Area Self Storage, an unprepossessing room with yellow walls, black plastic chairs, and a vending machine that offered bags of stale Doritos. Major Rick Harris, a trim black man, sat behind the counter, doing his best to look bored as he played solitaire on the old Dell PC where Joey O'Donnell had kept the center's records.

"Sir, there's no smoking in here," Harris said. His sister had died of lung cancer and one of his kids had asthma.

"Sure," DiFerri mumbled, grinding out the half-finished Marlboro Light under his heel.

"Can I help you?"

"Yeah," DiFerri said. "I'm looking for locker D-2471."

Harris nearly fell off his chair. This wasn't the guy he'd expected. Somehow he kept his face straight. "Sure. That's the second floor, off the main hallway toward the back. I can show you."

"I can find it myself."

"No problem. Lemme see your key."

Sure enough, DiFerri held up the key. D-2471. Harris pushed the green button, unlocking the steel grate that separated the office from the storage area. A few seconds later DiFerri was inside. Harris waited until he was out of sight, then clicked on the tiny microphone wired to his chest.

"Code Blue active," he said. "Repeat, Code Blue. *This is not a drill.* Bogey a white male, medium height, white T-shirt, overweight, approximately forty years old."

Almost involuntarily, the major found himself looking at the box under the counter that hid his radiological protective suit.

DIFERRI LUMBERED UP the stairs, wheezing as he pushed open the door to the second floor. He didn't have much wind. Or much time. His new friend Bokar had told him he needed to figure out what was inside the bag and report back by four-thirty P.M.

"I just check it and tell you what's inside?" DiFerri had asked.

"Precisely."

"It's not drugs or nothing illegal."

"No. Nothing illegal."

"That don't sound too hard. And then—"

"I shall give you another fifty dollars and explain your next task."

DiFerri didn't totally understand this game, but he figured if he didn't like what he saw in the bag he would just quit. Even if the whole thing was some joke, he'd already gotten fifty bucks. These Hollywood guys had plenty of cash, for sure. Besides, nothing this interesting had happened to him since the first time he got laid, and that was a long time ago. So after he caught his breath DiFerri started moving again, walking down the halls of the storage center, looking for D-2471.

EXLEY'S PHONE RANG. "Get over to the sports bar," Shafer said. "Something's up in Albany."

Encrypted satellite links gave the agency a real-time view of the storage center, ending up in an auditorium-sized room with three hundred flat-panel televisions, each capable of showing a different satellite feed. Officially, the room was known as the JTTF Secure Communications Presentation Center. But when Duto caught one of the center's technicians watching his beloved Miami Dolphins in a corner on a sleepy Sunday night, Shafer started calling the place the sports bar. The name stuck.

The sports bar was a ten-minute walk from Exley's office. Or a five-minute run. She ran.

DIFERRI MADE A couple of wrong turns before he found D-2471, near the northeast corner of the storage center's second floor. He paused in front of the locker, then slipped his key in, wondering what he'd see. Maybe there'd be a camera crew. Maybe the bag would be filled with money, crisp hundreds in packets like in the movies. Or maybe his key wouldn't work at all.

But the door opened easily, and when DiFerri turned on the overhead light he saw nothing but the oversized canvas bag that Bokar had told him to expect. He took a tentative step into the room and closed the door. It shut behind him solidly, and he wondered if he had locked himself in. But when he checked the handle the door swung open smoothly, and the corridor outside looked just as it had a few seconds before. DiFerri closed the door again, wondering why he felt creeped out. He'd watched *Fear Factor* plenty of times. Those stunts were weird. This was just a bag in a locker.

On his way to the locker DiFerri had seen a half dozen signs warning against smoking, but he didn't see one in here. Screw that guy at the front desk. He tapped a cigarette into his palm and lit up.

ONLY ABOUT A handful of civilians had been inside the storage center when the man with the key came in. They were not evacuated; Duto and Kijiuri had specified that the center should operate normally unless someone tried to remove the bag. Nor did the commandos approach D-2471. But everyone in the center was being shadowed. If the bomb detonated, the commandos would evacuate the civilians from the building, by force if necessary, and take them to a temporary decontamination center NEST had set up a mile away. There they would be checked for radiation exposure.

The computer simulations that NEST had run suggested a 70 percent probability that no civilian would be exposed to harmful levels of radioactivity, as long as everyone escaped the building within three minutes of an explosion. Of course, those odds left a 30 percent chance of harmful exposure, but that couldn't be helped.

AT THE SPORTS bar Exley found a dozen agency officials watching the monitors. Inside the locker a perplexed-looking white man puffed on a cigarette and nudged the canvas bag with his foot.

"This guy?" she said to Shafer. The guy looked like a mechanic, maybe an out-of-work trucker. Anything but a terrorist.

"You know as much as I do."

"What about the NSA?" The National Security Agency had recognition software that could match facial photographs with a database of suspected al Qaeda members.

"Nothing there. He's probably just a Dixie cup," Shafer said. "Hired in case we're watching."

"Charming term," Exley said. "Dixie cup" was agency jargon for someone disposable, someone who could be arrested or killed without consequence. "I don't get it," she said. "If they went to so much trouble to bring the stuff in, why are they treating it like this?"

On-screen, the guy in D-2471 poked at the bag, then squatted beside it.

"We're so screwed," Shafer said.

She knew exactly what he was thinking. The agency and the FBI were in an impossible position. The guy in the locker probably had no idea what he was playing with. Then again, he had the key. He might be a genuine al Qaeda operative, a true believer who happened to look like a trucker. Until they arrested him, they wouldn't know. They couldn't move too quickly or they might blow the operation. But if they moved too slowly, they risked letting the guy blow himself up, especially if he was a dupe.

Exley felt the way she had when she was seventeen and trying to learn to drive a stick. Lay off the gas, drop the clutch, slip the transmission into gear. Easy.

Only she couldn't do it. She had burned out the clutch on her brother's old Willys Jeep. Boy, had that day been awful. Worse because her brother was so locked up fighting his own demons that he hardly paid attention when she told him what she'd done.

She brought her attention back to the screen. The guy was still playing with the bag. "So . . . we let him open it?" she said to Shafer.

"If you've got a better idea now would be a good time to share."

She didn't.

DIFERRI STUBBED OUT his cigarette on the locker's concrete floor. Time to get to work. He cautiously opened the big canvas bag, pulling down its black plastic zipper to reveal the smooth metal top of the aluminum trunk inside.

He tried to lift the trunk out of the bag. It was heavier than he had expected. His grip slipped. He grunted and let go, and the trunk thudded against the floor and banged into his knee.

"Dammit," he yelped. The complaint echoed in the locker, and again he considered leaving, telling Bokar that he couldn't open the trunk. No. He'd always wanted to be on TV, and he wasn't going to blow this chance.

He tried again, turning the trunk on its side. He found a digital lock with a numeric pad instead of a keyhole. Just as Bokar had promised. The lock's red LCD flashed the time: 15:47:05 . . . 15:47:06. . . . Shit. He had less than an hour to get downtown. As Bokar had told him to do, he tapped the pound key on the pad three times. The clock disappeared, replaced by a blinking row of dashes. DiFerri pulled his battered wallet out of his pocket and found the piece of paper with the code that Bokar had given him. 4308512112-9447563-01072884.

DiFerri carefully punched the numbers into the pad. By the time he finished he was sweating, and not from the heat in the airless room. He hoped he had gotten the code right. He punched the pound key three times, as he'd been told. The code disappeared, replaced now by a timer.

10 . . . 9 . . . 8 . . . 7 . . .

Holy shit.

6 . . . 5 . . . 4 . . . 3 . . . 2 . . . 1 . . .

He lumbered to his feet and tried to back away.

LIKE EVERYONE ELSE watching in Langley, Exley could see exactly what was happening inside D-2471. The cameras were good enough to catch the terror on the guy's face as he stepped backward. Then the bomb blew. The explosion echoed inside the communications center, and the monitors went black.

The room was silent. Exley could not stop replaying the panicked look she had just seen. He was no terrorist, that guy. He didn't belong in that locker. She had just watched an innocent man die. For the first time in history, a radioactive weapon had exploded on American soil. And she and everyone in this room had allowed it. Their mistakes had no end. Shafer's joke about the Dixie cup seemed unimaginably callous now.

Then the ringing of a phone, and another and another, broke the silence. The communications center began humming like a casino on New Year's Eve, technicians shouting to the commandos inside the center. The mission wasn't over. The Delta units and the Albany police had to evacuate everyone within a quarter mile while NEST's scientists determined how much radiation the dirty bomb had released. Plus, they would have to figure out who the guy in the locker had been and track his movements and accomplices as far back as they could. Though Exley had little doubt that the trail—if they could trace it at all—would eventually lead back to one Omar Khadri.

Exley felt a murderous rage replace her shame. In all her years at the CIA she had never been so angry. She knew that personalizing these battles didn't help win them, but she couldn't stop herself. This man Khadri was toying with them and killing Americans for sport. He had to be destroyed. "Whatever it takes," she said to herself under her breath.

Shafer heard her. "Yes," he said.

KHADRI WAS BRUSHING his teeth in his motel room in Kingston when he heard the first television bulletin.

"This is Scott Yorne with breaking news from Channel 2, your capital area news leader. The Albany Police Department is evacuating parts of western Albany following an explosion in a storage center on Central Avenue. Authorities are advising everyone else in the region to stay inside for at least two hours. So far, police have been tight-lipped about the nature of the explosion, but they promise us more information as soon as possible . . ."

So Farouk had told the Americans about the bomb, Khadri thought. Otherwise they wouldn't be evacuating the city. They had been watching the locker and knew what it held. Or thought they did, anyway. They would be surprised when they got inside. Khadri smiled briefly as he looked at his reflection in the bathroom mirror. His precautions had been wise.

But his smile faded as he thought about Farouk's treachery. He had to assume that Farouk had told the Americans everything. At least one cell in Pakistan was blown. And probably all the nuclear techs that Farouk had recruited. Khadri had carefully compartmentalized his operations. He might be able to cut off the blown cells in time to save his other operatives in Pakistan. But he couldn't escape the fact that Farouk's capture was a major setback.

Pressure constricted Khadri's chest. He reminded himself that he had no real reason to worry. The bomb had surely killed that fool DiFerri. Still, he wanted to get as far from Albany as possible.

He trotted into the motel bedroom and began tossing clothes into his suitcase. Then he stopped. In control, he thought. Always in control. He emptied the suitcase onto the bed and began repacking, folding his clothes neatly.

WITHIN AN HOUR, NEST scientists wearing radiological protective suits were inside locker D-2471, trying not to gag as they picked their way around the pieces of Tony DiFerri scattered around the room.

What they found puzzled them. Or, more accurately, what they didn't find. Instead of the radioactive furnace they had expected, their detectors picked up only low levels of alpha rays and practically no gamma rays. No plutonium-239. No highly enriched uranium. No cesium-137 or cobalt-57. Instead the NEST team detected traces of plutonium-238, an isotope of plutonium that was practically safe enough to eat, as well as a few grams of low-enriched uranium. Those had apparently accounted for the traces of radiation they had found when they first scanned the locker. Nor did the area show any signs of biological or chemical contamination. No anthrax, no smallpox, no sarin, no VX.

This dirty bomb looked clean after all.

AT LANGLEY THE mood became slightly less grim when the news came in. After a consultation with the White House, Duto and Kijiuri decided to call off the evacuation and blame the local police for overreacting. With the promise of $35 million in extra federal aid, the Albany mayor and police chief agreed to take the heat. The explosion would be classified as conventional, which was close enough if not quite true, and Capitol Area Self Storage would remain the property of the federal government for the indefinite future. In twenty-four hours the national media would forget the bomb, and in a week it would be down to a paragraph even in the local papers. People blew themselves up all the time in America. In other words, nobody in the world except Tony DiFerri would have to know just how badly the agency and the Feebs had screwed up. That was the good news.

"The bad news," Shafer said to Exley, "is that we're back where we started. Nuclear material in the United States, and we have no idea where it is."

It was nearly two A.M., and they were back in her office. They had spent the last few hours on frantic conference calls that reached from the White House to Albany to Langley to Nellis A.F.B. and even Diego Garcia. The calls had been full of bureaucratic ass covering, but along the way the principals had found a few minutes to discuss what had happened in Albany, and what it might mean. They were now sorting through three possibilities, none entirely satisfactory.

The first was that Dmitri the Russian physicist had duped Farouk Khan, selling him the wrong plutonium isotope, atomic junk instead of the treasure he'd been promised. The White House had seized on this theory. After all, the president officially viewed al Qaeda as weakened and on the defensive, hardly worthy of attention compared to Iran and other troublemakers. The fact that the group had supposedly smuggled a dirty bomb onto American soil didn't square with this view, and so the White House was looking for evidence to discredit the bomb.

Maybe the optimists at 1600 Pennsylvania were right, Exley thought. The only problem with their theory was that Farouk was a trained physicist who had explained to Saul exactly how he had tested the material he had bought.

A second possibility was that Farouk had simply lied to Saul about the amount of radioactive material he had bought from Dmitri, hoping—as detainees sometimes did—to make himself seem more important than he was. The White House liked this theory too. In any case, it could be checked relatively easily. Farouk had already been thrown back into the hole. If he had lied they would know soon enough. Exley didn't even want to imagine what Saul did to people who tried to deceive him.

Then there was the third theory, the one the White House didn't like. The theory that Farouk hadn't lied to Saul about where the bomb was hidden. Not intentionally, anyway. The theory that someone else had lied to Farouk. Someone—call him Omar Khadri—had gone to the trouble to build a fake dirty bomb, maybe more than one. And why would Khadri do that? Both to hide the location of the real bomb and as a counterintel trap, so he could know whether the United States had compromised his operatives.

If the third theory was right, Farouk would have nothing more to tell them, no matter what Saul did. Which meant the trail to the bomb was dead. Worst of all, because the JTTF had tipped its hand by beginning the evacuation after the explosion, Khadri now knew that they had been watching the storage center.

Which meant that he knew that Farouk had been flipped, and that the United States government was aware that al Qaeda had a dirty bomb on American soil. Which made him more likely to blow it quickly.

No, the third theory wasn't comforting at all.

Shafer and Exley both believed it completely.

11

WELLS RAISED THE Glock and lined up his target.

With the pistol steady he squeezed the trigger. The Glock spoke to him the only way it knew, a short sharp bark. The slide popped back, ejecting a shell, and the weapon kicked in his hands as if it were angry he had fired. Wells controlled the recoil and squeezed the trigger again. And again. And again. And again, lower this time.

Finally he put the pistol down and looked downrange. Four holes punctured the center of the target, less than an inch from the bull's-eye. The fifth hole was six inches below, and slightly right. Not bad for fifty feet.

Since getting Khadri's message, Wells had practiced his shooting at American Classic Marksman, a little firing range in a strip mall in Norcross, a few miles from his apartment. He had forgotten how much he enjoyed having a pistol in his hands. He didn't think of the men he had killed; instead he remembered the hunting trips he had taken each fall with his dad, Herbert.

Once a year they had hiked into the Montana mountains, seeking deer and elk. Wells could almost smell the rich, dark coffee that they brewed each morning, hear the bacon bubbling in their frying pan. He hadn't eaten bacon since he'd converted. Even now he missed the taste. He and his father walked deep into the mountains, looking for a stand where they could wait in silence for the perfect shot. And the shot had to be perfect, since Herbert allowed Wells to target only one buck each season; if he missed he went home empty-handed. No sense in making the hunt too easy, Dad said.

In their third season, Wells finally bagged a whitetail. He could still remember how his pulse had quickened when he saw his shot ring true. The deer had reared back, then listed to the right and fallen. A clean kill. Before Wells had pulled the trigger he had wondered whether killing the buck would bother him. But since that moment he had never been afraid to shoot. He couldn't pretend he hated killing. Animals killed and animals died; that was the natural order.

WELLS PUT ASIDE the Glock and picked up the Makarov that he had bought at a gun show in Chamblee two weeks before. The pistol was identical to the one he had left behind in the hut on the day he'd first met Khadri. As he held it, unexpected memories from the North-West Frontier filled him: the thick stench of raw sewage on summer days; a tiny girl in a full black burqa holding her father's hand as he led her through the market in Akora Khatak; the not-quite-empty bottle of Johnnie Walker Black that he had found one night outside the mosque, and the shock of the whiskey's pungent aroma when he uncapped the bottle and poured it away.

He almost couldn't believe that he'd left Pakistan just six months ago. Usually he didn't think much about the place or Sheikh Gul or Naji and the other jihadis he'd known there. They seemed to belong to another life. Maybe it was the way he had left, disappearing so quickly. Or maybe forgetting the frontier was easy because living there had been so hard. Maybe he just didn't want to know what he would see if he looked back.

He was looking ahead now, getting ready for whatever was coming next. Besides the pistols, he had picked up an assault rifle at the show, a Chinese-made knockoff of an AK-47. But that gun stayed in his apartment, since he had illegally modified it from semiautomatic to full auto.

For close-in work he had bought an old 12-gauge shotgun, worn but mechanically perfect, and sawed the barrels down so far that the shotgun was now only a couple of inches longer than the Glock. He had to leave the 12-gauge at home too. Sawed-off shotguns were illegal too. And for good reason. Beyond ten feet they were worthless, but up close they were as lethal as a rocket-propelled grenade. With luck they could take out two or three men with one pull of the trigger.

Getting silencers had proved more complicated. The dealers at the Chamblee show didn't like talking about them, and Wells didn't want to push too hard and wind up buying one from an ATF agent. But with the help of a manual he'd bought at the show, he'd built one in his apartment. He had no illusions about how long it would last, and it wasn't great for accuracy. But it did quiet down the Makarov a little.

In any case, he didn't plan to use the silencer unless he had no choice. He preferred knives when silence was a necessity. He had bought a couple of those too, along with holsters, smoke grenades, and pepper spray, all legal in Georgia. From a store in Macon that advertised itself as "Specializing in Home Defense" he had picked up four police-style walkie-talkies, the hands-free kind that clipped to the shoulder. As well as a bulletproof vest, a flak jacket, and a gas mask in case he had to play defense. A trip to an army-navy surplus store had rewarded him with a green camo uniform, and for night work a black ski mask, black sweatpants, a black hood, and black leather gloves.

At a hospital supply store near Atlanta General, he had put together an emergency medicine kit: Ace bandages, Betadine, clotting agent, gauze dressings, latex gloves, scalpels, splints, sterile solution, surgical scissors, syringes. Even Cipro, Demerol, and Vicodin, ordered from an Internet pharmacy in Costa Rica. His Delta training had included advanced battlefield medicine, and during the fighting in Chechnya Wells had set bones and treated shrapnel wounds. He had bought a couple of books on emergency medicine to refresh himself.

He was getting ready, all right. He only wished he knew what for.

Wells looked at the Makarov in his hand, feeling the metal stubble of its grip. The Makarov was smaller and lighter than the Glock and sometimes got lost in his palm. Still, Wells liked having a pistol he could slip into his waistband. He pulled back the Makarov's slide, chambering a round, and sighted the target, imagining Khadri's face at its center.

The first shot pulled right about three inches. The Makarov just wasn't as smooth as the Glock. Wells sighted again. This time he was straight but high. Wells exhaled and stood utterly still, visualizing the bullet's path, seeing it plow into Khadri's cheek, just under the eye, blood trickling out, Khadri crumpling as quickly as gravity could pull him down. He squeezed the trigger. Bull's-eye.

He practiced for another half hour, then unloaded the pistols and slipped them into their carrying cases. On his way out, he bought oil and a chamois cloth. He didn't think they needed to be cleaned, but he wanted to break them down anyway, just to be sure.

"Good shooting today?" This from the owner, a tall, bearded guy named Randall.

"Just getting back into it."

Randall smiled. "Look like a pro to me."

BACK AT HIS apartment Wells broke apart the pistols and wiped them down. He whetted his knives until their blades seemed ready to bleed. Finally he made himself stop. Khadri—or his men—were due to arrive tomorrow at Hartsfield, and Wells couldn't ever remember feeling so anxious before a mission. He didn't care if he died, but he could not fail. *He could not fail.* He had failed to stop September 11, failed to stop the Los Angeles bombings. Not this time.

He had kept to himself since his ill-fated night out with Nicole, the bartender from the Rusty Nail. He had even quit working as a day laborer to get ready for Khadri. Money wasn't a problem; even after buying the guns and the gear, he had a couple of thousand dollars left from his stash. As far as he knew, Nicole had never called the cops; he had swung by the Kermex lot to check if anyone was looking for him, but nobody was. He wondered sometimes if Nicole had gotten back together with her ex-boyfriend. If they had, Wells figured he deserved the credit.

He was praying five times a day again too, examining the Koran with the intensity he had shown during his years on the frontier. In truth, his faith was weak. But he couldn't let Khadri see any cracks in his fervor. He wanted to be sure he had recovered the daily rhythm of the religion by the time his fellow jihadis arrived.

Mainly he worked through possible scenarios: What if Khadri's carrying a vial of smallpox? What if he says Qaeda has a nuclear weapon but won't say where? What if he comes with a dozen other men? Do I kill him on the spot? Try to play along with him so he'll open up? Turn him over to the agency? Wells wished he could talk things through with Exley. But he knew that calling her would only get her in trouble. When he had more information for her he'd reach out. He needed to be ready, because the show was about to start. Khadri's style seemed to be to wait, then move fast. He struck Wells as a man who would share information only at the last moment. When they'd met in Peshawar Khadri hadn't even hinted at the Los Angeles bombings. But at some point he would have to explain his plans, and then Wells would have a chance to stop him.

WELLS DIDN'T EXPECT to sleep that night. But he did, a dreamless sleep, and when his alarm buzzed he came alert immediately, just as he had on those crisp fall mornings in Montana, hunting beside his father. He brewed himself a pot of coffee and bowed his head before Allah. Then he strapped the stiletto to his leg and headed for Hartsfield, the giant airport on Atlanta's southwest edge.

The morning traffic on 285 was even worse than he'd expected, but he had given himself plenty of time. He clicked on the pickup's radio. Lately he had amused himself by listening to WATK, a crackly right-wing station far up the AM dial whose morning host, Bob Lavelle, was fond of conspiracy theories. For the last week Lavelle had talked about nothing but the explosion in Albany, the one that everyone else had already forgotten.

"Then why'd they evacuate the city?" Lavelle said. "I'm telling you, there's a lot we don't know about this." Lavelle's voice rose. "Listen to me for a minute. Stop what you're doing. Put down that liberal newspaper. Think for yourself for once. You don't start evacuating people because some two-bit loser blows himself to bits in a storage locker. That doesn't make sense—"

Wells turned the volume down. Lavelle was wrong about a lot of things—Wells believed that the moon landing had happened—but the guy was right about Albany. What had happened there made no sense. Wells figured the agency or the FBI had been watching the locker for a biological or chemical weapon. But Wells couldn't understand why they had let anyone into the locker at all. Khadri could probably fill in the missing pieces, but Wells didn't plan to ask.

Lavelle was still yelling as Wells flicked back down the dial. No point in having to explain to Khadri why he was listening to WATK, whose hosts hated Muslims even more than they disliked the Feds.

AT HARTSFIELD WELLS left the knife inside the truck; it could cause him trouble at a security checkpoint. He hadn't been inside an airport since the spring, and he didn't like being in this one. There were probably more cops and federal agents here than anywhere else in Georgia. His old friends at Langley could easily have sent a BOLO—be on the lookout—alert for him to the Transportation Security Administration.

In case they had, he had done his best to change his looks. He didn't put much stock in elaborate disguises, which usually attracted attention rather than deflected it. But he had grown out his hair since the spring, and today he was wearing a Red Sox cap and wire-rim glasses with clear lenses. As long as he didn't do anything dumb, he ought to be fine. The TSA officers were overwhelmed and mainly worried about keeping the lines moving. To protect himself further, he had told Khadri that he would wait in Hartsfield's main concourse instead of the terminal, which would have required him to go through a checkpoint. After a few minutes of pacing the halls, he settled down with a *Journal-Constitution* and tried to read about the Braves' latest win—six in a row—but he couldn't focus.

Eventually he gave up and let his mind roam. It settled on Exley. At this hour she was probably in her office. He had never seen where she worked, but he could picture it. She would try hard to keep her desk neat, but it would still be messy, thick with unclassified reports and maps and transcripts. In her safe she would have photocopies of classified documents—she wouldn't get the originals. She would have pictures of her kids and maybe some drawings they had made for her. He hoped so.

She wasn't married anymore. If she had a boyfriend, a lover, she might have a picture of him. But Wells was sure it would be discreet. She wasn't the type to bring her life into the office. Did she bring the office home? Nearly everyone at the agency was married. He couldn't picture her having some awful workplace affair, the kind that the secretaries know will happen even before it starts and the bosses figure out in a week. The kind that inevitably ends with the husband back at home with wife and kids. Exley was smarter than that. Had to be. But Wells knew better than anyone that loneliness in large doses could twist people so badly that eventually even they couldn't recognize themselves.

So did she have a lover? A boyfriend? After the way she'd opened up to him in the Jeep he couldn't imagine she was seriously involved with another man. Nobody lived with her, anyway. When he had called her that morning a month ago, she had picked up. And she hadn't sounded surprised. As if she had been waiting for his call. As if she had been thinking about him as much as he'd been thinking about her. He closed his eyes and imagined her, alone in her bed, sleeping nude beneath a thin cotton sheet, her windows open to the humid Washington night and a fan spinning slowly overhead. The vision made him shiver, and for a moment he could almost touch her.

Wells opened his eyes and looked at his watch. Eleven-forty. In five minutes Khadri would arrive on Delta flight 561 from Detroit.

THE FLIGHT CAME in on time. But Khadri wasn't on it.

The man who stepped off the escalator was younger, early thirties, tall, clean-shaven, wearing slacks and a loose-fitting polo shirt. He couldn't do anything about his olive skin and wiry black hair, but otherwise he blended nicely with the crowd of midday business travelers. Right down to his laptop. A professional. He glanced around, saw the Atlanta Jazz Festival T-shirt that Wells had promised to wear in his e-mail—a simple, foolproof way to make contact in public—and walked straight over.

"You must be Jack," the man said in clean, soft English with just a hint of a Saudi accent. "I'm Thomas."

The names were right. Khadri might not be here, but this was his man. "Good to meet you," Wells said. "How was the weather in Detroit?" A simple question, just to confirm what he already knew.

"Cloudy last night but clear this morning."

Wells extended his hand, and they shook.

THEY WERE SILENT until Wells swung onto 285, heading east, back toward his apartment. The man who called himself Thomas leaned forward to peek at the right side mirror, checking for tails. "Can you drive faster, in the left lane?" Thomas said. Wells did.

A few minutes later Thomas told him to move right and slow down. Then to speed up. Wells followed every instruction.

"Where do you live?" Thomas said as they reached the intersection of 285 and I-20.

"Doraville. Northeastern Atlanta. About fifteen miles. Should be there in twenty minutes."

"Where exactly?"

"The address?"

"Yes."

Wells told him.

"We're not going to your apartment. Get off here and go west on Interstate 20."

"Toward downtown."

"Yes." Thomas said nothing more. And Wells knew his wait wasn't over yet.

WELLS PULLED INTO the parking lot at a beat-up Denny's in southwest Atlanta. He'd been driving for hours, making endless loops on the highways that scissored the city. Now they were back practically where they had started, a couple of miles from the edge of Hartsfield. Planes flew low overhead, on their approach to the airport. Wells fought down his rising impatience, telling himself that a few more hours wouldn't matter.

Wells parked, and Thomas led him to the end of the lot, where a man stood beside a green Chevy Lumina. He was shorter than Thomas and dressed casually, jeans and a Falcons T-shirt.

"This is Sami," Thomas said. He hugged Sami and murmured something into his ear.

"Sami." Wells put out his hand. Sami let it hang in the air until Wells finally pulled it back.

"Give him your keys." Thomas didn't smile.

Without a word Wells flicked his keys to Sami, who caught them neatly and turned for Wells's pickup. Thomas got into the Lumina, indicating with a wave that Wells should follow.

Wells stayed cool as he watched his Ford disappear from the parking lot. These men were taking all this trouble for a reason. Khadri was putting him through one last test before finally lowering the drawbridge and letting him into the castle. Or so he hoped.

Again they drove aimlessly. The Chevy's little digital clock passed five P.M., and the traffic began to thicken. But Thomas showed no impatience. Wells figured he was giving Sami time to search the apartment. Fine. Let them play this game. No matter how hard they looked they couldn't go deep enough to break his cover.

Finally Thomas's cell phone trilled. He picked up. *"Nam."* He hung up and slipped the phone into his pocket.

"It's clean," Wells said.

"What is?"

"My apartment. Except for the guns. And those are for us."

For the first time Thomas smiled. "That's what Sami said."

THEY ROLLED PAST Turner Field and the golden dome of the Georgia capitol, until Thomas turned right onto Fourteenth Street, into the center of a neighborhood called Midtown, a jumble of tall office towers and low-rise apartment buildings. Thomas found a garage and circled up the ramps, nodding to himself as the floors emptied. Finally he parked on the top floor, in the middle of a sea of empty asphalt.

"Out."

"Thomas," Wells said. "Are we friends?" He was speaking Arabic now, enjoying the smooth feel of the words. Aside from prayers, he hadn't spoken the language since Pakistan.

"I think so," Thomas said, also in Arabic. "We're making sure."

"Then will you tell me your real name?"

"Qais."

"Qais. Don't you think I know there's a gun under the seat? Don't you think I could take it if I wanted?" Wells smiled tightly at Qais. I'm a professional too, he didn't say. Give me a little respect.

Qais showed no surprise. "You could try."

Wells couldn't help liking the guy's style. Neither of them said anything else. Wells slid out, and sure enough, Qais locked the doors and reached under the driver's seat, pulling out a little .22. He tucked the gun under his shirt and got out.

"Put your hands on the hood and spread your legs," he said to Wells, back in English now. He frisked Wells efficiently. "Good."

"Were you a cop in a past life?"

"Something like that. Let's go. Somebody's waiting. You'll be glad to see him."

THE SUN HAD slipped behind the office towers to their west by the time they left the garage. Qais moved easily now, comfortable that they weren't being tailed. In a few minutes they reached Piedmont Park, a one-hundred-acre expanse of grass and trees around an artificial lake. On the hilly lawn at the park's edge, shirtless college students tossed a Frisbee around in the twilight. Joggers in sports bras made their way along a path at the bottom of the hill. Beyond them a man sat alone on a bench, quietly reading The New York Times.

Khadri.

He stood as Wells and Qais walked toward him, folding the paper under his arm. He was one hundred yards away now, fifty, twenty-five, ten. And then he was close enough to touch. Kill him now, Wells told himself. Drop him and break his neck. Or take the gun from Qais and shoot them both.

Instead Wells merely smiled and held out his hand, as Khadri had at their initial meeting. Wells thought he could probably take Qais, but he couldn't be certain of getting them both. Khadri might have a gun too. Again he remembered those hunts growing up. He would have only one shot at Khadri. He had to be sure.

To Wells's surprise Khadri ignored his outstretched hand and hugged him instead, gripping him close, running his hands down Wells's back in a quick frisk.

He let go of Wells and stepped back. "Jalal." No one had called Wells that name since Peshawar. *"Salaam alaikum."*

"Alaikum salaam."

"You look different."

"I, ah—I grew out my hair. To blend in, you know."

Khadri looked at Wells's shirt. "Did you go to the jazz festival?"

His perfect English accent grated on Wells's ears. "For a couple of hours. They have it in this park, over there." He pointed west.

"You like jazz?"

Wells shrugged. "Sure. It was fun. It was something to do."

"While you waited?"

"While I waited."

"And Qais? No problems at the airport?"

Qais merely shook his head. He had retreated a couple of steps, but his hand was on his hip, casually, a few inches from his pistol.

"Shall we stroll, Jalal? Such a nice evening."

They walked slowly along the jogging path, Qais a few steps behind, out of earshot.

"It's pretty, this place," Khadri said. "I read it was designed by the sons of the man who built Central Park in New York. But Central Park is much bigger."

Wells wished he knew if Khadri was probing for something or just thinking out loud.

"You passed through New York on your way here, Jalal."

"Yes."

"What did you think?"

"New York? I thought it was one big target," Wells said truthfully. He wanted to grab Khadri's neck and squeeze until the man's face turned gray and his eyes rolled back in his head.

"Didn't you think it was exciting? Times Square?"

"Sure. It was exciting."

"But not your kind of place."

"I grew up in Montana, Omar. I had mountains to myself."

"How about this?"

"It's pretty, like you said." Khadri was just talking, Wells realized. Chatting about America. Even he must need a break some-times.

"It's strange that some places are so—pretty—and others so awful, isn't it, Jalal? Your people, they live so easily."

"Too easily," Wells said. "They ought to notice the world's mis-ery. So much ignorance is evil. And they're not my people."

"You always say the right thing, Jalal. Just right. You always sound like one of us."

This was the moment, Wells knew. If he couldn't convince Khadri now he never would. "Because I am. I don't know what else to say. Whatever you ask, I'll do."

Khadri stopped walking and turned toward Wells. "I want to trust you, Jalal. Otherwise I wouldn't have come here. Do you be-lieve that?"

"Yes."

"You can be incredibly valuable to me, to us. We have big jobs ahead. And I have so few good men—" Khadri broke off. He had problems he didn't want to reveal, Wells thought.

"In any case," Khadri went on. "You are unique. You fit in here"—Khadri waved his hand at the city around them—"in a way that I never will, Qais never will. It is a great gift."

"Yes."

"You've never given us reason to doubt you. In Chechnya, in Afghanistan, in Pakistan."

"I've always tried to do what's necessary."

"And yet. I don't understand you, Jalal. I have talked about you with the sheikh himself. And after we sent you here, I asked the men who knew you on the frontier about you. For all those years you studied and prayed and trained. You were never impatient—"

"I was impatient," Wells said.

"If you were you never let anyone see it. You never complained. You never took a drink or a smoke or had a woman. The perfect sol-dier. But I see that discipline and it frightens me. I wonder, how do I know whether you are fighting for us—or them?"

Wells gripped Khadri's arm, pulling the smaller man toward him. Qais strode toward them, but Khadri waved him off.

"Omar. I'm not the perfect soldier. The men who died in Los Angeles, who sacrifice themselves in Iraq every day. The martyrs. They are. All I've done is wait. I only want the chance to serve. And if I must I'll wait forever—"

Wells stopped. He had made his point. No need to go further. He let Khadri go, but Khadri did not step away. Instead he leaned toward Wells, looking up into Wells's face. Finally he nodded. "You want the chance to serve? Then you will have it."

Wells bowed his head. The drawbridge had dropped. He was in. All the years, all the waiting, they'd finally paid off. Was this how it felt to rise from the dead? "Thank you, Omar."

Khadri tapped his chest. "I must go. Qais will explain the mission. He speaks for me."

"Thank you," Wells said again. *"Allahu akbar."* God is great.

"Allahu akbar."

Khadri walked away, up the hill. He crossed out of the park and disappeared.

"He looks like he knows exactly where he's going," Wells said quietly to Qais.

"He always does."

AT THE GARAGE Sami waited in Wells's pickup.

"Salaam alaikum," Sami said.

"Alaikum salaam."

"So you're with us."

"Inshallah."

Sami smiled and tossed Wells back his keys.

WELLS DROVE THE Ranger, Qais in the passenger seat. Sami followed in the Lumina.

"Where's your hotel?"

"No hotel. We're staying at your apartment."

"The neighbors will wonder."

"We aren't staying long."

Wells waited for something more, but Qais didn't explain further.

"Who trained you, Qais?"

"The Saudi Mukhabarat. And I spent six months at Quantico with your FBI."

"No wonder."

"Thank you."

"So . . ." Wells said in Arabic. "You and Sami didn't come to Atlanta just to see me, did you?"

Qais laughed. "No. Nor just to waste gasoline."

"Then would you like to tell me the mission? Or should I guess?"

"You won't guess." Qais was much more relaxed now that Khadri had given Wells his okay.

"The CDC? Centers for Disease Control?"

"No."

"CNN Center? The Coke building?"

"No. Anyway, Omar likes Coca-Cola. It's all he drinks."

"Me too," Wells said. "The Georgia Dome? Turner Field?"

"I don't even know what those places are," Qais said. "Look, it's only you and me and Sami. And this isn't a martyrdom mission. Omar needs us alive."

"Then . . . it must be something simple. An assassination."

"Very good. Who?"

Wells had no idea. The mayor of Atlanta? A CDC scientist? One of the senators from Georgia? Nobodies. And anybody really important would have a ton of security.

"You're right, Qais. I can't guess."

"You've heard of Howard West? The general?"

Howard West had run the army's black ops and counterterrorism units during the 1990s. Wells had met him once, at a memorial service for a Delta officer who'd died. West had spoken briefly, then disappeared into a helicopter to do whatever it was that three-stars did.

He had retired a few months after that—Wells couldn't remember exactly when. Now he worked as a "consultant." That meant he collected six-figure checks from companies that peddled spy gear. In return, he connected them with his old friends at the Pentagon. He kept a low profile. Wells hadn't even known he lived in Atlanta.

Attacking him was a brilliant way for Qaeda to declare its equality with the United States. You hunt our leaders? We'll hunt yours. And since he was retired, West would have much less security than an active general. But killing West wasn't the big job that Khadri had planned, Wells thought. "Omar needs us alive," Qais had said. The assassination was a diversion. The drawbridge was only halfway down. Khadri was offering Wells a bargain: Kill West, or die trying, and I'll trust you. Kill West and you're in. If not, you'll never see me again.

An ache creased Wells's back. He felt like a puppet whose strings had been pulled too hard. Khadri had outsmarted him again. But maybe he could find a way out.

"We can get to West," Wells said to Qais. "It'll take some planning, though. When does Omar want it done?"

"Tonight."

"Tonight." As he said the word Wells felt the trap snap shut.

12

WELLS OPENED HIS apartment door to find that Sami had laid out his arsenal on the kitchen table, the guns and knives an invitation awaiting an answer. Aside from that, the place looked undisturbed, which didn't surprise Wells. Like Qais, Sami was a professional, a former Jordanian cop.

"Shall we say the *maghreb*?" Wells asked, using the Arabic word for the evening prayer.

"What about your neighbors?" Qais said. Through the walls they heard a television blaring in the next apartment, the jokes and canned laugher running together monotonously.

"Wendell's almost eighty," Wells said. "And almost deaf. As long as we're quiet."

He laid out a rug, and the three men said their evening prayers. Then they ate. On the way home Wells had stopped at a 7-Eleven and bought premade sandwiches and quart-sized tankards of coffee. He was ravenous, and he figured Qais and Sami must be too. But he felt no pleasure as he chewed his stale turkey hero, just the knowledge that the clock was winding down. He swallowed his last bite and looked at his watch. Nine o'clock. He had four hours, six at the most. No matter how hard he tried, he couldn't see a way clear. He couldn't kill West. Yet Khadri would never trust him if West lived.

With a week of notice, even a day, he could have warned Exley. Then the agency and the FBI could have set their own trap. They could have snatched up Qais and Sami and let Wells go. They could even have announced that Qais and Sami had been killed in the house, and that West had been shot and wounded. Khadri would have to accept that; he had no way to check.

But Wells couldn't get a warning to West now. Qais and Sami weren't going to leave him alone tonight. They knew that the real point of the mission was to test Wells's loyalty. Of course, he could just kill Qais and Sami now. But then he would lose whatever information they had, and the trail to Khadri would end. Turning them in would be better, but that was no sure bet either. They wouldn't exactly sit back and smile if he picked up the phone and called 911.

Wells wondered whether he should just let West die, pull the trigger himself if Qais asked. This was a war, and West had been a soldier once. Not just a soldier. A general. He was close to seventy. He had lived a full life. He might even understand.

Wells shook that thought from his mind. He had to make sure West lived tonight. For his own sake as much as the general's. There were some lines he could not cross. He couldn't murder the people he had been charged with protecting. He couldn't play God and sacrifice one of his countrymen in the hopes of saving others. No. He had to save West without blowing the cover he had worked so hard to build.

YET HE COULDN'T see a way out, no matter how hard he tried. Call 911? Can't. Shoot Qais? Can't. Kill West? Can't. Warn West? Can't. Call Exley? Can't. Call 911? Can't . . .

He pulled his attention back to the kitchen as Sami spread a street map of Buckhead over the table. Technically, the area was part of Atlanta, the northwestern corner of the city. In reality Buckhead was a lush suburb where the city's corporate gentry lived in oversized houses set back from winding tree-lined streets. Wells had done lots of landscaping work there.

"He's here." Sami pointed to a red sticker, a few hundred feet from the intersection of Northside Drive and Mount Vernon Road.

Qais slid a manila folder from his laptop case. "The property records say he bought it for two point one million dollars in 2001," Qais said. "Three floors, with a guest cottage on the side."

"Two point one million? The army pays better than I remembered. Do we have pictures of him?"

Qais pulled out pictures of West taken from the Internet. Wells recognized the general, a tall, bald man with thick, rubbery lips and a mass of wrinkles for a forehead. "How do we know he'll be there tonight? He must be on the road a lot."

Qais looked at another paper. "He'll be there. The Georgia Defense Contractors Association is giving him its lifetime achievement award at a dinner tonight. A town called Roswell."

"That's north of here."

"And tomorrow afternoon he's speaking at the City Club downtown. He'll be home."

Wells couldn't disagree. "What about bodyguards?"

"Only one," Sami said.

"You sure?"

"I've been watching him. When he's out he rides in a Jimsy"— Arab slang for a GMC Suburban. "The driver doubles as his bodyguard and sleeps at the house."

"More likely in the cottage," Qais said.

THE GLIMMER OF a plan took shape in Wells's mind. Maybe he could split Qais and Sami up, after all.

"Yeah," Wells said. "Probably in the cottage." He turned back to Sami. "You're sure West doesn't have more protection?"

"I've only seen one guard ever."

Khadri really did want them all to survive, Wells thought. He was surprised that West had so little security, but the guy had been retired for a while, and anonymity was his best defense.

"The house has a fence and a gate," Sami said. "I took pictures last week." He spread them across the table. The fence had a brick base topped with low ornamental spikes. Behind it, up a hill, a big Georgian house sat back about one hundred feet. A driveway separated the house from the guest cottage. Sami pointed to the fence.

"But only about six feet high, and no barbed wire."

"Not in Buckhead," Wells said. "The neighbors wouldn't approve. How big's the property?"

"A hundred and twenty meters long, sixty meters wide." Four hundred feet by two hundred feet, Wells mentally translated. About two acres.

"Big enough to give us a little privacy," Wells said. "What about dogs?"

"I think one. I've heard it a couple of times."

Wells shook his head. Dogs were a real problem, the biggest one yet. Dogs meant noise. "He married? Any family?"

"He's divorced," Qais said. "About a year after he retired. His wife lives in Houston."

"Only one wife?" Wells joked.

Qais smiled. "Only one."

Good. Fewer chances for mistakes. "And Khadri wants this tonight? It has to be tonight?"

Qais nodded. "He said you would understand."

Wells could only nod. "I do."

He pointed at the map. "I know this part of town from my landscaping work. The place looks more private than it is. Mount Vernon, that's a big road, a lot of traffic—we can cut across a couple of lawns and leave that way if we have to. Get back here in time to get a good night's sleep and get Qais back to Detroit."

FOR TWO HOURS, they talked through the mission. Wells would have liked more time to plan and a lot more information. Floor plans of West's house, including the room where he slept. The number of police cars and private security patrols that covered the neighborhood, and their usual routes. Whether West had a gun, and if so where he kept it. Instead they didn't even know whether the house had an alarm, or whether it was keyed to the fence.

They would need to move fast, making up with speed what they lacked in intel and firepower. They had to get out before the police arrived to pin them down. Wells figured they had five minutes at most from the moment they got to the house, even if the place didn't have an alarm. They should plan on being done in three. Escape was basically impossible once the opposition arrived in force. Especially in unfriendly territory, which Buckhead was.

"If we hear a siren, we go," Wells said. "Immediately."

Slowly, he guided Qais and Sami to his plan, letting them work out the details so they wouldn't realize how much of the idea was his.

"Enough," Qais said finally. "I feel like I'm back at your FBI. You know everything will turn to shit anyway once we get inside. These things always do."

"Sure," Wells said. "But we have to pretend it won't." Despite himself, Wells liked these guys. And when they woke up tomorrow on a flight to Guantánamo, they would have only themselves to blame.

SAMI HAD BROUGHT clothes for himself and Qais, black pullovers and black pants like the ones that Wells had bought at the army surplus store.

"We look like a mime troupe," Wells joked when they had dressed.

"Mime troupe?" Sami said.

"The guys who wear all black and—forget it."

Sami had brought his own guns too, .45s with silencers as well as an H&K machine pistol, a short-barrel automatic rifle with a thirty-two-shot clip. The H&K was inaccurate and showy but a nasty weapon nonetheless. Jihadis couldn't resist machine pistols, Wells remembered; they had seen too many action movies. The .45s were the real prize; they fired subsonic rounds, and with the silencers screwed on they were as quiet as a gun could be.

Wells didn't ask where Sami had gotten the guns. They looked brand-new, and for a moment he wondered whether the agency might be behind this, testing his loyalty with this crazy plot. Maybe Vinny Duto would be waiting for him at the house instead of West.

But Khadri had sent Qais and Sami to him, and if Khadri was an agency mole the United States would have captured bin Laden and destroyed Qaeda a long time ago. No. The guns were real and they were loaded and West was alone in that house. He would die tonight unless Wells could save him.

. . .

THEY WOULD TAKE both the Ranger and the Lumina, which Qais promised couldn't be traced if they had to ditch it. Sami had wiped it down to erase fingerprints. They would leave the pistols and ski masks in the Lumina's trunk in case they were stopped, though Wells figured the cops might find an excuse to search the car in any event. Three men, two Arab, cruising around Buckhead after midnight, dressed like a SWAT team. . . . No, they had better drive carefully.

"Do me a favor," Wells said to Sami. "No speeding."

"*Nam.*"

They prayed once more, asking Allah for his blessing, for the chance to bring the wrath of Islam upon the infidel general. Wells hoped that Allah paid no more attention than He had to the prayers that Wells had offered beside his parents' grave.

Just before one A.M. they rolled out, Wells and Qais in the pickup, Sami following behind in the Lumina. Despite the danger—or because of it—Wells's hands were steady on the steering wheel, his breathing slow and easy. How he had gotten to this place no longer mattered. *He* no longer mattered. Only the mission counted.

THEY MADE THEIR way west on 285, the wide highway mostly empty aside from the eighteen-wheelers burning through the night. Then southwest on Mount Vernon and southeast on Powers Ferry and southwest again on Mount Paran. The traffic got lighter with each turn they made, until finally they were alone. They made one slow winding loop around the block that surrounded the general's house, looking for security patrols or houses with too many lights on, listening for dogs barking or husbands yelling. But the good citizens of Buckhead were all asleep, or pretending to be.

Wells looked at his watch. One thirty-three. They wouldn't have a better chance.

"Now," he said to Qais.

"Now."

Wells held his left hand out the window, the sign that they were on, and parked his pickup in front of a half-built brick mansion around the corner from West's house. Sami popped the Lumina's trunk. They reached for the guns and the masks. Wells took his Glock and a silenced .45 for Sami; Qais grabbed the other .45 and the H&K. They slid into the Chevy. Sami rolled around the corner and stopped in front of West's house.

SAMI PUT THE car in park but left the engine running. They pulled on their masks and gloves. Wells tucked the Glock into a holster on his hip. Sami slung the H&K across his chest like the villain in a Steven Seagal movie. "Five minutes maximum," Wells said. "And if we hear sirens we're out."

"We know," Qais said.

"*Nam.*"

Wells looked again at his watch: 1:34:58 . . . 1:34:59 . . . 1:35:00.

"*Allahu akbar,*" Wells said. "Go."

They were out of the car. They closed the doors silently and ran for the fence.

Wells was the first to reach it. He pulled himself up and over in one fluid motion, then jumped down, landing easily. If the fence had an alarm, it was silent, a lucky break. The neighbors would sleep a few seconds longer. Qais followed quickly, but Sami was temporarily stopped when his H&K got tangled in the crown of the fence, something that never happened in the movies.

The lawn was as lush and green and perfectly cut as a football field before the season's first kickoff. Wells looked around for a dog, but the grass was empty. Then he heard the barking. The noise grew louder as Wells ran up the hill toward the big white house.

He reached the front porch and looked at his watch: 1:35:20. He would give himself fifteen seconds to pick the lock on the front door. If he couldn't, they would have to break a window. But when he grabbed the doorknob it turned smoothly. The door was unlocked. Weird, but he didn't have time to figure it out. The dog was yammering loudly now, one bark rushing into the next. He sounded like he was at the door. And he sounded like he was big. They would have to take care of him quickly.

Behind him Qais reached the porch just as Sami finally got over the fence, a delay that was fine by Wells. Sami ran up the hill, angling away from the house and toward the cottage, as they had planned.

"The dog," Wells said. Qais nodded and raised the .45. Wells turned the knob and kicked open the door.

The dog came flying out, a big beefy Rottweiler, leaping for Qais with his jaws wide open. Qais's first shot caught the dog in the chest and knocked him down. He whimpered and yet kept coming, protecting his turf. Qais shot him again between the eyes, the big round smashing the Rottweiler's skull, splattering fur and brains and blood across the porch. He collapsed and was still. Qais's eyes glittered behind his black mask.

THEY STEPPED OVER the dog's carcass and into the house. Wells closed the door and they both took a moment to let their eyes adjust. Qais turned toward Wells—

—and Wells was swinging the Glock toward him, holding the heavy pistol by its barrel. Qais tried to get a hand up to deflect the blow, but the Glock came too fast. The butt of the gun crashed into his temple just behind the eye, the softest spot on the skull.

"*La,*" Qais said. No. His face went slack. He wavered but didn't go down.

So Wells hit him again. The same spot. This time Wells could feel the pistol dislodging bone. Qais grunted, a sound not unlike the one the Rottweiler had made, and tottered over, unconscious before he hit the ground.

WELLS'S PLAN WAS simple. Split the jihadis up. Take out Qais, leaving him alive for interrogation if possible. Take out Sami before he got to West's bodyguard. Disarm the guard before he started shooting, and then find West and explain what was happening. Call Exley and tell her everything. Have the agency put out a cover story to convince Khadri that Qais and Sami had died in the raid. Maybe even fake West's death too. Do it all before the Atlanta cops showed up and blew his head off.

Well, "simple" might be the wrong word for the plan. But it was the best he could do under the circumstances, and so far it was working. "FBI!" he shouted up the stairs, hoping West wouldn't freak out and come down the stairs shooting. Or worse, drop dead of a heart attack.

"FBI! General, please stay calm—"

But there was no answer.

"General—"

The house was silent. Maybe West was hiding in his bedroom, calling 911 . . . though that wasn't how Wells expected a three-star to act, even one old enough to collect Social Security. Doesn't matter now, Wells told himself. I have to move. He turned and ran toward the guest house.

AS HE CROSSED the lawn he heard the rattle of Sami's H&K from the cottage, a half dozen shots, a break, and a half dozen more, echoing through the humid Georgia night.

He arrived at the cottage a few seconds later to find Sami grinning at him, the H&K held loosely in his hands. Wells could see lights flicker on in the neighboring houses. So much for the plan.

"Sami—"

"You're never gonna believe it, man," Sami said in Arabic. "Where's Qais?"

"In the house, looking for West."

Sami turned toward the house. "Take a look," he said to Wells.

Wells walked into the cottage.

Sami was right. Wells couldn't believe it. Even in his wildest imagination he wouldn't have expected this. But there they were. No wonder the front door had been unlocked. No wonder the house had been silent. And no wonder West's wife had divorced him when he retired.

A dozen rounds from H&K had done a lot of damage to West and the bodyguard, but not enough to obscure what had been happening in the cottage before Sami arrived. The bodyguard lay naked across the bed. A lubed-up condom hung on the end of his flaccid penis. West wore a studded black leather dog collar and what looked like a leather corset. One of his arms was handcuffed to the bed; the other hung limp at his side. Evidently the bodyguard had been trying to unlock him when Sami arrived. He had failed. And so had Wells.

·   ·   ·

WELLS GLANCED AT his watch once more: 1:36:43. Not that it mattered. West, dead. The bodyguard, dead. He would never be able to explain to the police what had happened here tonight. He would never be able to explain to Sami what had happened to Qais. He had only one way out of this mess, and no time to spare. He stepped out of the cottage. Sami turned toward him.

"Can you—"

Wells raised the Glock and shot him. Once in the chest, and then in the head, just to be sure. He left the H&K but grabbed Sami's .45. A good silencer might come in handy.

Wells ran to the house. In the distance he heard a siren. He had to finish Qais off. Qais would know now that he wasn't loyal to Qaeda, and so Qais would try to blame this attack on Wells to get the agency after him. The agency might be able to figure out that Qais was double-crossing him, but not if Qais gave up Wells just a little at a time, like he really wanted to protect him. No, Wells couldn't take that chance. Qais had to die.

Wells stepped over the dead Rottweiler and into the entry hall. Qais lay unconscious on the floor where Wells had left him. As Wells looked down Qais sighed faintly, as if he had already accepted his fate. "*Inshallah,*" Wells said quietly.

He shot Qais once with the .45 in the back of the head. A quiet pop. Another man dead. Then Wells did something he hated. He turned Qais over and aimed the .45 at his face. He stepped back so the blood wouldn't spatter his legs and pulled the trigger until he had blown Qais's nose and mouth and eyes into a bloody pulp. An unrecognizable pulp. Wells assumed that the surveillance footage at Hartsfield would show him with Qais, and that the police would check those tapes as soon as they could. But Qais wasn't carrying any identification, and with what Wells had just done the tapes wouldn't be much use.

WELLS JOGGED THROUGH the house to the kitchen, in the back. The sirens came louder now. He opened the kitchen door and sprinted through the garden behind the house. He pulled himself over the fence, landing on gravel in the unfinished backyard of the half-built mansion.

He whipped off his ski mask and ran around the unfinished house and down the driveway to the street where he had parked his pickup. The houses on this side were still dark. A lucky break.

He slid inside the Ranger, pulled his Red Sox cap over his head, and drove off. As he turned onto Mount Vernon he could see a police cruiser speeding toward him, flashers blazing, sirens screaming. The officer inside looked hard at him as they passed but didn't slow down. And Wells drove free into the night.

BACK AT HIS apartment he sat at the kitchen table, trying to control the faint shaking of his left hand. The adrenaline was gone now and he just felt tired. Beyond tired. Exhausted deep into his bones.

In April he had told Walter the interrogator that he didn't remember how many men he had killed. He had lied. He remembered every one. Now he had two more to add to his list. He thought of that first buck he had shot so many years before. No, he didn't hate killing. But he was sick of it, sick of being good at it. Sick of knowing that he would have to do it again. He had been around too much death for too long.

Wells forced the thought of death out of his head and balled his hand into a fist. When he opened it again, the shaking was gone. He couldn't blame himself for tonight. Khadri had put him in an impossible spot. He had played his cards as best he could. He couldn't have known that West would be with the guard. "Don't ask, don't tell," he murmured to the empty kitchen, and felt a faint ugly smile cross his face.

He considered calling Exley, turning himself in, trying to explain what had happened. But that was impossible. Things had gone too far tonight. He'd been involved in the killing of a three-star. No way to sweep this under the rug. Even if the agency believed him, it would have no choice but to lock him up. Or just make him disappear. No, he could never redeem himself unless he brought in Khadri, dead or alive. Nothing less would save him from the agency. Nothing less would save him from himself. All this killing had to take him somewhere.

Get the bad guy, save the country, get the girl. Simple, really. "Yeah, I'm right on track," he said aloud to the empty room.

. . .

THE GOOD NEWS was that the cops and the FBI would have a hard time figuring out what had happened tonight, Wells thought. Plus they would keep the details of the killings out of the media. No sense in ruining West's reputation.

So Khadri would know only that Qais and Sami had died alongside West and the bodyguard. Khadri wouldn't trust Wells more than he had before tonight, but he wouldn't trust Wells any less either. Wells figured he would hear from Khadri soon or not at all. And his next mission, if there was a next mission, wouldn't be a test run. In the park earlier today Khadri had looked like he was running short on time.

Wells knew just how Khadri felt.

13

THE CAT WAS in pitiful shape.

When Tarik picked her up from the animal shelter a week before, she had been runty but healthy, an energetic tabby whose fur was a mottled blend of black, brown, and white. Unlike most strays, she showed no fear of humans. She swiped playfully at him on the drive home. Even when he locked her in the cage in the bubble in the basement, she didn't fight.

"You'll really like her," the woman at the SPCA had told him. "She's a great choice."

AND THE WOMAN was right, though not for the reasons she would have liked. Three days after being exposed to an aerosolized mist of Y. pestis, the cat lay on her back, mewling quietly. Tarik could hardly bear to look at her. Her fur was matted and greasy with the blood she had vomited. Pus caked her green eyes. Open sores covered her stomach. She could hardly turn her head when he entered the bubble and approached her cage.

Enough, Tarik thought. He sank a syringe into a vial of sodium pentobarbital solution and carefully measured out two milliliters of the liquid. He grabbed the cat's back left leg and looked for a vein on her stomach. Under normal circumstances, she would have fought. Instead she waved her paws feebly in the air and closed her eyes. Tarik found a vein and jabbed the needle into it. The cat went limp a few seconds later.

"Poor cat," Tarik said. "I'm sorry."

He did not enjoy making animals suffer, especially cats. He would have preferred to experiment on a dog, but dogs were naturally immune to plague. So he had no choice. And despite his sorrow at the cat's awful death, he could not deny the pride he felt at the speed of his progress with the plague. He had stopped all his work on his other germs, even anthrax, to concentrate on *Yersinia pestis*.

Tarik would have liked to credit hard work for his success. But the truth was that the bacteria he had received from Tanzania appeared to be an especially virulent strain of plague. The germs grew quickly in brain-heart infusion broth and stayed alive for hours after he strained them into a weak solution of soy agar that flowed easily through his nebulizer. The bacteria were also more temperature-resistant than Tarik had expected.

Without a column chromatograph and a polymerase chain reaction assay he couldn't be sure, but he suspected that this *Y. pestis* strain included both the pPCP1 and pMT1 plasmids. Those were strands of DNA that produced enzymes that interfered with the immune system and the blood's ability to clot. A week before, seeing how quickly his mice and rats were dying, Tarik had started taking doxycycline, an antibiotic known to work against plague. As far as he knew, he had not been exposed, but he wanted to be doubly careful.

Looking at the cat's bloody carcass, he was glad he was taking the medicine. He carefully plucked her body from the cage and slipped it into a large glass jar of hydrochloric acid, where it would dissolve. He would go by the shelter for another cat tomorrow. Though maybe he'd be better off at a pet store. They'd have fewer questions. He had been surprised when the woman at the shelter had asked him what name he had picked out for the cat.

"I'm not sure yet," he'd finally stammered.

Yes, a pet store was the way to go, Tarik thought. But if his success continued, he would soon be done with cats. His next subjects would be monkeys, whose respiratory systems had more in common with humans'. Unfortunately, monkeys weren't easy to come by; biological supply companies would sell them only to licensed research centers, and very few people bred them for sale as pets. He had seen Internet ads from breeders in the United States, but he wasn't sure he could get across the border by himself, much less with a monkey in tow. And he strongly suspected that customs agents—maybe even the police—would pay his house a visit if he tried to order one online.

Still, even without the monkeys Tarik believed he now had enough skill with the nebulizer to infect people in an unventilated room—if he could figure out a way to release the mist without anyone noticing. Of course, that didn't mean he could cause a widespread outbreak. He had months to go before he could figure out how to stockpile enough Y. *pestis* for a big attack. And he worried that it would take months or years to overcome the technical problems associated with large-scale spraying. Creating an aerosol mist in a lab with a few milliliters of solution was far easier than spraying hundreds of liters of liquid from a crop duster or the back of a truck.

But he couldn't deny his progress. He had been spending six, eight, sometimes ten hours a day down here, sleeping only in short snatches as his excitement grew. He knew he should pace himself—he was surprised by how tired and disheveled he appeared when he saw himself in the bathroom mirror—but the plague filled his mind. The plague and Fatima.

As he thought of her his excitement faded. Fatima had grown even more distant from him in the last month, coming home late from work, hardly smiling when he tried to talk to her, pushing off his fumbling advances in their bed. The week before, he'd emerged from his work in the basement and again found her whispering on the phone in the kitchen.

"What do you care?" she'd said. "You're down there all the time anyway."

At that he had hit her, just a couple of times.

"Please, Tarik," she'd said. "What's happening to you?"

You and your wicked ways are what's happening, Tarik mentally answered her. He wished he could talk to someone about her, but Khadri was the only person he trusted enough to ask, and Khadri's advice was always the same: focus on your work. "It's your problem," Khadri had said the last time they spoke. "Deal with it."

Fine. I'll deal with it, Tarik thought. I'll deal with it tonight.

THE OXYGEN GAUGES on Tarik's regulator dipped toward empty. He headed back into the airlock and stripped, then hung up his respirator and wiped down the tanks with bleach. When the tanks were clean he dragged them outside of the bubble into the open area of the basement. There he hooked them up to an oxygen pump to refill them.

He showered and dressed slowly, savoring the rush of power that came from handling Y. *pestis*. He didn't want to leave the basement. This place belonged only to him, and no one could take that away.

Finally he headed upstairs. A strange trembling rose in him as he walked up the steps to face his wife. Fatima needed to support him, support his work, not disrespect him by coming home late. She had given herself to him as a good Muslim woman, a daughter of the Prophet, and she would keep her word to him and to Allah. He almost didn't care at this moment if she loved him, as long as she respected him.

He felt a mix of anger and relief when he opened the top door of the stairs and found her sitting at the kitchen table, writing on a yellow legal pad. His lovely wife. Still, his temper rose as he saw that she was wearing a skirt that showed her legs. When had she bought that? She looked like a *kafir*. He had warned her about dressing immodestly when she took her job at the law firm and stopped wearing robes. But she'd dismissed his complaints, telling him she needed to fit in at work. No more, Tarik thought. From now on she would do as he said.

"Hello, my sweet," he said, and walked over to kiss her. She turned her lips from his, offering her cheek instead. "How was work?"

She didn't respond.

"My sweet, we've talked about this many times before. Why are you so late? You must call—"

"Tarik—"

"Fatima." The anger on her face stopped him for a moment, but he decided to press ahead. "Listen to me—"

"Tarik!" she yelled. "I'm through listening! Now you listen!"

Her voice echoed in the tiny kitchen, and he found himself shocked into silence. She had never raised her voice to him before.

She pushed back from the table and stepped out of her chair. He noticed a small black suitcase at her feet, a cheap softsided bag he had never seen before. He tried not to think about what it might mean. He realized he had lied to himself. He didn't just want her respect. He wanted her to love him again, to smile the way she had when they had first met.

She took a deep breath, composing herself. The kitchen was eerily silent, and Tarik felt as if he had suddenly been given superhuman powers of sight and sound. He heard the slow drip of water from the leaky kitchen faucet, and saw the faint dark fuzz on the peaches that she always kept in a bowl on the counter, the grain of the cheap dishrag in the sink. He looked up and found that the light from the overhead bulb burned his eyes.

When Fatima spoke again, her voice was quiet and firm.

"Tarik. I can't live with you—"

His thoughts contracted to a single word: No. "My sweet. Of course you can live with me."

She laughed bitterly. "Don't you see you've proven my point? I say I can't live with you and you don't even let me finish my sentence—"

"Don't you love me, Fatima?"

A pained expression crossed her face. "Do you know why I married you, Tarik? I thought you were a scientist. That you would understand a modern marriage. But you're as bad as the rest of them. Worse."

"This is no way to speak." He tried to keep his voice steady.

"Tarik." Her voice broke. "Do you think I want to do this? Since spring I've tried to talk to you a dozen times, a hundred times, but you don't listen."

"I want to talk—"

"You say you want to talk, but you don't. You disappear into that hole"—she pointed accusingly at the locked basement door—"and don't come back for hours. Days. You don't tell me what you're doing. You never let me bring anyone over. I feel like a prisoner in this house."

"You're not a prisoner—"

"And you're changing, Tarik. You don't sleep—"

"I sleep—"

"You *don't*. You're not the same man you were even a month ago. I don't know what you're doing down there"—again she looked at the basement door, and Tarik felt his stomach clench—"but you've turned into someone who scares me. You beat me last week, Tarik. I never would have imagined that."

"I didn't beat you—"

She pulled up her shirtsleeve, exposing black-and-blue welts the size of credit cards on her left arm, above the elbow. "What would you call this?"

Shame and rage rose in him. "I didn't mean—" But even as he said the words he could feel his fist clench.

She picked up her suitcase. "I'm leaving, Tarik. It will be better for us both."

Now the shame was gone. A pure white rage filled him. He remembered finding his mother dead in her bed in their apartment in Saint-Denis. The yellow paint peeled from the walls, and Khalida's eyes yellow too, the needle still in her arm. He had hated his mother so much at that moment. But this was worse.

"You can't leave," he said. "Where will you go?"

"You think I don't have friends?"

"What kind of friends?" he said. "I won't let you. You belong to me."

At his words an ugly sneer formed on her lips. "You think I don't have a boyfriend? My poor little Tarik—"

Had she really said that? He slapped her hard, across the face.

"No more, Tarik—"

He slapped her again. She stumbled backward and banged against the kitchen counter. But she just shook her head and stood up straight, her brown eyes fierce. She was tiny, barely five feet tall, but as she reared back she seemed twice his size.

"Yes, a boyfriend," she said. "A *kafir* boyfriend. A real lover, not like you—"

And Tarik knew he would never have her back. He raised his hand to slap her again, but she put up her own hand. "Don't—"

He spat instead, a white glob landing on her cheek.

"Bitch. Worthless whore. The infidels have filled your head with rot. I won't divorce you."

The spittle trickled slowly down her cheek. She raised her hand and wiped away his venom. Her eyes never left his.

"Then I'll tell the police what you're doing down there." She pointed again to the basement. "Don't you think they'd like to know?"

"You said you didn't know."

"Of course I know. Am I a fool? Maybe I'll tell them anyway."

THEN THE KNIFE was out of the drawer and in his hand. A big butcher knife with a black plastic handle. A fevered god spoke in his head and he obeyed. Fatima began to scream even before he landed the first blow, slashing across her stomach so the blood sprayed out through her clean white shirt.

She turned to run but he stabbed her in the back and she fell and he was on her. He cut at her again and again, plunging the knife into her tiny body, stabbing into her back and neck, cutting through skin and fat and bone until she stopped screaming and her blood covered him. She was dead in less than a minute.

THE BUZZ IN his ears faded to silence. A bird chirped in the night outside, behind the blinds that he always kept drawn. He stood and looked at his wife.

"Allah forgive me," he said quietly. Had he really just killed her? He couldn't believe it, and yet there she was, unmoving, her legs splayed, her blood pooling thick as paint on the kitchen's white linoleum floor.

He dropped the knife. Already his rage was fading. He hadn't wanted to hurt her. Didn't she know he loved her? She shouldn't have pushed him, shouldn't have done this to him. *She* was to blame.

He knelt beside her and stroked her hair. "I'm sorry, Fatima," he said.

What would he do? Had the neighbors heard her scream? What about the people in her office? Her boyfriend? All of them must know that she had planned to leave. Soon enough the police would come. Tarik could stall them for a few days, tell them that she had left Montreal to see friends. But the boyfriend, whoever he was, wouldn't let this go. Eventually the police would come back with a warrant. And the basement would be the first place they would look.

Dear God. What had he done? His plans, his work. About to be lost. Because of this whore. Pity filled him, pity for her and for himself. He had nothing left now, nothing but a few days to work, not nearly enough time to take his revenge on this world.

But he couldn't give up. Not yet, anyway. Maybe he could salvage his plans, get his germs someplace far from the gray house, someplace the police wouldn't find them. At least find a way to make use of the *Y. pestis* he had grown.

He turned on the faucet as hot as the water would go and washed his hands and face until his tan skin lost its reddish tint. He knew he would be bloody again soon enough. He would have to take Fatima's body downstairs and wipe the kitchen floor. But for this moment he wanted to be clean.

He pulled a cellphone from his pocket. He punched in a number he had been warned never to use except in the most serious emergency. The phone rang three times.

"*Bonjour, mon oncle.*" A moment passed, and Tarik wondered if he had misdialed the number. Then he heard Khadri's voice, as calm as ever. "*Bonjour.*"

Tarik felt an immense relief. Everything would be fine.

14

"WE'RE SURE WE have the right apartment?"

"We're sure. Sort of."

"Because we're about to ruin someone's day if we're wrong."

"Either way we're gonna ruin someone's day," Shafer said.

He and Exley stood in the Secure Communications Presentation Center, watching a feed from Flatbush Avenue in Brooklyn on the six-foot-wide main monitor. Right on schedule, two New York City garbage trucks appeared on-screen, rolling slowly down the street. The whine of their diesel engines rumbled through the screen's speakers. Exley glanced at her watch: 5:12 A.M. They would go in three minutes.

"It's too early for this," she said to Shafer. She could feel her pulse pounding in her temples, a sure sign of a nasty headache coming on.

"It's too early for anything."

"No audio," Vinny Duto snapped at a technician. Mercifully, the noise ceased.

At this hour the street looked empty, or as close to empty as New York City could be. Dawn was an hour away, and the streetlamps provided the only light, a sickly yellow-orange glow. Graffiti-covered metal gates protected the silent stores. Black garbage bags were heaped in front of a Church's Fried Chicken, offering a feast for the rats that scurried along the curb. At the intersection of Flatbush and Clarendon, the garbage trucks stopped behind a livery cab looking for the night's final fare.

But the street's silence was deceiving. At the moment, more cops and FBI agents were on Flatbush Avenue than anywhere else in New York. Instead of trash, the garbage trucks held a dozen agents in their steel bellies. The homeless man lying in front of the Church's was actually an NYPD detective. Snipers covered the street from rooftops around the intersection.

The object of all this attention was a redbrick tenement fifty yards from the corner of Flatbush and Clarendon. Once again, Farouk Khan deserved the credit—or the blame—for what was about to happen. Two weeks before, acting on information from Farouk, an elite Pakistani army unit had swept through an al Qaeda safe house in Islamabad, catching two men. One quickly flipped, telling interrogators about an al Qaeda sleeper in the United States, an Egyptian who had entered on a student visa in 2000. The informant even remembered the Egyptian's first name: Alaa.

A search of immigration records by the Joint Terrorism Task Force revealed that nine Egyptians named Alaa had entered the United States on student visas in 2000. Four had left when their visas expired. Two of the other five still lived illegally but openly in the United States, according to public records. In two days, the FBI tracked down and arrested both. Neither was connected to al Qaeda, but both were immediately taken to federal detention centers for deportation hearings. Their bad luck.

The remaining three Alaas didn't appear on driver's license lists or tax records or arrest warrants or voting rolls. They'd been careful. But in this case not careful enough. The JTTF passed the information from the visa applications to the Egyptian Mukhabarat. The Egyptians needed less than twenty-four hours to find the families of the three missing men. One was easily cleared; he had died in a car accident. Another was living under a fake name in the United States, working at a convenience store in Detroit. He sent money home to his family and had no known connections to terrorism in either Egypt or the United States. The FBI arrested and interviewed him, then flew him to Cairo under emergency deportation orders signed by a friendly federal judge. When he protested, he was told to consider himself lucky that he wasn't being shipped to Guantánamo. He stopped complaining.

Then there was one. Alaa Assad. An engineer, a graduate of Cairo University, and a member of the Muslim Brotherhood, an Egyptian group that is half political party, half terrorist front. Alaa's family admitted that he had traveled to the al Qaeda camps in Afghanistan before getting his American visa. After he entered the United States he disappeared, they said. He never wrote and never sent money home.

But they were lying. Alaa had made a mistake. A natural mistake, but a mistake no less. He had stayed in touch with his family. When the Mukhabarat pulled the Assads' phone records, it found calls to a New York City cellphone. In hours the FBI tracked the phone, a prepaid model sold two years earlier at a drugstore in Queens. The phone would have been untraceable if Alaa had paid cash for it. But he had inexplicably charged it to a credit card in the name of Hosni Nakla, 1335 Flatbush Avenue, Apartment 5L, Brooklyn, New York. "Hosni" also had a New York State driver's license whose picture matched the photographs of Alaa in the Assad family's Cairo home. So the JTTF had decided to pay an early-morning call on apartment 5L.

A typical successful investigation, Exley thought. A little luck and a lot of hard work. And it had happened fast, the dominoes crashing one into the next, as the most productive investigations often did.

ON THE OTHER hand, the Albany and the Atlanta cases were stalled. The Atlanta shootings had proved especially messy. The killers remained unidentified and the motive a mystery. At first, Exley and everyone at the JTTF had assumed the shootings were related to terrorism. But the general's hidden life had forced them to reconsider.

The FBI, which was leading the investigation, had discovered that General West had slept with at least five enlisted men during his career in the army. He had once forced a sergeant to retire after their relationship soured. All five of those men had alibis, but other former lovers were surely lurking. One might have killed West for revenge. Even a busted robbery was possible; the Atlanta cops had found $200,000 in a safe in West's bedroom.

Making the case even trickier, the physical evidence proved that West and the bodyguard hadn't killed the Arabs. A third shooter had killed them, then escaped. But why? Terrorists didn't shoot their own. Maybe the third man had hired the other two to help him with a revenge killing, then taken them out so they wouldn't talk.

That was the FBI's theory, anyway. Exley and Shafer and the others at the agency who knew about Wells had their own suspicions. But at an emergency meeting two days after the shootings, Duto warned them all to keep Wells's existence secret. "He's our asset," Duto said. "There's no evidence that he did this. No need to tell the Feebs about him."

Another lie, Exley thought. Wells was nobody's asset right now, certainly not the agency's. But she didn't argue. If Wells wasn't involved in the shootings, making his name public would blow his cover. And if he was involved . . . Exley didn't want to think about that.

Meanwhile, Duto's team was still searching for Wells. As far as she knew, they had no leads, although she wasn't sure Duto would tell her or Shafer if they had. Exley hadn't helped. She still hadn't revealed Wells's early-morning call to her. Too much time had passed, she told herself. Talking about it now would just get her in trouble. But she knew the truth. She didn't want Wells sitting in an isolation chamber in Diego Garcia. When he was ready he would reach out to them. Reach out to her.

SO THE FBI never heard about Wells. And that wasn't the only problem the Atlanta investigators faced. The Pentagon had pushed to classify details of what had happened at the house, claiming that disclosing too much information could compromise national security. The Pentagon's real motivation—embarrassment about West—wasn't hard to figure. But the FBI had decided not to argue. Even the third shooter remained a closely kept secret. The lack of information had created a vacuum that bloggers filled with wild theories, though no one had guessed the real story. Even the craziest conspiracy theorists had limits.

The Albany bombing had also frustrated the JTTF. The bomb hadn't left any recognizable signature. The timer, the trunk, the battery, and the wires were available at any Home Depot. The C-4 was military grade, but military-grade plastic explosive was available for the right price all over South America and eastern Europe. The junk radioactive material in the bomb didn't match any of the samples the Department of Energy had on file from Russian nuclear labs.

The Albany investigators had managed to identify the man who'd died in the explosion. He was Tony DiFerri, an unemployed grifter with a half dozen arrests for burglary and cigarette smuggling, nothing that explained how he had ended up blown to bits inside locker D-2471. The best guess from the Joint Terrorism Task Force was that the man called Omar Khadri had duped him into opening the trunk. Unless they caught Khadri they wouldn't know how. DiFerri sure couldn't tell them.

IT WAS 5:14. One minute to go. On-screen, the garbage trucks had pulled over and turned off their engines. Exley sipped her coffee. "You think it's real?" she said to Shafer.

"You know as much as I do." Probably a lie, Exley thought, but she didn't argue. Shafer was especially irritable this morning. "Let's assume it's real. The problem—"

Shafer broke off. On-screen, men in black flak jackets, Kevlar helmets, and plastic face shields jumped out of the garbage trucks. They halted for a moment at the front door of the tenement, then blasted open the lock and ran inside.

THE RAID WENT smoothly. At 5:22 A.M. four agents came out of the building holding a dazed-looking man in a T shirt and sweatpants, his hands and feet manacled. They shoved him into an unmarked van and drove off, trailed by two police cars.

Inside the Secure Communications Presentation Center, a small cheer went up.

"Little early to get excited, don't you think?" Shafer murmured to Exley under his breath. "We don't even know if it's the right guy."

Shafer was probably right, but she didn't want to hear it. After everything that had gone wrong the last few months, the JTTF needed a break. "Can't you be happy for five seconds?" she said. "If we're wrong we'll cut him loose. He can get a lawyer and sue us. Like everybody else."

"Assume we're right. Assume he's real," Shafer said. "Somebody set up these cells very carefully—"

"Khadri," Exley said.

"Sure, Khadri, whoever he is. Somebody. John Wells. Anybody."

Exley put her hand on Shafer's shoulder and turned him so that she could see his face. "You don't really believe that," she said.

Shafer shook his head. "No. But the more time that passes, the more I wonder. Why doesn't he just call us?"

Exley could feel her temples throbbing as she thought of Wells. "He knows we'll bring him in if we find him," she said.

"Or he's turned into a damn mole rat. He's lived underground so long he can't do anything else. He wants to hide forever."

"If he had something, he'd tell us. I'm sure of it."

"How can you be sure of anything about John Wells?"

A very good question, and one she couldn't answer.

"Forget Wells," she said. "Go back to Khadri. Or whatever his name is."

"Whatever his name is, he's very good. We have no picture, no bio, nothing. And his network is airtight. We've had four hundred people working for five months to crack the L.A. bombing. Heck of a diversion, if that's what it was. What leads do we have? Same for Albany."

"His network's not airtight. It sprang a leak today."

"Even if he's real, that was pure luck."

"We caught a break. That's how it goes, Ellis. And maybe this guy is the thread that unravels everything else."

"I'll bet you he isn't. One dollar. I'll bet our new friend Alaa has been waiting for a phone call since he got here. That's why he got sloppy. He got bored. He's a drone. Khadri's too smart to give a drone anything important."

"No more bets, Ellis," Exley said. "You still owe me a hundred for Wells. And you can say what you like. I'm glad we caught this guy." She tried to keep her tone even, but she could feel her anger rising.

"Maybe."

"Maybe? The first time we capture an al Qaeda sleeper agent in America and you wish we didn't?"

"Jennifer, relax."

"I hate it when men tell me to relax."

"Then don't relax. But think it through," Shafer said. "Khadri can see us closing in. He has to figure the worst case, that we're right on him, right on Network X. I think he's going to move very soon."

"Before he's ready."

"You mean before we're ready. So it'll be five thousand dead instead of twenty thousand." Shafer laughed sourly. "Too bad we're not as close as he thinks we are."

Exley wanted to beat her head against the nearest wall. "You told Duto this?"

"I told him two days ago we should watch Alaa but not arrest him. Not tip our hand." Shafer looked at the main screen. The van holding Alaa was speeding over the Brooklyn Bridge toward the federal detention center in downtown Manhattan. "You can see what he thought of that."

"Let me guess. He said you were speculating. Pure conjecture. That we don't leave al Qaeda sleepers on the street. Especially after what happened in Albany. And Los Angeles. That there's no evidence anything we do will cause al Qaeda to change its plans. And that we won't know what Alaa knows unless we ask him."

"You forgot the part where he told me I was crying wolf."

"It's all true," Exley said. "Everything he said was true."

But she felt sick. Shafer was right. Finally, after all these years, the agency and the FBI had bumped against the edges of Network X. They had lit the fuse.

"You're right," Shafer said. "I'm just guessing."

"Like you did in 2001."

Nothing had changed since then, Exley thought. The agency and the JTTF were still stuck on small, showy operations instead of finding the men who really mattered.

"Duto reminded me that we don't second guess at the White

House anymore. We're an instrument of national policy. We do what we're told. I'd forgotten that."

He pulled out his wallet and counted out five twenty-dollar bills, shoving them into her hand.

"That's for Wells."

Exley flushed. "I was just kidding, Ellis," she said. "I don't want your money." She tried to push the bills back to him, but he stuck his hands in his pockets.

"Keep it," Shafer said. "Maybe it'll be good luck. Get the mole rat out of his hole."

"I thought you don't believe in luck."

"I don't." He walked away.

IN A MARRIOTT in Stamford, Connecticut, Khadri saw the arrest in Brooklyn on the local news from New York. The report was sketchy—the police hadn't disclosed Alaa's name or any details—but Khadri knew who had been arrested as soon as he saw the apartment building.

Even worse, he couldn't figure out how the *kafirs* had found Alaa. Only two people knew Alaa's real identity or where he lived. One was Khadri himself, the other the leader of Alaa's cell, a Lebanese named Ghazi who lived in Yonkers, just outside New York City. Khadri would have to make sure Ghazi was safe. But what if the Americans had already arrested Ghazi and were waiting for Khadri to call?

No. Ghazi's wife and children had been killed in the Israeli invasion of Lebanon in 1983. He hated the Jews and the United States more than anyone Khadri had ever met. Ghazi would die before he betrayed his al Qaeda brothers. The *kafirs* had found Alaa some other way. Fortunately, Alaa didn't know much, just the number of a cellphone Khadri would destroy as soon as he could, and an e-mail address that Khadri would never use again.

A knock at the door startled him. Khadri looked at his briefcase, where he kept his gun. Were the *kafirs* coming for him already? "Yes?"

"Room service."

Right. His breakfast. He opened the door, still half-expecting to see FBI agents lined up, guns drawn. But the only person outside was a waiter with a tray. "Just leave it, please."

"Yessir."

Khadri looked down at his food: hot coffee, scrambled eggs with the steam still rising, a glass of fresh orange juice. Normally he would have been ravenous. But this morning he had lost his appetite. In just the last month, he had lost three of the ten sleeper agents that al Qaeda had in the United States. Including Qais, his best operative.

Khadri had explained to Qais that he'd designed the mission in Atlanta to test Wells's loyalties. He had warned Qais to be careful, to kill Wells immediately if he felt at all threatened. So Khadri couldn't understand what had happened. Wells had e-mailed him afterward, explaining that the mission had gone wrong because West wasn't sleeping where they'd expected. He was outside the main house, having sex with his bodyguard. The bodyguard had shot Qais and Sami before Wells killed him and West, Wells said.

The story was so bizarre that Khadri almost believed it. Almost. He wished he knew if he could trust Wells. He had debated that question endlessly with himself, and he still wasn't sure. But he believed that the answer was yes. More important, he didn't have much choice, especially after what had happened in Montreal.

Yet another disaster, Khadri thought. Allah had not blessed him this month. Crazy Tarik Dourant. Khadri understood why Tarik had snapped. His wife had deserved what she'd gotten. But why couldn't Tarik just have waited? Khadri would gladly have taken care of Fatima and her *kafir* boyfriend in due time. Instead Tarik had lashed out—and now his work was about to be lost. The Montreal police had already interviewed him about Fatima's disappearance. Soon enough they would come for him. Before he was arrested, Khadri needed to get Tarik's germs into the United States.

Wells was his best choice. Khadri's other sleepers might have problems at the border, but Wells could cross easily. And Khadri thought he had found a foolproof plan, one that would work even if Wells was an American agent. A plan that would turn everything around and shock the world.

As soon as possible Khadri needed to get authorization from

Ayman al-Zawahiri for the new operation. Zawahiri wouldn't be pleased with the change. Al Qaeda prepared its attacks years in advance. An operation as important as this wasn't supposed to be revised on a few days' notice, and the new plan would cost al Qaeda all its American sleepers at once. But Zawahiri would understand. Better their men should die gloriously than be arrested one by one. Better to strike while they still had the strength to land a heavy blow. This attack might not be as elegant as his original plan, but it would kill just as many people.

Khadri leaned forward to pray. He couldn't delude himself. The noose was tightening. He would probably never see Mecca, his greatest dream. He would never be married or have a family. He would probably die in this alien land, surrounded by infidels. Yet he found himself more afraid of failure than death.

In this, at least, he and Wells were alike.

AS SOON AS the phone rang Wells knew. Khadri was the only person who had this number. He pulled the handset out of his pocket, took a breath, and accepted the call.

"Jalal."

"*Nam.*"

"Check your gmail account." Click.

"As you like, Omar," Wells said to the dead line.

Finally, Wells thought. Finally Khadri had decided to use him. He felt certain this was the real mission, the one he had awaited for so long. And even if Khadri was sending him down another false path, Wells knew now that they would meet again. This time he would destroy Khadri. Even if he had to tear out the man's throat with his bare hands.

Wells could see now that Khadri was Qaeda's linchpin, even more important to the group's plans than Zawahiri or bin Laden himself. Khadri and Khadri alone controlled Qaeda's networks in the United States. Without him Qaeda's ability to attack America would be set back at least five years. Maybe more. Not forever, but enough time for Major Glen Holmes and Wells's old friends in the Special Forces to root out the last of the jihadis in the North-West Frontier. To catch Zawahiri and bin Laden himself. To defeat Qaeda. Khadri was the key.

15

AT THE DORAVILLE Public Library, Wells logged on to his gmail account. The orders were simple enough. Drive—Khadri specified that Wells had to drive—to Montreal. Pick up a package at a hotel. Drive back. Khadri had included a phone number for the contact he would meet in Montreal. The meeting was barely twenty-four hours away. He would need to move fast.

Back home Wells packed an overnight bag with the essentials: His field medicine kit. His flashlight. His black leather gloves. His knife, strapped to his leg. The .45 he had taken from Sami. He wrapped the pistol and silencer in plastic and packed them in a separate bag. He would have to hide them before he reached the border, but for this trip he wanted a gun. He left his other weapons in the apartment. He had gotten rid of his Glock the week before, tossing it into a deserted stretch of the Chattahoochee River fifty miles north of Atlanta. The gun had splashed into the black water and disappeared without a trace. Wells wished he could forget Qais and Sami as easily.

Wells slipped his Koran into the bag as well. After everything that had happened, everything he had done, he wasn't sure what he believed. Still, the book was like an old friend he hadn't seen in a while. Maybe they didn't have much to talk about anymore. But they had understood each other once, and that counted for something.

He looked around the apartment one last time as he headed out. Lucy had died, but Ricky was still alive, swimming listlessly. Wells decided to give the fish a last meal. Somehow he didn't expect to see the place again. No great loss. It had served its purpose.

On his way out, Wells knocked on the door of his next-door neighbor, Wendell Hury, the old man whose television blared game shows through the walls of Wells's apartment every day. They weren't exactly friends, but Wendell was the only person in all of Atlanta who might notice that he'd gone. Wells felt oddly compelled to say good-bye. But though Wells could hear Wendell's television through the door, the old man didn't answer his knock. Wells waited a few seconds, then turned away.

WELLS ROLLED DOWN his windows as he passed through the suburbs and into the lush green woods of northeast Georgia. The September air was warm and humid, with thick clouds in the air promising a late-afternoon shower. Wells could feel sweat running down the small of his back. He flicked on the radio and skimmed between stations, not really sure what he was hoping to hear. Then he caught the fiddles of "The Devil Went Down to Georgia," a great hokey country song from the Charlie Daniels Band that Wells hadn't heard at least since high school.

> The devil went down to Georgia
> He was looking for a soul to steal

The song brought a grin to Wells's face, his first real smile in weeks. He stomped on the gas for a moment, feeling the Ranger's little engine rev and the pickup jump forward, then pulled his foot away and reminded himself not to speed. Even after the highway narrowed to two lanes outside the Atlanta suburbs, traffic was heavy and state troopers a constant presence. But the oversized signs and the road's smooth macadam soothed him. Through South Carolina he hummed "The Devil Went Down to Georgia," wondering what his comrades in the North-West Frontier would think of the song. Not much, probably. For the first time since he had come back to the United States he felt truly American.

IN NORTH CAROLINA the skies darkened. Rain broke against the windshield in sheets, and the traffic crawled forward through foot-deep puddles. Outside Durham Wells stopped at a giant Mobil station. As the Ranger's tank filled he punched Exley's number into his cellphone. He should tell her about the message from Khadri. He could hear the purr of her voice as he dialed. But before the call went through he canceled it. Khadri's message was too vague to be useful. The hotel could be a dead drop. As he had for their Atlanta meeting, Khadri would surely take precautions to make sure Wells wasn't being trailed.

Wells didn't want to involve the agency until he had something concrete, like the package—or, even better, Khadri. In any case no one at Langley would believe him. Even Exley would just tell him to come in, give himself up. No. To redeem himself he needed the package, whatever it was. He slipped the phone back into his pocket.

The rest of the drive went quietly. South of Washington, Wells turned east on 495, the route that would give him the widest possible berth around Langley. Again he fought down the urge to call Exley. He would have time later to tell her everything he wanted . . . if he lived.

THEN, FOR THE first time in weeks, Wells thought of his son. He squeezed the wheel as he remembered again that day almost six months before when his ex-wife forbade him to see Evan. Heather had been right. Wells had chosen to forsake his family, and nothing he said or did could salve that wound. For a moment he closed his eyes. When he opened them he had pushed his family out of his mind and resolved to think only of the job ahead.

He drove on, escaping the storm behind him, his little white truck passing silently through the night. When he reached the George Washington Bridge the Ranger's digital clock read 2:47 and the air outside was cool and moist. Wells was tired and sore from the hours on the pickup's hard bench seat, but he knew that if he needed to he could go at least one more day without sleeping. In Afghanistan he had once stayed up sixty-five hours straight. Though he had been younger then.

The girders of the giant steel bridge glowed white in the night. To his right, to the south, the towers of Manhattan shone over the Hudson River. In the distance he could just see the Statue of Liberty. Wells understood why Khadri had called the city beautiful. He did not doubt that Qaeda would do everything possible to destroy it.

He turned north on I-87, following the signs for Albany. A few minutes later, he reached the Tappan Zee Bridge, stretching across the Hudson like a snake floating on the water. Wells smiled to himself as he recrossed the river, realizing he could have stayed on the Hudson's west bank all along. Well. He would remember that shortcut the next time Khadri sent him from Atlanta to Montreal to pick up a secret package.

NORTH. THE EXITS came farther and farther apart. Wells rubbed his eyes and fought the temptation to speed. After Albany, the highway had an eerie, postapocalyptic emptiness. Wells turned up the Ranger's radio to fill the void, smiling to himself as he found a Springsteen song playing low on the FM dial:

> I've got my finger on the trigger
> tonight faith just ain't enough

But as the miles flowed on, the static worsened until Wells could no longer understand the voices he heard and finally he flicked off the radio and rode in silence.

The sun rose, revealing the Adirondacks, low mountains covered with the thick forests he remembered from his years at Dartmouth. By January these hills would be as cold and cruel as the eleven-thousand-foot peaks in Montana. But for now they looked gentle, easily manageable. Like so much else in the world, they were a trap for the unwary. At Chestertown, a hundred miles south of the border, Wells pulled off and found a no-name motel whose red neon light flashed VACANCY. He had made good time, and he wanted to nap before the border crossing. He paid for a room for four days up front, then flopped on the bed and slept a black sleep for three hours, until the alarm woke him. He showered, shaved, and dressed, then shoved the bag holding the .45 inside the room's cheap wooden bureau.

On his way out he hung the DO NOT DISTURB sign on the door. The gun would be safe until he got back. Even if a housekeeper did look inside, Wells was sure she wouldn't do more than change the towels.

HE PASSED CHAMPLAIN, the last exit on I-87 before the U.S.-Canada border. The highway divided, and Wells slowed as he approached the border checkpoint. He looked at his watch: eleven-fifteen. The sun gleamed in the clear blue sky. A perfect warm September day, a reminder that summer hadn't ended quite yet. He felt fresh and strong and ready.

The Canadian border doesn't require a passport. Wells handed over his driver's license.

The guard glanced at it, then looked him over idly. "From Georgia? Long drive."

"Don't I know it."

"Is the purpose of your trip business or pleasure?"

"Pleasure, I hope." Wells smiled. "Meeting a woman I been e-mailing. Jennifer's her name. In Quebec City. Hope she's as pretty as the pictures she's been sending."

The guard nodded. "How long do you plan to stay?"

"A couple days. It'll depend on how things go."

"Do you have a hotel?"

"I'm hoping I won't need one."

"Well, good luck. Have fun." The guard handed back Wells's driver's license and waved him through.

WELLS'S PHONE RANG as he piloted his Ranger across the Champlain Bridge and over the Saint Lawrence River, closing in on the skyscrapers of Montreal's downtown. He clicked on the phone. *"Nam."*

"This is Richard." The man's voice quivered. But he had the right name, the one that Khadri had e-mailed Wells to expect.

"Karl," Wells said.

"Yes. Good. Are you close?" Wells couldn't place the accent.

"Yes."

"Good. It's a new plan."

No surprise there.

The man coughed lightly. "Drive on to Quebec City. Next to the Hôtel de Ville, the city hall, is a big parking garage. You shall find it easily. Meet me there on the second level at four o'clock. I have a white minivan."

The words were proper, but the phrases were off. English wasn't this guy's first language, or his second. "I'll find it. I've got a pickup truck. Also white."

Click. An amateur, Wells thought. Or a pro playing an odd game.

TARIK WAITED FOR his hands to stop shaking, then slid the phone into his pocket. Jalal had come, just as Khadri had promised. Now Tarik needed to keep his own promise and deliver his package.

He had taken care of his wife, sealing her body in thick plastic bags and leaving her in the basement of the gray house. A temporary solution, sure, but Tarik was thinking short-term these days. The police had knocked on his door again this morning. He hadn't answered, but they knew he was home. They wouldn't wait much longer before they came back with a warrant.

But by then Jalal would have his package. The plan should work, Tarik thought. Technically, the delivery mechanism was simple. The germs were ready. Yes, the plan should work. As long as he could keep his nerve.

SO MY LIE at the border about Quebec City turned out to be true, Wells thought. He stopped for gas, picked up a map, and sighed as he saw that his new destination was another 150 miles away. Well, another couple of hours of driving hardly mattered. "Giddyup," he said as he turned the Ranger's ignition.

The garage in Quebec City was huge, and mostly empty. Wells drove through it slowly, doubling back twice. As far as he could tell he wasn't being trailed, but he knew the limits of countersurveillance. Finally he parked. He tilted his head back and immediately fell asleep. Best to conserve his energy.

WELLS JOLTED AWAKE. He snapped his head up to see a white Ford Windstar, a young man behind the wheel pressing the horn. The man swung open the minivan's passenger-side front door. Wells slid out of the pickup and into the van.

The driver was small and thin, rings around his dark brown eyes, a twitch in his cheek. He licked his lips nervously as they shook hands. "So you like jazz," he said.

"I listen to it every afternoon," Wells said, completing the code. The driver seemed to relax a little. He put the minivan into gear and they rolled slowly away. Wells slung his bag behind him in the van.

"I am Tarik."

"John. Or Jalal. As you like."

"*Salaam alaikum,* Jalal."

"*Alaikum salaam.*"

Tarik guided the minivan out of the garage, turning toward Canada 40, the highway connecting Quebec City and Montreal. He was a careful driver, constantly checking his rearview mirror and signaling long before he switched lanes.

"Back to Montreal?" Wells said. "You sure you don't work for Exxon, all this gas we're burning?"

The muscles in Tarik's skinny forearms jumped. If he wasn't scared he was doing a great job of acting. "I don't understand what you mean."

"It was a joke . . . forget it."

Tarik looked at Wells. "Can you put on your seat belt, please?"

Wells clicked in without comment.

"Could I turn on the air conditioning? I like the cool," Tarik said.

"You're driving, Tarik. You can do whatever you want."

Tarik flicked on the air and they rode for a few minutes in silence.

"I'm sorry I kept you waiting," Wells said casually.

"Kept me waiting? No, no," Tarik sputtered. "I just got there when you saw me."

Then why did we meet in Quebec City instead of Montreal? Wells wondered. Tarik wasn't using any countersurveillance tactics to lose potential pursuers. In fact, he drove so cautiously that anyone could follow him. "Where are you from, Tarik?"

"I grew up outside Paris." That explained his accent, at least.

"Now you live here?"

"Yes. Montreal." They were having an interview, not a conversation. Tarik was too nervous to ask any questions of his own. Wells could have switched to Arabic but decided to stay with English, to keep the kid off balance.

"You work there?"

"I'm a graduate student."

"In?"

"Neuro—neuropsychology." Again the muscles in Tarik's forearms twitched. Wells began to wonder if the Royal Canadian Mounted Police would be waiting for them in Montreal.

TARIK WAS TRYING his best to act scared, though he hardly needed to act. Khadri had warned him that Wells would probe him, and walked him through how to respond. If he kept the lies to a minimum he would be fine, Khadri said. All he needed to do was stay calm for a few hours, give Wells the package, and send him along.

Tarik desperately hoped Khadri was right.

"DO YOU LIKE it?" Wells said.

"What?"

"Graduate school."

"Yes."

"Are you married, Tarik?"

"Not anymore." He seemed to smile, though Wells was no longer sure about anything this kid did.

"Sorry it didn't work out," Wells said.

Wells waited, but Tarik said nothing more. "Tarik. You know who sent me. Is something wrong?" He switched to Arabic.

"Nothing is wrong. Everything is cool." The phrase sounded ridiculous coming from Tarik's mouth. He shook his head mulishly, like a sixth grader caught passing a note in class.

Wells shifted gears. "What's in the package, Tarik?"

"I don't know. They came yesterday. I didn't open them."

Again Wells waited. Still Tarik said nothing. Finally Wells asked, as smoothly as he could: "They? There's more than one package? How many?"

"I'm not allowed to talk about this."

"Where'd they come from? Who delivered them?"

"Jalal, please."

"Is there another courier, Tarik?"

But Tarik shook his head and said nothing.

SET THE HOOK and don't say too much, Khadri had told Tarik. I don't care what he thinks is happening. As long as he has the package when he leaves.

KHADRI WAS PLAYING games, Wells thought. As usual. Why hadn't he sent the packages, whatever they were, straight to the United States? Why use this kid, who looked like he wanted to vomit? Why multiple couriers?

Tarik sat rigidly in the driver's seat, his hands clenching the wheel. Wells could see that he was done talking, unless Wells put a knife to his throat. And as much as Wells wanted to take control, force the situation, he had to be patient. Tarik was only a courier. Wells would take the package, cross the border, and wait for Khadri.

THE SUN WAS low in the sky when they reached Montreal. Tarik turned off the highway into a run-down neighborhood. They passed a brightly lit Muslim community center with signs in English, French, and Arabic. A few minutes later Tarik turned into the parking lot of a run-down motel.

"Wait," he said, and got out. He walked into room 104. Wells figured Tarik had rented the room for a night as a place to store the mysterious package. A dummy location, one Wells couldn't trace. Smart.

Wells looked around for any signs they were being watched. He saw nothing. The street was quiet. No helicopters floating overhead, no UPS trucks cruising by, no Ford Crown Victorias parked away. On the other hand, if this really was a sting operation, the cops—or the agency—would wait until he had taken the package from Tarik. They might even wait until he got back to Quebec City.

So arrest me, Wells thought. Let this madness be the agency's doing. At least I'll know that Langley's a step ahead of me, and close to catching Khadri. But as he looked around again, he felt sure the agency was nowhere near him. Or Khadri.

Tarik reappeared from room 104 carrying a soft-sided blue travel bag, large enough to hold a week's worth of clothes, small enough to fit in an airplane's overhead bin. He carefully placed the bag in the back of the minivan. "It has a briefcase inside. Don't open it."

"What if they search it at the border?"

"Omar said that's up to you. He said he was sure you'd think of something."

"I'm glad he has so much confidence in me," Wells said.

Tarik said nothing more on the long drive back to Quebec City, and Wells didn't press him.

THE GARAGE IN Quebec City was almost empty when they rolled up to the little white pickup. Wells had never been so glad to see the truck. He stepped out of the minivan. To his surprise, Tarik followed. "May Allah smile upon you, Jalal," Tarik said in Arabic. He tapped his heart. Wells responded in kind.

"On you as well, Tarik."

"And may he make us victorious."

"*Inshallah.*"

Wells offered Tarik his hand. Instead the smaller man gave him an awkward hug. Wells pulled the blue bag out of the Windstar and set it in his pickup. He waved once to Tarik, then leaned against his truck and watched the minivan disappear.

When the Windstar was gone Wells slid behind the wheel of the pickup, but he didn't bother to start the Ranger for a while. If this was a sting, he'd give the cops plenty of time to arrest him without a fight. But the garage stayed empty, and finally Wells turned the key and rolled out of Quebec City and into the night.

· · ·

IT WAS 1:04 A.M. by the Ranger's clock when Wells rolled up to the deserted border crossing. He felt as if he'd been driving forever, but in truth he'd just begun the journey home.

The guard took a long look at his license. "You have a passport?"

"No sir."

"When'd you cross into Canada?"

"Just yesterday morning."

"You from Georgia?"

"Atlanta."

"Long way for such a short trip."

"I was visiting a girl in Quebec City," Wells said. "Met her on the Internet. It didn't work out so good. She was about twice as big as the picture she sent."

"Too bad, man." The guard laughed. "You can never trust those Canadians." He looked down at the Ranger's passenger seat. "What's in your bags?"

"Just clothes. I was hoping to stay a while. Took the week off."

"No drugs, guns, nothing like that."

"No sir."

"Well, better luck next time." The guard handed Wells back his license. "Welcome home. Drive safe." Just that easily he was back.

A HALF HOUR later Wells pulled over and pissed by the side of the highway, looking up at the night sky. This far north there wasn't much pollution. The glow of the stars reminded Wells of Afghanistan. He wondered if he'd ever see those mountains again, or what he would think if he did. Maybe he and Exley would vacation there one day. Adventure tourism.

He found his phone and punched in a number Khadri had e-mailed the previous day. "Leave a message," Khadri's voice said.

"I'm through," Wells said. "I'll be back in Atlanta tonight. Late." Click.

IN THE MOTEL room in Chestertown Wells sat on his bed and gingerly unzipped the blue bag. Inside he found a couple of T-shirts . . . a pair of jeans . . . some smelly socks and underwear. And a hard-shelled plastic briefcase clasped with a digital lock.

Wells wondered how he would have explained it to the border guard. He picked up the case, feeling its heft, maybe twenty pounds. Not nearly big enough for a nuke. But inside there could be enough plutonium for a bomb. Enough anthrax to annihilate a city. Sarin. VX. Smallpox. Anything. Pandora's briefcase.

Wells poked at it for a minute more, then gave up. He could probably force the lock, but why bother? If Khadri was using him as a decoy, the case would be empty or booby-trapped. On the other hand, if the case held something important, then Khadri would have to get it. And then. . . . The knife strapped to Wells's leg throbbed as if it were alive. Khadri wouldn't survive that meeting.

He lay back on the bed. He would sleep three hours and be on the road by dawn. But first he had a call to make.

EXLEY ANSWERED ON the second ring. "John?"

"Five o'clock this afternoon. Swimmingly."

"I'll be there."

He hung up.

She had said yes without hesitation. He loved her for that.

16

"LEFT AT THE sign," Ghazi said. "Third house down."

Khadri stopped his Ford Expedition in front of a neatly kept house in Yonkers, just north of New York City. A black Lincoln Town Car sat in the driveway, in front of the garage.

"You like it?" Ghazi said. He had bought the place three years before, and he was as house-proud as any first-generation immigrant. Ghazi was the only al Qaeda sleeper who lived openly in the United States, a former Lebanese army explosives expert who had emigrated legally in 1999. He had spent the years since building an American life. He drove for a car service, paid his taxes on time, even showed up for jury duty. And he never forgot the day in 1983 when an Israeli artillery shell landed in his living room in Beirut and splattered his family across the walls. Never forgot and never forgave. He blamed the United States as much as Israel. The Jews were nothing without the Americans. Ghazi had waited a very long time for Khadri's orders.

"VERY NICE," KHADRI said. In truth, Khadri didn't care for the house's green paint or its aluminum siding. But he saw no reason to explain its shortcomings to Ghazi, who would be in paradise soon enough anyway.

Khadri popped the Expedition's back latch, and the two men dragged a steel trunk out of the SUV. "Heavy," Ghazi grunted in Arabic.

"It's lined with lead," Khadri said. They had picked up the trunk at a storage center outside Hartford. Inside the garage they lowered the trunk to the clean concrete floor. Ghazi clicked the garage door closed. They were alone with the trunk. And the vehicle that Khadri thought of as the Yellow. Khadri walked slowly around the Yellow, examining it. Just as Ghazi had promised. Its tires were worn and its paint faded, but it had a new inspection sticker and the right license plates. No one would look twice at it. Perfect.

"It's ready?" Khadri said.

Ghazi slid a key into the ignition. The Yellow started without protest. Ghazi let the vehicle run for a minute before turning it off and handing the key to Khadri.

"Have the neighbors ever asked about it?"

Ghazi shook his head. "They know I drive a cab. They think maybe it's for a new business."

"So it is."

FROM THE OUTSIDE the Yellow appeared completely ordinary. But beneath its seats were wooden crates that held thick gray blocks of C-4, twenty-one hundred pounds in all. Khadri had originally expected to use the vehicle for a conventional bombing like the ones in Los Angeles, but since Alaa's arrest he had changed his plan.

Inside the Yellow, thick black wires led from detonators on the crates to a battery near the driver's seat. To prevent any chance of an accidental explosion, the wires were not hooked to the battery. When they were connected the Yellow would become a rolling bomb, smaller but far more powerful than the ammonium nitrate bombs that Khadri had used in Los Angeles. A ton of C-4 could take out a thirty-story building.

Khadri knelt before the trunk and punched a stream of numbers into its digital lock. He knew exactly what was inside, but he wanted to see once more. The lock clicked open. Khadri pulled out a small steel box held shut by a simple padlock. He twisted the lock's dial and opened the box. There it was. The gift of God. Two sealed jars, the first holding a half dozen pieces of gray metal, the second filled with a dirty yellow powder.

"That's it?" Ghazi said. He sounded disappointed, Khadri thought.

"It will be enough."

In truth, before his recent setbacks, Khadri had hoped to add to this stash of plutonium and highly enriched uranium. Perhaps even to accumulate enough material to meet his dream of a nuclear weapon. Then Dmitri the Russian scientist had died. Farouk had disappeared. And now the *kafirs* were closing in. Best to use what Allah had offered before the opportunity disappeared.

Khadri locked the box and returned it to the trunk, where even the most sensitive radiation detectors could not find it. When the C-4 blew, the explosion would vaporize the trunk, scattering plutonium and uranium for miles. A very dirty bomb. In the middle of Manhattan.

"Lift," he said. The two men lugged the trunk into the Yellow, where it fit nicely among the crates of C-4.

"*Allahu akbar,*" Ghazi said quietly. God is great.

"*Allahu akbar.*" Khadri was pleased with their work today. The first half of his plan was ready. The rest would fall into place when Wells delivered his package. Khadri thought briefly of the fate that awaited the American. If Wells's allegiance to al Qaeda was genuine, he would die a martyr, Khadri thought. If not . . . he would simply die. Either way, Wells would soon be in Allah's all-powerful grasp. He should be pleased.

CUT OFF FROM the rest of Washington by river and highway, the Kenilworth housing projects are a world unto themselves, a gravity well of addiction and poverty. The gleaming dome of the Capitol is barely two miles from the low-rise apartments of Kenilworth. It might as well be in another galaxy.

Yet a most unlikely oasis is tucked beside the projects. Created in 1882, the Kenilworth Aquatic Gardens are a lush, swampy forest thick with salamanders and snapping turtles and even the occasional armadillo. Wells would have liked to pretend that he'd chosen the gardens for his rendezvous with Exley because of their beauty. In fact he'd picked them because they were the most secluded place in Washington. If Exley planned to turn him in, the agency's surveillance would be hard to hide.

But as he steered the Ranger down Washington's Highway 295, closing in on the gardens, Wells felt sure that Exley would be alone. He had believed in her unconditionally since that night in the Jeep. Maybe even since the day they met at the Farm so many years ago, when they were both young and married.

In the end he supposed he had kept his faith after all. Not in the agency or in Allah or even in America, but in her.

HE DROVE UNDER a pedestrian bridge covered with a steel mesh fence, there to protect drivers from the neighborhood kids, who had a habit of dropping rocks onto the road. This was Kenilworth. He pulled the .45 out of his bag, unscrewed the silencer, slipped both inside his jacket. His phone trilled. He pulled it from his pocket, expecting Exley. Instead the number was a 914 area code. Westchester. Just outside New York City.

"Jalal." Khadri.

"*Nam.*"

"Where are you?"

"Our nation's capital."

"Just so." Khadri laughed.

"I'll be home tonight."

"Unfortunately not. I need you in New York. As soon as possible."

Wells felt as he had during his first few weeks in the army, buffeted by orders that seemed nonsensical. Khadri surely had a decent idea of his schedule. Why hadn't he called earlier, before Wells got to New York? But there was no point in arguing.

"New York City?"

"The Bronx." Khadri named an address.

"See you there," Wells said. He hung up, and as he did he realized something strange. Khadri hadn't asked about the package. Hadn't even hinted at it.

· · ·

TEN MINUTES LATER he turned into the gardens' parking lot. There were no signs of surveillance. He saw her immediately, leaning against a green minivan, arms crossed. She was wearing a navy blue shirt and gray pants that showed off her slim hips.

He parked beside her. She didn't smile, but when he got out of the truck she stepped toward him and hugged him tightly. "John," she said. She stepped back to look at him. He pushed her up against the minivan and kissed her, his arms around her. Their mouths locked as easily as two clouds merging and he felt the weight of her body against his, her breasts against his chest. Finally she pushed him away.

"You didn't come here for this," she said.

"Not *just* for this."

He took her hand and led her into the park. The forest and swamp surrounded them. The sounds of the city disappeared, and the air turned moist and rich. They walked silently toward the Anacostia River, not quite touching, content to be beside each other. Finally the path ended at the edge of the mud-brown river.

"How'd you know about this?" Exley said, watching the water roll lazily south. "I've never heard of it."

"I came here a couple times after the Farm. When I was getting my language training."

"With Heather."

"Jealous?"

She smiled. "Now why would I be jealous?"

He shivered as a breeze came off the river.

"You all right, John? You look tired."

"Too much driving," he said. "Khadri sent me to Montreal for a briefcase." He told her what had happened with Tarik the day before, and his suspicions of another courier.

"You don't know what it is?"

"It's locked. I haven't tried to open it."

"And you're meeting Khadri here? In D.C.?"

"No. I was heading south, but he just called. Changed the plan. Told me to turn around, go to New York. Something's about to happen. It's happening already."

"Shafer thinks so too."

He looked at her, then out at the river. "Care to share?"

She half smiled. "I was sort of hoping you would know."

"It's like we're in ancient Rome, sacrificing sheep, reading the entrails. Trying to figure out what catastrophe the gods have planned for us next."

"They're not gods."

"They want to be," he said. "Angry pagan gods who throw thunderbolts because they can."

"Do you believe in God, John? Not little-g gods but the big one?"

The question stopped him. He found himself looking at the sparrows flying over the river, thinking about the Koran in his truck, the men he had killed. "Yes," he said finally. "But I'm not sure he believes in me."

"I'm serious—"

"So am I. Can you do everything I've done and still feel grace? Still feel peace? And that's God to me. I'm afraid I've left Him a long way behind."

"When I was a kid I believed," Exley said. "Then my brother went crazy and I stopped. It seemed too cruel, to take someone's mind away that way. I remember one time, when his meds were working, joking around with him: 'How come God never just tells you to go shopping? How come it's always "The water's poisoned, there's a chip in your brain, the aliens are coming"?' He laughed, really laughed, and I did too. It just seemed so futile. But now that I have kids I want to believe again, if not for my sake then for theirs, believe that there's something more than this."

"I know what you mean." Wells touched her arm. "Jenny. Does anybody know I'm here?"

"Back to work, huh? No. Not even Shafer. You're toxic, John. Worse than toxic. I'm ending my career right now. Heading for jail, maybe."

"I'm sorry, Jenny."

"It's not your fault. Where have you been since April?"

"Sitting on my ass, mainly."

"Where?"

He didn't want to tell her, but he knew he couldn't lie. "Atlanta."

"Not just sitting on your ass."

He looked at her sidelong. "Tell your friend Duto I didn't shoot West," he said. "I tried to save him but I couldn't. Khadri set it up. To test my loyalty."

"And you passed," she said. "Khadri trusts you. That's why he sent you to pick up the case."

"He doesn't, though. Something's wrong. He's playing with me. I think maybe I'm some kind of a decoy." Wells paused. "Any of this fit with what you've got?"

She shook her head. "But we arrested a sleeper last week. In Brooklyn. And we think they have a dirty bomb." She told him about Farouk Khan, the explosion in Albany, Shafer's suspicions that al Qaeda planned to move fast.

"So when are you raising the alert level?" Wells said.

"We don't do that anymore. Not without specific intel. We're winning this war, remember? No need to upset anyone."

"A dirty bomb doesn't count as specific?"

"Not if we don't know where it is. We already embarrassed ourselves in Albany."

"Maybe it's in that briefcase in my truck."

She shook her head. "The radiation detectors at the border would have picked it up. And if the case was lined with lead you'd know. It'd be heavy as hell."

He was quiet. After a minute she looked at him. "What are you thinking, John?"

"I'm thinking it's time to get on the road." Back to New York. The day was still warm, but the trees on the opposite bank of the river were casting long shadows.

Her voice rose. "You're coming in."

"And cut the link to Khadri?"

"Give me the address. We'll get him."

"He won't be there. You know that. It'll be one of his guys, waiting for me. If I don't show, he won't either. And we'll all be scratching our butts in Langley when the bomb goes off. I've seen that episode before. Didn't like it much." He stepped toward the trail that led to the parking lot.

"You can tell it to Vinny. We'll get you up there tonight."

· · ·

BUT EXLEY KNEW she was lying. Duto would never use Wells on an operation this sensitive. For the same reason that Duto had insisted the JTTF arrest Alaa Assad right away instead of waiting. No one would fault Duto for putting Wells in a hole until the agency was sure he was loyal. The CIA director didn't get blamed for failing to prevent terrorist attacks; George Tenet, who had been running the agency on September 11, had gotten the Presidential Medal of Freedom after his retirement. No, the director got blamed for embarrassing the agency—or the White House. And letting Wells loose after he'd already disappeared once could be very embarrassing. Duto would never risk it. With a few weeks they might be able to change Duto's mind. But they didn't have a few weeks.

Duto wasn't evil, Exley thought. Just a bureaucrat, like too many of the folks at Langley, more concerned about his career and his reputation than anything else.

Wells seemed to read her mind.

"If you really think that, then call him," he said, and turned to walk away.

Suddenly Exley knew what she had to do. Some part of her had known from the moment she'd seen his truck roll into the parking lot. "Then I'm coming with you."

He looked at her, seemingly trying to gauge her seriousness. Then he shook his head. "Don't be stupid."

She was tired of men talking down to her. Even this one. "So fucking arrogant," she said. "I'll watch. If there's trouble, I'll call in the cavalry. If not, I'll wait while you play soldier."

"Don't do this—"

"It's not negotiable. Either I come or I'm calling Duto. Now." She pulled out her phone.

A crow screeched in the woods behind them. Wells turned from her, tilted his head to the sky. "Are you holding?" he said.

"What?"

"A gun? Do you have a gun?"

"No."

When he turned back to her he held a pistol, a thick gray .45. In his left hand a cylindrical tube. He slowly screwed the silencer onto the barrel. The river and the park were empty. No one around to see. No, she thought. This is impossible. He can't do this. He won't.

"John," she said. She held her breath.

AND THEN HE held the pistol out for her to take.

She exhaled. Did he know what he had just done? Had she simply misread the situation? Or had he intended to terrify her, to remind her of the years he'd spent in the field while she'd been behind a desk? She'd never know, and she couldn't ask. Either way, her fear, fading now, reminded her that they didn't know each other nearly as well as she wanted to pretend.

She pushed her fear aside and focused on the pistol. It was heavier than she expected. She held it in both hands to keep it steady.

"When was the last time you shot one of these?" Wells said.

She couldn't remember. She had learned to shoot at the Farm, of course, but that had been a long time ago. The agency didn't make analysts practice. "A couple months ago," she said evenly. "I go to the range every year."

She looked at the pistol, remembering her training. She racked the slide to chamber a round, racked it again so the round popped out. Wells caught it in the air and slipped it into his pocket. She flicked the safety on and off. She slid the magazine from the grip, then pushed it back in.

Wells took the gun, racked the slide again, handed it back to her. "Shoot it," he said. "Down the river. Hold on tight. It'll pop on you."

She hesitated.

"If you can't do it now, you sure won't do it with somebody in your face," he said.

She raised the gun and pulled the trigger. As he promised, the gun kicked sharply. The recoil pushed her back a step, but she kept her arms steady. With the silencer the shot sounded hollow, like a hand slapping a wooden table. The noise faded fast, no echo. "What about you?" she said.

"What about me?"

"Where's your gun?"

He pulled up his jeans to show her the knife strapped to his leg. "I'll make do," he said. "Listen. You need to know something about that forty-five."

"I'm listening."

"If you get to a place where you need it, *shoot first*. Don't get fancy. Don't tell anybody to freeze. Nothing like that. Not a word. Just shoot. Because if you get to that place and you wait, it'll be too late."

"How will I know if I get to that place?"

"You'll know."

She said nothing, only nodded. She wasn't sure she could shoot someone with no warning. But Wells would never let her come if she admitted that.

"Good," he said. He leaned in and tilted his head toward hers, opening his mouth to kiss her.

But she shook her head.

"When we're done," she said.

"When we're done."

They turned and walked back from the river, toward the parking lot. Toward New York.

17

WELLS TURNED OFF the Major Deegan Expressway into the heart of the South Bronx, long dark blocks only beginning to share in New York's renaissance. The open-air drug markets were gone, but women in skirts the size of handkerchiefs leaned against cars, looking for business. Outside brightly lit bodegas, men stood in clumps, sipping oversized bottles of malt liquor.

He wended his way through streets made narrow by double-parked cars, battered American sedans with tinted windows and NO FEAR stickers plastered on their windshields. Finally he found the address Khadri had given him. As he pulled over he saw in his rearview mirror that Exley had stopped a block behind. Not great tradecraft. She should have driven past and parked farther down. The slipup reminded him that she hadn't been in the field for a long time. She didn't belong anywhere near this.

But he had let her come, and now he was responsible for her, a complication he didn't need at this moment. He closed his eyes and allowed himself to think of her promise. *"When we're done."* If they made it through tonight, they would find a quiet room and a big wooden bed and make love until they both were sated. That would take some time.

He shivered and coughed, a thick gurgle from deep in his lungs. The driving had gotten to him; he felt as if he'd been awake for three days straight. And he had developed a nasty headache somewhere in New Jersey. Adrenaline would have to carry him the rest of the way.

He opened his door, coughed again, spat a wad of phlegm onto the asphalt. He had given up trying to predict what Khadri had planned. Tonight he would end Khadri's games. He cocked his head left and right. The street was empty. He stepped out of the Ranger and walked to the building, one slow step after the next.

The tenement was battered and gray, its bricks covered with sprawling whorls of graffiti whose meaning Wells could not decipher. Its front door was set back from the street, black with a porthole-shaped window, the glass reinforced with chicken wire.

The door opened easily, the brass knob loose as if the lock had been forced. Wells stepped inside and found a narrow hallway dimly illuminated by flickering fluorescent lights.

"Jalal."

A man Wells did not recognize sat at the top of a narrow set of stairs, cigarette in his mouth, gun held loosely in his lap.

"*Nam.*"

"Come."

Without another word the man stood and turned away.

Wells let the front door fall shut behind him and walked up the steps.

EXLEY SAT IN her minivan, fighting the impulse to run into the tenement and bang on every apartment door until she found him. She had covered the digital clock in the Caravan to stop from being maddened by its slow march; she had never been so bored and so anxious at the same time. Wells had gone inside around midnight. Now four hours had passed with no sign from him. Or anyone else. The building had been silent since he went in. Where was he? she asked herself. What was he doing? She couldn't wait much longer. Another hour? Until dawn? Perhaps she should have gone in already, but she didn't want to blow his cover, the cover he'd worked so many years to build.

If only the agency hadn't alienated Wells. If only he'd been able to convince Duto of his value. If only he hadn't disappeared for so long. He ought to be wearing a wire. These blocks ought to be swarming with FBI agents and police. Though even that wouldn't lessen the danger he faced. He was on the other side now, in a place where no one could get to him quickly enough to make a difference if something went wrong. Khadri—or whoever was up there—could put a gun to his head and pull the trigger in a second. All the cops in the world couldn't stop that. No wonder Wells didn't have much use for Duto and the rest of the Langley paper pushers.

Exley looked up as a black Lincoln Town Car rolled past her van. The Lincoln stopped in front of the apartment building and double-parked, its blinkers flashing. She held her breath. The Lincoln's door opened. A man wearing a blue blazer—an unlikely sight in this neighborhood at this hour—walked out, looked around quickly, and stepped into the building.

APARTMENT 3C was small and shabby, a railroad flat with a windowless living room and a tiny bedroom that looked into an airshaft. Mold stained the peeling orange wallpaper, and the refrigerator produced a maddening electric hum. On a broken coffee table, a small television silently played a DVD of the hajj, the pilgrimage to Mecca. But even the jihadis around Wells looked bored with the tape.

Wells sat on a sagging couch in the living room, his hands cuffed in front. He had fallen asleep briefly after they cuffed him, fatigue overtaking him until the thought of Exley downstairs jolted him awake. Now he was hardly talking, harboring his energy while he waited for Khadri. The men with him didn't seem to mind. There were seven, but only two had introduced themselves. Ghazi was the oldest and seemed to be the leader, a heavy man with a close-cropped beard and dark pouches under his eyes. The man who had been waiting for Wells called himself Abu Rashid—father of Rashid. He smoked constantly, flicking ashes onto the floor, putting his cigarette down only to spit into the sink. In fact all seven men smoked, and the room's air was stale and heavy, worsening Wells's nagging cough. He wished someone would crack a window.

With the possible exception of Ghazi, the seven men in here had never been professionally trained, Wells could see. They weren't nearly as aware as Qais and Sami had been. Only three of them had pistols, the guns tucked loosely into their pants: Ghazi and Abu Rashid and a dark-skinned Arab with a long beard whose name Wells didn't know. Most importantly Abu Rashid hadn't found Wells's knife because he hadn't patted down his legs.

But Wells wasn't about to make a move. Not yet. Not until he saw Khadri.

"Water?" Ghazi asked him.

"Please," Wells said.

Ghazi looked him over with concern. "Are you all right? You seem unwell."

"I could use a good night's sleep." Wells sipped the water Ghazi offered and closed his eyes, shutting out the room's dim light. Around him the men spoke quietly in Arabic about the World Cup; for an hour they had debated Jordan's prospects.

"Is Khadri coming?"

"Soon, my friend, soon."

And then Wells heard the steps on the stairs.

KHADRI TOOK A single step into the apartment and closed the door. A surgical mask covered his nose and mouth. "Jalal."

"Omar. My friend. *Salaam alaikum.*" Wells began to stand. A wave of dizziness passed through him. Why the mask? he wondered.

"Don't get up," Khadri said. "You need your strength."

Wells stood anyway. A violent cough shook him.

"I'm sorry about Qais and Sami—"

"You're here now. That's what matters. And you have the package?"

"There." The briefcase sat on the kitchen counter.

Khadri smiled. "I knew they wouldn't keep you at the border." Khadri punched numbers into the briefcase's digital lock. The latch popped open.

"Your secret's in there," Khadri said. "See for yourself."

He sent the case skittering toward Wells across the pocked wooden floor of the living room. My secret isn't in this apartment, Wells thought. She's sitting outside in a green minivan.

Wells sat back on the couch and fumbled with the briefcase. "Ghazi, will you uncuff me?" he said casually. "I can't open it like this."

Ghazi looked to Khadri. After a moment, Khadri nodded, and Ghazi unlocked his cuffs.

Wells lifted the lid of the case. Inside, nothing. He ran a hand along its inside walls, looking for a false bottom. But he couldn't find anything. He had been a decoy after all.

He shook his head wearily. "I don't get it," he said. "Who's the courier? Where's the package?"

Khadri pointed at Wells. "You are."

"But—" Wells coughed again. He looked at Khadri's mask. And suddenly he understood.

"I'm infected." The words came out as quietly as the final fading notes of a symphony that had gone on much too long.

Khadri's smile was the only answer Wells needed. He considered the possibilities. Anthrax didn't spread person to person. Smallpox had a longer incubation period.

"Plague, right?" He kept his voice steady, as if the question were of only theoretical interest.

"Very good, Jalal."

For a moment, only a moment, Wells felt the deepest panic overwhelm him. He saw his lungs filling with blood, his skin burning from the inside out. Unthinkable agony. But he kept himself still and waited for the fear to pass, knowing that remaining calm was his only hope of beating Khadri now. The panic subsided, and when he spoke, his voice was steady.

"But why like this? Why not just have me bring the germs in?"

"What would I do with a vial of plague? I'm no scientist. And plague is fragile. At least outside the body. Or so Tarik tells me."

"I thought Tarik was a neuropsychologist."

"He's a molecular biologist. A very good one. Though he has some problems of his own." Wells couldn't be sure, but behind the mask Khadri seemed to smile. "He said infecting you would be the best way to make sure the germs survived."

Another cough ripped through Wells.

"It seems he was right," Khadri said.

Wells looked around. "Seven men. Where will you send them?"

Khadri considered. "I suppose I can tell you now, Jalal. Four here, on the subways, mostly. Times Square, Grand Central. The other three to Washington, Los Angeles, Chicago. Lots of plane rides. Seven martyrs. Eight, including you. The sheikh will be pleased."

Seven men coughing clouds of plague bacteria into packed subway cars. Boeing 767s and Airbus 320s. Department stores and office lobbies. How many people would they infect before they died? Thousands? Tens of thousands?

"Brilliant, Omar." And despite himself Wells couldn't help but be impressed with the plan's boldness. Then he remembered. "But . . . isn't plague treatable with antibiotics?"

"*Nam.* If it's diagnosed in time. But in three days your people will have something besides plague on their minds. And the germs move very fast. As you can see better than anyone. The hospitals will be full before the Americans recognize what we've done."

"Another attack?"

Now Wells was sure he could see Khadri smile. He's chatty, Wells thought. He's talking to a dead man.

"Anthrax?" Wells wondered aloud. "Smallpox?"

"Jalal. You are not thinking clearly, I'm sorry to say. Would I use a biological attack to distract the Americans from a biological attack?"

"A bomb then. Like L.A."

"Not exactly. This bomb is special."

Wells's fever seemed to rise. He mopped at the sweat that had suddenly beaded on his forehead. "A dirty bomb?" The agency had been right after all.

"I just think of it as the Yellow."

"The Yellow?"

"You would have been very impressed with the Yellow, Jalal. I'm sorry you won't be alive to see it."

Wells wondered if he could get his knife, make it across the room, cut Khadri's throat before he was tackled. Probably not. Seven men stood between them. In any case, killing Khadri would make no difference now. The other men surely knew where the dirty bomb was hidden. Wells couldn't even slit his own throat and kill himself to stop the plague from spreading. He'd been coughing in this room for hours; he'd already infected the others.

"Will you tell me something, Jalal?" Khadri said from behind his mask. "Now that your martyrdom is certain. The truth. Are you one of us?"

Wells didn't hesitate. "*Nam*. With my heart and soul. *Allahu akbar.*"

"*Allahu akbar,* Jalal. We'll meet again. In paradise."

With that, Khadri walked out.

EXLEY DRUMMED HER fingers against the wheel of the minivan, listening to the same stale news WCBS had been recycling all night. The Lincoln had been double-parked for fifteen minutes. She was desperate to go inside the tenement. But she held back. Wells would come out soon enough, she thought.

The door to the apartment building opened, and the man in the blazer walked out. Alone. He stepped into the Lincoln and drove slowly away. So much for her intuition. She turned off the radio and considered her options. She had told Wells she would call in the cavalry if he got in trouble. She had to assume he was in trouble now, that he was being held captive and the man in the blazer had been checking on him.

But she didn't know which apartment he was in. If she called the agency, the JTTF would surround the building, start kicking down doors. The al Qaeda operatives would know they were caught and kill Wells immediately. No. She would go in, find the apartment for herself. Then she would decide what to do.

She reached into the glove compartment and pulled out the .45 and the silencer that Wells had given her. She held the gun in both hands. This was insane. She didn't even know how many men were with him. What would her kids do if she got herself killed? Walking into an apartment full of terrorists? Insane.

Yet she began to screw the silencer onto the barrel of the .45. Insane or not, she couldn't let him die in there. She would find out where he was. And then? said the nasty little voice in her head, the one she hated. Then what?

She ignored the voice and finished attaching the silencer. She would leave a message on Shafer's voice mail at work, explaining what had happened, where she was. He always checked that mailbox when he woke up. Worst-case, the JTTF would only lose three hours. Anyway, al Qaeda wouldn't attack now, with the streets empty. Whatever they had planned wouldn't happen before morning.

She tried to tuck the pistol into her pants. It wouldn't fit. She unscrewed the silencer and tried again. Still too big. A sure sign that she belonged behind a desk, not out here. But the frustration only made her more determined to prove them all wrong. Duto. Khadri. Shafer. Even Wells. These men who thought their war was too important for her to fight.

She dumped out her purse, everything, the detritus of her life, lipstick, wallet, cellphone, Luna bar, makeup mirror, a wadded-up pack of Kleenex, all of it falling onto the seat and the Caravan's dirty carpets. Luckily she'd brought an oversized bag, a black leather purse. She screwed the silencer back on. She racked the pistol's slide. She dropped it and the keys to the van into her purse, sweeping everything else under the seat. If these guys captured her she'd be better off without any identification, especially her CIA badge. She called Shafer's voice mail and left her message.

Then, before she could reconsider, before her better judgment could take over, she stepped out of the minivan and onto the empty black street.

WELLS COULD ALMOST feel the germs multiplying inside him. He was husbanding his strength, and he still believed he could survive if he got the right antibiotics. His fever was under control. He wasn't coughing blood. But in a few hours he would pass the point of no return. If Exley or the police didn't show up before then, he would go for his knife and kill as many of the men in this room as he could. In the commotion the neighbors would surely call the cops, and if he survived until they arrived he would tell them what was happening.

Exley. He hoped she would be prudent and call in the professionals. Be smarter than he had been. He couldn't blame any higher power for putting him in this place, only his stiff-necked hubris. Pride before the fall. If only Duto hadn't pushed him so hard back in April. If only he had killed Khadri in Atlanta. If only . . .

None of the hypotheticals mattered now. He was dying in this dirty apartment, the bacteria in his blood proof that he and the agency had misunderstood each other as badly as they misunderstood their common foe. He had never earned Khadri's trust, and he never would. With his parting question, Khadri had showed that he suspected—or at least wondered if—Wells was still working for the agency. He had used Wells as a courier at least in part as an ironic gesture, a final twist of the knife. You can die for us but you'll never be one of us. Wells had always hated irony, the favored drink of wannabe intellectuals. He hated it more now.

No matter. He still had his knife. Don't bring a knife to a gun-fight, the marines always said. But he thought he would be okay. He was quicker than these amateurs, and now his hands were free. As he had expected, Ghazi hadn't bothered to cuff him again after Khadri left. And Exley was out there too. *Everything depends which side of the shotgun you're on.* His mother and his father, lying in their graves in Hamilton. He missed them, but he wasn't ready to join them just yet. Wells rubbed his wrists. He wanted nothing more than to reach for his stiletto, but he restrained himself. He glanced at his watch. Almost five A.M., the night nearly over. He would give Exley until the sun rose. Then he would start some unironic knife twisting of his own.

EXLEY STEPPED INSIDE the tenement and looked around the dim first-floor hallway. Her purse hung unzipped on her left arm, close to her body, so she could reach quickly for the pistol inside. Still, she wouldn't be as quick as somebody with a holster. She remembered what Wells had said in Kenilworth, a world away now. *Shoot first. You'll know.*

Her eyes adjusted to the semidarkness and she saw a roach skittering down the corridor. She followed it, ignoring the stairs for now. She walked slowly, resisting the temptation to turn and see if anyone had slid in noiselessly behind her. She was predator, not prey.

At the end of the hall she could hear music playing quietly from behind apartment 1F, a gospel hymn seeping under the door. She hesitated, then tapped lightly. Inside the apartment heavy steps shuffled toward the door, then stopped. Exley tapped again.

"Howard?" an old woman's voice whispered from behind the door. "That you?"

"No ma'am," Exley said as quietly as she could.

"Howard?"

"Wrong address, ma'am. Sorry to bother you."

The door creaked open, a chain holding it in place. An old black woman in a housedress peeked out, her eyes glazed with cataracts behind thick plastic glasses. "Where's Howard?"

"Ma'am, please go back to sleep," Exley whispered, thinking, Please don't raise your voice.

"Why'd you knock on my door?"

"I'm looking for someone."

"Howard?"

"No ma'am. Someone else. A man."

"Join the club." The woman smiled, a big toothless grin.

"A man in this building. Upstairs." Exley pointed up. "Maybe you heard him come in tonight. Not too long ago."

The smile turned into a scowl. "They was banging up and down before."

"Can you think what floor?"

"The third. Maybe the second."

"Goodnight, ma'am. Thank you."

"If you see Howard—"

"I'll tell him."

"Promise?"

"I promise."

The door closed, and Exley was alone again.

SHE WALKED UP the stairs noiselessly. Until now, she had never been grateful for the ballet lessons that her mother had forced on her in grade school. She would have to thank Mom properly tomorrow. If she got the chance. At the top of the stairs she stopped. Up here both overheads were working, throwing their harsh light on the dirty yellow walls of the hallway. A dozen cigarette butts lay in a pile at her feet. Someone had been sitting here tonight, smoking. Waiting.

The floor was silent, the apartments dark. Outside a car rumbled by, its speakers pumping bass. Exley found herself shrinking against a wall. Then the noise faded, and the tenement was still.

She looked down at the cigarette butts again. Of course. Cigarettes meant smoke. She sniffed for a moment. There. The faint odor of smoke grown stale after hours in this hallway. She moved forward slowly, following the scent, as obvious to her now as a trail of bread crumbs.

When she turned up the stairs to the third floor, the smell grew stronger. She slipped her hand inside her purse and found the .45. Without taking the pistol out of the purse, she slid down the safety. Slowly, silently, she climbed the stairs.

"JER-RY! JER-RY!"

A woman. In the hall. She knocked once, paused, then hammered furiously on the door of the apartment as if her fists could break the door off its hinges. "Jerry, you come out right now! Jerry!"

Wells recognized her voice immediately. How had she found him? No matter. He leaned forward, moving his hands closer to his knife. He could feel the adrenaline rising in his blood, overcoming the germs. Ghazi pulled out his pistol and leaned over Wells. Too close, Wells thought. He doesn't know he's too close.

"What do you know about this?" Ghazi said in Arabic.

"Nothing."

Ghazi smashed his Makarov into Wells's skull, just above the ear. A starlit pain flashed through his head. He grunted and leaned back but kept his arms forward.

"Is she with you?"

"I swear I know nothing."

"It's just one woman," Abu Rashid said, his eye at the peephole. "There's no one else out there."

"Jer-ry!" Exley screamed outside. "Leave that whore and come out RIGHT NOW or I'm calling the cops!"

The knocking began again, then a crash.

"She's drunk," Abu Rashid said. "She dropped her bag."

"Fuck," Ghazi said. "Crazy American woman. Get rid of her."

"How?"

"I don't know. Just get rid of her."

A BEARDED ARAB man opened the door. A second man stood just behind him, a cigarette hanging from his mouth.

"You're not Jerry," Exley said. *Shoot first.* She leaned over her bag and reached inside, feeling the pistol.

"This isn't the apartment you're looking for," the man said. He began to close the door.

NOW. WELLS COUGHED, leaned over, reached down with his right hand for his knife. As he came up he flicked open the knife. With his other hand, he grabbed Ghazi's arm, pushing the gun away.

"Exley!"

Ghazi fired. Too late. The bullet missed Wells, blew through the couch, lodged in the wall. Wells forced the stiletto into Ghazi's belly, feeling the fat and muscles tear underneath the blade, then ripped the knife upward, tearing viciously through Ghazi's stomach. When the knife had gone as far as it could go, Wells reversed downward, widening the wound into the intestines. Ghazi screamed, dropped his gun, pressed his hands to his stomach, the blood already pouring out, black in the dim light.

WHEN WELLS SHOUTED Exley's name, the man at the door looked back for a moment. She heard an unsilenced shot from the apartment. Without hesitation she lifted her purse and squeezed the trigger of the .45. The pistol fired through the bag, its echo muffled by the silencer and the leather. The round tore into the man's hip, pushing him into the door.

The man tried to close the door, but Exley raised the gun inside the purse and pulled the trigger again. This time the shot caught him in the center of the chest. He stumbled backward, his bearded mouth forming a silent furry O as he fell. Exley wrenched the .45 out of the bag to get a clear shot at the second man, the man with the cigarette in his mouth. But now he was reaching into his waist-band for a gun of his own.

She fired again, hearing another shot from the apartment as she did. This time the gun kicked high on her and her shot caught him in the neck as he pulled the gun out of his pants. He began to fall, his cigarette dropping from his mouth

—and Exley heard him shoot and felt the agony in her left leg all at once. The bullet seemed to have caught her just above the knee. She could no longer hold herself up. She screamed and fell forward, toward the apartment. She grabbed for the door with her left hand as the man collapsed, blood spurting from his neck

—and now a third man came forward, a fat shoeless Arab, step-ping toward the two in the doorway, reaching for the gun on the ground. Exley forgot the pain in her leg and focused on the fat man. She pulled the trigger of the .45 as he bent over, groping for the gun. But the heavy gray pistol kicked up on her, and her shot flew over his head.

The recoil pushed her backward and she lost her balance and fell, dropping the .45. It kicked away from her, down the hallway. She crawled for it. Her leg seemed to be on fire and she screamed. The fat man in the doorway picked up the pistol. A small smile formed on his face as he turned toward her and raised the gun. Exley turned toward him and began to raise her hands, hating herself for her use-less, pointless surrender even as she did

—and the top of the fat man's head exploded and he collapsed, falling obscenely upon the first two men she'd killed.

Then Wells shouted. He seemed to be a long way away.

"Exley! Stay out there!" Like she had a choice. The hallway spun, faster, faster, and the blackness filled her eyes and she passed out.

AS GHAZI SCREAMED and fell, Wells dove for the Makarov Ghazi had dropped beside the couch. Wells grabbed the pistol and twisted around to see two men almost on him. With his right hand he fired, the shot catching one of the men in the chest, puncturing his heart, sending blood spurting through his shirt. The man groaned and rolled over, his legs twitching as he died.

The other man, a skinny Pakistani who hadn't spoken all night, reached Wells and jumped toward him, close enough for Wells to see the tiny veins in his eyes and feel his hot desperate breath. The Pakistani grabbed for the Makarov with both hands. With his left arm Wells hit the Pakistani with a forearm shiver, snapping back his chin. Wells grabbed the man's scrawny neck and the Pakistani forgot the gun. He gasped for air, his hands pulling hopelessly at Wells's wrist as his mouth opened and he begged for breath. And now Wells's right hand was free. The hand that held Ghazi's gun. Wells shoved the pistol into the Pakistani's mouth, watching his eyes widen in the moment before Wells blew out his brains.

Wells looked toward the door, where two more men lay in a heap—and a third had just grabbed Abu Rashid's gun. He would have time for only one shot. He aimed across his body as the fat man stood. He squeezed the trigger.

The man went down. One shot, one kill.

"Exley!" he yelled. "Stay out there!"

AS QUICK AS that, they were done. The room was quiet, its rough wood floor slick with blood and brains. Ghazi was still moaning, but weakly now. Wells was certain he would be dead in minutes. The other five were already gone. Wells didn't see the seventh jihadi, a Saudi college student who had bragged earlier in the night about reading *Mein Kampf*. But he could hear the kid inside the tiny bedroom, begging in Arabic, "Please."

"Get in here," Wells said. He could feel his adrenaline fading, the plague rushing back. The Saudi appeared in the doorway, his hands up.

"Lie down." Wells pointed to the corner. "Hands on the back of your head."

"Please." The Saudi was crying now.

"Lie down."

The Saudi lay on his stomach, his arms on his head. Wells hoisted himself to his feet and walked toward the man. His trigger finger ached. This one surely deserved to die. He raised the Makarov and took aim.

Don't, he thought. Keep this much of yourself at least. He had killed men in cold blood. But never this way. Never when they had already given themselves up. He lowered the gun, pulled himself back from the abyss.

He heard Exley sighing softly in the hallway, the neighbors beginning to rustle. Time to move. He grabbed the handcuffs and cuffed the Saudi to the steel radiator in the corner of the room.

WELLS STEPPED OVER the bodies in the door and walked into the hall. He felt as though he had recrossed the River Styx. Exley lay pale and quiet, her eyes closed, the left leg of her pants dark with her blood. Wells tore off his shirt and tied a crude tourniquet around her leg to stanch the bleeding. Her eyes fluttered open.

"Jennifer. Jenny." She moaned softly. He leaned down to hug her. She was cold. "You'll be okay." He hoped he was right. A cough racked him and he turned away. Though she was surely already infected, thanks to their kiss in Kenilworth. "We did it, Jenny."

"Nobody but you calls me Jenny," she whispered. "Why is that?"

"They don't know you like I do." He smoothed her hair. "I have to go."

"Khadri?"

"Promise me you'll hold on."

She nodded, weakly.

"Promise," he said.

"I promise." He kissed her on the cheek as she closed her eyes.

WELLS CHECKED THE clip on Ghazi's pistol to see how many bullets were left. Six. Should be plenty. He had just one man left to kill. He popped the clip into the pistol and tucked the gun into his jacket.

If he told the neighbors about the plague, they would panic. There would be time to get them antibiotics. He would call the police from the Ranger. He could already hear distant sirens through the walls of the tenement. As quickly as his poisoned lungs would allow he ran down the stairs.

18

THE STREET WAS empty, the sky above just beginning to break. The sirens were at least a half mile off; at this hour even the New York police department, with its thirty-five thousand cops, was spread thin. Wells shivered in the night air and trotted for his Ranger.

In the truck he reached into his bag and with a shaking hand grabbed a clean shirt and his medicine kit. He pulled the shirt over his head. Then he found his Cipro bottle and tipped four, five, six of the big white pills into his mouth. He swallowed them dry and sat up straight. Cipro was a potent, broad-spectrum antibiotic; Wells couldn't be sure that it would work against the plague, but he hoped that he had just bought himself a few hours. Still, he would need to get to a hospital soon.

He remembered seeing *The Price Is Right* as a kid, watching Bob Barker tell the contestants they had to guess the price of the prize as best they could without going too high. "Whoever is closest without going over," Barker always said. Wells figured he was playing that game with the plague now. As close as he could without going over.

Wells twisted his key in the ignition and the Ranger kicked into life. He pulled into the street. At the first light he turned right—south—then right again. West. Toward Manhattan. He was sure that Khadri would try to blow up the Yellow dirty bomb, whatever it was, as soon as he learned what had happened to his men. Which would be very soon. The media would be all over the bloodbath in apartment 3C.

WELLS CROSSED OVER the Willis Avenue Bridge into Manhattan as the sun rose in his rearview mirror. Time to call in the cavalry. He grabbed his cell and punched in 911. As he did the phone beeped. Low battery.

"Nine one one emergency."

"There's been a shooting on One Forty-sixth Street in the Bronx."

He could hear the dispatcher clicking on her keyboard. "Yes, sir. Emergency units are on the scene."

"Make sure they have biohazard gear. The apartment's contaminated with plague."

"Plague?"

"Yes."

"Sir, are you certain—"

"Yes." Wells hung up.

He didn't know how to reach Shafer or Duto, but he hadn't forgotten the number for the Langley crisis desk, which was always staffed. He punched it in. After a single ring a man picked up.

"Station." An odd tradition that had lasted almost since the agency's creation.

"This is John Wells."

"And how may I help you, Mr. Wells?"

"I need to talk to Vinny Duto." Again his phone beeped.

"There's no one here by that name," the man said smoothly. "Are you sure you have the right number?"

Wells punched the steering wheel in frustration. Of course the guy wouldn't just put him through. He had probably never heard Wells's name before. And Wells no longer had the emergency codes that agents used to prove their identities to the desk.

He coughed viciously and spat a fat glob of phlegm onto the Ranger's passenger seat. It was still gray, at least. If he started coughing blood even the Cipro couldn't save him.

"Hello? Hello?" The man had hung up. Wells called back.

"Station."

"Please. Get Duto for me. Or Ellis Shafer."

The man hesitated. Duto's name was public record, but Shafer's wasn't. "Tell me your name again?"

"John Wells. I'm an agent. My EPI is Red Sox."

"I'm sorry, Mr. Wells. I have no way of checking your EPI. Whatever that is. If you have something else to tell me, please do it."

"Look, I don't have the codes anymore, but please believe me."

"Mr. Wells, someone will have to call you back. Can you be reached at this number?"

"No. The battery's going."

"Mr. Wells—"

"Tell them to put out a BOLO"—be on the lookout—"for the Yellow."

"The yellow what?"

"It's a dirty bomb," Wells said. He felt clouded and weak. The Cipro and the plague were at war inside him, and the plague was holding its own. At least. "I know I'm not making much sense, but that's all I have for you. The Yellow. Also there's a man in Montreal named Tarik who's infected with pneumonic plague, a scientist—"

"Thank you, Mr. Wells. Someone will call you back."

Click. Wells looked down to see that his phone had gone dead. Even if the guy sent the message up the line, the agency couldn't reach him. For a little while he was on his own.

ON HIS WAY home Khadri stopped for steak and eggs at an all-night diner on Webster Avenue. He found himself ravenous. He could hardly wait for his men to begin their travels this morning. Nothing could stop the plan now.

He had just pulled into Ghazi's garage when he heard the first bulletin on his radio. "And we have some breaking news for you from 1010 WINS. There's been a shooting at an apartment building on One hundred and Forty-sixth Street in the South Bronx. Police have cordoned off the block, and neighbors say at least two men have been removed on stretchers. Stay tuned. We'll update this important story as soon as we have more details."

Khadri shook his head, slowly at first, then faster and faster, until his head fogged and he had to stop. "No," he said quietly. "No." He sat back in the Lincoln and breathed deeply, trying to calm himself. How could he have been so foolish? What had the American done in that apartment?

He had to assume the worst, that Wells had killed his men and called the police. After so many years, Wells had fooled him, undone all his work. The plague would never leave that apartment now. Khadri cursed himself for his arrogance. And John Wells, that lying infidel. Allah would surely send Wells to the hottest fires of hell, and Khadri would deserve to join him there for losing this opportunity.

It wasn't just the plague, he thought. The Yellow was registered in Ghazi's name. The police could trace it easily once they identified Ghazi. He would need to blow the bomb this morning, before the police made the connection. He looked at the Lincoln's digital clock: 6:29. Until now Khadri hadn't planned to die in the attack; he had intended to leave the Yellow in a garage near the target and be in Mexico by the time the bomb blew. But he couldn't take that chance now. He would have to blow the bomb himself.

At that thought, Khadri's stomach fluttered. He pushed his fear aside. He had promised paradise to his jihadis; now he too would discover whether Allah awaited. And with that thought Khadri stepped out of the Town Car.

AT LANGLEY WELLS'S message was passed to Joe Swygert, the overnight head of the duty desk. The warning troubled Swygert; the caller knew the agency's procedures, but none of the current codes. And the information he had offered didn't make sense, Swygert thought. The daily hot sheet that listed the top current threats had never mentioned a Yellow attack.

He looked over the message again and sighed. The duty desk got calls like this a couple of times a year from nut jobs who somehow found its number. He punched up the agency's Level III classified directory, looking for a John Wells. He couldn't find the name, but he knew that absence didn't necessarily mean anything. The directories didn't stop at Level III.

Swygert looked at his watch: 6:32. In three years, he had woken Duto only twice: once when Farouk disclosed the dirty bomb to Saul and once when an agent died in a suspicious car crash in Beijing after meeting a high-level mole in the Chinese government. Swygert didn't plan to call Duto or Shafer unless something else crossed the wires.

KHADRI WEAVED HIS way south through the Bronx on the Major Deegan. Already the traffic was picking up, box trucks loaded with vegetables to stock deli shelves, McDonald's tractor-trailers with giant Big Macs painted on their sides. Khadri drove slowly. He planned to reach his target by eight. He would have liked to wait longer, make sure the buildings in midtown were full, but he couldn't afford to delay. His arrogance had already cost him too much. Better to hit early than be caught and miss his chance entirely.

AT 7:03, WELLS parked his Ranger in a taxi-only zone on Forty-fourth Street in Manhattan, just off Eleventh Avenue. He ignored the cabs honking at him as he washed his hands and face with the last of a gallon of water he had bought the night before. He felt sick and weak, and his coughs were coming more quickly now. Soon he would need intravenous antibiotics more powerful than the Cipro if he were to have any chance to survive.

"This showcase can be yours," he muttered to himself. He wondered if he would ever see Evan again. Probably not. But then a lot of fathers and mothers wouldn't see their children after today if he couldn't find Khadri. "Watch him, Lord," Wells murmured. "Whatever happens today, please watch him." He didn't care whether he was praying to the Muslim God or the Christian anymore, and he supposed God didn't care either.

Wells tucked his Red Sox cap low on his forehead, slipped Ghazi's gun into his waistband, and covered it with his shirt. He stepped out of the truck, blinking in the cloudy morning light. He leaned against the truck, unsure where to go. He had heard the shootings in apartment 3C reported on the radio, but so far there were no signs of a dragnet by the police, no roadblocks or sirens screaming. Obviously Exley was still unconscious, and no one had linked his call to Langley with the bloodbath in the apartment. The agency and the NYPD would make the connection soon, he knew. Probably in the next couple of hours. But a couple of hours might not be soon enough.

He wondered if he should find the nearest police station, explain who he was, ask them to put out a bulletin for Khadri. But the cops wouldn't issue an alert right away, not on the word of a disheveled man off the street who said he was a CIA agent and had a story about plague and a dirty bomb. His showing up in person might even slow the process of getting an alert out. Especially since the cops would mostly be interested in him as the apartment shooter. No. When the police put out a public alert for him or Khadri he would turn himself in and get the antibiotics he needed. Until then he would stay on the streets and try to find the Yellow, whatever it was.

But where to go? The United Nations and the New York Stock Exchange were too well guarded. The Empire State Building? Citigroup Center? The Time Warner Center? Grand Central? Then Wells remembered what Khadri had told him when they'd met in Atlanta, in Piedmont Park. *"Didn't you think it was exciting? Times Square?"* Times Square was the only place Khadri had ever mentioned by name. It was the best-known address in the world. And it would be far easier to reach than the others. It was Ground One.

Of course, he could be wrong. Khadri might hate the Empire State Building for reasons Wells didn't know. And Wells couldn't even be sure he would recognize the Yellow when he saw it. But he was out of options. He could go to Times Square. Or turn himself in.

"Times Square," Wells said aloud. Four blocks east. He turned and walked into the rising sun.

THE COPS ON 146th Street didn't need long to see that the massacre in apartment 3C was more than a drug deal gone bad. The NYPD immediately dispatched antiterrorist units to scour the building. The department also notified the FBI's New York City watch center, looking for any information the Feds might have on the apartment or the men inside. The FBI reported that none of the men showed up on its main terrorism watch list, but that didn't necessarily prove anything. The detectives badly wanted to question the woman who'd been found in the hallway. Unfortunately, she was in surgery. Meanwhile, the man they'd found chained to the radiator refused to talk.

Wells's warning about plague was passed to the police tactical command center at One Police Plaza in Manhattan. The officers on the scene were warned, and a police biohazard unit was dispatched to the building to test for contamination, standard practice whenever a plausible bioterror warning was received. Still, the officers in the apartment didn't panic; bioterror hoaxes were all too common in New York.

The NYPD biohazard unit was one of only six civilian units in the United States equipped with an experimental polymerase chain reaction assay capable of detecting plague. The test took roughly an hour.

At 7:26, its results came back positive.

THE OFFICIAL SNOWBALL immediately began rolling. Apartment 3C was declared a possible bioterror site. The building was placed under quarantine, no one allowed to enter or leave. The doctors operating on the woman from the hallway were warned. Blood samples were taken from her and the nameless man who'd been captured in 3C. The police flashed a bulletin to the FBI, the Joint Terrorism Task Force, and the White House. And Joe Swygert, the Langley duty officer, realized that he had better find Vinny Duto and tell him that a man named John Wells had called.

In minutes, the JTTF pieced together what was about to happen on the streets of New York. At 7:41 an all-points bulletin went out to every New York City police officer and FBI agent on duty in the city, telling them that intelligence indicated an imminent terrorist attack, probably with a radiological—a.k.a. dirty—bomb. The bomb's exact delivery method remained unknown, but cabs, Ryder trucks, and Yellow freight trucks were to be considered especially dangerous. The bomber was also unknown, though he was believed to use the alias Omar Khadri.

A separate bulletin was issued for John Wells, a white American male, six-two, approximately two hundred pounds, dark eyes and hair, as a material witness in a six-person homicide in the Bronx earlier that day. At Langley, the agency scrambled to find a picture of Wells to give to police and television stations. The bulletin advised officers to consider Wells armed and dangerous, and warned that he might be infected with *Yersinia pestis,* or plague bacteria.

The president immediately ordered onto high alert the army's biowar defense center and the secret army teams that had the job of responding to a nuclear or radiological attack on U.S. soil. The White House press office called the networks, asking them to make time at eight-thirty A.M. for an announcement of critical national importance.

There were just three problems with all this activity.

No one had a picture of Khadri.

No one knew what the Yellow was.

And they were all too late anyway.

AT 7:43, KHADRI swung the Yellow from Central Park South onto Seventh Avenue. The traffic was hardly moving, but even the worst New York gridlock couldn't keep him from his target, he thought. He looked out through his vehicle's high square windshield at the *kafirs* elbowing one another on the sidewalks, rushing to their offices so they could fatten their pockets.

If they only knew the fate that awaited them, the fire and ash, the deadly smoke. Then they wouldn't be so worried about getting rich. But it was too late for them. He looked back at the trunk, then at the detonator, hidden at his feet, where it couldn't be seen. These people would have to hope for mercy from Allah, he thought. They would get none from him.

The light at Fifty-eighth Street turned green. Khadri eased down on the gas. The Yellow rolled ahead.

WELLS LEANED AGAINST the western edge of the TKTS booth, in a traffic island on the northern edge of Times Square, on Forty-seventh Street between Seventh Avenue and Broadway. In the afternoons the booth sold discount Broadway tickets to tourists, but in the morning it was closed, the only empty space in the maelstrom that stretched from Forty-seventh to Forty-second. Instead of fighting the crowds, Wells had decided to conserve his strength and wait at the booth, where he could cover the vehicles heading south into the square on Broadway and Seventh Avenue.

He knew he wouldn't be out here much longer anyway, and not just because of the plague. In the last five minutes police sirens had been screaming to the east, the north, the south, all over. As Wells watched, two cops pulled their pistols and ordered the driver out of a cab double-parked by the Morgan Stanley headquarters on the corner of Forty-seventh and Broadway. The word was out. He would soon be irrelevant. But not just yet. Wells shivered and turned his attention to Seventh Avenue.

He knew, somehow, that Khadri was very close. The Yellow. It had to be some kind of vehicle, Wells thought. A cab made sense, but it was too obvious. Khadri had been so pleased when he'd said those words in the apartment. Not a cab. And not a truck. A truck was too big, too hard to hide. The Yellow was something else, something that was big enough to hold a good-sized bomb without attracting attention. But what?

A police car turned onto Forty-seventh Street and stopped in front of him. The officers inside looked curiously at him. The driver rolled down his window.

"You okay, buddy? You look a little sick."

"Fine," Wells said. He tried not to cough.

FIFTIETH STREET . . . Forty-ninth . . . Forty-eighth . . .

Khadri kept both hands on the wheel and tried to contain his adrenaline as the Yellow headed south. The traffic was so heavy that the people on the sidewalks were walking as fast as he was driving, but that didn't matter now. Nothing could stop him. His hands were shaking, but not from fear. He should have been scared, he knew, but instead he felt only excitement. The world would long remember this day.

THE TRAFFIC CAME to a stop on the corner of Forty-seventh Street and Seventh Avenue. Three black Lincoln Town Cars, a UPS

delivery van, a Range Rover, a battered Volkswagen Jetta, and a little school bus—what the kids in Montana called a short bus. The
bus was empty except for the driver, but it was riding low on its
wheels, like it was carrying a heavy load.

Wells looked at it and knew. Khadri. The ironist. Of course. And
no one would look twice at a school bus.

The Yellow was second at the light, on the west side of Seventh
Avenue, behind a Lincoln. Maybe sixty feet away. Three seconds if
he ran. Ten if he walked. Wells tucked the cap down on his head and
began to walk east, toward Seventh Avenue. Khadri was half right,
he thought; they were meeting again, but not in paradise. In Times
Square.

"Hey, buddy," the cop said. Wells kept walking, crossing behind
the police cruiser and through the taxis that were moving slowly
across Forty-seventh.

Forty feet. He coughed, a vicious rib-shaking eruption he didn't
try to cover. If he didn't get to the bus, the people around him would
have bigger problems than plague.

"Hey. I'm talking to you." The cop wasn't yelling, not yet.

Wells reached the north side of Forty-seventh and turned right,
cutting between clots of men in suits who were scurrying west
toward the Morgan Stanley headquarters. Thirty feet. Not close
enough, not yet. Khadri would surely have the detonator in his lap.
Wells slipped a hand into his waist and grabbed his gun, holding it
under his jacket.

He peeked back and saw that the cops were getting out of their
cruiser. He began to trot toward the bus.

Twenty feet. "Stop!" he heard the cops yell, but an enormous
honk from a UPS truck drowned them out. He could see Khadri
now behind the driver's seat of the otherwise empty bus, sitting
straight up, head held high, as if he could already see paradise.

Ten feet.

A FEW SECONDS, Khadri told himself. This light would turn
green, he would drive two blocks, and in the heart of the square, at
Forty-fifth Street . . . he would be complete. A few seconds. Two
blocks. The detonator was still at his feet. He wasn't allowing him-

self to touch it, so he wouldn't have the temptation to blow it too early. He wanted this to be perfect.

And then he saw the man in the Red Sox cap, running toward the bus, a gun in his hands.

Khadri screamed, pure animal rage. He reached for the detonator—

Wells's first shot ripped through his chest, knocked him back toward the window. Khadri felt no pain, just enormous anger. He wouldn't let the *kafirs* take this from him. He reached down for the detonator that was so very close. But Wells kept coming, firing, and as he kicked open the door of the bus and jumped inside Khadri knew he had failed.

Wells leaned over Khadri, his hot feverish filthy breath in Khadri's face, and Khadri knew. Wells was the angel of death. He tried to stay angry, but the black wind came for him and he closed his eyes. A dribble of blood spilled from the corner of his mouth. A final agonal breath rattled his chest. He died.

WELLS FELT THE shot even before he heard it. The muscles in his back seemed to explode. He twisted and fell forward. Onto Khadri. The cops. Doing their jobs. Getting the bad guy. So they thought. No. He had to live. He had come too far to die. He'd done his job too. All those years in the wilderness. He tried to lift his hands, but the effort overwhelmed him.

Wells could feel his blood, his hot dirty blood, pumping slowly down his back. As he closed his eyes and the world went black his last thought was Exley.

EPILOGUE

EXLEY WOKE. HER left knee burned as if a shark had bitten off half her leg. But when she opened her eyes she saw her foot in the air. A sling held her leg in place. A hospital bed. Two women stood beside her, one wearing a white doctor's coat, the other a nurse's uniform. Surgical masks hid their mouths.

As consciousness found her, the pain in her leg turned to agony. The electrical fire inside her burned endlessly, every nerve in her knee sending an individual message of grief to her brain. "Hurts," she choked.

Beyond her leg, the rest of her body ached terribly. And though she'd just woken she felt enormous fatigue, as if she'd been running for days on end. Exley clenched her fists against the pain and the nurse ran a hand down her arm, carefully avoiding the intravenous line plugged into her elbow.

The doctor stepped forward. "You were shot," she said. "Do you remember?"

Now Exley did. "In the hall."

"Would you like some ice?"

Exley nodded. Even talking was an enormous effort; her mouth seemed to lack any moisture. With her gloved hand, the nurse slipped a chip of ice into Exley's mouth. Exley sucked on it, a cold piece of paradise. She began to remember more, her hours in the van, Wells shouting her name—

"What happened?" Panic rose in her, under the pain. Wells. Where was he? Her last memory of him, leaning over her in the dirty yellow hallway.

"Can you tell me your name?" the doctor said.

"Jen. Exley."

The doctor nodded. "I'm Dr. Thompson. Julie. I have some good news for you, Ms. Exley. Your children are here."

"Where's here?" She licked her lips, dry again.

"The infectious disease unit at Bellevue. New York. You've been here about sixteen hours. But we want to be sure you're not contagious before we bring David and Jessica in."

At the doctor's second mention of her children Exley felt a strange sorrow overtake her. They shouldn't see her like this. She had come so close to dying, giving them up. She had been absent from them for too long. The drugs and the pain and the shame melded in her mind and she felt hot tears running down her cheeks. The doctor—Exley had forgotten her name already—pulled off her glove and put a cool hand on Exley's forehead.

"There's no reason to worry," she said. "You were infected with some nasty stuff, but it looks like we caught it in time. You can probably see them tomorrow."

Exley thought again of Wells. "Where's John?"

The doctor glanced at the nurse. "Also here. He's very sick."

Very sick. Exley closed her eyes.

"I know you're in a lot of pain," the doctor said. "We need to be careful about how much medication we give you, but if it hurts too much, tell us. When you feel better there are a lot of people who want to talk to you. To thank you. In the meantime try to sleep. Please."

THE NEXT DAY passed in a haze, Exley slipping in and out of consciousness as the nurses adjusted her medication. The doctors briefly brought in her kids and her mother, and Exley's joy at seeing them overcame her shame. Still, she was glad when they left. She saw in their faces that they were shocked by the way she looked. The effort of trying to smile for them exhausted her. She passed out almost as soon as the door closed behind them.

When she woke again Shafer was crouched beside her bed. "Ellis," she croaked. For the first time she felt a trace of energy returning, although her knee burned as if it were being torn apart from the inside out.

"Jennifer." For once he seemed at a loss for words. He wrung his hands together and hopped around the room on his spindly legs.

"What happened out there?" she said. "They won't tell me."

"It was close, but you did it, Jennifer," he said. "You and Wells."

"What did they mean when they said I might be contagious?"

"I'm probably not supposed to be the one to tell you this, but Wells infected you with plague."

Plague. Exley's body ached at the word. Shafer rubbed her shoulder. "It's okay. We think we've tracked down everyone who was exposed, here and in Canada."

Canada? Exley decided not to ask.

"I need to see him, Ellis."

"He's in bad shape," Shafer said. "He was exposed a lot longer than you, and he was shot in the back."

"Khadri shot him?"

"No. The police." A strange half smile crossed Shafer's face. "Things got messy at the end, but it worked out all right. Our boy's a hero and you must be too. The president's coming up here next week. Meanwhile Duto's taking all the credit, and I'm letting him."

Duto's name provoked a flare of anger in Exley, but the emotion faded as quickly as it came. She was just too tired. Shafer seemed to read her mind. "Don't waste your energy, Jennifer. If it's not him it'll be someone else."

"He's going to make it. Right, Ellis?" In her haze she imagined trading her leg so Wells would live. Or both legs. Sure. Who needed legs anyway?

"I'm not going to lie. They're saying fifty-fifty. But that's better than yesterday."

· · ·

THE NEXT MORNING she felt stronger, and she asked that they take her to his bed. They told her no, but she insisted. So they rolled her in her bed to a room watched by four New York City police officers wearing blue dress uniforms and white gloves. An honor guard.

Wells lay on his side, an intravenous drip in his arm, oxygen tubes in his nose, a catheter poking out from the sheets by his waist. He was pale and gaunt and his breath came slowly, but the steady beeping of the pulse monitor and oximeter above his head reassured Exley.

"I know he doesn't look great, but he's doing much better," Dr. Thompson said. "He's been trying to say something, mumbling. We think he could regain consciousness today."

In the bed Wells twitched and sighed.

"Can you bring me closer?" Exley said.

WELLS STOOD OUTSIDE a gleaming white skyscraper, the biggest he had ever seen. Its marble walls seemed to have no end. He wanted badly to get in though he didn't know why. Something was impelling him, something he couldn't fight. He was too tired to fight anyway. He looked for an entrance but the building had no doors or windows, only a single push-button entrance bell. He pressed the bell. It began to beep and a man in a blue blazer and a surgical mask materialized in front of him.

Please, Wells said without speaking. Yet he knew the man would understand.

The man pointed at Wells's belt, where a dozen pistols hung. Makarovs, .45s, Glocks, even a couple of old revolvers. As Wells watched, the pistols morphed into each other. They were alive, he realized. He'd never seen living guns before. Yet the sight didn't surprise him.

Take them off, the man thought-said.

I can't, Wells replied. He looked down. A vast pit lay beneath him, filled with men and cranes and earthmovers building a neon city. You don't know what it's like down there.

Take them off, the man said again. Behind him the marble skyscraper lost its shine and began to fade. Wells desperately reached for the man in the blazer, but the man raised a finger, a single finger, and pain flooded Wells, radiating from his back into his shoulders and then across his body.

Wells looked up. The skyscraper was almost gone. He knew he would never get in if he kept his guns. He tried to pull them off but couldn't: they were bound to him like leeches.

The building disappeared. The man shook his head and waved his hand angrily. And Wells fell.

HE LANDED ON his back on hard, rocky ground. The neon city had vanished, and the sky above was black. Wells closed his eyes and saw stars, but dimly, like fireflies. He was looking at his own brain through a thick gauze curtain. Again he felt a surge of pain in his back. He looked at the stars. They were dim, too dim. They weren't the stars he remembered from Afghanistan.

Afghanistan.

And once he understood that word everything came back, everything, all of it, all at once, as bright and wicked as a fever dream, only real; he could remember everything, and the pain from the hole in his back scorched through the morphine or fetanyl or whatever it was that they were giving him and—

—he opened his eyes. And there she was.

ACKNOWLEDGMENTS

This book could not have been written without my brother David, who helped conceive the idea of a CIA agent inside al Qaeda and think through ways to tell this story. He too is a writer, but when I asked him if I could take a shot at this book, he told me to go ahead. For that encouragement, and for the ideas he offered each step of the way, I cannot thank him enough.

Thanks also to:

Ellen and Harvey, my parents

Mark Tavani, an editor who edits

Heather Schroder, who somehow convinced Random House to sign a contract on three chapters and an outline, giving me the confidence (and legal responsibility) to finish, and Matthew Snyder, who performed a similar trick with the movie rights

Jonathan Karp, who bought in early

Pilar Queen, Deirdre Silver, Andrew Ross Sorkin, and Jennifer Vanderbes, who offered wise and gentle criticism on the first draft

Dorian and Eric Nerenberg, who showed me the Buford Highway

Douglas Ollivant, Kelly Pippin, and other soldiers and officers too numerous to mention, who shared their stories (and their chow halls) in Baghdad and Najaf

Zaineb Obeidi and all the translators and drivers at the Baghdad bureau of the *Times*

And, finally, all the war reporters and photographers who risk their lives every day. I worked with them for only a few months, but my respect for them grows daily.

ABOUT THE AUTHOR

ALEX BERENSON is a reporter for *The New York Times* who has covered topics ranging from the occupation of Iraq to the flooding of New Orleans. He graduated from Yale University in 1994 with degrees in history and economics. This is his first novel. He lives in New York City.

ABOUT THE TYPE

This book was set in Sabon, a typeface designed by the well-known German typographer Jan Tschichold (1902–74). Sabon's design is based upon the original letter forms of Claude Garamond and was created specifically to be used for three sources: foundry type for hand composition, Linotype, and Monotype. Tschichold named his typeface for the famous Frankfurt typefounder Jacques Sabon, who died in 1580.